BEHIND the MASK

DARE DEMUREN

AMVPS

This is a work of fiction. Names, characters, businesses, places, events and incidents are either the products of the author's imagination or used in a fictitious manner. Any resemblance to actual persons, living or dead, or actual events is purely coincidental

This novel is dedicated to the memory of two wonderful
persons:

Herbert Akinlolu Odelola, uncle in-law, exemplary teacher and
pharmacist
and
Mabel Olusanu Alli, cousin, friend and brilliant physician

"Gone but not forgotten"

CHAPTER 1

Mike had been swotting for days on end in his father's massive library. He sat behind the ornate table where his father had clinched many deals in his days as the Head of the Senate, in his hey days as the kingmaker, before a stroke emasculated him. After the inauspicious time Mike had spent in London, he returned to Lagos to start his postgraduate studies. Ever since he enrolled in the medical school, he had the ambition to become an obstetrician and gynaecologist. He thought it was glamorous to have the ability to bring new lives into this world. Right now, he was finding the going too tough. He stretched his long arms and legs, and almost fell off his chair. As he struggled to maintain his balance, his limbs scattered the things on the table and he sent his father's whiskey flask flying off and smashing against the wall, exploding with a bang.

His mother was nearby and overheard the commotion. She hurried into the library and found her son clearing the mess on the floor.

'Mike, what's the matter?'

'Mum, there is nothing serious. I am just fed up with all the useless information I have to cram,' replied Mike.

'My son, no knowledge is wasted. Just look ahead to the gain. As they say, no pain no gain.'

'I know, but it is clinical anatomy that is driving me nuts. I want to become a gynaecologist but I have to memorise a lot of rubbish.'

'Don't give up my son. Take a break and come back to your studies later.'

'Good idea mum. I am going to join dad's friends and observe their meeting.'

Mike's mother returned to the kitchen to supervise the cooks who were preparing the menu for the 'committee of friends,' a motley group of loyalists and business associates of Chief Femi Lawanson within the People's Party of Nigeria. Mike exited the library, hopped down the stairs and slipped quietly into the massive living room. At least fifty men and women were seated and listening attentively to Senator Abisayo mapping out their strategy for the coming local government elections. The list of prospective candidates was being compiled and would be ratified in a final meeting to be held at the City Hall at the end of the following month. Senator Femi Lawanson and his group still held sway in the South West of the country and they had therefore been mandated by the party to present the list of candidates. The meeting drew to a close after two hours, and guests retreated to the giant marquee for a sumptuous dinner. As they walked towards the marquee, Mike caught a glimpse of an old school mate ahead.

'Ahmed, how are you?' Mike asked when he finally caught up with him.

Ahmed turned round and embraced him. They rocked right and left for minutes before disentangling. They had not seen each other since they completed their secondary school education almost ten years earlier.

'Ahmed, I am delighted to see you after all these years. What have you been up to?'

'After my secondary school certificate examinations, I worked in a bank for a few years, and was half way through my banking diploma course when I had the good fortune to meet our leader, your dad, who mentored and led me into politics. I am now the chairman of Lagos central local government. What about you, Mike? What are you up to?'

'As you are aware, I studied medicine and qualified as a doctor three years ago. I am now preparing for my postgraduate examinations in Obstetrics and Gynaecology,' replied Mike.

'How long will that take?'

'If all goes well, I will complete my studies in four years time, and become a Fellow of the Postgraduate College, and hopefully a Consultant Gynaecologist within a year or two,' replied Mike.

'You are not serious, you must be joking.'

'No, I am not joking. I've got four to five years to become a Consultant,' replied Mike.

'Mike, you are my good friend. Can I ask you a personal question?'

'Go ahead.'

'When you become a Consultant, how much will you be paid?'

Mike gave the range of salaries from newly qualified specialists to senior consultants.

'Wow, I am shocked. Our local government councilors are paid more than your consultants.'

'That is life,' replied Mike.

'Mike, let's forget about work for now and get something to eat.'

They joined the others in the marquee and ate with relish.

They rounded off with ice cold Star beer. Mike watched as Ahmed engaged numerous colleagues and supporters in discussions interspersed with jokes all evening. Finally, it was time to go home, and Ahmed looked round for his friend.

'Mike, where is Mike Lawanson?'

'He is sitting in that corner,' said one of the guests pointing towards Mike downing yet another bottle of ice cold Star beer. There will be no more studying tonight.

'Mike, most of the guests have already left. I have thoroughly enjoyed myself, and seeing you again after all these years is a delight, a bonus. Where's the leader?'

'Who is the leader?' enquired Mike.

'Who else? Ahmed retorted. Your father of course. He will always be our leader. I owe my political fortune to him and I have to pay my respects before I depart.'

Mike led him across the compound through immaculate corridors to the massive reception room where Femi Lawanson was chatting with his trusted aide, Senator Abi. As they walked in, the two friends stopped talking and shifted their gaze towards the door. Ahmed instinctively prostrated full length in front of Senator Lawanson, in the Yoruba tradition of complete respect for a superior. He repeated his action in front of Senator Abi, although the latter protested feebly that this was unnecessary, and of course Ahmed didn't prostrate as fully as he did before the leader.

As Ahmed exited the room, he whispered to his friend.

'Your father is a great man; it was not for nothing that he was known as the kingmaker. To the committee of friends, he is still a kingmaker.'

Ahmed flicked open his mobile phone and pressed a speed dial code. A few minutes later, a gleaming metallic black Mercedes 280 saloon arrived. The chauffeur jumped out and opened the door for Ahmed. Ahmed said his goodbye to his old mate, and handed over his business card.

'If you need anything, call me. If I can't help, I'll know someone who can.'

With the final statement, Ahmed sat in the so-called owner's corner, rear seat away from the driver. The car eased away and Mike could only marvel at Ahmed's status.

Mike ambled to his bedroom. He kicked off his shoes but didn't bother to change into his pyjamas, or more accurately was by now so inebriated that he was incapable of changing his clothes. No sooner was he on his bed than he fell asleep, and was soon snoring heavily. He woke up around noon with a splitting headache. The first thing he did was to pop two Aspirins even though he knew he shouldn't take analgesics on an empty stomach. The examinations start tomorrow and he still had a lot of ground to cover. He grabbed a sandwich and a cup of black coffee and then buried himself in his books. He was determined to give a final push to the line. His mother had to persuade him to go to bed at 12 midnight so that he could be fresh and attentive in the morning. He was up again by 5.00 o'clock, well before the rest of the house rose, brushing up on some facts.

The first paper was good. Mike felt he did well in the essays. After lunch, there was a 2 hour multiple choice question paper on clinical anatomy and physiology. This was an unmitigated disaster. First he didn't manage to answer all the questions, and he then committed the indefensible error of altering many of his answers because as fatigue set in and the headache returned, self doubt manifested. When he left the examination hall, cursory review of the questions showed that most of the final answers he altered were wrong. When they went in for the final paper of the day, his confidence was shot to pieces. He scribbled some unintelligible stuff on the answer sheets and left the hall within half an hour. That was the end of this examination. He made up his mind he would not bother to show up for the oral examinations the following week.

CHAPTER 2

ike spent the days following the examination debacle like a zombie. He spoke little, ate little and hardly slept. He couldn't tell his parents he had flunked his exams. They thought he was still studying for part two of the examinations. After three days, he snapped out of the trance, and made up his mind to seek help. He retrieved Ahmed's card and placed a call to him.

'Ahmed, how are you?'

'Who is this?'

'This is Mike Lawanson. I need to see you as soon as possible.'

'I have an important meeting all morning. Can the matter wait till later tonight?'

'Of course, it can.'

'I have been invited to be the guest of honour at the annual Institute of Journalists award night at the Shangri La Hotel in Victoria Island tonight. My wife is away in London, so we can go together.'

'How do I get there?' asked Mike.

'I'll send the driver for you at 6.00 p.m. The event starts at 8.00 p.m. This is a black tie or complete traditional attire event. You can sleep over in my house after the event. That will give us the opportunity to talk.'

'That's fine with me,' replied Mike.

The chauffeur arrived for Mike by half past five. When Mike came out, he was astonished so see that Ahmed had sent a Mercedes

ML 350 SUV. They left just before 6 p.m. The turbo diesel engine roared into life purring like a wild cat down Ikorodu road on to the third Mainland bridge leading on to highbrow Victoria Island. Thirty minutes later they drove into Ahmed's exclusive gated compound.

Ahmed met him at the door and led him through the lobby into a massive living cum dining room.

'Mike, join me at the table. My cook has prepared rice, fried plantain, and beans with stewed meat and fried fish. I recall you were crazy about rice and beans during our schoolboy days.'

'I am still crazy about the combination.'

Mike flung his coat on the sofa and joined Ahmed as they tucked into the food. They washed the food down with fruity red wine.

'Mike, it's now 7.30 and we should be on our way.'

They were soon on their way and drove into the hotel with few minutes to spare. As they stepped into the hotel lobby, they were met by a beautiful lady.

'Chairman Ahmed, you are welcome, Sir. I am Mosun Martins. Let me lead you to your table.'

'Thank you.'

She led them through the hotel lobby wiggling her bum as she walked in measured steps in her Jimmy Choo shoes, like a catwalk model. Mike's gaze alternated between her derriere and her shapely legs. This got his pulse racing, and he drew close to Ahmed, whispering into his ears.

'Ahmed, I really like this lady.'

'Chill my friend,' Ahmed replied.

I really like this lady. I don't care what Ahmed says. She looks like a princess, an ebony black beauty, Mike thought to himself.

As they sat down on the special guest table the lady addressed Ahmed.

'Sir, I'll look for Queen and tell her you've arrived.'

'Who is Queen?' asked Mike.

'That's Nkechi, the co-ordinator of this programme. She was a beauty queen during her university days and her close friends call her Queen.'

Shortly afterwards Nkechi arrived and greeted Ahmed warmly.

'Nkechi, meet my good friend Doctor Mike Lawanson.'

'Pleased to meet you,' Nkechi said as she offered her hand. Mike took her hand and felt the smooth silky texture of her palm.

'I am truly pleased to meet you,' replied Mike.

Nkechi smiled, flashing gleaming white teeth. Mike's gaze dropped from her face to the plunging neckline which revealed just enough of well rounded cleavage to get men drooling.

As she walked away to attend to other matters, Mike's gaze was fixed on Queen's figure with her fair complexion.

I think this is the woman for me. The Queen trumps the Princess any day.

'Oh my God, this lady is beautiful,' muttered Mike.

Ahmed overheard and admonished his friend.

'Take it easy Mike. So you want both of them. Forget about the ladies and let's enjoy the evening.'

Mike tried hard to concentrate on the proceedings but in reality his thoughts were only on one thing, or more precisely one person.

The climax of the evening was choosing the journalist of the year followed by a short speech by Ahmed whose local government had financed the event. Whilst Ahmed was giving his speech, Mike engaged Nkechi in discussion and was able to exchange phone numbers with her. He promised to call her soon. Nkechi didn't think much about the promise because she regularly had such encounters with men. The ML350 growled and roared down the nearly deserted streets of Victoria Island reaching home in only fifteen minutes, just before midnight. Mike was quiet on the trip home.

'Mike, you are unusually quiet.'

'I am just tired,' Mike lied.

I have been wasting my time swotting and sitting for exam after exam. I have been really stupid. Ahmed barely passed school leaving certificate in Grade three whilst I had a very good Grade one, and went on to A levels and university. Today, he earns more and lives better than our professors.

As they entered the living room, Ahmed removed his traditional cap and flowing robe, flinging both on the sofa.

'Mike, can I get a cold beer for you?'

'No, just get me a glass of water.'

'You can't be serious.'

'I am dead serious. No alcohol for me tonight. I want to think straight.'

'O.K. let's talk.'

'Ahmed, I have decided I need a change of career.'

'What do you mean?'

'I am abandoning medicine for politics. I want to serve the people.'

'Really, Mike, that's news to me.'

'My friend, I want to contest the next local government election as a councillor.'

'It seems that you are serious.'

'I am not joking. I am going to seek the party nomination at the next meeting.'

'Have you spoken to your father about it?'

'That's no problem. Once I convince my mum, she'll win over my dad.'

'Time is of the essence. You need to do that tomorrow. Once this is done, give me a call and I'll talk to Senator Abi so that we can find you a safe seat in Lagos.'

'Thank you Ahmed, you are a true friend. Let's celebrate this landmark decision. You can now give me ice cold beer.'

The following day Mike resigned his appointment at the teaching hospital. He then broke the news to his mother who was at first disappointed with the decision but finally came round.

Mike flipped open his mobile phone and punched in some numbers.

'Hello, who is that?'

'Lawanson, Doctor Mike Lawanson. We met last night.'

'Oh yes, doc. How are you?'

'I am fine. I will like to meet you soon. Are you free tonight?'

'I am sorry I've got an important engagement tonight.'

'What about tomorrow?'

'I am sorry, I am busy all week.'

'Can I send you the proposal for a project I am planning, for your comments?'

'Oh yes, you can.

'Thank you very much Nkechi. Bye for now.'

'Goodbye, doctor.'

CHAPTER 3

There was a massive turnout at the National Stadium, venue of the free polio immunization programme financed by Lagos State branch of The Peoples Party of Nigeria (PPN). Mike was the face of the programme. His portrait adorned the banners and flags all over the venue. Hundreds of rented hands wearing uniformed vests ushered the women and their children. At the end of the first day, thousands of children had been vaccinated. The programme continued for a whole week. By the third day, Mike had become a celebrity. Various newspapers and magazines were falling over each other to interview him. Then it happened. The FRCN tried to interview him but his diary was so full that Mike's manager could not accommodate the radio station. Word got to Nkechi and she told her boss she could secure an early appointment.

Nkechi flipped open her GSM phone and punched in the number Mike had passed to her at the gala night. It was late at night and Mike was already drifting off to sleep after a long day at the stadium when his phone rang.

'Hello, who is that?' Mike asked.

'Nkechi.'

'Nkechi who?'

'Nkechi Obi, Queen.'

'Hi Queen, to what do I owe this special honour?'

'I need a favour.'

'Favour? What can I do for you?'

'FRCN wants to interview you.'

'When?'

'As soon as possible, Mike.'

'No problem. I'll clear a slot in my diary tomorrow.'

FRCN got the interview the following day. As Mike walked out of the interview room, Nkechi was waiting by the door.

'Doc, thanks for granting my request.'

'You are welcome. Can we have dinner together one of these evenings?'

'What about tomorrow?'

'Tomorrow is fine replied Mike. I'll pick you up around 7 o'clock.'

When Mike ditched medical practice for politics, Senator Lawanson upgraded his son's mobility, replacing his Toyota Avensis saloon with a BMW X5 SUV. The day after the FRCN interview, Mike set out at 5 o'clock from their Ikeja GRA mansion for Lagos Island, waltzing through the traffic on the busy Bank Anthony way, on to Ikorodu Road. One hour later, he was still stuck in the usual Lagos 'go-slow' on Anthony Village road, the frustrating nerve jangling snail pace closing time traffic jam. He inched his way slowly through the road on his way to the Third Mainland Bridge linking this part of mainland Lagos to the Island. He finally got on the bridge at half past six. He pressed the throttle and the Beemer responded, zooming towards the Island. He didn't want to be late for his first date with Queen. He exited the bridge towards Ikoyi, arriving at the flat Queen shared with a colleague just before seven. Queen was already waiting. They were soon on their way to the posh floating restaurant on Marina. The floating restaurant was a converted luxury ship moored by the quayside. Mike had reserved an exclusive berth for two. They were treated like royalty to a four course dinner with jazz music and blues from greats like Duke Ellington and 'Satchmo' Armstrong in the background. When they finished deserts, as black coffee was being served, Mike turned to Queen.

'Would you like to dance?'

'No, not to this type of music,' replied Queen.

'I'll give you something you can't resist,' replied Mike.

He pressed a button on the side of the table, and the room lights dimmed. At the same time pre-picked music wafted slowly from hidden surround loudspeakers. It seemed as if Marvin Gaye had resurrected as the room was immersed in the evergreen love song, 'Let's get it on.' Mike held Queen firmly but gently as they danced cheek to cheek. When Lionel Ritchie's 'Hello' came on the air, Mike sang along serenading Nkechi. It was now past ten.

'Mike, thank you for a wonderful evening.'

'I should be thanking you instead for being such great company. One last dance, and then we can go home,' replied Mike.

Mike held her close as they had the last dance.

'Thank you, thank you very much,' he whispered in her ear as the music ended. Nkechi was quiet on the way back home. As he stopped the car at the entrance to the block of flats, she leaned towards him and kissed him gently on the cheek, and then she was gone. Mike was confused but on reflection, he concluded the evening had gone as well as could be expected. He could not risk being lubricious, as he was laying the foundation for a serious relationship. At this time of the day, the roads were clear and he arrived home by midnight.

Before he went to bed, he texted her: 'My beautiful queen. Thank you very much, you were wonderful tonight.'

On the other side of the city Nkechi was in turmoil. She couldn't sleep. Her life was relatively stable before Mike came on the scene. For the past year she has had a steady relationship with Chris Paul, a banker. He worked long hours during the week so they generally saw each other at weekends. He was rather dull but very reliable. Mike brought a level of excitement she had long forgotten existed, and she was now confused.

By the time Nkechi woke up, her colleague was already dressed and ready to leave for work.

'Queen, what's the problem?'

'Nothing. I am fine.'

'You are not fine. I know you too well. What is the problem?'

'I am just tired.'

'Is this anything to do with last night's outing?'

'Pat, I am confused. Chris has been good to me but my life with him is dull, too predictable. This new guy has rekindled a fire in my belly. He has brought a level of excitement and fun I had long forgotten existed.'

'Queen, be careful. Remember things are not always what they seem. Has Chris wronged you?'

'No, that's the problem. Chris has not done anything wrong. But life with him will be dull and boring. Mike seems to be the type of man I need.'

'So, has Mike asked you to be his girlfriend?'

'Not really but I get the impression things are moving inexorably that way.'

'What do you mean by that?'

'Look at the text he sent to me last night after he got home.'

'So, he wants you or loves you. What are you going to tell Chris?'

'I don't know. I don't know what to tell him. This is a really messy situation.'

Pat returned home from work before Nkechi. Shortly afterwards, the flat door bell chimed. She wondered whether Nkechi left her key at home. She pressed the intercom.

'Who is that?'

'It's the courier. I've got a delivery for Miss Nkechi.'

'Delivery from who?'

'It is from Doctor Mike Lawanson.'

'O.K. the door is open, please come in.'

The man brought in twelve long-stemmed red roses, and a wrapped gift. Affixed to the gift was a card with a love poem, handwritten by Mike. Queen was coy when she saw the roses and gift on her return from work. She said little but her flat mate could see a glint in her eye when Mike phoned her one hour later. The following morning Mike phoned her again as she was about to have breakfast. Pat was in her bedroom when the phone rang. She overheard Queen talking in a hushed tone to someone. By the time Pat emerged from her room, Queen had dropped the phone.

'Who is that,' asked Pat.

'It's Mike. He wants to see me again tonight.'

Queen and Mike continued to see each other regularly after this. She found that she was enjoying his company and becoming emotionally attached to him. Mike lavished her with flowers and expensive gifts and their romance seemed to blossom almost overnight. One night, a few weeks after she started going out with Mike together, Queen approached Pat for advice.

'Pat, Mike has asked me to escort him to a party in the family home at the end of the month.'

Queen paused but when Pat didn't say anything, she asked a direct question.

'What should I do?'

'Do you love him?' Pat asked.

'I don't know, but I am so happy in his company.'

'Queen, what about Chris?'

'What about him. I am afraid it's all over between us.'

She was still in a daze when her mobile phone rang. She picked it up and it was from Chris. She ignored the call and he left a frantic message wondering why she hadn't returned his call over the last 7 days. The phone rang again and she ignored it, wondering why Chris was bothering her. As soon as the caller started leaving a message, she grabbed the phone and interrupted the message when she heard Mike's voice.

'Hello, how are you?'

'I am fine, thank you.'

'I've missed you.'

'I've missed you too. Thank you for the flowers. They are so beautiful.'

'You are welcome. But the flowers are not half as beautiful as you.'

Nkechi blushed. They continued chatting for the next hour, blowing kisses and mouthing sweet nothings to each other. Before they signed off, Nkechi said she would be very busy with a project for the next three days and he might find it difficult to reach her but after that she would like to invite him to dinner.

Nkechi was uncompromising in her encounter with Chris. She arranged to meet him at one of their regular joints. Chris ordered his regular drink but was surprised that Nkechi asked for tonic water. Nkechi had a sullen look.

'What's the matter, dear?' asked Chris.

'It's over, Chris.'

'What is over?'

'Our relationship is dead. I am sorry but it's all over.'

As soon as it became clear that she was not joking, Chris was dumbfounded. When he recovered from the shock, he turned to her in deliberate halting speech.

'You and I have plans for the future. We.....'

Nkechi held up her hand, in a gesture to shut him up in mid-sentence.

'There is no you and I. There are no plans for the future. I hope we can stay friends, but there is no future for us.'

'Have you found another man?'

'How dare you? No one else is involved,' she lied.

A few minutes later, Nkechi got up, picked up her handbag and walked out of the restaurant. Chris hurried after her offering to take her home but she refused the offer. She hailed a taxi and headed home. For the next few days, Chris tried to rekindle the flame of love to no avail. He enlisted Pat's help but she knew the situation was hopeless. Nkechi came up with all manner of excuse, dredging up long forgotten failings and arguments. Eventually Chris gave up, but he couldn't concentrate at work and had to take a week's emergency leave to recover.

Once Nkechi had disposed of Chris, she and Mike became an undisputed item. Any spare time they had outside of work was spent in each other's company. She continued her work as a newsreader and announcer at FRCN, whilst Mike was engrossed in his quest to become a councillor. With the backing of Senator Lawanson and his friends, Mike was nominated to stand for councillor in the Lagos Mainland local government. The publicity from the polio immunisation campaign had enhanced his profile. He narrowly missed nomination for chairman's post but the deputy chairman's post was reserved for him, as long as he won his constituency election. Nkechi's mass communication skills came in handy. She helped direct the publicity blitz. Mike won the election and became deputy Chairman of Mainland local government. He was now earning more than the Professor of Obstetrics and Gynaecology in the teaching hospital where he had worked, a position that would have taken him at least another ten years and success at several examinations to attain.

A week into the new job he decided he needed a short break to recover from the rigours of electioneering. Spontaneity and surprises were some of the attributes that kept Nkechi pining for Mike. Even Nkechi could not have foreseen the stunt Mike was about to pull. As soon as the election results were announced, Mike collected Nkechi's passport and asked her to take a week off duty so they could travel to Accra for some important meetings. One of the perks of Mike's new job was the provision of an official car. The chauffeur picked up Nkechi from her flat and headed for Mike's Ikeja residence. One hour later they were at the airport.

Nkechi was surprised when Mike led her to the British Airways First Class desk.

'Mike, you've got the wrong desk.'

'I don't think so,' replied Mike.

'I think this is the London flight.'

'In that case we'll go to London instead.' Mike winked at her and then burst out laughing.

'Oh, you are just amazing. You had me fooled, but I don't mind at all.' Nkechi drew close to Mike and pecked him on the cheek, and then whispered into his ear.

'I love you too much.'

'Me too,' replied Mike.

Checking in and collecting boarding passes only took a few minutes. As they were about to go through the immigration fast track section, Mike caught a glimpse of his former boss on the economy queue. He walked over to greet him.

'Good morning Sir.'

'Morning, Mike. Congratulations on the election victory.'

'Thank you Sir. Where are you going?'

'My wife and I are off to London to attend the scientific congress of the Royal Society of Obstetricians and Gynaecologists. I am being honoured with the fellowship of the college.'

'Congratulations Sir. Good morning ma. I'll see you on the flight.'

As he turned to join Nkechi he couldn't help thinking he was lucky to have escaped the dreary and unrewarding life of an academic.

'That's my professor and his wife travelling economy to London. That could have been me ten years from now.'

They landed at Heathrow airport just before five. They passed through immigration fairly quickly and picked up their suitcases. As they exited the arrivals lounge, Mike spotted the limousine taxi driver carrying a board with his name. They were soon on their way to the majestic Jupiter hotel in central London. The couple were a bit tired from the six hour flight and the tortuous airport transfer through the streets of London with interminable traffic lights.

Nkechi sat on the edge of the king size bed, kicked off her high heeled shoes and stretched her curvy torso on the bed with cool breeze from the exclusive climate control system blowing across her face. Mike threw his coat on the sofa, loosened his tie and sat beside his woman, planting a kiss on her fleshy lips. She smiled and pulled him on to the bed. Before long, they were tearing their clothes off each other's backs. She slipped her hands southwards and felt his turgidity. He caressed the silky smooth skin whilst she responded with sighs of delight. When he entered her she was ecstatic. He was strong but gentle, patient and methodical and when the torrent finally came, she climaxed simultaneously. They held on tightly to each other, exhaling deeply. Then they went limp and relaxed their grips. She smothered his face with kisses and then playfully bit one of his ears, and whispered into it.

'Thank you, thank you very much. That was fantastic.'

'My Queen, thank you too. You were marvellous.'

They fell asleep in each other's arms. Queen was the first to wake up an hour later. She got some body lotion and gently massaged her man. When he stirred, she melted in his arms and he took her once more. They then soaked themselves in the bath blowing bubbles and smearing each other with soap suds like kids. It was 10 p.m. before they felt some pangs of hunger and then ordered supper from room service. They ate slowly, taking turns to feed each other like a newly married couple. They topped the food with a bottle of sparkling wine whilst watching a movie on TV. Queen drank slowly with her head on his chest.

That was fantastic. I was afraid that I was destined to die unfulfilled. This is the first time I have climaxed, and Mike is the best man I have ever known. He is as strong as a stallion.

That night Queen slept like a baby. She woke up with a start after nine, rushing to the bathroom, thinking she had been dreaming and was late for work.

'Good morning, Queen.'

There was a delay before she answered.

'Good morning dear. Thank you for yesterday.'

'Thank you too. I hope today will be better.'

She noticed that he was already dressed and reading a U.K. newspaper.

'How long have you been awake?'

'I woke up at 7 o'clock and decided to let you rest. Once you are ready, we'll set out for London's West End. We've got a busy day.'

'Give me thirty minutes and I'll be ready.'

'You can have one hour.'

'Thank you darling. You are so thoughtful.'

They left the hotel at 11 o'clock. Mike had warned that they would do a lot of walking, so they both wore sensible flat shoes. They took the underground to Bond Street station, exited and then walked down the street checking out the restaurants and cafes along the way. They finally settled for a small Chinese restaurant. They tucked into their brunch with relish. One hour later they left the restaurant several pounds heavier. They decided to burn the calories by walking. They strolled down Bond Street and then turned into Oxford Street, one of the busiest shopping precincts in the world. They became lost in the teeming crowd of thousands of shoppers and tourists. Nkechi had never been to England, and was amazed at what she saw. They walked into Selfridges, the largest departmental store on Oxford Street.

'Queen, this is our destination. Jimmy Choo shoes, Burberry purses, Loius Vuitton luggage, Versace business suits. Whatever you want, they've got it.' Mike picked up a piece of paper from the floor and scribbled something on it. Then he showed Nkechi.

'Queen, this is what we've got to spend here. I am not buying anything, so it's all yours.'

'Really?'

'Yes, so let's start.'

Two hours later they stumbled out of Selfridges, struggling to carry the shopping bags in both hands. They had wanted to walk down the street to 'House of Fraser' but they decided to give this a miss, and took a London black cab back to their hotel.

Nkechi was so excited. She again tried on all the new clothes and apparels, with Mike sitting down and admiring her. She looked good in all of them. Eventually, she folded the clothes and placed the shoes and bags in the new suitcase she bought at Selfridges. They both went down to the hotel restaurant for dinner and stayed back to listen to the pianist in the hotel bar whilst they sipped exotic cocktails. They returned to their room when the pianist closed at eleven. If Nkechi thought they were going to have a quiet night, she was wrong. No sooner were they in the room than Mike started serenading her. Then he turned on the music channel on the flat screen TV, and they started dancing. Before long they were locked in an embrace on the sofa, like the anaconda and its prey. From the sofa, they rolled on to the floor and continued canoodling until they were tired. When they disengaged, Nkechi was effusive in her praise of Mike.

'You are amazing darling.'

'You are wonderful yourself, a real queen.'

The next day, the couple went to Madame Tussauds in Baker Street, and then hopped on the open London bus. It was late summer and the weather was excellent for the tour of London. The next three days were equally fun filled. A week after they arrived, Mike and Nkechi were on the British Airways flight back to Lagos.

Once back in Lagos, Mike threw himself into the work of the local government. His medical training made him particularly methodical. He quickly built up a reputation as a thinker and doer. His parents were impressed with his dedication and the reports reaching them about his achievements. Nkechi was equally busy at FRCN, and was soon promoted into the editorial team. They hardly saw each other socially during the week, but occasionally their paths crossed in the course of their work. They kept in touch by phone and texts on weekdays but they were virtually inseparable at weekends.

When Mike became a councillor, Senator Lawanson reckoned he would need some space of his own and therefore allowed him to move from the main house he shared with his parents to the detached guest lodge in the same compound. This was in itself a fully furnished self-contained two bedroom bungalow with its own living room and other facilities. Soon after Mike and Nkechi returned from London, Mrs. Lawanson noticed that a red Toyota Celica car was parked in front of Mike's apartment on Friday night. It had not been moved at all throughout Saturday. When it remained in the same position on Sunday morning, Mrs. Lawanson walked across to find out who the car belonged to. She knocked on the door and then tried the lock. The door opened and she entered the living room. To her consternation, Mike was seated at the dining table having breakfast with a lady.

'Good morning ma,' said Nkechi, getting up from the table and curtseying as she greeted Mrs. Lawanson.

'Good morning mum. Queen, please set the table for my mother.'

'No thank you, I have already eaten. I saw the strange red car and I wanted to make sure all is well.'

'This is Nkechi Obi, my girlfriend. The car belongs to her. We were planning to visit you later today.'

'Hello, my daughter. Hope all is well.'

'I am well ma, thank you.'

'Goodbye. By the way, your father would like to see you after the church service.'

'O.K. mum I'll come over around 2 o'clock.'

Mike walked across the lawn to the main house just after 2 o'clock. He met his parents having lunch.

'Mike, grab a plate and join us.'

'Thank you mum, I am not hungry.'

'Oh I see, your woman has fixed something for you.'

'Which woman?' Senator Lawanson enquired.

'You haven't told your dad.'

'Tell me what?'

'Daddy, don't mind mummy. She is talking about my girlfriend.'

'Your girlfriend? Do I know her?'

'Don't think so dad. But you'll meet her soon enough. She helped me a lot during the campaign.'

'Mike, when did she arrive at the lodge?'

'Leave him alone Ajoke, he is old enough to have a girlfriend,' interjected Senator Lawanson.

'I know he is old enough to get married, and that is exactly why I wanted to talk to him. I want to be a grandmother.'

'Are you serious with this lady?

'Of course mum.'

'Then we should be thinking of meeting her parents. We have to do things properly in accordance with our traditions. First, the family introduction followed by the traditional engagement ceremony.'

'Slow down mummy. We are not ready for that.'

'I thought you said you loved each other.'

'Yes we do, but we are taking things slowly, one step at a time.'

'Okay, but don't wait too long.'

'We won't, but give us at least two years,' replied Mike laughing as he left the dining room to return to his apartment.

CHAPTER 4

David and Daniel Lawanson were Senator Mike Lawanson's younger twin brothers. David was a barrister in Ibadan in Western Region of Nigeria whilst Daniel was a Consultant Urological Surgeon who had stayed back to practice in London after completing his postgraduate training in surgery, and had only recently returned to work at the University Teaching Hospital in Ibadan.

David had joined the Peoples Party of Nigeria (PPN) when his brother was the Head of the Senate, and a confidant of the country's president. David's stature had risen astronomically when he successfully defended some union leaders who had been wrongly detained for organising industrial action. At great personal risk, he had fought the State Government and the police force. This made victory in the courts especially sweet. When he announced his candidacy for the Western Region Governorship elections scheduled for early the following year, the unions swung their support behind him. He still had to win the nomination of the party, but the Western Region was a bastion of the PPN and it was assumed that whoever won the party nomination was likely to be elected. Mike also threw his support and political machinery behind his uncle. David's running mate was Dauda Adams. David and Dauda were classmates in primary school. Dauda had enrolled in the police force after leaving the secondary school. He attained the rank of deputy inspector of police but retired early from the police force to go into local government politics. The partnership was designed to take into consideration the religious balance in the region, hence a Christian Governorship candidate with a Muslim standing to be the deputy Governor. The Western State wing of PPN confirmed their nominations on the eve of the National Congress in Jos where the various regional nominations would be ratified.

Team David flew to Jos in the middle belt for the congress. The weather in the plateau region was excellent in late September, before the cold chilly harmattan weather set in towards the end of the year. The congress duly ratified David and Dauda's nominations. The team decided they would spend another two days in Jos relaxing and attending to other matters before returning to Ibadan. David was due to address a special night vigil service organised by the Scripture Union of Nigeria at a local church in the suburb of Jos. David was a national executive member of the Scripture Union.

The night vigil commenced at 9 o'clock and was scheduled to end at 1.00 a.m. It was just before midnight with the service in full swing when there was persistent noise outside the locked doors of the church. The Sexton of the church offered to investigate. He slipped out of the door and was mortified by the sight which confronted him. He saw an irate mob numbering almost a hundred wielding cudgels, sticks and machetes. It was difficult to hear their grouse above the ruckus but he managed to hear that they were looking for someone alleged to have defiled the Holy Koran.

The Sexton escaped from the mob and managed to slip back into the church through a side door. Whilst anger boiled outside with the noise reaching a crescendo, the elders gently lowered the congregation into the bush through the vestry window at the rear of the church. The rear of the church was not readily accessible from the front or sides as a result of a deep gully with thick shrubs and trees. From the back of the mob, a voice rang out.

'The music has stopped. They must be planning something. Break down the doors. Death to the infidels,' he shouted.

'Death to the infidels, death to the infidels, death to the kaffirs,' the mob shouted as they stormed the building. Some pelted the windows with stones whilst others battered the doors with heavy wooden and metal rams. The front door soon gave way and the mob rushed into the porch leading to the aisle. The pastor in his white cassock exited the aisle and confronted the mob in the porch trying to assuage their anger. The two leaders brushed the pastor aside and ran into the main church hall looking for the worshippers. Meanwhile the mob descended on the hapless pastor.

The pastor managed to break free and fled into the surrounding bush. 'Get him, get the infidel,' shouted the mob. They rushed after him, throwing stones and other missiles at him. Just as he reached the edge of a gorge one of the attackers caught up with him and hit him on the back with a cudgel. He tumbled headlong into the gorge and only then did the mob turn back. In the meantime the two gang leaders found their targets in the vestry. Pa Abraham, the sexton was in his seventies. His hip and knee joints were riddled with arthritis and he walked gingerly. His infirmity made it impossible for him to climb out of the high vestry window through which the other worshippers escaped. He had urged their visitor and the pastor to escape, leaving him alone in the church. They would have none of this, and the younger man was trying to lift the sexton through the window when the mob leaders burst into the room. One of the attackers delivered a crushing blow across the nape of the visitor, and he fell across the room with the old man tumbling and smashing his head on the floor. The assailants dealt with the two men. Once the attack started, there was no stopping them until both victims were dead. They exited the church and ordered the mob to disperse. They left jubilant and triumphant.

News of the attack reached Jos city through some of the worshippers who managed to escape. By the time the police reached the site, all the miscreants had long since disappeared. They did some forensic work and then summoned ambulances to remove the corpses of David Lawanson and the Sexton. The Pastor was rushed to hospital in a coma. It was reported in the morning newspapers as a religious attack by fundamentalists. The police promised to get to the bottom of the crime. Dauda Adams as a retired police officer liaised with investigating police officers. He took personal charge of bringing David's corpse to Ibadan. This was a devastating blow to the Lawanson family and the PPN in the West. Dauda Adams led the delegation from the West to commiserate with the patriarch of the Lawanson family, Senator Femi Lawanson in Lagos. He promised to do his utmost to bring the perpetrators of the dastardly act to book. Thousands attended the funeral service at the Cathedral Church of St. James, and tens of thousands lined the streets as the hearse was driven slowly through the streets of Ibadan to the cemetery. The unions David had spent so much time and energy to defend in his lifetime were prominent in paying their last respects to him.

Gloom descended upon the Lawanson household in Ikeja. Senator Lawanson spoke little and ate little. He mourned the loss of his younger brother for a long time. Their father had died several years ago but their aged mother Grace Lawanson, now in her eighties had relocated to their village soon after her husband died. Femi and his surviving twin brother, Daniel, travelled together to bring their mother to Lagos before she learnt about the disaster from an outsider. The moment she laid eyes on them, she knew something was amiss.

'Where is David?'

'David is fine. He is busy preparing for an important court case,' Femi lied.

'I don't believe you. David is not that type of person. He is never too busy to visit his mother.'

'He has malaria fever, and the doctor asked him to rest,' Daniel lied.

'Thank you my son. Don't mind your brother. I knew something was wrong,' replied their mother.

They left late in the afternoon, arriving at the Lawanson Ikeja residence at dusk. When Mama walked into the living room, she noticed that the room was eerily quiet. Even at her age, she remained extremely perspicacious. When she saw a Reverend sitting amongst members of the family she became suspicious.

'Femi, tell me the truth. What happened?' Mama demanded to know.

'Mama, please sit down,' Femi pleaded. His mother sat down.

The Reverend started to speak.

'Mama, you are welcome.' He sighed and then continued.

'Apostle Paul tells us in his epistle to the Thessalonians not to be ignorant about those who have fallen asleep, lest we sorrow like those who have no hope.' Before he could continue, Mama let out a frightening shrill sound, and then fainted on the sofa. When she came round some minutes later, she was flanked on the sides by her surviving sons.

She looked to her right and directed her question to Daniel.

'Who died? Where is David?'

Daniel could no longer control himself. Tears rolled freely down his cheeks.

'Mama, David is no more. My twin has gone.'

Mother and child held each other tightly and cried intensely. In between sobbing and wailing, she made a strange pronouncement.

'How can this happen again? A mother is not supposed to know the grave of her own son, to bury two is terrible but three is immeasurable disaster.'

Eventually, Mike was able to sedate his Nan.

Mike was as confused as Daniel at Mama's utterance. After Mama fell asleep, the two of them approached Senator Lawanson. Daniel was the first to broach the subject.

'Brother, what did Mama mean about burying two sons?'

'It's a long story.'

'I am all ears. This is important family history and

I need to know.'

'Me too,' added Mike.

'Okay, get me a cup of water and then sit down. I'll start from the beginning.'

CHAPTER 5

'The relevant part of the story started in 1960. I remember this period vividly because it was the year of our country's independence from Great Britain. The gaps in the story were filled by my father just before he died. After he told me the story, I gave him my commitment that I would look after my mother and brothers. So you see why I feel guilty that I couldn't protect David.'

'It's not your fault,' replied Daniel.

'I should have known better. In my active electioneering days, I would never have gone out late at night or outside my base without adequate personal security. I should have insisted that David employ and travel with personal bodyguards.'

Senator Lawanson cleared his throat and started the story

'As the cock crowed at dawn on the first day of October 1960, I rolled over in bed, opened my eyes and peered at the alarm clock on the side table. It was only 5.30 a.m. but chinks of the rising sun had started to pierce into the bedroom through gaps in the curtain. I stretched in bed and then got up. My father was already awake. He tiptoed around the house, careful not to disturb his heavily pregnant wife, who was still asleep and snoring heavily. When in full throttle, Papa likened Mama's snoring to the locomotive engine of the Lagos to Zaria train he travelled in during his teacher training course in Zaria. He went into the bathroom to get ready for the day. Half an hour later, he walked out of the bathroom clean shaven and half dressed with his hair well groomed. Papa walked across the corridor to my room. As he turned the door knob, Papa was surprised that I was already getting dressed. There was none of the usual reluctance to get ready for school.'

"Good morning papa."

"Good morning, Femi," replied my father.

"Get ready quickly, today is a momentous day. After today, things will never be the same again, continued my father."

'Little did he know how prophetic this statement would turn out to be.'

'The entire country was waiting in anticipation of the handover of power from Great Britain to Nigerians after almost hundred years of colonial rule. Nowhere were the plans more elaborate than the capital city, Lagos. Papa was the headmaster of the Lagos Waterside Church Missionary Society village school. The best pupils from select primary and secondary schools in Lagos and environs had been chosen to march at the ceremony to be held at the racecourse on Lagos Island. I had been chosen to lead the contingent of twelve pupils from my school in the march past. The team would be accompanied by my father. The pupils had spent the last month in marching drills supervised by him, bringing to bear all his experience as a Scout leader. We also memorised the new National Anthem, and all of us could recite it anywhere and at any time of the day.'

'By 6.30 a.m. my father and I were ready to leave for the meeting point in front of the school. I turned out in heavily starched and well ironed khaki shirt and shorts, and well polished, glistening brown sandals.'

"Bye bye mummy," I said, addressing my mother who was now tidying up in the kitchen.

"Goodbye Femi," replied mummy.

"Grace, are you all right?" asked dad.

"Yes dear, I am fine thank you. Have a nice day. See you later," replied mum.

'We left home, turning round to wave to mum as we exited the gate. We hurried down the dirt road to the school, about four hundred yards away. We got to the meeting point with time to spare. By 7.00 a.m. the pupils and dad left in the Lagos Municipal Transport Service bus arranged for the occasion. Half an hour later, we stopped briefly at another school to pick up another batch of pupils. Then we took off finally for the Independence ceremony venue. The pupils quickly struck up friendship with each other, and before long, we were all singing merrily in the bus. The streets were sparkling clean and decorated with buntings and flags – the Union Jack of colonial Nigeria and the Green-White-Green flag of the new Nigeria.'

"Wow," I exclaimed as we disembarked.

'I was admiring the resplendent uniform of the various wings of the Nigerian Armed Forces, as they prepared to march into the arena. In colonial Nigeria, soldiers were not seen in public, at least not in uniform. The weather was excellent. The skies were clear and the sun shone brilliantly. When the ceremony started, the armed forces and the police marched with incredible grace and dexterity to the music of the army and police bands. The children found the Scottish bagpipe players of the Nigerian police band to be the most intriguing. How could such beautiful music come from such funny contraptions? The children marched with zing past the dais where a member of the British royal family standing in for Her Majesty the Queen, and the new Nigerian leaders stood. The Northern People's Congress and the National Council of Nigerian Citizens had formed an alliance following the pre-independence national elections, and they would provide the Prime Minister and Governor General respectively in the new Nigeria. A couple of hours after the ceremony commenced, it reached the climax when the Royal Princess handed over the instruments of office to the Nigerians as the Union Jack was lowered in Lagos for the last time, and the Green-White-Green flag simultaneously raised. The military band struck the first note, and the whole arena exploded with a rendition of the new National Anthem.'

> Nigeria we hail thee,
> Our own dear native land,
> Though tribe and tongue may differ
> In brotherhood we stand,

Nigerians all,
Are proud to serve,
Our sovereign motherland.

'As soon as the singing ended, the crowd burst into thunderous applause. The ceremony was broadcast live on radio and on television. Men and women were hugging each other and dancing in the streets. The marching school children returned to their schools to sumptuous dinner of jollof rice, fried rice, fried plantains, beef stew and mineral drinks. Elsewhere, people partied all day and night the length and breadth of the country.'

'My father was supervising the Independence dinner at the school when a neighbour ran into the staff room looking dishevelled and panting, unable to make any sense with her utterances.'

"Headmaster, where is the headmaster?"

"Madam, how can I help?" asked the teacher.

"I want to see Mr. Joseph Lawanson now," the neighbour replied.

"Tell him his wife, his wife, em em his wife..." added the woman, running frantically back and forth like a headless chicken.

"Calm down, what is the matter with Mrs. Lawanson?" the teacher asked.

"By this time the woman had created such a scene that my father had been attracted to the staff room to investigate."

"What's the matter Mama Olu?" dad enquired.

"It's Mama Femi, come quickly, Mama Femi is at the health centre," replied the neighbour.

'Dad had a quick word with his deputy and then hurried along to the main road where he hailed a taxi, and made for the health centre.

When he arrived at the health centre, mum was being attended to by the doctor and the midwife, and he wasn't allowed to see her for what seemed like eternity. In reality, he only had to wait for ten minutes. He paced up and down the corridor sweating and murmuring. When he was eventually allowed to see mum, he was overcome with emotion and rambled on, not making any sense. Ironically, it fell to mum to calm him down.'

"Don't worry Joe, I'll be all right," mummy managed to say, in a voice barely louder than a whisper.

"What happened?" dad was finally able to ask.

"Soon after you left this morning, I started having lower abdominal cramps. I took a pain killer but this gave only transient relief. I decided to rest in bed, but soon afterwards my water broke," explained mum.

"But you are not yet due," replied dad.

"You are correct. I still have five weeks to due date," replied mum before she suddenly screamed and doubled up in pain, from uterine contractions.

'The midwife hurried along.'

"Mrs. Lawanson, how do you feel now?" the midwife asked.

"Drop the formalities, just call me Grace."

"O.K. Grace, how do you feel?" she asked again.

"The pain is searing, it's just too much for me," replied mum.

"I'll get my trolley ready and give you an internal examination."

'The midwife was back in a few minutes with a small trolley covered with a drape. She pulled the screen to give her patient some privacy and then palpated her abdomen.'

"Head is down but not yet engaged," stated the midwife, giving a running commentary as she continued her examination.

'She grabbed the foetal stethoscope and listened for the foetal heart beats first on the right side of the lower tummy, and then on the left.'

'She then slipped on size 7 sterile gloves, swabbed the perineum with chlorhexidine solution and then carried out internal digital examination. As she withdrew her fingers, she muttered:

"Only one finger dilated."

"What did you find?" mum asked.

"The baby is fine, the head is down and heart beats are good but there is still a long way to go. You are only one finger dilated and the head is not yet engaged," replied the midwife.

"The pain is coming back," mum managed to reply amidst groaning and grunting.

"I'll give you something for the pain and this will also help you relax."

'The midwife retreated to the nurse's room, returning a few minutes later with a hypodermic syringe filled with Pethidine. She uncovered mum's bum and injected the drug. Minutes later, mum calmed down and fell asleep. Dad kept vigil at his wife's bedside all through the night. He refused to heed the advice of the nursing staff that mum was in good hands and he could go home to rest. By the time the doctors and nurses went on their ward round, mum had been in labour for twenty four hours. She was making very slow progress, and dad was starting to get agitated. In the village, dad was known to be uxorious. He had decided he wasn't going anywhere until his wife delivered the baby.'

'Dad told me that ten years earlier, labour for my delivery had lasted less than four hours, and mum was back home in twenty four hours. Since then, the couple had gone through turbulent obstetric history. When I was three years old, the couple tried for another baby. Mum promptly became pregnant but she miscarried when she was twenty weeks pregnant. A year later, she became pregnant and gave up work so that she could rest properly as advised, but once again she suffered a mid-trimester miscarriage. Mama agba, my paternal grandmother and the head of the family intervened at this point. She consulted a powerful diviner in her hometown in the west of the country who concluded that the child was an abiku, literally translated as "born to die." These children die at birth or early in infancy and re-enter their mothers' wombs to be re-born only to torment their parents again by dying in infancy. Mum was confused and became depressed. She only pulled through by throwing herself into church activities after the intervention and spiritual guidance of the village church minister.'

'Even though he did not show it, the medical officer had become worried about the slow progress of mum's labour and had contacted the Consultant Gynaecologist in the Specialist Hospital on Lagos Island. As he went back to the clinic to await her arrival, he saw dad sitting astride a chair hunched over the back of the chair. He looked dishevelled with blood shot eyes.

"Mr. Joseph, everything is under control. You can go home to rest and have a change of clothes," suggested Dr. Johnson.

'Dad looked at him with incredulity, but said nothing.'

"Mr. Joseph, you can come back to see your wife later in the day. There is nothing to worry about, but I have asked Professor

Rebecca Harris to review your wife. We are expecting her arrival any moment from now."

"Thank you, thank you," replied dad, who then readjusted himself on the chair and turned his gaze towards the maternity ward.

'Dr. Johnson gave up and shuffled along to his office.'

'Half hour later, the imposing Professor Harris arrived and walked briskly into the labour room, followed by Dr. Johnson and the hospital matron. Mum was now fully dilated but tired. The presentation was cephalic and foetal heart beats were still strong and regular. Professor Harris decided to carry out assisted forceps delivery of the baby. The baby was delivered within an hour, and he cried promptly. The afterbirth was delivered without any complication. Dad was elated, and he smiled broadly for the first time since he came to the health centre the previous day. Mother and child were discharged home later in the day.'

'Dad took some time off work whilst mum slowly regained her strength. Mama agba came down from the hinterland to help with the house work and child care. Three days after delivery, they were back in the health centre. It was mum who first noticed that the baby had slightly yellow sclera, and drew dad's attention to it. He tried to reassure her but by evening of the second day the skin had a yellowish tinge. At daylight on the third day, Grace and Joseph took the baby back to the health centre. Dr. Johnson said it was jaundice of prematurity, not uncommon in premature and low birth weight babies. They were referred to the Children's hospital in the city where the baby was admitted. The baby's eyes were covered with eye pads and the baby was treated with phototherapy and a combination of oral and parenteral medications. Daily blood tests were performed. By the sixth day of life, the serum bilirubin level had fallen to normal level and with this the baby's jaundice cleared. He was discharged home same day. On the seventh day, the traditional naming ceremony took place at the Lawanson home. Dad and mum named my brother Ope-Oluwa meaning "God deserves our thanks," and Mama agba named him Rotimi meaning "stay with me." Mama agba still held strongly to her belief that this child was an *abiku*. By naming him Rotimi, she was imploring him to stay alive this time and cease tormenting her parents. Mum did not really believe in the *abiku* theory but she could not openly oppose Mama agba. Well mannered, properly brought up wives were not supposed to oppose or try to discredit their mothers-in-law. If dad disbelieved Mama agba, he never said so. In fact, no one knew where he stood on this matter.'

'Ope-Oluwa Rotimi continued to thrive and steadily gained weight. Mama agba had her plans to strengthen the boy and banish the spectre of recurrent childhood death. Mama agba usually washed the baby every morning giving mum the opportunity to have a lie in. At age two weeks, she put her plans into operation. After washing the baby, she took a brand new razor blade and made three small lacerations on the child's chest barely drawing blood. She then took a black powder wrapped in paper with black thread and rubbed it into the scars, as she uttered some incantations. The whole procedure lasted less than five minutes. Mum rushed out of her bedroom to the bathroom when she heard her baby screaming but by the time she got to the bathroom, the baby was only whimpering.'

"Mama, what's the problem with Ope-Oluwa?" asked mum.

"There is no problem," replied Mama agba.

"Mama, what's that discoloration on his skin?" enquired mum, pointing at the bloodied marks on the baby's chest.

"Ah, that! That is *gbere* for his protection," Mama replied.

'Mum opened her mouth to say something, but changed her mind. She waited whilst Mama agba finished dressing the child and she then took the child for breast feeding. The rest of the morning mum held on to the child, apart from the spell when the baby had his morning nap.'

'When dad returned from work, the house was eerily quiet. There was none of the usual noisy welcome from mum. He saw Mama agba shredding some waterleaf vegetables in the veranda.'

"Good afternoon, mama."

"Good afternoon, how was school?" asked Mama agba.

"Good, very good," replied dad.

"Where is Grace?" asked dad.

"In the bedroom," replied Mama agba, pointing towards the room.

'Daddy could sense that something was amiss.'

"Dear, how are you doing?" dad asked as he strode across the living room into the bedroom.

Mum heard him loud and clear but did not utter a word.

"Grace, what's the matter?"

"This is the matter," replied mum, undoing the baby's dress and pointing at the scars on his chest.

"What's that?" dad demanded to know.

"Ask your mother, just ask her."

'Dad lifted the baby from his cot, and examined the chest closely.'

"Your mother said she was fortifying Ope with native insurance because he is an *abiku*," said mum with disdain.

"Oh my God, Oh my God," was all Joseph could say.

'He sat on the bed hugging his son, who was now awake and crying. The scars were still raw and sore. Mum administered half a teaspoon of Paracetamol syrup, and then rocked the baby back to sleep. Dad left the room to have a word with Mama agba.'

"Mama, I'll like to have a word."

"What's the matter," she demanded to know.

"Mama, why did you inflict those cuts on the baby's chest?" dad asked in an uncompromising mood.

"What type of question is that? You are following your wife blindly. Don't forget that I gave birth to you and brought you up. Or do you think I don't know what I am doing?" Mama agba replied defiantly.

'She continued after a short pause.'

"Look, that baby is 'born to die'. The Ibos call them *ogbanje*. All I was doing was to make sure he stays this time. Don't you know how many times he has come and gone, all those miscarriages and the stillbirth?"

"Mama, there is nothing wrong with him. We don't believe in that superstition."

"Thank you, thank you very much. I know I am an illiterate but I am still your mother."

With this Mama agba knelt beside the bed and pulled out her suitcase. She opened it and started arranging her clothes within it.

"Mama, what are you doing?" asked dad.

"What do you think I am doing?" replied Mama agba.

'Dad did not reply.'

"I am leaving for the village tomorrow morning."

"Mama, you don't have to go. We want you around,' replied dad, imploring my grandmother.

"Ah, no, you don't need me any longer. You and your wife are better informed than me."

'Mama agba finished packing her clothes and then slammed the suitcase shut. Joseph was dumbstruck. He was now in the middle of a tiff between the two women he loved. Mama walked out on him and went out to the balcony, rested her forearms on the railings and just gazed at the skies. Dad entered the living room and dropped into the arm chair, closed his eyes while his mind raced up and down wondering what his next move should be.'

The following morning, long before the rest of the household woke up. Mama agba had showered and tidied up her room. When mum ventured into the living room just after 6.00 a.m., Mama agba was sitting precariously on her battered suitcase.

"Good morning Mama," with mum half kneeling down as she greeted her mother-in-law, in the traditional way.

"Good morning my daughter," Mama replied.

'Mama, why are you up so early?'

"Didn't your husband tell you?" asked Mama agba.

'Tell me what?' replied my mother.

"Well, I am leaving this morning. I am returning home," replied Mama agba.

"Why?" asked mum.

"Why not?" replied Mama agba. Your husband has made it clear that you don't need me any longer. Can I say goodbye to my grandson?"

"He is still asleep but I'll bring him," replied mum.

'By now dad was awake and getting ready for work. He had concluded he would not try to dissuade his mother. He will make a detour and drop her at bus station on his way to work.'

'As they left for the bus station, Mama agba and mum exchanged greetings. Mama agba looked back one more time as dad drove out of the compound and she saw mum carrying Ope. I was oblivious of all the tension and ran after the car waving goodbye to my grandmother. She waved back and fought back tears. Little did they know that Mama agba would never again set foot in the house.'

'The next week was uneventful in the Lawanson household. Mother and child continued to do well, and they soon forgot about the encounter with Mama agba. Ten days after Mama left, mum noticed the baby was listless and not feeding well. They assumed it was just a mild viral infection which would soon improve. "It's the weather," dad said reassuringly.

"Every time the seasons change, there is usually outbreak of cold," mum added, nodding in agreement.

'Mum managed to push some Paracetamol syrup down the baby's throat. By nightfall there had been no improvement in the condition of the baby. The baby was lying prostrate on the bed and they were wondering what to do when suddenly he stiffened and had a seizure.

'Mum screamed, and dad panicked. He grabbed the baby and hugged him tightly.'

"Grace, please get me the car key. We must take our baby to the hospital immediately."

"It's now almost ten, and Femi is fast asleep in his room. We can't leave him alone in the flat," stated mum.

"Can you ask our neighbour to have him for the night," suggested dad.

"We've got no choice. I'll go ask Mo. Her boys and Femi are good friends."

'Mo obliged, and with that matter settled, they set out for the Queen Street Children's Hospital.'

'Dad drove at breakneck speed. They were in the hospital within thirty minutes. As they brought the child into the waiting room, he had another convulsion. This time the episode was more prolonged and definitely more frightening. The nurse gave them priority over the other waiting patients, and took them straight to the doctor.'

'Mum was now openly distressed, and in tears.'

"Doctor, doctor, please save my child," Grace pleaded with tears streaming down her face.

"Doctor, what is wrong with our son?" dad added.

"Please, stay calm. I will be in a better condition to answer your questions once I have examined him."

'The doctor was meticulous. He took a full clinical history from dad. Mum was not in a position to speak coherently. The doctor then proceeded to examine the child. He noticed the healing scars on the child's chest. When he palpated the abdomen, he noticed it was hard and board-like. He placed his stethoscope on the chest and listened to the breath sounds, and then proceeded to check the heart. The doctor looked up, shifted in his chair and then pointed at the scars in the chest.

"What is that?" asked the doctor.

'Mum looked at her husband, and sighed, as if to say, you tell him.'

"It is called *gbere*, native protection," replied Joseph.

"What were you protecting him from?" asked Dr. Gold.

"Well, my mother said that our son was an *abiku*, so she made those marks to protect him from premature death," replied dad.

"Three years ago, my wife delivered a son who died at birth. My mother said the new child looked exactly like the deceased son and must have come back to torment us."

The doctor did not respond. He just set about treating the child and then handed over the treatment chart to the nursing sister. As the doctor left the treatment room to attend to other matters, dad followed him.'

"Doctor, please tell me what you think the diagnosis is?" dad asked.

"I am not sure yet, but I think your son has tetanus, neonatal tetanus," replied Dr. Gold.

"What is that? And is it curable?"

'Dr. Max Gold spent the next few minutes giving a brief description of neonatal tetanus and possible causes.'

"Do you mean the infection could have entered his body through the chest scars?" dad asked.

"Yes," replied the doctor, nodding his head as he spoke.

"Thank you doctor, thank you very much."

"You don't need to thank me. I am just doing my job," replied the doctor.

"Doctor, do you believe that some children are born to die?"

"I am afraid, I don't," replied the doctor.

"There are many causes of infant deaths our people do not understand. I think *abikus* fall into this category," continued the doctor.

CHAPTER 6

'The Lawanson baby's condition remained serious but stable. Eventually, after several days in the neonatal intensive care unit, he was well enough to be moved to the general ward. At last, mum was relaxed enough to go home at night. The convulsive spasms were now few and far between. Then one night, soon after my parents left for home, the baby had a seizure and regurgitated his feed, part of which he aspirated. My parents returned to the hospital the following morning and Ope was re-admitted to the intensive care unit with severe bronchopneumonia. My parents were alarmed at the breathlessness of my brother. Despite all treatment measures, he died from sheer exhaustion and respiratory distress before noon.

'Just before the baby expired, the couple were led out of the intensive care unit into the waiting room as the doctors struggled to resuscitate him. The Consultant Paediatrician entered the waiting room half an hour later, my parents jumped from their seats. As the Consultant opened his mouth and uttered the words,'

"I am sorry..."

Mother did not let him finish. She let out a loud harrowing cry, which pierced the humdrum of the ward environment. She swooned and Joseph caught her in the nick of time. Grace was laid out flat on the couch whilst the doctor worked hard at reviving her. She came to in a short while, and managed to sit up. She started sobbing, at first low level crying interrupted by unintelligible sounds, eventually rising to a crescendo which drowned all other sound. Dad was confused and sad at the same time, eyes welling with tears. He knew he had to be strong for his wife.'

'Mum went into a prolonged period of depression following their child's death. She hardly spoke. Whenever she was coaxed to speak, she started with the same words.

"Parents are not supposed to bury their children. It should be the other way round."

'Then she would retract into her shell, and go quiet for days. In keeping with the tradition of the Yoruba of Western Nigeria, neither my father nor mother attended the burial of my brother. My uncles and aunties took care of all the arrangements and the baby was buried within days of his death.

'A month later, the gloom had still not lifted. Mum hardly spoke, and ate very little. She lost a lot of weight and my dad was alarmed. This was another disaster in the making. Mum seemed to be disinterested in life and had virtually ceased caring for herself and for me. Dad had to take an extended leave from work as he was afraid to leave mum alone. News soon reached the Bishop that their primary school headmaster's wife was suffering from severe depression. He sent a message to dad that he would arrange for a Consultant Psychiatrist to visit them at home. Dad was grateful for the concern but wasn't expecting any quick intervention. After all, he was only an ordinary primary school head teacher. To his surprise, the following morning as he was coaxing mum to eat some food, there was a knock on the door. Dad looked through the door peep hole and saw his vicar accompanied by a gentleman in black suit carrying a black briefcase. He turned the key and released the extra latch on the door.'

"Good morning Sir."

"Good morning Joseph," replied the vicar. The gentleman just smiled in response.

"Come in Sir, please come in," dad stood aside holding the door ajar for the men.

"Joseph, we've come to see your wife. Where is she?" asked the vicar.

"This is Doctor Anthony Obu, professor of psychiatry at the

University Teaching Hospital. The bishop has asked him to have a look at your wife."

"I am pleased to meet you Sir. I am Lawanson, Joseph Lawanson. Thank you for coming."

"Where is your wife?" asked the vicar.

"She is in the bedroom," replied dad. "Please sit down, I'll bring her out."

A few minutes later, mum joined them in the living room. The vicar was shocked but tried not to show it. This was not the Mrs. Lawanson he knew. Elegant, well nourished ebony black beauty. She was now haggard, with a mournful look.

"Mama Femi, quite an age. How are you?" asked the vicar.

'He had uttered those words before he realised how inappropriate they were.'

'Mum just looked at him, and gave a perfunctory virtually inaudible reply.'

'The vicar quickly backtracked and decided he would leave the business of delving into her clinical condition to the experts. He knew how important the issue of faith was to the Lawansons, so he decided to open the deliberations with prayers. Once this was over, he conferred with Professor Obu before announcing that he had important matters to attend to and would be back in an hour. In reality, he wanted to give them some privacy to enable the psychiatrist to get to the bottom of the matter.'

"Hello, Mrs. Lawanson. I am Professor Obu."

"Good morning Sir," replied Grace.

"I have come to talk to you," continued Professor Obu.

'Grace did not respond or show any emotion.'

"Do you want your husband to stay or will you like to talk to me alone?"

'She didn't answer but gestured with her shoulders that she didn't mind either way. The professor gestured to Joseph to sit down. For the first fifteen minutes or thereabout, the professor skirted round the main problem fielding bland questions, before finally confronting the main issue. For the most part, Joseph kept quiet, only occasionally encouraging his wife to answer questions whenever she was unresponsive. The doctor was perspicacious. Joseph likened him to a world boxing champion, methodically jabbing at the opponent to soften him before landing the killer punch.

"Mrs. Lawanson, what is the main problem now?" asked Professor Obu, with his gaze fixed on mum. He made eye contact, and through the horn rimmed spectacles his eyes seemed to bore a hole into the patient.

"I see him every time I close my eyes," replied mum.

"Who do you see?" asked the doctor.

" I see Ope every time I close my eyes. He just lies there staring at me. My son died because I am a bad mother."

"Not at all, I have heard nice things about you. You are a very good mother," replied the doctor.

"If I am good, why did my son die in such a horrible way?" mum demanded to know.

"His death had nothing to do with you. You did your best. Sometimes these things happen, and we do not know why," Doctor Obu replied.

'The dialogue continued for the next half hour. The professor knew there was a lot of work to do but he was deft and had laid the foundation for future therapy sessions.'

'In one hour, mother had spoken more words than she had done in the previous two weeks. Professor Obu checked his wristwatch. He had already spent an hour on this case when the vicar drove in.

"Joe, this is not going to be easy. It's a marathon and not a sprint, but I am confident that your wife will get better."

"Thank you Sir, God bless you," replied dad.

"Our students are having their final examinations, and I am going to be very busy in the hospital in the next two days. I will be back to see your wife in three days time between 10 and 11 a.m. but if any serious problem arises before then, please feel free to bring her to our accident and emergency department." The doctor opened his black bag and handed over an envelope to dad. "Give your wife one tablet to be taken with water, twice daily for the next 3 days and I'll review the situation on my next visit."

"Thank you Sir. Goodbye," replied dad.

'Then my father turned to the vicar who had now entered the living room.'

"Thank you very much for bringing the professor, and please extend my utmost gratitude to the Lord Bishop."

"I have an appointment to see him tomorrow, and I will convey your message to him," the vicar replied.

'As Joseph escorted the professor and his vicar towards their car, he tugged on the vicar's robe and whispered into his ear.'

"Can I see you for a minute, Sir?"

"Prof., excuse me, I'll be with you in a minute," said the vicar.

"Sir, I thank you for bringing the professor to see my wife. He is undoubtedly an excellent doctor as I can already see my wife opening up but I have a problem."

"What's the problem," the vicar demanded to know.

"You know I am an ordinary primary school head teacher. I am already dreading receiving the bill for this first session from the professor."

'The vicar cut him short, and told him the Bishop was Professor Obu's good friend and old classmate, and the professor had agreed to treat mum gratis.'

"Thank you Sir, Thank you very much. God bless you and your family. God bless Professor Obu and his family, and may God bless our Bishop and his ministry," uttered my father, profusely thanking and praying for the three of them. Such was the measure of his delight that he continued to pray for the trio, even after the vicar's car had disappeared from view.

'Three days later, Professor came back as promised, and spent another hour with my mother. She was making slow but steady progress. After the session, they returned to the teaching hospital together where mum was enrolled in his clinic. The fresh air seemed to rejuvenate my mum. She had not left their house for weeks. Professor Obu encouraged her to get involved in volunteering and affairs of the community. Christmas was fast approaching, and the choir was practising regularly for the carol service. Both of them had been in the choir in their different churches in their younger days. They first met at a choir festival, where they were introduced by a mutual friend. Involvement with the choir did mum a world of good, and her old self slowly returned.'

'After several weeks of treatment by Professor Obu, the couple were advised to have a change of environment. Dad took emergency leave and they travelled to Ibadan where they spent two weeks with relations. It was a refreshing break, and by the time they returned home Professor Obu was able to wean her off her drugs, and she returned to work. Mum decided she didn't want the hassle and trauma of another pregnancy and child birth, and her doctor inserted an intra-uterine contraceptive device.'

'My parents settled into the humdrum of suburban life. I made good progress in the grammar school, and excelled in sports and academics. I was in my final year, preparing for the school leaving certificate examinations when hell broke loose in the Lawanson household, with the potential to derail my preparation for the examinations. Mum had been feeling a bit under the weather and decided to visit their family doctor. When dad returned from work, he noticed that the house was unusually quiet.'

"Grace, darling where are you?" shouted dad as he walked into their apartment.

'There was no reply, only a muffled sound came from the bedroom.'

"Grace, hope all is well. What did the doctor say?"

'Mum looked at her husband, half rising from her supine position, eyes welling with tears.'

"What's the matter dear?" dad asked.

"I can't go through the stress again," mum replied.

"What stress?"

"Joe, I am pregnant. I am 8 weeks pregnant."

"Impossible, impossible," replied dad.

"That is exactly what I thought, but the doctor confirmed his diagnosis with clinical examination and urine pregnancy test," replied mum. "The doctor said the contraceptive coil must have been spontaneously expelled from the womb."

"How am I going to cope?"

"I can't risk the trauma of another child death," lamented mum, now sobbing.

"My darling wife, all will be well this time. I will do everything in my power to ensure this."

"Is Professor Obu still working in the teaching hospital?"

"I think so," replied dad.

"I will like to talk to him. Can you arrange an appointment?" mum asked.

"I will get in touch with his office and try to set up an appointment."

'One week later, they were sitting in front of Professor Obu in the clinic. Mum felt much better after the consultation. Professor Obu referred her to the Teaching Hospital Ante-Natal clinic for expert management of the pregnancy. She had an uneventful pregnancy, and was delivered of a set of twin boys at thirty nine weeks gestation. They were christened David and Daniel.

'Daniel, this is the story of your birth, and Mama's travails.'

'A day after your naming ceremony, word reached dad through the driver of one of the buses plying the route from his village, that his mother was planning to travel to Lagos to see the babies and help with child care. When he told mum, she slumped in the chair and started hyperventilating. Dad was alarmed and started panicking. He grabbed a wet towel and wiped his wife's brow, and then turned on the electric fan, all to no avail. I heard the commotion and joined them in the living room.'

"Mummy, what's the matter? What's happening dad?"

"I am not sure," replied dad. "Keep an eye on your mum whilst I get some help."

'I held on to mother and started rubbing her back, urging her to calm down. Dad shot out of the flat, and started banging on our neighbour's door. He was back in a few minutes with Mrs. Hearne, a matron at the General Hospital. The matron took control of the situation, and in half an hour Grace's breathing settled down. She then turned to Joseph.'

"Papa Femi, do you know what triggered the hyperventilation?"

"Not really," replied dad.

My mother looked at her husband disdainfully.

Then dad back tracked.

"I told her that my mother was coming to visit us and help with child care."

"What's the problem with that?" Matron Hearne asked, looking perplexed.

'Mum did not allow her husband to answer the question. She lifted her hand in a gesture to shut him up and then started speaking.'

"When we had our last baby, Mama came to help with child care. She said our child was an *abiku* and carried out some fetish practice and incantations to prevent premature death. In the end the child died. I don't want a repeat of all that,"

"Papa Femi, is that true?" Mrs. Hearne asked.

"Yes, well more or less," replied dad.

"Oh dear!" she exclaimed.

'After a short pause, she changed the topic and engaged mum in ordinary chitchat. She brought up the latest gossip in town, and the two ladies joked and laughed heartily for the next twenty minutes. Soon it was time for Mrs. Hearne to leave.

"Grace, I need to get ready for work. I'll see you when I return from the hospital," Mrs. Hearne said. As she departed, dad followed, thanking her profusely for her help. She beckoned to Joseph just as she exited the flat, and he followed her.

"Papa Femi, you have a potentially explosive situation which requires wisdom."

"What should I do?" asked dad.

"Is there somewhere your wife can go and spend some time?"

"Yes, she has an older sister in Ibadan. We were planning to visit her next Christmas," replied dad.

"That's it, ship her and the babies off to Ibadan as soon as possible, tomorrow if you can," advised Mrs. Hearne.

"What about Mama?" dad asked.

"Send a telegram to Mama to postpone her visit because Grace and the babies had travelled to her sister's in Ibadan, for change of environment on doctor's advice."

"Thank you, thank you very much Mrs. Hearne. God bless you. You've just saved my bacon."

'The following day mum travelled with both of you to Ibadan, and dad sent a telegram to his mother in the village. You all spent the next month in Ibadan, and mum was relaxed and full of life when she returned to Lagos. My grandmother never visited us again. A few months later, she suffered a stroke and was dead in a matter of days.'

CHAPTER 7

Dauda Adams placed a call through to Senator Lawanson from Jos. He would be in Lagos later in the day to brief him on the latest on police investigations into the murder of David Lawanson. The moment the plane landed at Ikeja Airport, Dauda drove straight to the Lawanson residence.

Senator Lawanson was expecting Dauda.

'Good evening Sir.'

'Good evening Mr. Adams.'

'I have been in Jos for the past three days, and I had several meetings with the divisional police officer leading to the investigation of my friend's murder. I also met the Deputy Commissioner of Police who was my course mate at the Police College.'

'What have they found?'

'I am pleased to inform you that they have apprehended two suspects, and one of them has confessed.'

'Good, very good,' replied Senator Lawanson.

'When will they be charged to court?'

'The police are grilling the culprits so that they can catch the other criminals before prosecuting them.'

'I hope that won't take too long.'

'No, it won't take long,' replied Dauda.

'Thank you, Dauda. Thank you very much.'

Dauda Adams declined to join them for supper as he had to be in Ibadan before nightfall. He promised to keep in touch.

Dauda moved quickly to establish his credentials as the main man in Ibadan branch of Peoples Party of Nigeria. With the blessing of the Lawanson family, Dauda Adams was chosen to replace the late David as the governorship candidate. When the campaigning got into top gear a few months after David's burial, the Lawanson political machinery threw its weight behind him. Mike even campaigned for him and his deputy, who was a protégé of his father. Buoyed by a lot of sympathy for the late David, Dauda won the governorship election in a landslide. One of the first decisions he made was to rename the main road leading to the parliament house, David Lawanson road. The Labour Congress which David had supported fiercely during his life time honoured his memory by naming the auditorium in their headquarters after him.

After a month of mourning, Daniel returned to his job as a Senior Consultant Surgeon at the University Teaching Hospital. He found it difficult to concentrate at work. His mind kept drifting to events of the last few weeks. This was especially dangerous for a surgeon, and sooner or later he was bound to make a terrible professional mistake. It was worse any time he drove through David Lawanson Road. He finally decided he needed a change of environment and sat down to discuss his options with his wife, Anita, a Permanent Secretary in the Western State government.

'Anita dear, I keep thinking of David.'

'That is only natural, he was your twin and you were very close.'

'I know but I am worried that I can't concentrate at work. I am afraid that I am not functioning at peak efficiency at work. Each time I see his friends or hear his name, my heart bleeds. This is potentially dangerous, a disaster waiting to happen.'

'I understand your concerns, but what are the options?'

'My dear, I have to leave Ibadan for some time.'

'Do you want a transfer to Lagos?'

'No, I think I have to leave Nigeria to work abroad.'

'What?'

'I saw an advert for a vacancy in Saudi-Arabia, and I am strongly considering applying. That is if you don't mind. A good number of my colleagues are now working in the Middle East. They say it's financially more rewarding than working in Britain, and of course you don't have to pay any tax.'

'Daniel, let's sleep on it and talk about it again tomorrow.'

'O.K. but we need to make a decision soon. The closing date for applications is next week.'

Anita reluctantly agreed to support the move to the Middle East. Daniel sent the completed application form and his curriculum vitae by courier to the recruiting company in London. He was shortlisted and three weeks later he was on a flight to the United Kingdom for an interview. The interview went well and he was appointed to the position of Senior Consultant Urologist. He returned to the agency the following day to sign the contract. Fortunately, he had friends who had advised him that he should not be ashamed to haggle for better terms. If the Saudis desperately wanted him, they would pay well above the going rate, but once on the job it was unlikely that any demand for pay rise would be entertained, even if his colleagues were on higher pay.

Daniel was offered a tax-free monthly salary of thirty-five thousand Riyals, approximately six thousand pounds sterling, with a free fully furnished three bedroom villa and business class ticket once a year for himself, his wife and up to three children. He told the recruiting agency he only travelled first class. This was not true of course. How could a doctor in government service afford to travel first class? Fortunately, he had travelled first class on British Airways at the expense of his brother, the senator. He dipped his hand into his coat pocket and brought out his ticket, dropping it on the table of the chief head hunter. Then he helped the manager out of his predicament. He only had one son, and the savings on the two children's tickets should be used to top up their tickets. He also wanted forty thousand Riyals monthly and not thirty five.

'I will have to discuss these variations with the Human Resources head in Taif. Please give me a minute while I try to get Taif,' the head hunter requested.

'By the way, you haven't said anything about my annual bonus,' added Daniel, as the recruiting agency boss left the room to place his call to Taif.

He returned fifteen minutes later and confirmed that the hospital had accepted Daniel's terms. The hospital wanted to know when Daniel would be available to start working for them.

'I will need to give my current employer a month's notice, and another month to tidy up my affairs.'

'Can we say three months, because it will take you about two months to get your Saudi visa from the embassy in Lagos.'

'That is fine,' replied Daniel.

'I will prepare your contract, and you can either pick it up in the office in the afternoon or we can put it in the post to Nigeria, but you have to sign our copy and return it to us before we can authorise the hospital to send your visa number to Lagos.'

'I'll pick it up in the afternoon, and sign your copy,' replied Daniel.

'Any other questions Mr. Lawanson?'

'Please tell me a bit about the job.'

'You will be based at a brand new centre of excellence, the Kingdom Medical Centre in Taif. Taif is the unofficial summer capital of Saudi-Arabia and it lies about six thousand feet above sea level on the slopes of the Sarawat Mountains, approximately 160 kilometres from Jeddah. This part of Saudi-Arabia has perhaps the best climate in the Arabian Peninsula. At the height of summer when the peak day time temperature in Riyadh is a punishing 48 degrees Centigrade, occasionally topping 50 degrees with heat stroke a major risk for outdoor workers, peak temperature in the Taif region hardly ever reaches 40 degrees, hovering around peak of 30 degrees most of the summer, and a cool 10 to 15 degrees in winter. It is a beautiful town and a wonderful place to work. The hospital is equipped with state of the art machines, and most of the doctors and nurses are either British or North American trained.'

Daniel called at the office later in the day to sign the contract and pick up his copy. Two days later, he returned to Nigeria and immediately resigned his appointment at the Teaching Hospital. Over the next two months, he made several visits to the Saudi embassy before he obtained his work visa. He found out that his family would have to wait for him to start working in Saudi Arabia before their visit visas can be issued. Ten weeks after the London interview, Daniel and Anita set out early one Thursday morning from Ibadan for the Lagos airport. Daniel boarded the early afternoon Ethiopian Airways flight for Addis Ababa en-route to Jeddah. He was travelling first class of course. The Boeing 767 landed in Bole Airport in Addis Ababa at 6.30 p.m. The airline lodged him at the Hilton Hotel for the night, and put him on the Jeddah flight early the following morning. The plane landed two hours later at King Abdul Aziz International Airport.

Daniel had arrived in Jeddah during the Umra, lesser Hajj season. When he entered the immigration hall, he was mortified by the mass of people ahead of him. There were over twenty rows waiting for immigration processing, each row with more than fifty passengers. Daniel joined the queue. He glanced at his watch and it was 11 o'clock. After one hour, only about twenty people ahead of him had been processed. Then loudspeakers boomed with what he was later to learn was a prayer call. To his horror, his immigration officer and most of the others got up and disappeared into the wash room for their ablution, and then congregated on prayer mats laid at one end of the hall. After prayers, the officers took their time resuming their duties. Half an hour after the prayer call, work resumed. Finally, at 1.30 p.m. it was his turn. The immigration officer was pleasant and his processing uneventful. It was all over in about four minutes because he was a highly qualified professional, with all the required documents. The traders and unaccompanied female pilgrims tend to run into much greater trouble, and many of them are denied entry into the kingdom.

After he passed through immigration, he retrieved his suitcase and this was then subjected to thorough search by Customs officers. He had been warned at the embassy in Lagos that alcohol was forbidden in the Kingdom, and you could not fail to see the warnings on the walls of the embassy waiting room in bold letters in English and main Nigerian languages that the penalty for drug trafficking in Saudi-Arabia is death by beheading. Finally at around 2 o'clock, he exited the hall, and was relieved when he saw his hospital staff carrying a cardboard with his name.

As Daniel walked towards the man carrying his name, he smiled.

'Doctor Daniel, you are welcome to Saudi Arabia.'

'Thank you,' replied Daniel.

'I am Hussein, the KMC travel officer. You must be exhausted.'

'Oh yes, I am tired and famished. I have been on my feet since we landed three hours ago.'

'Let me help you with your suitcase. Our vehicle is in the car park.'

When they got to the car park, the driver was fast asleep in the car with his feet on the dashboard and Arabic traditional music coming from the car speakers. Hussein tapped him on the shoulder through the open side window, jolting him out of his slumber. The driver disembarked and greeted Daniel warmly.

'Salaam Ailekum, doctor.'

'Ailekum Salaam,' replied Daniel.

That was the only Arabic he knew, from his contact with Muslims back home.

'Doctor, I'll ask Fahd to take us to a fast food outlet, so you can eat something before we set out for Taif.'

Fahd placed the suitcase in the luggage compartment, and they took their seats. He switched on the ignition key of the GMC Suburban and 5.7 litre V8 engine roared into life. He eased the automatic gear into drive and the vehicle pulled out of the car park, quickly gathering speed. He soon left the airport road and drove through the streets of Jeddah. Daniel was impressed with the beauty of the city with wide well laid out double carriage roads and rows of trees and flowers. He was still lost in thought and amazement when the driver veered into a driveway and ended in a fast food village.

'Which do you prefer?' Hussein asked. 'We've got Wendys, Subway, Mc Donalds, Kentucky Fried Chicken, and Burger King.'

Daniel was amazed at the number and variety of fast food outlets they passed by.

'Mr. Hussein.'

'Doctor, just call me Hussein.'

'O.K. Hussein, it looks like we are in an American city with all these fast food outlets, the wide roads, and the huge American cars.'

'Oh, yes, there is a strong American influence but things are not always what they seem.'

'What do you mean?'

'I hope you know that alcohol is forbidden in the Kingdom.'

'Oh yes, I do.'

'There is more. I'll show you something eerie. I don't really want to frighten you but I want you to be aware of the realities of life here.'

Hussein gave instructions to Fahd in Arabic who responded by making a sudden U-turn and then drove down the street they had come from. He made a few turns and then drove into a massive square with a big imposing mosque in the middle. The car park was at one end of the square. Hussein got down from the car and beckoned on Daniel to follow. They walked to the other side of the square where there was a tiled central portion. Hussein stopped at the periphery and pointed to the centre.

'That is "chop-chop" square.'

"Chop-chop, square?"

'Oh yes doctor. That is what the expats call this place.'

'Why?'

'Doctor, this is where death sentence is carried out.'

'How?'

'I want to spare you the gory details, but death sentences are usually carried out by beheading in public, in squares like this.'

'Argh,' responded Daniel with a mixture of shock and horror, almost choking on his burger. He suddenly lost his appetite. Hussein noticed the change in Daniel's countenance.

'Doctor, let's go. We've got a two hour trip to Taif.'

They set out on the journey to Taif. Daniel was quiet for most of the journey. He was deep in thought. Then as they neared Taif, Daniel sat forwards in amazement at the sheer brilliance of the engineering feat involved in building the winding road up the Taif road escarpment. In the last 21 kilometres on the Jeddah-Taif road, they drove winding round the hills from sea level to 6,000 feet above sea level. As they neared the peak, baboons clambered over the hillside and sat perched on the road side. It was such a beautiful natural sight to behold. Five minutes later Fahd drove into Taif town. He made a few turns and drove towards the suburbs of Taif. He had now left the traditional part of the town where ordinary people lived and made a detour through Al-Khalidyah, the exclusive area where the princes had palaces they stayed in during the summer months when they moved to Taif to escape from the unbearable heat of Riyadh. Daniel watched in awe and amazement as they drove through the tree lined avenue with flamboyant palaces with glistening marbles walls rising well above the high surrounding walls. The palaces were located in massive compounds with big villas for the servants and staff maintaining the palaces all year round. There were several such palaces on both sides of the avenue. Daniel had never seen such opulence. Fahd soon exited Al-Khalidyah and turned on to the Airport Road. A few minutes later, Fahd turned off the main road to a private road. One hundred yards down the private road, Fahd slowed down at the entrance to a gated compound to identify himself. He was waved through by the private security guard. Fahd drove past beautiful white villas with well manicured lawns and hedges with hardy shrubs and date palm trees. He stopped in front of house number nine. There were twenty such villas in the compound, with two roads, each with five houses facing each other. Hussein led the way.

'Doctor, please disembark so that I can show you your villa.'

Hussein opened the main door, and led the way through the entrance lobby into the living room.

'This is your living room, and the dining room and kitchen are this way. All the rooms including the kitchen are air conditioned. There are three bedrooms upstairs, all fully furnished,' Hussein added.

'Mr. Hussein, how do I settle my electricity and cooking gas bills?'

'You don't have to worry about any bills. The electricity and gas bills will be settled by the hospital. Local telephone is also free. If you would like to have an international telephone line, let us know and we'll help you get one. The only bill you will have to settle is your national and international phone bill.'

'There is a starter pack of bread, fresh milk, tea, sugar and fruit juice in the kitchen.'

'How do I get to work tomorrow?'

'Our bus runs every half hour from seven to five from the main entrance to the hospital, and then hourly from six up to nine o'clock.'

'Work normally starts at 8.00 a.m. but take your time tomorrow. I'll be expecting you in the manpower department around 10.00 a.m. Please come with your passport and two passport photographs. Don't forget to bring your medical certificates for sighting. Good night, see you tomorrow.'

'Goodnight and thank you Mr. Hussein.'

Daniel was tired after twenty four hours journey by road and air from Lagos to Taif, and fell asleep as soon as he dropped on the bed. He slept soundly and didn't wake up until the sun rise the following morning. He had a shower and was ready for the hospital by 6.30 a.m. He had a cup of tea and got on the 7 o'clock bus for the hospital.

CHAPTER 8

aniel eventually found his way through the maze of corridors in the administration block and located Hussein's office in the manpower department.

'Good morning, Mr. Hussein.'

'Good morning Mr. Daniel. Did you sleep well?'

'Thank you. I slept soundly like a baby.'

'Please have a seat and let's go through your documents.'

They sifted through the documents one by one with Hussein ticking the appropriate boxes in Daniel's file.

'All the academic certificates are O.K. Now let's sort out your residence status. Where is your passport?'

Daniel produced his passport and pushed it across the table to Hussein. He picked it up, took a photocopy of the identity and visa pages and then walked to a massive safe in the corner of the room and locked Daniel's passport in it. Daniel was bemused. Hussein noticed his countenance.

'Doctor, I am sorry I forgot to tell you that all employers in Saudi-Arabia are bound by law to collect the passports of all their foreign staff, and apply to the Ministry of Interior for official identity booklet called iqama which they must carry at all times.'

'You're joking.'

'No, I am dead serious.' Hussein dipped his hand into his pocket and brought out a small white booklet.

'I am a Sudanese national and this is my iqama. My passport photograph is on the first page, and my family's photograph on the second page. Muslims get a white iqama but your iqama will have a brown cover. This makes it easier for the authorities to differentiate between Muslims and non-Muslims.'

'Thank you for the clarification.'

Hussein then proceeded to issue Daniel with a temporary Kingdom Medical Centre identification document, and they then completed the form for the iqama to be sent later in the day to the Ministry of Interior along with Daniel's passport photograph and the appropriate payment.

Hussein popped out of his office for a few minutes. When he returned, he said the Head of Manpower would see them in five minutes.

'Mr. Daniel, let me tell you a little bit about the boss. I call him the boss but most hospital staff refer to him as Mr. G or the governor. Mr. Darren Gould is a quiet man with an inscrutable mien. His munificence knows no bounds but this must not be misconstrued as a sign of weakness. Those who made this mistake have rued the decision. He is from Essex in England but has lived in the Kingdom for over fifteen years. He has administered some of the best hospitals in the Kingdom, and has a lot of influence and clout in high places. By the way he is fluent in Arabic. Let's go. One thing Mr. G demands is punctuality.'

'Mr. Daniel Lawanson, you are welcome to Kingdom Medical Centre,' said Mr. Gould.

'Thank you, Sir,' replied Daniel, as they shook hands warmly.

'Doctor, please sit down.' He beckoned to Hussein to sit down.

'How was your journey?'

'It was fine. Mr. Hussein met me at Jeddah airport and he has been extremely kind and helpful.'

'Hussein excels at his job. If you have any problems, just approach him.'

'You would have noticed some peculiarities already. For instance, our week starts on a Saturday and the weekend is Thursday and Friday. There is segregation between the sexes on many fronts especially in public but we work together as a team in the hospital, just like any top hospital in Europe or America. Hussein will process the application for your official identity document, the iqama. I hope Hussein has told you about the iqama.'

'He has,' replied Daniel.

'This is a book on the traditions and culture of peoples of Saudi-Arabia. Please read it so that you do not fall foul of the laws. I am sure you will enjoy working with us. We have a modern hospital with state of the art machine. This is a 300 bed hospital, and more than 50 per cent of our medical and nursing staff were recruited from Europe or North America. Professionally, you will report to the Director of surgery, Professor Hans Becker. We are responsible for all non-medical matters. Do you have any questions?'

'No question, thank you very much.'

'Hussein will take you to Professor Becker who will arrange your induction over the next few days before you commence your professional duties.'

Daniel commenced full duties two days after he arrived in Taif. He introduced innovative laparascopic techniques into urological surgery at Kingdom Medical Centre, reducing operating time and patient morbidity following major surgery. By reducing patient length of stay in hospital, Daniel made more profit for the hospital and improved the patient experience. His reputation spread quickly after he was interviewed on Saudi TV.

In mid December, Daniel's wife Anita and their ten year old son arrived to spend some time with him. Christmas was not celebrated in the kingdom, so they would have to create their own festive atmosphere. Daniel had bought a Toyota Cressida saloon just before they arrived. He met them at King Khalid International Airport in Jeddah. He had told his wife to dress in a reserved way fully covering her body from her neck to ankle, in accordance with the tradition in the Islamic state. As soon as she emerged through immigration, she rushed forward to embrace her husband who held her at bay with outstretched arms. Such open show of affection was haram, forbidden in the Kingdom.

'Welcome darling. I am sorry we can't embrace openly in the Kingdom. Such show of affection has to be behind closed doors.'

He was however able to embrace his son. He passed the abaya to Anita to wear over her dress. The abaya is a black loose over-garment worn by women in the Arabian Peninsula, covering the body from the shoulders down to the ankles. It can be worn with the niqab, a face veil covering all but the eyes. Some women also choose to wear black gloves so that their hands are covered as well. Daniel didn't have any choice with the abaya but drew a line at buying the optional niqab or black gloves for Anita.

Daniel drove his family round the city of Jeddah, through the Corniche Road and past several tourist attractions. They marvelled at several monuments including the King's Fountain, said to be the tallest fountain in the world. Anita commented that Jeddah looked very much like an American city. After driving round the city for an hour they were famished, and Daniel threw the invitation to his family.

'It's time for food. What would you like? Burger and fries at McDonalds or something more salubrious in a proper restaurant?'

Before Anita could reply, Ade shouted: 'McDonalds.'

So, Daniel drove into the fast food village Fahd had taken him to when he first arrived.

'Wow,' exclaimed Ade, when he saw the variety of fast food outlets. They went into the family section of the McDonalds where they tucked into Quarter pounders, chicken nuggets and French fries, and topped these with large cups of coke. One hour later they exited the outlet.

'Dad, can we come again soon so that we can eat at Kentucky Fried Chicken?'

'I'll think about it,' replied Daniel.

'It's time to start our journey. We've got a long trip ahead of us. If we were Muslims, we'll get to Taif faster.'

'Why is that?' Anita asked.

'We'll drive straight through Makkah to Taif. That will cut about seventy kilometres from the journey,' replied Daniel. 'Unfortunately non-Muslims aren't allowed to step on the soil or even pass through the Holy cities of Makkah and Medinah.'

They then set out on the two and a half hour trip to Taif, driving for the first ten kilometres on the Jeddah –Makkah road and then turning right on to the ring road which circumvents Makkah.

Ade was soon fast asleep. As they neared Taif, Anita marvelled at the genius of the engineers who built the escarpment road. The baboons scampered around as they neared the peak of the hill.

It was dusk by the time Daniel drove into their compound. Anita was blown away by the beauty of the compound. When she entered the gleaming white villa with the plush carpets and ornate furniture, she smiled as she embraced her husband hugging him tightly. He responded, planting his lips on hers.

'This is a haven of peace. We are going to have a well deserved rest. Did you say you've taken the week off?'

'Oh yes,' replied Daniel.

The following day after a long lie in and brunch, Daniel took his family out on a drive round the town, first through the old traditional sections and then through the modern opulent sectors.

'Why are many shops closed? And the local market looks deserted,' remarked Ade.

'It is dangerously hot in many parts of the Kingdom between noon and early evening during summer months, with temperature topping 48 degrees Centigrade. It's more bearable in winter, but still a bit harsh. Therefore, the shops and souks close at noon, and reopen at 4.30 p.m. We'll check out the souk later tonight. The souks and shops remain open till late at night, closing about 10 o'clock. During Ramadan, shops and souks open when fast is broken around 5 p.m. and remain open till 2 or 3 a.m.'

'Really?'

'Oh, yes,' replied Daniel.

After supper they left for the souk. As they disembarked from their car, the call for the isha prayer blared from loudspeakers on top of the mosques. Many shop owners quickly pulled down the shutters, and hurried away for ablution.

As the trio walked along the pedestrian sidewalk in front of the souk, they saw a policeman, a sub machine gun slung over one shoulder and a whip in the other hand. He cracked the whip against the pavement from time to time, as a group of women in their abayas and some with the niqab sat quietly in front of the deserted shops. The policeman marched up and down the street and seemed to be looking after the women, presumably protecting them from harassment by strange men.

The policeman was under 5 feet tall, possibly only 4 feet 10 inches, and it looked like the gun was almost half his height.

'That policeman looks like Napoleon Bonaparte,' remarked Ade.

'Why?' asked Daniel.

'Because of his height. He reminds me of the way Napoleon was described in our history book.'

They were engrossed in their discussion when an old bearded man followed by two armed policemen confronted Daniel and shouted: 'Salah, Salah.'

'I am not a Muslim,' replied Daniel.

'Then go home or hide behind the shops,' replied the man in impeccable English. Daniel beckoned to Anita and Ade and they returned to their car.

'Who is that man? What is that about? Anita asked her husband.

'He is a *mutawa.* He is a sort of enforcer of the Islamic values of the land. The official title of their office is Ministry for the Promotion of Virtues and Prevention of Vice.'

'What would have happened if we had disregarded him?' Anita asked.

'I would have been arrested. I would have gone straight to jail.'

'Really,' exclaimed Anita and Ade in unison.

'Oh yes,' replied Daniel. 'You don't mess with them.'

After prayers, Daniel took them to the gold souk. Anita was mesmerized by row after row of glittering 18 and 21 carat jewellery. She tried on necklace after necklace. Eventually Daniel bought her a set of matching 21 carat set of necklace, ear rings, and bangles costing a few thousand Riyals.' She was thrilled beyond words.

After one week at home, Daniel went back to work, but he continued to treat his family to various attractions. Ade had become hooked on the takeaway menu of kabsa rice, barbecued whole chicken and fresh Afghani bread straight from traditional earthenware ovens.

A week after his family arrived, they had a scary incident which almost pitched them into trouble with the police authorities. Daniel returned from work about 6.00 p.m. on Saturday. Ade was glued to the TV, watching a premier league match which was being shown on the sports channel. Daniel and Ade were ardent Arsenal fans, and their team was playing an important match against Manchester United. Not surprisingly, no sooner had he arrived home than he joined his son in the living room. He kicked off his shoes and settled down to enjoy the game. Anita had no interest in soccer and kept herself busy in the kitchen. Daniel and Ade were unaware of what was going on around them. Suddenly, Daniel was startled by the sound of a car engine roaring into life.

'What is that?' Daniel asked.

'What?' replied Ade.

'That engine sound. Where is your mum?'

'Don't know,' replied Ade.

Daniel jumped up and dashed for the door, like one possessed. He flung open the door and saw his wife reversing the car out of the driveway. He called and frantically waved to Anita but she wasn't looking his way. She continued to reverse the car. Soon she would turn round and make for the compound gate. If the security guy is not very attentive, he would let her out on to the main road. He vaulted the hedge and sprinted across the lawn barefooted. His wife had started to drive out towards the gate. He hurdled over their neighbour's hedges and landed on the road only a few yards in front of the Cressida, frantically waving his arms in the air. Anita slammed on the brakes and the car screeched to a halt only inches from ramming into Daniel. She switched off the ignition and came out from the car.

'Dan, what's wrong with you.'

He was panting and incoherent. He was pointing at the car and jabbering.

Finally, he was able to make some sense.

'Anita, you could have landed both of us in jail.'

'Why, what did I do wrong?' she demanded to know.

'Women don't drive in Saudi-Arabia. If you had been caught on the road, you would have been arrested and deported, and I would have been jailed for failing to control you.'

'Really!' exclaimed Anita.

'Oh yes, no doubt about it. Where were you going anyway?'

'We had run out of fresh milk and I wanted to get some in the supermarket down the road. I didn't want to disturb you and Ade.'

'Let me get dressed properly and I'll take you there.'

Three weeks after they arrived in the Kingdom, it was time for Anita and Ade to return to Nigeria. Hussein had obtained 'exit and re-entry' visas for Anita and Ade. That would enable them to leave the Kingdom and return, not later than six months from their departure. They were scheduled to fly out on a morning flight to Addis Ababa, and from there to Lagos. Anita had acquired an extra suitcase filled with designer clothes and gifts for friends. The travellers now had three huge suitcases in addition to their carry on hand luggage. They could not fit all the stuff into the Cressida and he therefore requested transport from the KMC travel department. So, early on a Friday morning they set out for Jeddah in a GMC Suburban. They arrived in King Khalid International Airport a couple of hours before departure. They were travelling first class and therefore checking in was smooth and uneventful. They proceeded immediately for security and immigration checks. Daniel had to stay behind in the departure hall but he could see his family on the queue. Soon it was their turn, and he expected that the checks would not take more than a few minutes, and then they would walk through into the departure lounge. Daniel became worried when his family stayed longer than ten minutes with the immigration officer, and Anita repeatedly looked back towards him. There was an argument but Daniel could not make out what they were arguing about. Then Anita beckoned to him to come. As he moved forward, he was stopped by the policeman at the entrance but the immigration officer waved him on, and he was allowed in.

'Officer, what is the problem?' asked Daniel.

'*Mafi mushkila,* No problem,' he replied.

'If there is no problem, why don't you stamp their passports and let them proceed. Their flight will soon depart.'

'I can't do that. Your wife has changed her place of birth. '

'What do you mean by that?'

'The computer says your wife was born in

Rawalpindi,' the officer retorted as he pointed at the PC monitor.

'What!' Anita and Daniel exclaimed in unison.

'Look in her passport. She was born in Lagos,' Daniel protested.

'I have never been to Pakistan,' added Anita.

The officer grabbed the mouse and flicked through his monitor.

'You see, when your wife entered the Kingdom computer showed she was born in Lagos but now the computer says she was born in Rawalpindi.'

'It must have been a mistaken entry in the Ministry of Interior in Taif. Please rectify the error on your system,' implored Daniel.

'That is not possible.' Immediately afterwards the officer drew a big cross across Anita's immigration card. Daniel knew that Anita's case was closed.

'What about my son?' asked Daniel.

'No problem with his entry, he was born in Lagos,' replied the officer.

'The boy can travel.'

This is a foolish man. How can the boy travel on his own? Daniel thought to himself but knew better than to voice such thoughts.

Daniel collected the two passports and left with his family to seek the Ethiopian Airlines manager. He was sympathetic and two seats were reserved for them on the next flight, the following day. He advised them to move quickly to rectify the error at the Ministry of Interior in Taif, as the mistake could not be corrected anywhere else. Daniel was determined to sort out the problem the same day, even if they had to pay another fee for a new exit visa. They left immediately for Taif. The KMC Manpower department was extremely helpful and sent a Saudi to the ministry to deal with the matter, as foreigners were not allowed into this section. Daniel wasn't taking any chances and he went with the officer wearing his doctor's white coat. He was pertinacious and eventually the security guards allowed him to enter the premises. Someone had erroneously entered a Pakistani passport details under Anita's name. The old visa was cancelled and Daniel paid for a new visa. They collected the passport with the new visa with only minutes to spare before the ministry closed for the day. The following day they departed for Lagos on an Ethiopian Airlines 767.

CHAPTER 9

With the family gone, Daniel threw himself into his work churning out a phenomenal amount of activity. He continued with innovative oncologic surgical techniques, undertaking more surgery than his colleagues. He had great rapport with the physicians and radiologists, often running joint clinics and one-stop service. He was the super man of KMC.

A month after Anita left, the council of foreign ministers of the Gulf Cooperation Council, GCC, a loose political and economic alliance of the six Gulf States was meeting in Jeddah. The private secretary to the Saudi Foreign Minister, a diplomat and a very important personality in GCC circles had arrived in Jeddah two weeks before the meeting to plan for it. He brought his family along from Riyadh, including his fifteen year old son Abdullah who had been hit in the crotch during a football game in school. This had resulted in a painful scrotal swelling. He was seen at one of the top hospitals and a diagnosis of post-traumatic right testicular inflammation was made. He was placed on treatment and requested to undergo a follow up ultrasound examination after two weeks. At the follow up examination, the pain and tenderness had diminished considerably but the swelling persisted. Another follow up was scheduled for two weeks. On a previous trip to Jeddah, Mr. Al-Zahrani had heard about the new wonder doctor at the KMC, and made up his mind to take his only son to see him.

Professor Becker informed Daniel that a VIP was bringing his son to see him the following day.

'What does that mean?' Daniel asked.

'It means they've heard about your skills and expertise, and want to give you a try rather than flying him to the UK or United States.'

'Is that so?'

'I'm afraid that is the usual scenario.'

'Okay, what is the clinical history?'

'All I know is that the patient is a fifteen year old boy with scrotal swelling following football trauma.'

Just before noon, a stretch limousine pulled up in front of the hospital. The armed police guard disembarked and opened the door for the important visitor. Ambassador Al-Zahrani stepped out followed by his son. The hospital director came out to receive him. They walked briskly to the hospital director's office where Daniel was waiting. After a quick introduction, the Ambassador handed over a file containing a summary of the diagnosis and treatment given in Riyadh to Daniel. Daniel disappeared with Abdullah, whilst the hospital director took his father on a tour of the hospital.

Daniel spent the first five minutes reading through the documents he had been given. Then he took a full clinical history, and then examined the boy. Next, he took him to the Radiology department where he observed as the Consultant Radiologist performed an ultrasound scan of the testes.

'Doc, it appears there are some focal echo-poor masses in the middle of the right testis,' interjected Daniel.

'I think you are right,' the radiologist replied.

'Let's check the colour flow,' added Daniel.

The radiologist flicked the colour Doppler switch, and a burst of colours appeared on the screen. Eventually the surge of colours settled down and a pattern appeared.

'Doc, what do you think,' Daniel asked.

'It looks like there are a few focal slightly hypervascular masses in the right testis.'

'That was what I suspected. But I think the left testis is normal.'

'You are right, Daniel, the left testis is normal.'

'I'll perform a quick scan of the abdomen and groin.'

A few minutes later the radiologist declared that the abdomen and groin were normal. Daniel put a call through to the hospital director. They terminated their tour and returned to the director's office. When they arrived Daniel was already waiting for them.

'Mr. Lawanson, where is Abdullah.'

'He is in the hospital restaurant with my secretary. I thought that would give us the opportunity to discuss the case without frightening him,' replied Daniel.

'Doctor, I am anxious to know what you've diagnosed.'

'Sir, I reviewed the medical notes from Riyadh, examined him fully and then organised ultrasound of the abdomen and scrotum. I believe he has a testicular tumour.'

'Are you saying you think he has cancer?' the Ambassador enquired.

'Yes sir, I think he has testicular cancer, probably a seminoma.'

'What? He is only fifteen years old.'

'This is a type of cancer that affects young people, from about the age of fifteen years to thirty.'

'But the doctors in Riyadh diagnosed orchitis, and they placed him on anti-inflammatory drugs and a week later added antibiotics. How can you now say he has cancer?'

'They could be right Sir. The football trauma could have caused orchitis, which then masked the small tumour. It was fortuitous that he had that football injury, otherwise we might not have detected the tumour in time.'

'Your Excellency, Mr. Lawanson is correct,' the hospital director added.

'So, what is the treatment?'

'Surgical removal of the right testis,' replied Daniel.

'Oh my God! Isn't there any other treatment?'

'That is the best option. The tumour is small, and it appears it has not spread, so removal of the testis will be curative.'

The Ambassador was alarmed and it showed in his countenance, he turned to the hospital director and spoke to him in Arabic. Suddenly, he remembered that Daniel did not understand what he was saying and he apologised profusely, and then resumed in English.

'Ali, this is my boy, my only son. You know what our people say about a man without balls. A man without balls is not a man. It's better to die young. Who will inherit all my business and money?'

the Ambassador continued, turning from the director to Daniel, his arms in the air as if in supplication to Allah.

'The situation is not hopeless Sir. In fact, we will remove only one testicle and he will remain fertile. All he requires for fertility is one testicle. In a few years time, once he gets the all clear, we can insert a prosthesis in the right hemiscrotum and no one will know that the right testis had been removed.'

'Ali, what do you think?'

'Your Excellency, Daniel is the best we have. I daresay he is probably the best urological surgeon in the whole of Saudi-Arabia. If my son has such a condition, I will be happy for Daniel to treat him.'

'All right, Mr. Daniel, when do you want to operate?'

'I would have liked to operate today, but it's now too late because I want to arrange Computed Tomography scan of the Chest and Abdomen this afternoon as a baseline study. I want to operate tomorrow morning, and he should be home in three or four days.'

'Why so fast? I will like to talk to his mother about it.'

'The earlier the better, Sir,' replied Daniel.

'Ali, will you talk to my boy and reassure him that he is in good hands and all will be well.'

'I will Sir.'

'Thank you, *shukran*.'

CT scan was performed within the hour, and the Ambassador and Abdullah returned to their suite at The Sheraton Hotel in Al-Hada on the outskirts of Taif.

They were back in the hospital by 7.30 a.m. the following morning. Two hours later, Abdullah's right testis had been removed. Frozen section histopathology examination in the theatre had confirmed that the testicle contained cancer cells before it was removed. He wanted to be doubly sure as he could not afford to remove a non-cancerous testicle, given the Ambassador's comments the previous day. Three days later, Abdullah was discharged, and he travelled to Jeddah to stay with his father who was now engrossed with the GCC ministers conference which had just commenced. Ali arranged for Daniel to pay them a visit at home in Jeddah ten days after the surgery. The wound had healed well, and he cleared Abdullah to return to Riyadh. He gave him a six months appointment.

Six months later, Abdullah walked sprightly into Daniel's clinic beaming with smiles.

'Salaam Ailekum Abdullah.'

'Ailekum Sallam Doctor Daniel.'

'How are you?'

'I am fine. I have no complaints at all.'

'That is very good.'

'Come over to the couch, let me examine you.'

Daniel carried out a thorough physical examination.

'Everything looks good but I'll like you to have some imaging to confirm this, and for our records.'

'*Mafi mushkila*, No problem,' replied Abdullah.

Daniel then requested urgent ultrasound of the scrotum and CT scan of the chest and abdomen.

'What are your plans?' Daniel asked.

'I want to return to Jeddah tonight because dad and I are travelling at dawn to Washington. The foreign minister is having a meeting with the U.S. Secretary of State next week, and dad is going ahead to do some ground work.'

'O.K. Come over to my office once you've had your scans. We'll go together to review the images, and you can then leave for Jeddah.'

The ultrasound and CT scans were normal and Abdullah was on his way to Jeddah before five o'clock.

The following day a parcel addressed to Daniel was delivered to the hospital director's office. When Daniel opened the parcel, it contained two small gift wrapped boxes and a card with a short message:

'Mr. Lawanson, thank you for everything, from Ambassador Zahrani.'

What could this be?

He ripped the wrapping paper and opened the first box. It contained an Omega Constellation steel-yellow gold wristwatch. He flipped the watch round and saw his name inscribed on the back. He was speechless.

'Dr. Ali, this is unnecessary. I can't accept it. I was only doing my job.'

'Yes, you were only doing your job but the gentleman is only showing his appreciation for an excellent job. You can't return the gift. That would be very bad, an unwise move. These are very powerful men and you never know when you'll need them. Such an act would be regarded as unfriendly in our culture. Go ahead and open the second box.'

Daniel opened the box and found a matching lady's Omega Constellation wristwatch. Instinctively, he turned the watch over and read out the name inscribed on it.

'Anita Lawanson.'

'I am gobsmacked. How did he find out my wife's name.'

'Now you see what I was saying. These people make it their business to know everything.'

'Daniel, surprise your wife with that gift next time you see her. Don't forget to send a thank you note to the Ambassador.'

'I will, of course,' replied Daniel.

With Abdullah Zahrani doing well and back at school, Daniel returned to the mundane life of a surgeon. It was a regular cycle of clinics, ward rounds, surgical operations, then more post-operative ward rounds, and then the cycle started again, punctuated occasionally by surgical challenges in theatre. Daniel was an exceptional doctor and rose up to whatever challenge was thrown at him.

Daniel was looking forward to the summer visit of Anita and Ade. He was hoping there won't be any hiccups at the Immigration department in Jeddah airport. His family had a smooth passage through Customs and Immigration, and they were soon on the way to Taif, after a quick drive through the fast food pick up at Kentucky Fried Chicken at Ade's instance. Daniel always had a whiff of mischief about him. He didn't hand over the Omega wrist watch directly to his wife. He hid it under her pillow and left written clues about the house. After half an hour treasure hunt, she finally found the gift under the pillow in their bedroom. She was thrilled beyond words as the masterpiece adorned her wrist. When they went shopping, they saw Napoleon matching up and down the kerbside with his rifle slung over his shoulder, with an eye on the women in their abayas waiting for their husbands to pick them up.

It was the height of summer and with Riyadh's day time scorching heat, many of the ministers shifted their base to Taif.

Daniel had just finished the clinic on Wednesday evening, and was about to go home for a well deserved weekend rest with his family when the phone rang. The medical director wanted to see him in his office urgently.

'Daniel, what are your plans for tomorrow?'

'It's my family's last weekend and I had planned to take them shopping in Jeddah,' replied Daniel.

'I am sorry you have to shelve your plans,' replied Ali.

'Why?'

'Your reputation has preceded you. You are now a national treasure.'

Daniel was nonplussed.

'I'll spare you from further bewilderment. Prince Rasheed, the Minister for works and planning would like to see you in his palace at Al-Khalidyah tomorrow morning.' The hospital director noticed the change in Daniel's countenance, so he continued.

'You've done nothing wrong. He has heard about your sublime skills and wants you to see his mother-in-law. I understand she has blood in her urine. Don't worry, I'll accompany you. The Prince will send his driver to pick us up in the hospital at 10 o'clock.'

'I'll be ready by nine,' replied Daniel.

'If you wish I can arrange with our transport department to take your family to Jeddah. Your wife won't have any problem because your son will be her escort. The driver will take them anywhere they want.'

'That would be appreciated,' replied Daniel.

At nine the following morning, Daniel arrived in the hospital as promised. Ali arrived half an hour later, just as the minister's driver arrived in a metallic black Mercedes 500 saloon. They were soon on their way to the palace. As they reached the gate of a huge compound with high marble walls, the steel gate swung open. If the exterior of the compound looked impressive, the interior was truly palatial. The road was paved with tiles adorned on both sides with date palm trees, and beautiful flowers. They were driven to the guest villa to the left of the compound whilst to the right stood a massive white marble building, the main residence. Ali and Daniel were led into a large living room to await the arrival of the Prince. About fifteen minutes later, Prince Rasheed walked in.

'Gentlemen, Salaam Ailekum.'

'Ailekum Salaam your Excellency,' replied Ali and Daniel in unison, rising from their seats as soon as the Prince entered.

'Please sit down gentlemen.'

The doctors sat on the same sofa. The prince pulled a chair and sat close to them. He signalled to his aides to give them some privacy and they exited the room.

'Dr. Daniel I have heard a lot about you. Someone, whose judgement I respect said you are the best surgeon in the Kingdom.'

'Thank you Sir,' replied Daniel. 'I am very comfortable with urological problems but I may struggle with other surgical specialties.'

'I like you. You are a very modest man. The problem is with my mother in-law. In the last month, she has been having burning sensation when passing urine, and now says there is occasional blood in her urine. She was treated in Riyadh with antibiotics for urinary tract infections. At first the treatment seemed to work, but the symptoms are now back.'

'Your Excellency, has she been fully examined and the urine tested? Daniel enquired.'

'I am not sure,' replied the Prince.

'Can I talk to her?'

'Yes, of course. That is why you are here. My wife is very worried and we need to resolve this matter.'

'Your Excellency, I'll wait here. Can we have a chaperone for Mr. Daniel?' requested Ali.

Daniel was taken to a private room to wait for the mother in-law. She soon arrived with her maid. They were introduced and soon settled down to talk. After twenty minutes of full clinical history and examination he had a provisional diagnosis. He opened his doctor's bag and retrieved a sterile bottle. He gave it to the maid and instructed her on how to collect the sample. Minutes later he collected the sample from them and bade them farewell.

He returned to the guest living room where Ali was still sitting. He conversed with Ali whilst they waited for the Prince to return. The Prince returned shortly after.

'Doctor, what is your verdict?'

'Your Excellency, I think I have the answer but I need some

tests to confirm my suspicion.' He paused but the Prince urged him to continue speaking.

'I found out that your mother in-law has visited Egypt yearly for the past five years, staying in the Nile River area. She admits wading in the waters on her holidays. This is an area endemic for schistosomiasis also known as Bilharzia. The worm lives in infected waters in endemic areas and penetrates the human skin, finally lodging in the bladder where it may cause irritation and bloody urine. I suspect this is what she's got but I need to carry out a few tests to confirm.'

'What exactly do you want to do?' the Prince asked.

'I have already collected a urine sample which I'll take to the hospital. We may be able to identify schistosoma eggs in the urine sample. I'll like her to come into hospital so that we take some radiographs and possibly carry out an Intravenous Urogram. If this turns out to be chronic schistosomiasis, I will also like to inspect the interior of the urinary bladder.'

'How will you do that?'

'I will perform direct inspection of the bladder looking through a special tube under general anaesthesia. It's called cystoscopy. The reason I want to do this is to make sure there is no growth in the bladder because cancers have been known to develop after chronic schistosoma infection. If I find any growth, I will remove such. There is no need to worry.'

'How soon can I know the results of the urine test?'

'Your Excellency, we'll call in the laboratory staff and we can have the result by this evening,' replied Ali.

'Can you do the X-rays today so we can have a definite answer as soon as possible?'

'Yes Sir, we can,' replied Ali.

They returned to the hospital immediately and the laboratory staff started working on the urine specimen.

When the Prince's mother in-law arrived in the hospital an hour later, the radiographer was waiting. Daniel requested plain X-ray which showed faint calcification in the bladder wall. Immediately Daniel saw the radiograph, he exclaimed: 'Oh yes.'

Daniel proceeded with intravenous urogram to demonstrate the kidneys. The kidneys and ureters were normal.

Shortly afterwards, the laboratory results came through. Schistosoma ova had been detected in the urine sample.

Immediately, he dialled the hospital director.

'Dr. Ali, I was right. We have confirmed schistosomiasis.'

'Excellent, I trust you. I think it is better we return to the palace to tell the Prince in person rather than telephoning.'

'Whatever you decide,' replied Daniel.

'What about treatment?' Ali enquired.

'I have checked with our pharmacist, unfortunately the drug of choice is not in stock. But he can get the drug by Saturday if we want. I hope you don't mind, but I asked him to place order for the medicine.'

'Of course, I don't mind. You've made the right decision.'

One hour later they were back in the palace briefing the Prince. They were surprised when the Prince broke with tradition and first hugged Daniel, and then Ali.

'You guys don't know what you've done. My wife has been so downcast about her mother's illness, and was giving me grief over it. Now I can sleep soundly.'

He shook his head in amazement, and then continued.

'Dr. Daniel, I won't forget this gift from you. One day I will repay you. So, what's next? What about treatment?'

'Dr. Ali and I have placed order for the drug which should arrive on Saturday morning. I will like to perform the cystoscopy on Saturday morning at 8 o'clock. She can report at our day unit at 7 for pre-admission checks. She'll be ready to go home by noon with her drugs. I'll like to see her again a month from now to ensure that we have eradicated all the worms and the ova.'

'That's no problem,' replied the Prince.

The cystoscopy was normal and she was started on her drugs before discharge from the day unit. A month later, the blood in the urine had disappeared and urine analysis was normal. She was accompanied to the clinic by her daughter, the princess, who was full of praise for Daniel, and left a package for Daniel and Anita as a token of their appreciation.

CHAPTER 10

Mike Lawanson had a remarkable two years as local government councillor. He remained in the public eye by making the polio immunization campaign an annual event. Jostling had now commenced for party nomination for the elections to the Federal House of Representatives and the Senate, due to be held early the following year. The assumption had been that Mike would wait to stand for the post of local government chairman, but that was by those who didn't know him well. He was gunning for higher stakes. He put himself forward for election to the House of Representative, and there was no shortage of supporters in the Lawanson camp.

The Lagos branch of the PPN was due to host the annual congress of the party. Mike and many of the state parliamentarians and councillors were tasked with organising the event. Mike was responsible for publicity and the press. Understandably, he had enlisted the services of Nkechi. The team did a brilliant job, and the three day congress was a roaring success. It was rounded off with a dinner and dance party at the congress venue, the five star Eko Atlantic Hotel on the Marina. After the sumptuous dinner, hundreds of party members were entertained to a rollicking time with traditional highlife music by Emperor Rex Kotoka and his highlife chiefs from Ghana and juju music by King Kenny Thompson from central Lagos. Nkechi let her hair down dancing with zing and really enjoying herself. She wore out Mike on the dance floor and he soon retired to their table in the corner, drinking ice cold beer and looking on in admiration at his queen. Nkechi continued dancing with Ahmed and other friends. Mike could not help wondering where she got her stamina from. She really enjoyed the juju music, digging down and rolling her derriere as the juju music exponent twanged his guitar. Her beauty and exploits did not escape the notice of many lecherous men. Those who knew she was Mike's partner envied him, whilst others unaware of her relationship schemed and fantasised on what they hoped could be. It was one of the party leaders who dared to try his luck. Senator Patrick Osazuwa had been watching Nkechi with interest from the high table. He came down and started mingling with the other dancers greeting them as he cleverly inched his way towards the centre of the hall where Nkechi was dancing with one of Mike's friends. He timed his move perfectly and struck with the speed of a cobra which had been eyeing its prey. As soon as the music stopped the Senator shot out his hand to greet Nkechi.

'Good evening.'

'Good evening Senator.'

He was rather taken aback that she knew who he was, but he quickly recovered.

'Can I have the next dance,' he requested.

'Okay, Sir,' she replied.

They danced to the highlife tune. The Senator tried to hold her close but Nkechi managed to wedge her elbow between them to keep a decent space between them. When the music ended, the Senator tried to engage her in discussion but she cleverly extricated herself, but not before he slipped his business card into her palm, asking her to give him a phone call the following day. Nkechi walked straight to Mike and sat close to him, resting her head on his shoulder.

'Hope you are having a swell time.'

'Of course I am,' replied Nkechi, and then she continued.

'I am just amazed at lecherous old men.'

'What happened?'

'This is what happened,' replied Nkechi as she passed Senator's Osazuwa's card to Mike.

'How did you get that?'

'The shameless old man gave it to me as we danced. He said I should call him tomorrow, that he would like to go out with me.'

'That's vacuous. He must have known that you came here with your partner,' replied Mike in disgust.

'How did such a man become the head of Senate?' Nkechi enquired.

'It's a long story but it's unfortunate that we ended up with him as one of our leaders,' Mike replied.

It was now well past midnight and the revellers were starting to depart. Mike and Nkechi bade Ahmed farewell and retired to their penthouse suite on the tenth floor of the hotel. They sat on recliner chairs on the balcony looking out towards the Atlantic Ocean, canoodling and watching the lights from ships passing in the distance as the cool Atlantic breeze wafted across the balcony into their living room. They soon fell asleep in each other's arms on the balcony, waking up at dawn when it started to drizzle, and rain drops blew on to their bodies. Nkechi fixed cups of coffee which they drank to warm themselves before dropping off to sleep again. They had a relaxing Sunday morning, having a late breakfast in their suite. They checked out at noon, Mike dropped Nkechi off at her flat in Ikoyi, and then drove home to get ready for work the following day.

Mike returned to the humdrum of life in council politics. He was busy looking through files which had been dumped in the store room, gathering dust whilst they planned the party congress, but now had to be dealt with. The council accountant was waiting for his input into preparation of next year's budget. As he painstakingly plodded through the figures and economic projections his mobile phone rang. He flicked open the phone and the name of one of his good friends based in the party headquarters flashed on the LED screen.

'Charles, how are you doing?'

'I'm fine thanks.'

'What's up?'

'First, let me congratulate you and your team for hosting a successful congress, and that party was just fantastic. It was a great show. The main reason I called is to brief you on the rumour making the rounds here. I have it on good authority that the Senate leader has decided to invite all prospective candidates for the House of Representatives election for a seminar in Abuja. It is ostensibly to ensure that only the smartest and most electable are chosen.'

'But that is unconstitutional. We have never chosen our candidates centrally,' Mike protested.

'I know but who is there to stop him? You have to play the game and report in Abuja when you are summoned,' Charles advised.

'Thanks, thank you very much.'

The following Sunday, Mike boarded an early flight to Abuja, arriving just before noon. He immediately started setting out his stall. The programme would be held at the party headquarters. He wondered how the auditorium would accommodate the three hundred plus aspirants. As they arrived on Monday morning for the briefing, he was intrigued that the invitees barely numbered fifty. When Senator Osazuwa mounted the rostrum to welcome them, he solved the riddle. Incumbent parliamentarians were not invited. Only new candidates needed the seminar and tutorials to enhance their knowledge of history and politics of the land, and to improve their chances of election if chosen by the party.

That's bullshit. Rubbish and nonsense. All of us are battle hardened campaigners. We know the grassroots better than most of you.

This was what ran through Mike's mind, but of course he kept his thoughts to himself.

They sat through sessions as academicians and senior civil servants espoused various theories on politics and government. Finally, at 6 p.m. the torture was over. During the lunch break, one of the party officers slipped a note to Mike.

'Senator Osazuwa would like to see you in his office on the top floor as soon as you finish your lunch.'

What does he want? I have got no business with this man. Perhaps he wants to apologise for his unseemly behaviour at the party. It can't be that. Big men don't say sorry to small boys.

Mike knew that the Senator's boys were likely to be observing him and his demeanour. He wasn't going to be harassed. He remembered his father's philosophy, that when you are sweating you mustn't let your adversary know you are sweating, stay cool. He took his time with his main course, and then topped it with dessert. When he was done, he walked up the steps to exercise his muscles and ready himself for the unknown.

As he walked into the outer office, he found the Senator waiting to meet him. He walked across and greeted him warmly and then invited him into his more private inner chamber.

'Dr. Lawanson, thank you for honouring my invitation.'

'It's a pleasure Sir,' Mike lied.

'Mike, you are a very intelligent and perspicacious man, and I look forward to your help and cooperation.'

'Sir, let's cut the chase.'

'Okay Mike, I have met the woman of my dreams but I need your help to make our union a reality.'

'Me?' Mike asked in bewilderment.

'Yes,' replied the Senator, and then he pressed on.

'I met this lady at the party last week and I was informed that she is your acquaintance. The moment I set my eyes on her, I knew we were destined to be husband and wife.'

'But you already have a wife,' Mike replied unabashed.

'Young man, you still have a lot to learn. This is Africa. If you have the means to provide for many women and your offspring, nothing should debar you from marrying as many wives as you can care for. My first wife was married under the native law and customs act, so polygamy is not a crime. My father had four wives and he lived to a ripe old age before he joined his ancestors, and his children have done well. Anyway, back to the main issue. I met this lady called Nkechi Obi and I have fallen in love with her.'

Shameless, lubricious old man.

Mike was taken aback and was lost for words.

'Mike, say something.'

'What can I say? Nkechi is my woman. I am looking forward to the day we tie the knot.'

'Come on Mike. Everybody knows you are a playboy. To you Nkechi is just a play thing to be toyed with and disposed when you tire of her, but I want to build a life with her. I need her by my side at state occasions.'

Why am I sitting down listening to this rubbish? I am tempted to thump him and teach him a lesson he will never forget, but he is lucky that this is not my home turf.

'So, what do you want me to do?'

'Break up with her. When you return to Lagos, tell her you are no longer interested in the relationship and leave the rest to me.'

'I don't think I can do that,' replied Mike.

'Look, Mike, you are young and have a long career ahead of you. You will need helpers along the way. I promise you I will not forget your good deed. I guarantee you will be chosen as our House of Representative candidate for Lagos, and I can fast track you to stand for the senate seat at the following election. I have all the power and clout. Think about it and call me in a week with the good news. Goodbye and enjoy the rest of the seminar.'

Mike left the room without uttering a word. He was lost in thought.

This is a bad dream. It can't be happening to me. This is abuse of power and position. There is no way I am going to capitulate and surrender to this bully. I am fighting him to the end.

Mike went through the motions, completing the afternoon session like a zombie. As soon as the session ended he dashed to the airport and was soon on a flight to Lagos. He had wanted to sleep in Abuja but the encounter with the Senator made him yearn for Nkechi. He desperately needed to hold her in his arms. From Lagos airport, he took a taxi to Nkechi's residence in Ikoyi, not bothering to stop at home. When the door bell rang, Nkechi was already in her nightdress sipping a hot chocolate drink. She wasn't expecting anyone so she ignored the bell. When the door bell ringing persisted, she dragged herself up and went to the intercom.

'Who is that?'

'It's me, Mike.'

'Mike who?'

'Come on Queen, it's me.'

'I am sorry, please come in.'

As Mike walked up the stairs and entered the flat, Nkechi fired a torrent of questions.

'What are you doing in Lagos? Aren't you supposed to be in Abuja? I hope you are alright?'

'I am fine. I have just returned from Abuja and wanted to see you.'

'You couldn't wait till tomorrow.'

'No, I couldn't wait. I missed you too much.'

'Why have you brought your travelling case?

'I came here straight from the airport.'

'Mike, do you mean you drove here bypassing your house?'

'I didn't drive. My driver was not at the airport when I arrived, so I took a taxi from the airport.'

'Mike, this love is too much.'

'Queen, you deserve all the attention. You are too much.'

'Let me fix you something to eat before you return home.'

'Nkechi, I am sleeping here tonight. I'll go to work from here. Hope you don't mind.'

'Of course, you are welcome to stay. But why did you change your plans?'

'That's a long story. One day I'll have the time to tell you. Right now I am famished.'

After a meal of ground rice and vegetable stew with assorted meat, Mike stretched out on the sofa laying his head on Nkechi's lap. They listened to the National Network news as she gently stroked his face. Within minutes he was asleep. Nkechi operated a hidden lever and converted the sofa into a sofa bed, and gently eased Mike on to it, partially undressing him and then pulling a sheet over him up to his chin. She switched off the lights and slipped in beside him, abandoning her bedroom.

The couple left for work together early in the morning in Nkechi's car.

'Mike, it's pretty strange going to work in the same car with a man.'

'You'd better get used to it quickly. That's what we'll be doing when we get married.'

'Are we getting married?'

'Oh yes, we are. Or don't you want to marry me?'

'Mike, is that a marriage proposal?'

'Yes. I am sorry I couldn't arrange a more romantic encounter. Nkechi will you marry me?'

'Yes, oh yes I will.' As Nkechi leaned over and kissed him on the cheek. Her bright red lipstick smudged on his cheek.

'Careful, careful, I am still driving. We can save that for later. I promise to get the engagement ring soon, so that we can do things properly.'

'No worries. The most important thing is the commitment we have made to each other,' Nkechi replied.

Mike walked into his office beaming with smiles and attending to his duties with zing. Then his mind drifted back to the encounter in Abuja and he became morose. He grabbed his mobile phone, and flipped it open and placed a call to Ahmed.

'Good morning, Ahmed.'

'Good morning. How was Abuja?'

'Not good. That's why I am calling you. I need to see you urgently.'

'I've got a busy schedule today, but I should be free by 4 o'clock. Let's meet at "Temptations" at half past four for drinks, and you can tell me all about Abuja.'

'Okay, I'll be there by four.'

The rest of the day Mike was in a zombie-like state, doodling and repeatedly glancing at his watch. On days like this time seemed to stand still. After what seemed like eternity his alarm went off. He had set his mobile phone alarm to half past three. As if he could forget the most important matter in his life at the moment. He grabbed his briefcase and was soon on his way to the restaurant. The traffic was unusually heavy, and the drive which would normally take fifteen minutes dragged past thirty. By the time he drove into the car park it was already half past four. When Mike entered the restaurant, Ahmed spotted him from the vantage position in a far corner table. At that time of the day, the restaurant was almost empty. Most people were still at work.

'Hey, Mike cheer up.'

Ahmed beckoned to the waiter.

'Two bottles of cold beers, please.'

'No beer for me please, just apple juice,' interjected Mike.

'Mike, what's the matter? I have never known you to refuse a beer, especially free beer.'

'This is serious matter, and I want to think straight.'

Ahmed continued with small talk. As soon as the waiter brought their drinks and the complimentary nuts, Ahmed drew close to Mike and in a low voice, not audible beyond their table, he started off the conversation.

'Mike, what is the matter.'

'It's that vacuous, lecherous Senator Osazuwa.'

'Hey, he is our boss. What has he done to warrant such venom from you?'

'He is a snake, a venomous reptile.'

'Okay, tell me what happened in Abuja.'

Mike then narrated his experience with the Senator. When he

finished, Ahmed was speechless for minutes. When he recovered, he just kept muttering:

'Incredible, incredible, unbelievable. What on earth was he thinking?'

'I told you the man is a lubricious idiot. I am going to fight him to the end. I am not giving up my woman to him.'

'What did Nkechi say?'

'I have not told her what happened in Abuja but she was not impressed when he tried to proposition her at the party despite knowing that she came with someone else.'

'I hear the man can be vicious so you have to handle this matter with wisdom. I suggest you keep away from him, and for the foreseeable future don't take Nkechi to any political party event that you think he is likely to attend. Hopefully, he'll forget about her and latch on to another woman. In any case, what are your plans for Nkechi?'

'I have proposed to Nkechi.'

'Really?'

'Oh yes, I did so this morning.'

'And what did she say?'

'She said yes.'

'That's great, congratulations. Get cracking with preparations for the ceremony. Once you tie the knot with her, he'll have no choice but to lay off.'

Mike felt better after chatting with his friend.

'Ahmed, I'll have my beer now.'

'That sounds good. I'll keep you company and have another one. I am not driving so I can relax. What about you?'

'I am going to see Nkechi.'

'Of course, lover boy,' replied Ahmed.

'I've got to return her car.'

'So, how will you get back home?'

'My car should be at Nkechi's by now. I sent my driver to pick her from work and take her back home. So we'll swap cars when I see her later.'

'That's brilliant. You are already living almost like man and wife. Let's enjoy the beer so that you can be on your way.'

The men drank up and were soon on their way. Mike and Nkechi spent the evening spoiling each other, and he finally left for home about eleven o'clock. The coming days were the same for the love birds. Apart from time spent at work, they were virtually inseparable. Mike had virtually forgotten about the Abuja encounter when he was jolted back to reality, two weeks after his meeting with the Senator. The previous day his secretary informed him that he had a phone message from the party headquarters in Abuja, and he was expected to return the phone call. He asked his secretary to find out who it was and to say that he was out of town. They found out that the call originated from the Head of Senate's office. Mike did not return the phone call.

When Mike arrived at work the following morning, he found one of the party officials waiting for him in the secretary's office.

'Good morning Dr. Lawanson.'

'Good morning. How can I help you?'

'Can we go in to your office? I've got a confidential message for you.'

'Please come in. Can I offer you a cup of tea?'

'No thank you, I am fine.'

'Please sit down,' Mike beckoned to the gentleman to sit down, whilst he settled into his swivelling office chair.

'How can I help?' Mike asked.

'I am Moses Brown, principal personal secretary to the Head of Senate. I have got a note for you from the boss.' He then slipped an envelope across the table to Mike. Mike picked it up, his pulse rising as he ripped open the envelope. The enclosed contained a terse message. It read:

Dear Dr. Lawanson,
You have failed to keep your promise. I will be waiting for your call this morning. The bearer of this note will call me and hand over the phone to you. I trust you will do the right thing.

Yours truly,

P. Osazuwa.'

Mike was fuming but he tried hard not to show it. He kept quiet bobbing up and down in his chair.

'What's the matter doctor?' Before Mike answered, Moses continued. 'The boss asked me to call him and hand over the phone to you. Are you ready?'

'This is bullshit.'

'Pardon me, Dr. Lawanson, there is no need for such language.'

'Look Mr. Brown, if we were not in the same political party, I would have asked my boys to lock you up or give you the "Lagos Isale Eko treatment".' He paused and then continued.

'If you want to phone the Senator you can do so but I am not ready to talk to him.'

'Sir, the boss is a very powerful man, I will advise you as a friend, not to cross him.'

'Okay, I will send a reply to him. Here is a sheet of paper and a pen.'

Mike pushed the blank sheet of paper and ballpoint pen across the table to Moses.

'Write this down. There is nothing that the chicken can do to the hawk.'

'I am sorry I can't do that,' replied Moses.

'Okay, I think you really want me to arrange the Isale Eko treatment for you. I'll call in my boys if you don't start writing immediately.'

Moses picked up the pen immediately.

'What do you want me to write?'

'Good man, I knew I could count on you.'

'Write the following: "There is nothing that the chicken can do to the hawk," and also, "Our elders say that the needle may be small but woe betide the fowl that swallows it."'

'Now put the message in this envelope and seal it.' Moses did as instructed.

'Now call your boss and tell him that I am unable to talk to him but I have sent a written reply to him. Then you will have no choice but to deliver the letter.'

'Sir, you are declaring war on him.'

Mike was furious. He got up and called in his bodyguard. He was a burly six foot six man.

'Go ahead and phone him.'

Moses did as he was instructed. Mike then asked the bodyguard to leave the room. Mike was now surprisingly calm. He turned to Moses.

'Mr. Brown, I am sorry for my inhospitable behaviour but I will give you a background to my grouse with your boss.'

'Are you married?'

'Oh yes, replied Moses.'

'What would you do if a big man tells you that he likes your wife and asks you to kick her out so that he can cohabit with her?'

'God forbid. Impossible, I will fight the big man. Better to die than to be disgraced.'

'Ah! That is what your boss is trying to do. I am about to get married to a lady, but your boss has asked me to abandon her so that he can make her his second wife.'

'Don't quote me, I don't want to lose my job, but that is very bad.'

'Mr. Brown, so you see why I am ready to fight your boss to the end.'

'Again, don't quote me, but be careful. Best of luck and goodbye, I'll deliver your letter.'

Mike asked one of the local council drivers to drop Brown at the airport for his return trip to Abuja.

CHAPTER 11

'Mike, why do you look so worried?'
'I have a lot on my mind.'
'What's bothering you? Money problems?
Mike shook his head.
'Have you got any misunderstanding with your girlfriend?'
He shook his head again.
'Dad, I think I am being followed.'
Mike's dad stiffened in his seat.'
'Are you sure?'
'Yes, I am sure. Yesterday, I suspected that I was being followed by a motorcycle rider, so I stopped briefly at a petrol station. The guy rode past and stopped at the next junction. I made a U-turn and returned the way I came, and the rider did the same. When I flagged down a police patrol car, the motorcycle rider sped off.'
'We can't take chances.'
Femi Lawanson remembered what happened to David.
'Lightning must not strike twice. I'll get Abisayo to provide you with protection. I'll call him right away.'
'Thanks dad.'
When Mike left home for work the following morning his car was followed by a Toyota land cruiser carrying four burly bodyguards with bulging muscles and dark sun glasses. This team accompanied him everywhere he went, day and night. The trailing of Mike's car stopped or so it seemed.
A month later, the security guards decided to assess the threat,

and determine if it had gone away. They swapped their security vehicle for a white van, which was parked down the street from Mike's home. Mike drove to work whilst the van followed at a distance. As a further precaution, the van did not follow Mike's car into the local government compound but was parked round the corner in a side street with the guards keeping in touch with Mike by mobile phone. Mike had a meeting at Agege local government headquarters on the outskirts of Lagos that afternoon. The white van again followed at a distance, as they snaked through the Lagos traffic. The meeting ended at five o'clock. As Mike exited the building, he received a call from a lookout that there was suspicious movement just outside the gate and they wanted to trap them by routing their journey home through desolate village roads. As Mike left the compound, he swung the car to the left away from the shortest route home. He then turned left into the Abiodun village road. He looked up at his mirror and saw a motorcyclist and a pillion rider gaining speed on him. He turned into a side street and the biker followed suit. Mike slowed down and checked the side mirrors and then stole a quick glance back through the rear window. Mike thought he saw the pillion rider holding an object.

This looked like a hand gun but Mike couldn't be certain. His heart beat quickened and palms became sweaty as he held tight to the steering wheel.

Where are the guys supposed to be guarding me?

At that moment the white van came into view and Mike breathed a sigh of relief. Mike accelerated down the deserted road and the motorcycle raced after him. The white van driver hit the pedal and the eight cylinder engine responded, gaining distance on Mike and the motorcycle. As the pillion hit man raised his arm, the Glock pistol was recognised by the van driver. After all, this was one of their tools. He nudged the motorcycle with his bumper, and the bike careered off the road into the ditch and the shooter discharged his gun into the air as he flew off the seat with arms flailing in the air. The motorcycle engine spluttered in the ditch with wheels still revolving, pinning down the rider. The bodyguards disembarked from their vehicle to inspect the scene. The rider pinned down by the bike was dead. There was a smell of burnt flesh from where the silencer had seared his abdomen, but that was not the cause of death. Fresh blood and grey matter oozed from a clean hole in his occiput, whilst there was a big gash in front of the head from where the bullet exited. His companion had accidentally shot him when they fell off the bike. They looked sideways and the shooter was groaning and breathing heavily. He was a crumpled mess. Both legs were broken and he was impaled by the stake he fell on, which was sticking out through his torso. He tried to talk but blood gushed out of his mouth, and he gurgled and then convulsed before expiring.

'Let's get out of here,' shouted one of the bodyguards.

'Not until we've checked their pockets,' declared the other.

'Be careful. Leave no clues.'

The bodyguards were careful not to leave any clues. They looked through the pockets of the victims and retrieved Mike's photograph from the pocket of the shooter. There was no other document. These were professional assassins, hired killers as they are known in Nigeria. The bodyguards didn't want to be embroiled in messy police investigations, so they left the site undisturbed removing only Mike's photograph.

Mike was truly shaken. It was a subdued Mike who entered his father's living room an hour later. Femi and his wife were watching TV when he walked in.

'Mike, why are you so quiet?'

'Mum, I thank God and I thank daddy,' replied Mike.

'What is the matter?' Femi Lawanson asked.

Mike then narrated the events of the last three hours.

His mother got up and started singing praises to God.

The men ignored her.

'Mike, do you have any idea who sent them?'

'I am not sure, but I think it must be someone from our party.'

'Impossible, it can't be,' replied Femi.

'Let's look at the photograph. There may be some clues in it.'

'Such as...' Mike enquired.

'Just bring the photo.'

Mike retrieved the photograph from his pocket and handed it to his father. His father studied it for a few minutes, and turned it over. There was no name or inscription on it.

'Mike, look carefully at the photograph. Where was it taken? When did you wear that attire?'

'Oh yes, yes I get it,' exclaimed Mike. 'The photograph was taken at our party congress in Lagos two months ago. So you see dad, it must have been supplied to the killers by a party member.'

'Who did I offend? What have I done that they want to extinguish my light?' Mike's mum cried, with her arms held high as if in supplication to a higher power.

'Ajoke, calm down, everything is under control,' Femi tried to assuage his wife's concerns.

'Mike, allow your mum to rest. Let's talk in the library.'

The men retired to the library leaving Mrs. Lawanson in the living room. No sooner were they settled in the library than Femi started probing deeper. Mike recounted his Abuja experience whilst his father listened intently. Mike did not bother with the Lagos visit of Osazuwa's emissary. When Mike finished Femi kept shaking his head in disbelief.

'Mike, do you know what our elders say about the cry of the witch?'

'I don't know.'

'I'll tell you. The witch cried last night and the child died this morning, there is no doubt in anyone's mind that the witch killed the child. This is the handiwork of Osazuwa. Don't worry Mike. He will hear from me. I will tell him we are watching him, and if he wants a fight I'll give him one. Meanwhile, we'll have to beef up our defences. You don't go anywhere without your bodyguards. Not even to your girlfriend's place. And another thing, don't be predictable. Change your route to work regularly.'

Femi ended the conversation by reverting to his native Yoruba tongue.

'*Ko si ohun ti adie, to le fi eiye asa se.*'

Mike smiled. This was the very proverb he quoted to Osazuwa's emissary.

Mike became more security conscious and watched his rear at all times. He never went out without his guards in the accompanying security vehicle. They were the most fearsome that the leader could recruit. Two of them were ex-marines, and they could snuff the life out of grown men with their bare hands. They fortified their skills with appropriate firepower, tucked away beneath their jackets. The other two were daredevil drivers, graduates of the Kirikiri maximum security prison. One drove Mike's car and the other the security vehicle. Following the encounter with the motorbike assassins and Femi's cryptic message to Osazuwa, Mike was left alone. His car was no longer trailed but he knew better than to let down his guard. He moved Nkechi to a new flat in a gated compound in Ikoyi with security guards. Mike also resorted to all manner of subterfuge. When he visited Nkechi at weekends without his bodyguards, he went in a disguise and swapped cars. He never went in his BMW X5, but took his mother's Mercedes sport utility vehicle.

Mike's enemies were formidable and indefatigable. They withdrew their surveillance of his Ikeja house but after a few months they turned their attention on Nkechi's residence. They planted a spy amongst the security guards. All he had to do was record the movements of Nkechi and Mike, and forward to an intermediary, who then passed on the information to his godfather. It soon became clear that Mike was untouchable whilst his guards were around. Initially, they were surprised that Mike didn't visit Nkechi at weekends. It did not take long before the spy became suspicious of the old man visiting in the Mercedes ML 350. He reported this to his minder who traced ownership of the car to Mrs. Lawanson through the Vehicle Registration Authority. The sleuth was armed with a camera with high powered telephoto lenses. He was alone on duty when the ML 350 drove in the following Sunday afternoon. He opened the gate and waved the driver in. He retreated into the guard house and started clicking away with the hidden camera. He focused on the driver's face, and as he disappeared towards the door, on his gait. When the photographs were analysed by the minder, it confirmed their suspicion. Mike had fooled them for over a month. Mike was clever but not clever enough. The cobra had stalked its prey and was now about to strike.

The following Sunday the 'old man' came again to visit Nkechi arriving just after noon. They had lunch and then sat on the sofa canoodling as they watched weekend TV. Mike briefed Nkechi about the planned publicity blitz to ensure he would clinch the party nomination to represent Lagos Central in the Federal House of Representatives election.

'Nkechi, it's now 7 o'clock and it's been raining heavily for the past two hours. I think I should make a move before Ikorodu Road gets flooded.'

'Aren't you a good swimmer? You just abandon the car and swim all the way home,' Nkechi joked.

Mike held on tightly to his woman, kissing her and whispering sweet nothings into her ear.

'Wish I could stay the night, and not have to go home.'

'Why don't you stay?' Nkechi asked.

'I've got a lot of work to do at home, and the deadline is looming. I'll make it up to you when the nomination is in the bag.'

'Bye darling.'

'Bye sweetheart,' replied Mike.

He put on his hat, dark glasses and grabbed his walking stick before he exited the flat. He was the old man once again.

The ML 350 roared into life and he slowly drove to the security gate. He waved to the guard as he opened the automatic door. The guard returned the greeting. As he exited the compound and zoomed down the street, the guard dialled a number and delivered a cryptic message. Ten minutes later, Mike was on the Third Mainland Bridge on his way to Ikorodu Road. Visibility was poor as a result of the heavy tropical rain. Mike did not see the lorry. As he descended the ramp to join the link road leading to Ikorodu Road, a five ton tipper lorry zoomed out of the side road, aquaplaned and rammed the Mercedes SUV front passenger door. The ML 350 took off like a meteor flipping over and somersaulting twice before coming to a rest on its side on the other side of the road. The sight was frightening with its crumpled bonnet and partially collapsed roof. The front passenger tyre had burst on direct impact with the lorry and the spare tyre had flown out through the front windscreen. Mike was in severe pain, groaning and pleading for help. He was bleeding from lacerations to the face. The doors were jammed shut by the force. The seat belt and air bags had done their jobs largely protecting the chest and torso of the victim but his right leg was trapped by the pedals. The rescuers hacked away and eventually freed his trapped leg. It was evident that the ankle had been shattered by the trauma. Mike was trying to be brave but the pain from his leg was excruciating. By the time he was removed from the car and laid in a shed by the road side, he no longer felt any pain in his leg. Soon afterwards, the police arrived and radioed for an ambulance. When the paramedics arrived, they quickly assessed Mike and couldn't elicit any sensation or reflexes in his lower limbs. They came to the conclusion that he had sustained spinal injury, and would require management by a neurosurgeon or spinal surgeon. The paramedics conveyed Mike to the Federal Specialist Medical Centre in Yaba. The police then set about investigating the accident. It soon transpired that the lorry driver absconded immediately after the accident. The heavy rainfall meant that most of the tyre markings had been washed away. Police took eye witness accounts, photographs of the site and then set about removing the two vehicles for forensic examination. The police soon found out that the lorry had been reported stolen two days before. The police now pinned their hopes on forensic analysis of the lorry.

At the teaching hospital, Mike was examined by the Emergency Department Consultant, Doctor Francis Carr and the Orthopaedic Surgeon on-call. The right ankle and fibula fractures were the least of their worries. Mike had wet himself as they brought him into the ED suggestive of the loss of sphincter control. Dr. Carr catheterised Mike's bladder and then requested urgent Computed Tomography (CT) scan of the neck, chest, abdomen and pelvis. The doctors needed to find out why Mike had lost all sensation in his lower limbs, and quickly too. The CT examination revealed narrowing of a disc space in the lower thoracic spine but there was no fracture or dislocation in the spine. There were a few rib fractures with moderately contused lung and small bilateral basal pleural effusions, presumed to be haemorrhage from the contused lungs. The abdomen and pelvis were normal. The findings could not explain the lower limb paralysis. There was a quick conference by the specialists and they ordered Magnetic resonance imaging of the thoracic and lumbar spine. The MRI revealed the presence of a large disc prolapse at the thoraco-lumbar junction severely compressing the lower end of the spinal cord. This was responsible for the urinary incontinence and lower limb paralysis. The spinal cord compression would have to be relieved urgently to prevent permanent neurological damage.

As the doctors prepared for the operation, Senator Lawanson and wife hurried into the emergency department. Mike was now hooked on to numerous machines, with tubes down his throat and intravenous infusions running into both arms. Mike was almost unrecognisable and Mrs. Lawanson let out a harrowing cry when she saw her son. Her husband fought back tears as he engaged the doctors in a discussion on Mike's condition and prognosis. He signed the operation consent form. Thirty minutes later, Mike was wheeled into the theatre. It was a delicate and painstaking surgery because the team had to make sure that vital structures were not damaged in the small operating field. The hospital had the best neurosurgeon in Lagos, perhaps in the whole country, and he was being assisted by a visiting consultant orthopaedic surgeon from Cardiff. Two hours later the prolapsed disc had been resected and the operative wound closed. The orthopaedic surgeon then fixed the right ankle fractures with a metallic plate and screws. Shortly afterwards, Mike was wheeled to the Intensive Care Unit. His respiration would continue to be assisted by a mechanical ventilator whilst his body recovered from the massive battering it had received. He was expected to make full recovery, albeit slowly. They would only be able to assess how well his neurological deficit had improved after weaning him off the muscle relaxant and sedation.

Mike's parents kept vigil by his bedside all night, save for a short time when his father took leave to make a phone call to Senator Abisayo. He gave him specific instructions on what to tell Senator Osazuwa. Femi Lawanson had come to the conclusion that this was the handiwork of Osazuwa. When Abisayo tried to be dispassionate and suggested they should assume it was an accident until there was evidence otherwise, Femi replied with the same Yoruba proverb he had told his son a few months earlier.

'The witch cried last night, and the child died the following morning, is there any doubt that the witch killed the child?'

Abisayo agreed, and would get in touch with Osazuwa in the morning. He wasn't looking forward to the conversation as it was bound to become acrimonious, but he had to carry out his mentor's wishes.

All through the night, Nkechi tried unsuccessfully to get through to Mike. He called her every night before he went to bed, even when he was out of town. Surely, something was amiss. She hardly slept, and kept checking the clock at intervals. At 5.00 a.m. she couldn't bear it any longer and called Mama Lawanson, as she referred to Mike's mother. The phone rang once and then went dead. She was now thoroughly confused and afraid. She didn't know what else to do, so she phoned her friend Mosun Martins.

'Who is this?' asked Mosun.

'It's me, Nkechi.'

Mosun was still sleepy, sat up groggily and glanced at her clock.

'Oh my goodness, Nkechi, it's just 5.00 a.m.'

'I know and I am sorry. There is a problem.'

'What is the matter?'

'Something is wrong with Mike.'

Mosun stiffened when she heard that.

'What happened, what's the matter? Mosun asked.

'I don't know but something is seriously wrong. I have tried to reach him by phone without any success. Even Mama Lawanson is not answering her phone. Mike left here last night in the heavy rain and I have not heard from him since.'

'Nkechi, this love is too much. Perhaps he was tired and forgot to phone you before he fell asleep.'

'Impossible. He never fails to phone. Something is wrong and I am on my way to their house. I would like you to accompany me. I am on way to pick you up.'

'Isn't it too early? Why don't you wait a little longer?'

Nkechi did not reply. She had already dropped the phone and was on her way to pick up Mosun in Ebute Metta. Mosun got up and had a quick shower. She was still getting dressed when Nkechi pressed the door bell. Five minutes later they were zooming down Herbert Macaulay Road towards Ikeja. At this time of the day, the Lagos roads were still almost deserted with only some early risers on the roads. An hour later, it would be bedlam on these same roads with traffic jam and the cacophony of street hawkers and drivers, vying for ownership of the roads. Just after 6 o'clock, Nkechi drove up to the Lawanson compound gate. She was well known to the security guard, who waved them in. As soon as he locked the gate, he ran after Nkechi's car. Nkechi saw him in the rear mirror and stopped abruptly. Before Nkechi could speak, the guard rattled on.

'Good morning madam. How is Oga Mike?'

Nkechi glanced at Mosun, as if to say I told you so.

'What is wrong with Mike?' asked Nkechi.

'Madam, you never hear? Oga Mike get serious accident last night,' the guard replied in pidgin English. Nkechi screamed and started crying. Mosun tried to calm her friend and urged her to stop crying.

'You need to be strong. Mike will need you to be calm and strong at this time.'

Then Mosun took over the questioning.

'Which hospital did they take him to?'

'Madam, I don't know,' replied the security guard.

Mosun and Nkechi disembarked and walked to the main house. Mosun pressed the door bell and the housekeeper opened the door after seeing Nkechi. They spoke for a few minutes and then left. Nkechi was so distraught that Mosun decided it was not safe for her to drive. Mosun slipped behind the wheel and they were soon on their way to the Federal Medical Specialist Hospital in Yaba medical compound. The roads were now getting busier and their drive to the hospital seemed to take forever. In reality, it took only thirty minutes.

Nkechi and Mosun rushed into the hospital reception, and were shown the way to the Intensive Care Unit. They had to wait in the ICU relatives room because Mike's parents were still seated by his bedside, and each patient could only have two visitors at any time. A nurse gave Nkechi's message to Senator Lawanson who then withdrew, allowing Nkechi to see Mike. She stood speechless when she saw Mike with all the tubes and machines keeping him alive. She shuddered as tears rolled down her cheeks. Mama Lawanson stood up and took Nkechi's hand, she then held her tightly with Nkechi's head resting on Mama's ample bosom whilst she sobbed quietly. Eventually, she calmed down and they both sat down. Mama told her all they had garnered about the accident. Shortly afterwards the Lawansons departed after Nkechi offered to stay. The Lawansons would have a little shut-eye and be back at noon. The doctors planned to remove the endotracheal tube and get Mike breathing on his own in the afternoon. If all goes according to plan, Mike should be able to talk by the evening.

The Lawansons returned by noon as promised. They found Nkechi and Mosun sitting quietly in the waiting room. The doctors had decided to remove the endotracheal tube and get the patient breathing spontaneously. The doctors succeeded but Mike was heavily sedated and almost in a state of stupor. Mike did not seem to recognise anyone and the ladies left soon afterwards. Nkechi said she would be back later in the evening. When Nkechi returned, Mike was on his own. The sedation had worn off and Mike promptly recognised Nkechi. He smiled when he saw her. He muttered a few inaudible words. Nkechi had to strain her ears combined with lip reading to understand what he was trying to say.

'Mike, just nod or blink if I get it right.'

'Are you saying, you can't feel your legs?'

Mike nodded. Nkechi slipped her hands beneath the bed sheet and stroked Mike's leg.

'Can you feel my touch?'

'No,' replied Mike, shaking his head.

Nkechi slipped her hand upwards and held his manhood. It was limp with no reaction despite her touch.

'What do you feel?'

'Nothing,' replied Mike.

Oh my God, I can cope with paralysis but not impotence. Nkechi thought to herself.

'Don't worry, all will be well. It is still early days, and you will soon recover fully.'

'I hope so,' muttered Mike.

Mike was struggling to keep awake. The nurse came round and told Nkechi that Mike needed to rest. Nkechi decided it was time to leave. She bent over and kissed him on the cheek whispering into his ear: 'Good night and sweet dreams darling. I'll be back tomorrow.'

Mosun and Nkechi were back the following day after work. Mike was more lucid though still in some pain from the rib fractures and at the operation site. There was however no change in the paraplegia. Mike's parents arrived just as they were about to leave. Nkechi pulled Mama Lawanson aside and told her she was worried that the paralysis had not improved despite surgery. Mama confessed she was perturbed too, and had only been putting up a brave face in order to keep Mike's spirits up.

'Mama, you and daddy will have to ask the doctors what they are going to do about the situation. If they don't know what to do, perhaps we can get a second opinion from other experts.'

'Thank you Nkechi, that's exactly what I told my husband on our way to the hospital this evening. We'll have to sit down with the doctors as soon as possible.'

CHAPTER 12

The following morning, Senator and Mrs. Lawanson arrived well ahead of time for their 10 o'clock meeting with Mr. Ade Thomas, the Consultant Neurosurgeon, and Professor Jonathan Boone, the visiting Orthopaedic Surgeon from Cardiff in Wales, and waited in their car. At five minutes to ten, they walked into the hospital and were led to the surgical department. Professor Boone was already waiting for them in Mr. Thomas's office.

'Good morning, Mr. and Mrs. Lawanson.'

'Good morning Professor,' they replied in unison.

'Ade will be here in a minute. He is just finishing a quick ward round. He wanted to reassess Mike so that he can give you the latest report on his neurological status.'

'Thank you,' replied Senator Lawanson.

'Can I get you tea or coffee?'

'No thank you,' replied the Lawansons.

Mr. Thomas breezed in about ten minutes past ten, apologising profusely for his lateness.

After the pleasantries, Senator Lawanson cleared his throat and addressed the doctors.

'Gentlemen, my wife and I thank you for all you have done for our son since his admission. We thank you for saving his life but we are very worried about his continuing lower limb paralysis.' He paused and then continued. 'We have noticed considerable improvement in his breathing and chest wall bruising but his paralysis has not improved despite the surgical operation.'

Then his wife interjected.

'I have spoken at length with some of your nurses and they confirmed my suspicion that the paralysis has also affected his manhood. We can't sit and watch our only child become impotent.'

'We are doing our best,' replied Mr. Thomas. Professor Boone chipped in.

'Sometimes the best course of action is to do as little as possible. To wait and let the body recover from unusual trauma and swelling is a prudent line of action, especially when dealing with the spinal cord.'

'I know you are doing your best but it's been five days since the accident and we are understandably anxious. To say we are anxious is putting it mildly, we are downright distraught,' replied Senator Lawanson.

'So, what's the plan?'

Mr. Thomas was the first to respond.

'We'll carry out detailed clinical neurological examination later today, and then obtain a CT scan. Unfortunately, we can't carry out MRI so soon after spinal surgery, and will have to make do with CT. Depending on the outcome of the tests, we may continue to watch and wait or decide to operate again.'

Mrs. Lawanson stiffened and couldn't hide her alarm upon hearing that the doctors may undertake another spinal surgery.

'Can we take him abroad?' Mrs. Lawanson asked.

'Is that what you want?' asked Ade Thomas.

'Yes, but I want to emphasize that there is no suggestion of incompetence or failure on your part. I have the utmost respect and regard for your expertise and skills, but we think the total care in the United Kingdom is superior to what we can deliver in Nigeria,' replied Senator Lawanson.

'In fact, we would like you to help us arrange urgent referral to the best centre in the UK.'

'The Neurological Hospital in Queen's Square is one of the best in the world. The head of spinal surgery is an old classmate and good friend. I'll place a call to him once we finish this meeting. He does some private work in the hospital but the only problem is his fees. His fees are extremely high. Apart from his fees, there is the direct payment to the hospital for use of its facilities, and of course the cost of the air ambulance to transport Mike to London.'

'Mr. Thomas, money is no object,' replied the Senator.

'Please set the ball rolling. This is my business card. Please give me a call as soon as you hear from your friend. Can we work towards transferring Mike on Sunday? I guarantee I will have the air ambulance on standby at Ikeja airport by Sunday morning.'

With that the meeting was concluded.

Mr. Thomas immediately set to work whilst the Lawansons walked up the stairs to see Mike. They had agreed at the meeting not to tell Mike of the impending transfer until everything was in place. They spent less than an hour with Mike before leaving for the Victoria Island office of the Grand Phoenix, jointly owned by the Senator and his trusted friend, Maxwell Osita. Maxwell immediately started making calls to their overseas partners. Senator Lawanson left the hiring of the air ambulance to Maxwell, and soon left for home with his wife. Initial contacts suggested it would cost between twenty five and thirty thousand pounds sterling. The Senator had an important political matter to deal with, and his wife visited Mike alone in the evening. She met Nkechi and Mosun by Mike's bedside. Nothing seemed to have changed, and she took her leave after a short time. The three of them said their goodbyes and promised to meet again the following evening.

Mosun had a busy day at work and was a bit late arriving at the hospital. Visiting time commenced at 4.30 p.m. but Mosun didn't walk into the ITU until 6.30 p.m., half an hour to the end of visiting time. Mike's parents had tried to cheer him up, but he was restless, troubled by something. He betrayed his emotion immediately Mosun walked in.

'Where is Nkechi?'

'I don't know. I thought she would be here. We haven't seen or spoken to each other today,' replied Mosun.

'I'll call her as soon as I leave the hospital. I suspect she must have had a very busy day at work, or some unexpected assignment.'

'Cheer up, lover boy, I am sure she'll be here to see you tomorrow,' Mosun teased him.

Soon it was time for all the visitors to leave. As the three of them walked down the stairs, Mosun moved close to Mrs. Lawanson, and held her hand.

'Mama, can I ask you a personal question. Please forgive me if it appears I am too forward.'

'Go ahead.'

'I don't know how to put it, but have you considered taking Mike to London for further treatment. I know these doctors are good but I think the total care will be better in England. Of course, that is if it is not too expensive.'

The question stopped Senator Lawanson dead in his track. His wife glanced at him, and their eyes met.

'Thank you, my daughter. God bless you. We are already looking into it,' she replied.

Senator Lawanson nodded his head in admiration.

What an amazing lady. Extremely thoughtful.

He said nothing, and continued walking towards his car.

Mosun bade them good night and walked briskly to the taxi rank. As the Lawansons pulled away from the car park, Mrs. Lawanson spotted Mosun hailing a taxi. She wound down the side window and called out to Mosun. Mosun walked towards their car and bent down to talk to Mrs. Lawanson.

'I thought you came in your car.'

'I took it in for service this morning, but they didn't finish fixing it this afternoon as planned.'

'So how did you get to the hospital?'

'I took a taxi,' replied Mosun.

'Ajoke, the questioning is enough. Please let her come in.'

'Oh, I am sorry, please come in,' said Mrs. Lawanson, as she opened the rear door for Mosun.

'We'll drop you at home. Where do you live?' the Senator asked.

'I live in Ebute Metta but I am not going home,' replied Mosun.

'Oh, I am sorry. I hope I am not being intrusive. Where can I drop you?'

'I am going to church. We hold a vigil service with special prayer sessions on the last Friday of every month. I wasn't planning to go but I have a special request. I am going to pray for Mike's recovery.'

Mrs. Lawanson turned to face Mosun, and smiled at her.

'God bless you, God bless you my daughter, thank you very much.'

'Where is the Church situated?' Senator Lawanson asked.

'It's the Gospel Church in Apapa Road,' replied Mosun.

'Oh, yes I know it.'

Senator Lawanson swung his Jaguar saloon car on to Clifford Road and zoomed towards Apapa Road. The service had just started when they dropped Mosun off. The Lawansons could hear the congregation rendering praise and worship songs as Mosun opened the door and then disappeared inside the church.

'Papa Mike, that girl is a wonderful human being.'

'I agree with you. She is so intelligent and thoughtful,' replied her husband.

What his wife didn't say but which crossed her mind was that she would have preferred Mosun to Nkechi as her son's partner.

Mosun couldn't visit Mike on Saturday. When she entered the ITU on Sunday she panicked and started sweating profusely when she didn't see Mike in his cubicle. Her mind was in turmoil as she feared the worst. She stood dazed and speechless in the middle of the ITU. The ward sister walked up to her and spoke to her, jolting her from her trance-like state.

'Can I help?'

'Yes sister, I am here to see Mike Lawanson.'

'Come with me. I'll lead you to his ward. He had improved considerably and we moved him to the high dependency unit yesterday.'

'Thank God for that,' was all Mosun could say.

As Mosun walked into Mike's cubicle, Mike suddenly broke away from the conversation he was having with his parents. His eyes lit up, and his parents who had been backing the door turned to find out what was happening.

'It's a pleasure to see you.'

'Me too,' replied Mosun.

'I missed you and Nkechi yesterday.'

'I'm sorry I couldn't make it. I was so tired after the all night vigil service that I slept most of the day. When I finally dragged myself from my bed, I had to run errands for my parents.'

'Okay I forgive you,' Mike joked.

'But where is Nkechi? I haven't seen her or heard from her since last Thursday.'

'I haven't spoken to her either. When I couldn't get through to her I drove to her house. Her car was parked in front of the building but her flat was deserted. As I was about to leave I saw her neighbour who told me she travelled to the East on Friday afternoon.'

'Really?' Mike asked. He couldn't hide his disappointment.

'Mike, don't be too hard on her. It must have been an emergency. In any case you didn't have your mobile phone on you in the ITU.'

'That's true, but she could have called you.'

'Mike, there must be a good reason. I am sure she'll tell you all about it when she returns. Anyway, I am happy you are getting better, and they could move you out of ITU. As I prayed on Friday night I knew you would get better, slowly but surely. I have no doubt in my mind that you are going to walk soon.'

'Mum, tell her the news.'

'What news?' asked Mosun, now facing Mrs. Lawanson.

'Mike leaves for London tonight.'

'Thank you Lord, thank you Jehovah,' was all Mosun said in response to the news.

Then Mrs. Lawanson continued.

'Mike is to be transferred to Queen's Square Neurological Hospital in London. The air ambulance is already at Ikeja airport, and we leave for the airport in two hours time.'

'Mum, do you know why I was thanking God?'

They were now so familiar that Mosun had started referring to Mrs. Lawanson as mum, in the tradition of the Yoruba people of Western Nigeria.

'As we worshipped and praised God on Friday, our Reverend asked us to write down two prayer requests each and pray along with him on the requests. My first request was for it to be possible for Mike to be transferred to the UK for expert treatment as soon as possible. God has granted that request. The second request is my secret. One day I may be able to share it with you.'

'Thank you my daughter.'

'Mosun, thank you for concern and kindness,' added Mike.

'Mike, you need to rest before your trip so I must leave soon. Do you want me to pray with you before I leave?'

Before Mike could answer, his mother answered in the affirmative.

The three of them stood up around Mike's bed holding each other's hands and Mike's, as Mosun prayed for Mike's recovery. Then Mosun picked up her bag and prepared to leave but not before giving Mike a small prayer book.

'Promise me you'll use this prayer book. There is a prayer for every day of the month. I've got another copy at home. Promise me you'll use the book and I'll pray along with you daily,' requested Mosun.

'I promise,' replied Mike.

'I've written my phone number in the prayer book. I'll be expecting your phone call within a week or two. I am hopeful you will have good news to tell me. Once I have your phone number, I'll pass it on to Nkechi. Mum, this is my phone number. If you want me to do anything, do not hesitate to call me.'

Then as she turned round to leave, she shook Senator Lawanson's hand.

'Thank you Sir, and have a safe trip.'

Then she was gone.

The Lawansons were quiet for several minutes after Mosun left. Mike broke the ice.

'Isn't she a wonderful person?'

'Yes she is,' replied his mother.

'Dad, you didn't say anything.'

'I am still dazed. She has blown me away. I have not met such a caring and selfless person in a long time.'

'What does she do for a living?' asked Senator Lawanson.

'She is a senior geologist with Levron Petroleum Company,' replied Mike.

'Do you mean she is a graduate?'

'Of course she is. She graduated with first class honours in geology.'

'Yet she is so polite and humble,' Mrs. Lawanson added, before keeping her thoughts to herself.

May God open my son's eyes before it is too late. This is the sort of girl he should be courting, not that high society model.

CHAPTER 13

ike had a thorough clinical review the moment he was admitted into hospital in Queen's Square. The Professor of Neurosurgery, the Chief Consultant Spinal Surgeon and the Chief of Radiology held a conference where all imaging performed in Lagos were reviewed and compared with CT scan obtained soon after his admission in the London hospital.

By nightfall, Mike was wheeled into theatre for an operation on the spine. Two hours later, he was back in the recovery room.

It was an optimistic Chief of Spinal Surgery who walked into the relatives waiting room to brief the Lawansons on the outcome of the operation.

'Mr. and Mrs. Lawanson, the surgery went well.'

'How is Mike?'

'He is in the recovery room. We want him to rest tonight but you'll be able to talk to him tomorrow.'

'Doctor, what did you find?'

'He had bled around the conus of the spinal cord, possibly after his first surgery. This haematoma or blood collection was compressing the spinal cord.'

'So, was this the cause of his paralysis?' asked Mrs. Lawanson.

'We can't say for certain. The cord was probably bruised and swollen from the trauma of the road traffic accident and prolapsed disc. The prolapsed disc was completely excised in Lagos, but the haematoma would not have helped matters. It did not allow the cord swelling to subside. It's a long journey but I am hopeful that

Mike will make a complete or near total recovery. The degree of recovery will depend on his determination to persevere with the arduous physiotherapy regimen we will prescribe once the wound heals.'

'Thank you doctor.'

'Please go home and rest. You've had a long day. You can look at him through the glass screen on your way home. Please come with me so that you can see that he is asleep and resting.'

When the Lawansons arrived the following afternoon, they met a groggy and rather incoherent Mike. He had been heavily sedated to allow his body to recover from the stress of the trip from Lagos and the surgery. They sat quietly at his bedside. Suddenly, Mrs. Lawanson remembered something and started rifling through Mike's drawer. She soon found what she was looking for. She opened the pocket book to the day of the month, drew her chair close to Mike's head and started quietly reading the prayer for the day. When she started, Mike smiled. This was taken as a sign of approval. When she finished, she whispered into his ear that she would do this daily until he was fit enough to pray for himself. He nodded to show his delight and agreement. His parents left shortly afterwards for their home in Regent's Park.

Meanwhile, Nkechi returned to Lagos on Monday morning. She had the day off work and therefore drove to the hospital to see Mike. She was surprised to learn that Mike had been transferred to London. She concluded that his condition had not improved or might have worsened. She phoned Mosun but couldn't get through to her. She was anxious to learn more about Mike. She sent a text to Mosun that she was back in Lagos and would visit her in the evening.

The two friends were delighted to see each other, hugging each other like long lost friends. They had been away from each other for only four days. After the pleasantries, Mosun started the inquisition.

'Nkechi, why did you go away without telling me or Mike?'

'My parents sent word that they needed to see me urgently.'

'How are they? Hope they are well?'

'Thank you. They are in good health.'

'Nkechi, I know you too well. What is it you are not telling me?'

'Nothing,' replied Nkechi.

'Don't give me that. Something is wrong,' insisted Mosun.

'Okay, I'll tell you what happened. My parents in their wisdom felt I was messing around and wasting my time in Lagos, instead of settling down with a man.'

'Why didn't you tell them about Mike?'

'Well Mike hasn't proposed properly, has he?'

'But the two of you are an item. It is only a matter of time,' replied Mosun.

'Mosun, we can't go there now. I couldn't tell my parents that my husband to be is lying in a hospital bed, paralysed and impotent.'

'That's a cruel thing to say. Definitely, his situation is temporary and he will soon recover.'

'Are you sure about that?'

'You should always hope for the best. Anyway, what happened in the East?'

'Nothing much. Someone came to ask my parents for my hand in marriage.'

'Impossible. Nkechi, I don't believe you. If this is your idea of a joke, it's not funny at all.'

'So what did you tell your parents or this man? By the way do I know this man?'

'I don't think so.'

'What do you mean by you don't think so.'

'Okay, you don't know him.'

'So, did you accept the wedding proposal?'

'No, I didn't,' replied Nkechi.

'Thank God for that. You owe it to Mike to wait for him to recover, and then try to rekindle your love. You have to be patient and prayerful.'

'Mosun, you know that patience is not one of my virtues.'

'You'll have to cultivate it. I'll give you Mrs. Lawanson's phone number in the UK so that you can call her and send a message to Mike. It will cheer him up.'

'O.K. I'll call phone her tomorrow.'

The friends had their supper and spent the rest of the evening watching TV before Nkechi left for home around 10 p.m.

The following day Nkechi placed a call to Mrs. Lawanson. She apologised for having to travel suddenly to see her parents without telling anyone. It was an emergency, she reiterated. They talked about Mike, the new operation and his present condition. Mike was doing well but hadn't yet regained sensation or movement in his lower legs. The doctors were hoping to transfer him to the general ward later in the day. Nkechi sent her love to Mike and promised to phone him as soon as he was out the Intensive Care Unit and able to use a mobile phone. She could call him on the same number because she intended to leave her phone with him. Mum conveyed Nkechi's message to Mike. This cheered him up as he waited in anticipation for her phone call. He was dying to hear her voice once again.

Mike was transferred to a side room in the general surgical ward as promised, just before hospital visiting time. time. He was feeling much better apart from soreness in the lower back, at the site of surgery. He was a bit tired but struggled to keep awake. He didn't want to miss Nkechi's phone call. The phone call never came and finally he dropped off to sleep. His parents got up quietly and left for home. The phone finally rang at dawn the following morning Mike stretched out and grabbed the clam shell phone, flipping it open with his thumb as he placed it against his ear.

'Hello, good morning mum.'

'Good morning, this is not mum,' replied Mike.

'Hello Mike, how are you? This is Mosun.'

'Hello Mosun, I am delighted to hear from you.'

'I wanted to call mum to find out how you are doing before leaving for work. It's great talking to you directly.'

'It's always a pleasure talking to you. Your voice is like a tonic. It invigorates me.'

'Thank you,' replied Mosun.

'I am much better. The surgery went well. The doctors said they evacuated what they called a haematoma around my lower spinal cord. The legs are still numb but the doctors expect a slow but progressive improvement.'

'Mike, all will be well. Your healing will be complete. I know it in my heart.'

'Thank you for your constant encouragement,' replied Mike.

'What about our deal?'

'What deal?' asked Mike.

'We had a deal. You promised to use the book I gave you,'

'Oh yes, I promised, and I will keep my promise. Mum has been using it to pray for me daily, but from today I will start using it personally.'

'That's good, very good. Get well quick. I'll call you again tomorrow morning.'

The phone call lifted his spirit. The physiotherapist found a positive and cheerful Mike when she arrived to start the prescribed exercise.

Mike soon settled into a daily regimen of special diet, neurotrophic drugs and exercises. Mosun phoned him early every morning before she left for work and this cheered him up tremendously. Nkechi hardly phoned and it soon dawned on Mike that perhaps the flame of love had been extinguished. He was perplexed and couldn't understand why, but he had come to accept the situation. He never mentioned her name again in the presence of his parents, and only rarely did her name come up in conversation with Mosun. His focus now was on getting well again.

CHAPTER 14

It happened two weeks after the London surgery. Senator Lawanson and his wife were visiting Mike in hospital. The Senator was on his way to Heathrow airport to attend a key meeting of the political party national executive committee before the national elections. He was one of the six national vice-presidents of the party, representing the south-west zone. Mrs. Lawanson would stay behind in London to cater for Mike's needs.

Mike's parents chatted quietly whilst Mike was more interested in the league match between Arsenal and their North London arch rival Tottenham Hotspurs. Mike was a diehard Arsenal supporter. The game was hard fought but half way through the second half it remained goalless. The Spurs team kept their opponents pinned to their half and unleashed a sustained barrage of shots which the Arsenal defence just managed to keep out of the goal mouth. Almost all the Tottenham players were in the Arsenal half of the field. Suddenly, an Arsenal mid-fielder latched on to a loose ball and dashed down the Spurs half out running the Spurs defenders who were caught unawares. As he approached the Spurs penalty area, he unleashed a blinder which sailed into the far corner of the net. The senator was backing Mike and it was Mrs. Lawanson who noticed the sudden movement. As the Arsenal player struck the ball Mike had thumped an imaginary ball, and there was a ripple in the bed sheet covering Mike's legs. Mike had moved a leg for the first time since the car accident.

'Mike you moved your leg,' Mama Lawanson shouted ecstatically.

'Yes! Mum I moved it.'

'Thank you Lord, thank you Lord,' Mike's mother uttered repeatedly, as she broke into a spontaneous dance.

Senator Lawanson was speechless but he held his hands up, as if in supplication to a higher power.

'Mike, where is the phone.'

'It's over there.'

'Who do you want to phone? Senator Lawanson asked.

'Mosun, I want to tell her the good news. She has been so supportive and positive.'

'That's true. Go ahead.'

Mrs. Lawanson placed a call through to Mosun. She was exhilarated and rejoiced with the three of them, talking to all of them in turn. The senator said he would be in Lagos the following morning and would like to see her in the Grand Phoenix headquarters on Victoria Island in the afternoon if she could make it. She would be there immediately after work, between 4 and 5 p.m.

Mosun was able to get away a bit early from work in Lekki, just before the closing time traffic jam. A little after four she drove into the Grand Phoenix car park. Once through the reception, she hurried up the stairs to the Chairman's office. The Senator was waiting in his office as she walked. He greeted her warmly, like one of the family.

'Sir, how was your journey.'

'It was good. Very smooth flight and I was able to sleep on the flight.'

'How is mum?'

'She is fine. She is extremely happy at the turn of events with Mike's condition.'

'I can imagine how happy and relieved both of you are,' replied Mosun.

'We owe you a debt of gratitude. You have done more than anyone to encourage Mike and keep his spirits up.'

'I was just doing my duty as a friend.'

'You can't say that about all friends. After all where is Nkechi today?'

Mosun didn't reply to that question. Some questions do not require answers.

'Sir, there is something I had wanted to tell you but I didn't know how to broach the subject.'

'Okay, fire on.'

'You've got a very good set up at Grand Phoenix, and you can diversify into oil exploration and marketing, so that Mike doesn't have to return to politics when he recovers.'

'I am listening. I know you've thought this through, and you have more to say.'

'Okay Sir. You've got the contacts and the wherewithal. My suggestion is that you ask the President and the Oil Minister for an oil prospecting licence. We call it OPL in our line of business. I am aware that some blocks are about to be issued to a few top Nigerian businessmen and government functionaries to look for oil in the Niger Delta. Try to secure an OPL for at least 500,000 acres. What I will suggest is that once you get the OPL, the company enters into a joint venture agreement with an established international oil exploration company, to act as your technical adviser. Some Nigerian businessmen are short sighted, and just sell their OPL to foreign companies for fast bucks. They get a lot of money from these companies but only a fraction of what they could eventually earn if they find oil and manage the business on their own. Once you get a technical adviser, you keep 60 to 70 percent stake, and offer 30 to 40 percent to the technical adviser.'

'Mosun, that's a brilliant idea. Why didn't I think of this before? I am having a private meeting with the President in Abuja tomorrow, and the Oil Minister is my man. I nominated him for the post, to represent our zone.'

'Sir, I prepared a document just in case you showed interest. It will give you an overview of the project and the preferred areas in the Niger Delta. Good luck Sir.' Mosun handed over the document to Senator Lawanson.

'Thank you very much.' Then he broached another subject.

'The reason I asked you to come is that my wife and I wanted to say thank you for all you have done for Mike and for us.' Before Mosun could say anything, he pulled open his drawer and handed a small packet to her. Mosun placed it on the table, and protested that she couldn't take it. There was no need for any gift.

'Please open the package,' urged Mr. Lawanson.

She tore the wrapping and her mouth fell open when she saw the content. It was a Cartier gold plated lady's wristwatch.

'I can't keep it. It is far too expensive,' protested Mosun.

'My wife bought it for you. She will be offended if you reject it. This is nothing compared to what you have done for us. Turn the watch over and look behind it.'

Her name had been engraved on the back plate. She had to accept the gift.

'Thank you Sir, and have a safe trip to Abuja. If you need more information about the matter we discussed, please feel free to phone me.'

The Senator introduced Mosun to Maxwell Osita, and she then left for home.

Senator Lawanson placed a call to the oil minister's office in Abuja. He needed to see him the following morning for a very important matter, which he couldn't discuss on the phone. The minister empathized with him on Mike's condition, and cleared his diary for the morning to accommodate Senator Lawanson. The Senator was punctual and went straight to business. It transpired that the minister was on the verge of submitting the list of successful applicants for OPL to Mr. President. He had whittled the number down to four big guns. He confessed that the bidding and lobbying was tough but he couldn't say no to his mentor. He would add his name but he required some paperwork to be completed and sent to him before the end of the week. Lawanson assured the minister the paperwork would be delivered by hand to his office within two days. Lawanson said he was going to have private lunch with the President before the party executive meeting later in the day. The minister suggested it would help if he just dropped a hint to Mr. President that he had applied for an OPL and would appreciate the President's approval.

The executive committee of the Peoples Party of Nigeria met at the party headquarters till late into the night. They ratified the names of all the candidates standing for the upcoming Federal House of Representatives elections. Mike Lawanson's candidacy had been withdrawn following his serious road traffic accident, and his good friend Ahmed was now standing instead. Senators Lawanson and Osazuwa sat at opposite ends of the table. They exchanged only the most perfunctory of greetings and avoided each other like the plague. The meeting ended at about 1.00 a.m. Walking stick in hand, as Senator Lawanson ambled towards his car, he thought he saw a familiar figure in the distance. He rubbed his eyes and squinted in the dark. It was only the silhouette of a lady but she looked very familiar. Before he could decide what to do, a car drove by and the lady entered and the car zoomed off. That was Senator Osazuwa's car, so he had to be wrong about the lady's identity. He brushed aside the thought and then continued to his car. His chauffeur drove him to his hotel. He was tired but couldn't sleep. The silhouette kept flashing in his memory. Finally, he decided to take action. He called one of his loyalists based in Abuja. He wanted to know the identity of the lady who went away from the executive meeting last night with Senator Osazuwa. He demanded immediate action and woke up his security boys. They swung into action with surveillance cars and night goggles and cameras with infra red capability. They traced the car Lawanson had seen to Osazuwa's official residence and laid siege down his street, masquerading as a police patrol car. In the morning the car was replaced by dishevelled sleuths walking up and down the street. They took photographs of all cars and occupants entering and leaving the compound. Later in the morning, Osazuwa drove out in company of a lady matching the description they had been given. They used their telephoto lens to snap frontal photographs of the duo. The guys even captured them chatting animatedly and laughing. They phoned their boss and were called off. The boss drove straight to Lawanson's residence and handed over the camera to him. As Lawanson scrolled through the images, he stiffened and exclaimed, shouting expletives. Then he calmed down.

'Incredible, my eyes didn't deceive me. This is unbelievable perfidy. Indefensible wickedness.'

'Is that all Sir?'

'One more thing, please down load the photographs I have marked on to my laptop, and then erase all the images from the camera.'

'Consider it done, Sir.'

He passed his laptop to the man who promptly carried out his instruction. He was dismissed and then left the Senator to wallow in his misery.

The Senator spent the next hour considering his options. Finally, he dialled his wife. He knew she would still be at home.

'Ajoke, how are you?'

'I'm fine. How did the meeting go?'

'It went very well.'

'How is Mike doing?'

'Thank God. He is getting stronger by the day. The doctors are now talking of discharging him next week, to continue physiotherapy as an outpatient.'

'That's good news. Tell the hospital accounts office that I'll transfer another twenty five thousand pounds to the hospital bank account tomorrow.'

'Thank you dear.'

'Ajoke, are you sitting down?'

'What sort of question is that,' replied Mrs. Lawanson.

'Please sit down. I've got something important to tell you.'

'Okay I have sat down. I am all ears.'

'Ajoke, I thought I had seen it all. In all my sixty plus years, I have never seen such treachery, such perfidy and lecherous behaviour.'

'Femi, I am waiting anxiously. What happened?'

'You will not believe what I saw. Nkechi is now going out with Osazuwa,' replied Senator Lawanson.

'Which Nkechi?' asked Mrs. Lawanson.

'The same Nkechi. Your son's girlfriend.'

'That can't be true,' replied Mrs. Lawanson.

'My dear, I saw it with my own two eyes. I thought I was dreaming but my boys trailed them to Osazuwa's house. She slept there last night. The boys showed me photographs to prove it.'

'*Ye pa ripa,*' exclaimed Mrs. Lawanson in her native Yoruba language. Then she continued her lamentations, asking questions which did not require any answers.

'Ajoke, Mike must not know about this. We don't want anything to set back his recovery.'

'I agree. My lips are sealed.'

'Ajoke, I believe that Mike is lucky not to have married Nkechi.'

Mosun was elated at her promotion at work and decided to mark it with a luncheon on Sunday for her close friends, Binta and Nkechi. It would be an opportunity for the friends to let their hair down and catch up on the latest gossip in town. Binta's husband dropped her at Mosun's flat ahead of time. Binta helped her friend with the cooking as she excitedly announced that she was expecting her first baby. The bump was not yet evident but she was blooming and more curvaceous than ever. This actually made her more attractive than ever. She giggled as she confessed that since she became pregnant Godwin couldn't keep his hands off her. They were having more adventurous encounters than ever.

'Binta, I am happy for you but you need to tell him to take a cold shower occasionally, so that you can rest properly during your pregnancy.'

'Don't worry. I now work part-time and I sleep and rest when he is at work. I've also told him we have to slow down when the bump becomes big.'

'Isn't Nkechi coming?'

'Oh yes she is. She should be here any time from now.'

Shortly afterwards her door bell rang. Mosun looked through the window but couldn't see Nkechi's red Toyota Celica. Instead a gleaming white Mercedes C class coupe was parked in front of the house. She was still wondering who drove the Mercedes when she heard Nkechi rapping on the door and shouting to be let in. Mosun ran down the stairs to open the door for her friend. They hugged each other as they hadn't seen each other for some time.

'Where is your car?' Mosun asked, after they finally let go of each other.

'It's out there,' replied Nkechi.

'Out where?' Mosun asked.

'There,' as Nkechi opened the door and pointed to the white Mercedes car.

'Congratulations. That's really posh. Binta, come down and let's admire Nkechi's new car.'

Nkechi opened the car remotely, and for the next ten minutes showed off all the gizmos in the luxury car to her friends. As they walked up the stairs, Mosun was the first to sour the conversation.

'This car must have cost you a hefty sum.'

'Not really,' replied Nkechi.

'What do you mean?' asked Binta.

'It didn't cost me a penny. My boyfriend bought it for me.'

'Your boyfriend?' Mosun asked, confused.

Before Nkechi could speak, Mosun continued.

'How come? How did Mike manage that from his sick bed in London?'

'Did I say Mike bought it? Nkechi retorted, now getting irritated.

'My partner, my future husband bought it for me.'

'Nkechi, you can't be serious. Tell me you are joking,' replied Mosun.

'I am not joking. I have met the man I'm going to marry.'

'I thought Mike was your man,' continued Mosun.

'Let me be. Did you invite me to your house to face an inquisition?'

'This is not an inquisition. I am just talking to you as a good friend. I feel that even if you wanted to leave Mike, you would wait for him to recover. Can you imagine the shock and deleterious effect on his recovery when he finds out you have left him in his hour of need.'

'Mosun, stop judging me. Mike is now free and you are single. You can have him if you want.'

'Nkechi, that's a cheap shot. You know I never wanted Mike. I always wanted the best for both of you'

'Nkechi, that's not fair,' Binta chipped in disappointed.

'Mosun, I am sorry. I didn't mean that. Please forgive me.'

'You are forgiven,' replied Mosun. Then she went quiet. Then Binta broke the ice.

'Mosun, let's have something to drink whilst Nkechi fills us in.'

Mosun laid out drinks on the table. Nkechi poured herself a glass of fruity red wine from Bordeaux, whilst Binta objected patting her lower abdomen when Mosun tried to pour her some wine, and settled for apple juice.

Then Binta resumed her probing.

'Who is the lucky man?'

'His name is Osazuwa.'

'Which Osazuwa?' Mosun asked.

'The same Osazuwa, Patrick Osazuwa the Senate leader,' replied Nkechi.

'You can't be serious,' insisted Mosun.

'Oh yes I am. I have found true love.'

Mosun was dumbfounded and kept her thoughts to herself as Binta continued probing.

This is shocking. Wonders will never end. Was this not the same man Nkechi described as a feckless lecherous old man? The same man suspected of having a hand in Mike's predicament.

'Tell me more. How did the relationship start?'

'Binta, Patrick was persistent and wooed me for two months before I agreed to meet him. What he did next bowled me over. You know I went out with Mike for almost two years but he was never serious about marriage. We had a good time but at my age I need more than that. I need security, I need stability and commitment. Patrick asked to meet my parents. I wasn't sure whether this was a good idea. I employed all manoeuvres to stymie Patrick but he didn't give up. Then on my last birthday I woke up to find a brand new Mercedes car parked in front of my flat with a note slipped under my door asking me to collect a package from the compound security office. I was curious and when I retrieved the package it contained the car keys and documents in my name, and the car was fully taxed with comprehensive insurance. There was a short note that it was from Patrick with love, to mark my birthday.'

'Wow, that's incredible. It's like a fairy tale,' interjected Binta.

'That car costs a whopping eight million Naira, and possibly nine million considering all the extras,' continued Binta.

Binta paused and Nkechi continued her explanation.

'So, I agreed to talk to him. That was the least he deserved. Before we went further I quizzed him about Mike's accident. I couldn't go out with any man who could be involved in such a dastardly act. He denied categorically. He swore that he had no hand in Mike's car accident. I quizzed him on his marital status. He confessed that he was married but his wife resided in their village. He had married her under the "Native Law and Custom Act" when he was a village teacher, long before he went to university and then embarked on a political career. Under the Act you can marry more than one wife. Unfortunately, his first wife has not been able to bear him a child but he still takes care of her. I admire a man who does not shirk his responsibilities.'

'So, what happened next,' Binta asked excitedly, much to Mosun's discomfiture.

'Patrick travelled to the East to meet my parents. What I thought was going to be a mere introduction metamorphosed into a traditional engagement party. Patrick surpassed himself. He came with his heavyweight friends and a traditional dance troupe from his home state. During the introduction of the two families, Patrick asked if we could upgrade the event to a traditional engagement because he was desperate to tie the knot with me. My parents asked me and I said I didn't mind, and so the event turned into an engagement party. Patrick had been prepared for this eventuality as he sealed the deal by presenting me with a newly built duplex bungalow which he had bought in a new development in the town. He apologised that he was not being presumptuous but had taken the chance by buying the property in my name. My parents have now moved from our old family house to one wing of the duplex whilst the other wing is reserved for me.'

'This means you are virtually married.'

'Oh yes, but I told Patrick I am not moving in with him in Abuja unless we have a marriage certificate. We've fixed the registry marriage for the end of the month in Lagos. Then I'll relocate to Abuja.'

Mosun had heard enough.

'Girls, the food is getting cold. Let's eat.'

'Oh yes, I am famished. Let's eat,' replied Nkechi.

They tucked into the delicacies Mosun had prepared. The girls relaxed with their favourite tunes and as dusk approached, Godwin arrived to collect his wife. Nkechi left soon after.

CHAPTER 15

'Gring gring, gring gring, gring'
Mosun picked up her phone as she was getting ready to leave for work on Monday morning.

'Hello, good morning, who is speaking.'

'Good morning, this is Lawanson, Senator Lawanson.'

'Good morning Sir. You sound very distant.'

'Oh yes I am. I am on a business trip in the United States.'

'I hope all is well.'

'Oh yes, that's why I am calling. I've got double good news.' He paused and then continued.

'The government gave us the OPL.'

'Wow, that's good news,' replied Mosun ecstatically.

'I have got even better news,' continued Senator Lawanson. 'Mike has ditched the wheel chair and is now able to walk with the aid of crutches.'

'Thank God for that. That's fantastic news,' replied Mosun. 'Congratulations Sir. I rejoice with you.' I'll phone London later to talk to Mike and mum.'

'Mosun, we would like you to be involved in our plans to expand our business. Specifically we want you to lead the OPL project.'

'That's going to be difficult Sir. I've just been promoted at Levron to head a new department which will be involved in new exploration and collaboration with our American parent company. I leave on Saturday for the United States to spend a month at our head office in Dallas.'

'Congratulations on your promotion. That shouldn't stop you working with us later. We'll double whatever Levron is paying you. Please think about it. We can discuss our offer further when you return from the United States. We want the right person for the leading role, someone intelligent and reliable and I believe you are that person. Don't let me keep you any longer, have a good day at work'

'Good bye Sir.'

Mosun was not due to report in the Dallas office until Monday, so she altered her itinerary so that she could transit in London on Saturday to see Mike and his mother for the first time since he was airlifted for treatment from Lagos. That was two months ago. In that time they had spoken innumerable times on the phone that they were now more like family.

'Good evening mum. I was thrilled to hear that Mike can now walk. I am on my way to the US, and will be in London on Saturday for about twelve hours. If you and Mike are available, I'll call on you to say hello around noon.'

'We'll be thrilled, and we'd like you to join us for lunch,' replied Mrs. Lawanson.

'Where is Mike?'

'I am afraid Mike is out, gone for his physiotherapy session. I'll give him your regards when he returns.'

Over In Saudi Arabia, Anita had just arrived for her six months visit to keep her residence status valid. When she landed at Jeddah Airport, little did she know that this was going to be a holiday of a life time. Daniel had something special up his sleeve. Following the successful treatment of Prince Rasheed's mother in-law by Daniel, the Prince had sent a package to Daniel in appreciation. When Daniel opened it, he was flabbergasted. The package contained two return first class tickets on Saudi Arabian Airlines from Jeddah to London, and one week all expenses paid complementary stay in an executive suite at the 5 star Kingdom Hotel in Park Lane. Daniel had visited the hotel's website and found out that the cheapest room in the hotel costs six hundred pounds a night. The Kingdom Hotel, possibly the most prestigious hotel in London was owned by Prince Rasheed and one of his brothers. Prince Rasheed had enclosed a handwritten letter to the Hotel manager that Daniel and

Anita were his personal guests and were to be treated thus. Daniel had been requested to inform the Prince's office once they fixed their travel dates so that the hotel could make arrangements for their London airport transfer and room reservation.

Anita arrived from Lagos on Sunday but by Friday morning they were on a Saudia 747 bound for London Heathrow Airport. Once through immigration, they were met by the hotel luxury limousine driver who drove them in a stretch Mercedes 500 S class to the hotel. Everything about the hotel showed opulence. Daniel and Anita weren't used to this type of pampering, but the hotel manager had stayed late to meet them, and emphasised that they only needed to ask for whatever they wanted. When they said they wanted to visit a relative the following day at 1.00 p.m., the manager said the Mercedes 500 was reserved for their use for the entire week, and would be on standby 24/7 in case they changed their mind and decide to go out suddenly.

Daniel and Anita arrived in style at the Lawanson Regent's Park home around noon. They had just settled down and were chatting with Mike when the intercom bell rang. Mike eased himself out of the chair, leaned on the back and heaved himself up on to his feet steadying himself with his crutches. Once steady he ambled his way towards the intercom.

'Who is that?'

'It's me, Mosun.'

'Good afternoon Mosun, the door is open. Just push the door and come in.'

As soon as Mosun walked in, Mike's face lit up. Anita noticed but said nothing.

Mosun winked at Mike and then smiled. She went over to greet Anita and Daniel.

She then turned to Mike.

'Congratulations and well done. Do you remember what I said when you were lying on that hospital bed in Yaba? We'll come back to that. Where is mum?' asked Mosun.

'Mum is in the kitchen, supervising the cook.' Mike pointed the way to the kitchen, and Mosun moved across the living room towards the kitchen. She could be overheard greeting Mike's mum in a very familiar tone. You would have thought she was talking to her own mother.

Anita beckoned to Mike, and then whispered.

'How long have you known each other?'

'Only since my accident,' replied Mike.

'That's amazing. You are a lucky man, your wife and your mother being such great friends.'

'Auntie, she is not my partner?'

'Then, what is she?' Anita asked.

'Anita, stop being so inquisitive. You are embarrassing Mike,' Daniel stated.

'Mike, ignore your uncle. Please answer my question before she returns.'

'She is a friend, my best friend.'

'What did she tell you on the hospital bed?'

'She said she was confident I would walk again.'

Before Anita could say any more, Mosun walked in with Mike's mother.

'Mosun, let me show you my skills.'

With the aid of the crutches, he walked smartly around the living room.

'Mike, that's just wonderful. This calls for a celebration.'

Mosun walked half way across the living room towards Mike.

'Let's leave the toast till later, when dad returns home. If you can walk across the room without any crutches, I'll give you a massive hug.'

Mosun had thrown down the gauntlet. This was a duel of mind and body. Mike struggled and finally propelled his body forwards. He took a few faltering steps before he seemed to lose his balance but he was never in any danger, as Mosun had moved towards him and caught him in her arms. She hugged him and kissed him gently on one cheek.

Anita winked at Daniel, as if to say didn't I tell you these two want each other.

Senator Lawanson soon returned home. He was visibly pleased to see Mosun. He was full of praise for her support and steadfastness during the dark days of Mike's incapacity.

'Anita and Daniel, let me introduce you formally to Mosun Martins, one of the most reliable and dependable persons I have ever met. She was a rock when we despaired. I hope that one day we can reward her for what she has done for us.'

'Mosun, meet my brother a Consultant Surgeon and his wife, a Permanent Secretary in Western State of Nigeria.'

'Thank you Sir, thank you for all the kind things you've said about me. I am truly honoured but I was only doing my duty as a friend.'

'Okay, dinner is served. Let's eat,' announced Mama Lawanson.

'After the three course dinner, they retired to the living room for drinks. Anita and Mosun stuck to Apple Juice whilst the others downed lager beer and wine. Mosun engaged the others in conversation but she did more listening than talking. She appeared to be particularly relaxed with Senator and Mrs. Lawanson. It seemed as if she was talking with her parents.

As the clock struck five, Mosun got up and announced it was time for her to leave.

'Mum and dad, thank you for having me in your home. My flight is later tonight, so I have to get my things from my hotel and leave for the airport by eight o'clock. Dr. and Mrs. Lawanson, it's a great pleasure meeting you. I look forward to meeting you again in future. Mike, keep doing your prescribed exercises. By the time I finish in the US, you should be back in Nigeria.'

'Mosun, how are you getting back to your hotel?' asked Anita.

'My taxi will be waiting downstairs. I told the driver to be here by 5 o'clock.'

Just as she finished speaking, the bell rang. It was the taxi driver. She curtseyed to the Senator and his wife, shook hands with the others and made a quick exit. Mike saw her to the door and then retired to his room to rest.

Anita was the first to speak.

'What a well-mannered and lovely lady.'

'She is truly amazing,' replied Mike's mother, and the Senator nodded in agreement.

Then Anita dragged Mike's mother to the kitchen.

'Auntie, what's the relationship between Mike and Mosun?'

'They are just friends,' replied Mike's mother. Then she continued. 'She was a good friend to Mike's girlfriend who abandoned Mike after his accident, and is now going out with a married man. I don't think Mike knows that last bit, so please keep that to yourself.'

'Really, I think Mike is lucky not to have married his ex,' replied Anita.

'I agree with you.'

'Has Mosun got a serious boyfriend?' asked Anita.

'I don't know. She has never mentioned being in a romantic relationship with any man. She promised to phone every day when Mike was being transferred to the UK, and she has kept her promise.'

'You don't say?'

'Oh yes, that is why my husband said he has not found anyone as reliable and trustworthy as her.'

'Why doesn't Mike try to start a serious non-platonic relationship with her?'

'Anita, that is what I am hoping he'll do before another man wins her heart.'

'I'll broach the subject with him and find a way to persuade Mike to make a move.'

'Thank you Anita.'

CHAPTER 16

The American Airlines Boeing 777-300ER taxied to a stop at Dallas Fort Worth International Airport early in the morning. Mosun was met in the arrivals hall by staff of Levron International, and was driven straight to her hotel, arriving there by 10.00 a.m. After completing her registration, she was handed a bouquet of flowers by the hotel reception staff. She thanked the staff for their hospitality and carried the dozen long stem roses whilst the porter hauled her luggage into the elevator on the way to her 10th floor room. It was only as she was about to place the flowers in a vase that a small folded note dropped to the floor. She picked up the note and unfolded it. She was gobsmacked. The note indicated that the flowers were from Mike. It read:

'To my best friend and the most beautiful person I have ever met. Thank you for everything. You mean the world to me, Mike.'

She was thrilled but marvelled at Mike's ingenuity. How had he managed to pull this off? She only gave him the hotel name and address during her visit yesterday. She was fatigued from being in the air for much of the previous two days, and soon fell asleep. When she woke up it was late afternoon and she quickly set about making important work related phone calls, and getting ready for her new job the following day. Mosun placed a call to her parents and after a little chat, she sent a text to Mike thanking him for the flowers. She tucked herself in and was already drifting off to sleep when her phone rang. She picked up the phone and viewed the number. It was Mike.

'Hello, Mike.'

'Hello, beautiful,' replied Mike.

'Mike, how are you?'

'I am better than yesterday, especially now that I've heard your voice.'

'You are back to your old self, flirting already,' replied Mosun.

'Mosun, I've got something to ask you but I don't know how to go about it.'

'Fire on.'

'We are good friends, right?'

'Oh yes Mike, we are very good friends. I feel relaxed in your company.'

'Mosun, I think I am falling in love with you.'

'Mike, stop teasing. Alright, I'll play along. I love you too, true platonic love, almost like brother and sister.'

'That's not the sort of love I am talking about. I want us to be closer, as close as two people can ever be. Please will you be the love of my life?'

'That will not be possible. What about Nkechi?'

'What about her? I know the truth,' replied Mike.

'What do you mean?'

'I know that she has been cohabiting with the enemy.'

'Who told you?' asked Mosun.

'I have my sources. Don't forget that as a politician, I have my own network.'

'Some of my boys wanted to teach her a lesson. They said they knew her movements and could easily arrange an unfortunate set of events, that would teach her a lesson.'

'What sort of lesson?'

'They were going to smash her feet with a sledge hammer, break many pedal bones so that she would end up using crutches. She would be unable to wear high heeled shoes for a long time, and possibly end up with a limp.'

'Oh my goodness,' exclaimed Mosun. 'I am worried about the company you keep. Those friends of yours are vicious.'

'They are not my friends. They are party operatives, sometimes referred to as personal bodyguards or thugs. I forbade any action.'

'Good. That's a relief.'

'So, why don't you fight for her love when you return to Lagos.'

'I don't love her any more. You are the one I love.'

'Mike, let's stay good friends. I think it's too early for you to rush into a new relationship. Isn't that what psychologists call the rebound phenomenon?' In any case, I've got a confession to make.'

'What is it? Are you committed to someone else?' Mike asked, alarmed.

'There is nobody else.'

'That's a relief,' replied Mike.

'Mike, I have not been lucky in love. When my last relationship ended two years ago, I vowed that my next relationship will be with the man I'll marry. I have had many advances since then but I am yet to find the one.'

'Mosun, I am the one.'

'Only time will tell whether you are the real deal or not? For now, your main goal should be to regain your strength and return to work.'

'I am convinced I am the one for you and won't relent. I'll give you some time to warm to the idea though.'

'Alright Mike, I'll give it some thought.'

'By the way, dad thinks I should quit politics and join his company.'

'And what do you want?' asked Mosun.

'I was enjoying politics.'

'Were you enjoying politics or the trappings of power and the accompanying benefits?

'I tried my best to serve my constituents well,' replied Mike. 'Do you think I should quit politics?'

'The choice is yours but your father is a very experienced and wise man. Don't disregard his counsel without good reason.'

'Thank you. I now know what to do.'

'I need to get some rest Mike. Good night,' uttered Mosun as she stretched and yawned.

'Good night, my dear.'

The next week was exciting and exhausting at the same time. The group comprised twenty geologists and engineers from Levron partners in South America and Africa. The sessions started early at 8 o'clock with lectures and briefings all morning till lunch at noon, followed by workshops and simulations all afternoon till 5.00 p.m. The following Monday, all twenty were whisked off on a helicopter to offshore oil fields to put into practice all the things they had learnt. It was tough grimy work, but this first-hand experience would turn out to be invaluable later. Three weeks later, by the time they were airlifted from the offshore field to Dallas for the last time Mosun had formed friendships and alliances with colleagues from Mexico to Mozambique. Mosun left Dallas on Sunday afternoon for a three day stay in New York, sightseeing and shopping.

Mosun returned to Lagos mid-week, giving herself ample time to relax before resuming work the following week. She spent the whole of the first day back resting at home and reading her mails. A big envelope caught her attention so she grabbed and ripped it open. It was from Grand Phoenix. The company brochure outlined the operations of Grand Phoenix and the projections for growth over the next few years. Then there was Phoenix Oil, a new subsidiary incorporated only in the last few months. It appears that the intention was for Phoenix Oil to be semi-autonomous within the group. There was a personal note from Senator Lawanson for Mosun to get in touch with the company's Managing Director as soon as she returned from Dallas. She thought it might be a good idea to get this out of the way before going back to work at Levron, so she booked an appointment to see Mr. Maxwell Osita the following morning.

Mosun walked into the Grand Phoenix building just after ten and took an elevator straight to the fifth floor office of the Managing Director, Mr. Maxwell Osita. She was shown into his office by his PA.

'Good morning, Miss Martins.'

'Good morning Sir.'

'Welcome back from the States. I hope you had a good trip.'

'Yes I did. It was a great trip, very worthwhile. I learnt a lot of new things about oil exploration and spent 3 weeks on an offshore rig.'

'That's brilliant,' replied Maxwell.

'Let me show you round our company.' With that Maxwell got up and led the way.

'You've met my PA, Mr. Marcus.' Mosun nodded and acknowledged Mr. Marcus's presence with a smile. He reciprocated with a smile, standing as a mark of respect.

They exited the room and turned right. He turned the door knob and they entered a small unoccupied room, and a further door led to a massive office space with an ornate table in one corner.

This is the office of the boss, our chairman Senator Lawanson.'

'Very impressive,' muttered Mosun.

'There are two more offices on this floor. Here is the office of our new Business Development and Public Relations Manager. Unfortunately, he is not in today. He has gone to hand over to his successor at his old job. You'll meet him when next you are here.'

'What's his name,' asked Mosun.

'He is Dr. Mike Lawanson. Our Chairman's son,' replied Maxwell.

'So, Mike joined the group after all.'

'Do you know Mike?'

'Yes, I do.'

'Over here is the company board room.'

They walked down the stairs, and Maxwell showed Mosun round the offices where the staff were hard at work. There is a staff cafeteria in that corner where you can have lunch at subsidised rates.

'So, that's the Grand Phoenix machine.'

'Impressive but from where do you want to run the oil business?' asked Mosun.

'Oh, I almost forgot,' Maxwell replied jokingly.

'This way,' as Maxwell led the way down another flight of stairs to the third floor.

'Welcome to Phoenix Oil,' announced Maxwell.

He retrieved a bunch of keys from his pocket and opened the main door.

'This is the Phoenix Oil reception desk. The operation and technical rooms are all on the left side. The first room on the right is the board room, and next to it is the office of the Director of Operations, your office and that of your Personal Assistant, if you agree to join us. That's the tour. Let's go back to my office so I can present our offer. The Chairman will link up with us by phone. He's in Port Harcourt clinching a deal.'

Mosun sat across the table from Mr. Osita. He grabbed the phone receiver and pressed a speed dial code. The response was prompt.

'Hello, Maxwell.'

'Hello, Sir. Miss Martins is in the office with me.'

'Turn on the speaker phone so we can hear each other.' Maxwell pressed the speaker phone button and replaced the phone receiver.

'Miss Martins, welcome back from the States.'

'Thank you Sir,' replied Mosun.

'Mr. Osita will brief you about our plans for Phoenix Oil. We think you are the right person to lead this new company, and we are willing to wait for you if you wish to work through your notice with your present employer. Please give our offer serious consideration. Mr. Osita has all the power to negotiate with you.'

'I will do so Sir. Thank you.'

Senator Lawanson clicked off and Maxwell then sat down with Mosun to discuss the offer on the table. After one hour of bargaining, they reached an accord. Mosun would return to Levron for a month to lead her new department and utilise the skills acquired on the Dallas trip, and then resign giving 3 months notice. In four months, she would be available to take up appointment as the operational head of Phoenix Oil, on double her present salary. In addition, there would be an official chauffeur driven car and a generous housing allowance. They agreed a formula for end of year performance related bonus once Phoenix Oil starts making a profit. Finally, Mosun asked that this agreement be kept secret till she resigned from Levron in a month's time. It was almost 1 o'clock when Mosun finally left the Grand Phoenix premises.

Senator Lawanson was so thrilled with the news he received from Maxwell that he promptly called Mike to share his joy. The news was to be kept secret though. Mike had not spoken to Mosun in over three weeks. There was no mobile phone signal on the oil rig, so Mosun couldn't phone anyone. Mike didn't know that but had missed her phone calls and wondered whether she was trying to avoid him or playing hard to get since he tried to get closer to her. Mike dialled Mosun's telephone number. She answered the call.

'Hello.'

'Hello, Mosun. It's Mike.'

'Hello Mike, how are you doing?'

'I am fine thank you. Welcome back.'

'Thank you.'

'Why did you cut me off for three weeks?'

'I was stuck on an offshore rig with no mobile phone signal.'

'Mosun, I missed you and your lovely voice. So I threw myself into my physiotherapy, and here I am back in Lagos, walking once again without crutches.'

'Congratulations Mike.'

'Thank you.'

'I understand you are joining the group.'

'Shush, that's supposed to be a secret. I need to be discreet and do things properly.'

'You can trust me, my lips are sealed.'

'Would you like to attend a dinner-dance party with me tomorrow night?'

'I am sorry Mike, I've got an important prior engagement.'

'In that case, let's meet each other half way. We go for the dinner and then you can leave the party early for your engagement.'

'That won't be possible.'

'What party are you attending?' requested Mike.

'It's not a party. I am going for the all-night vigil service in our church.'

'I see, enjoy the service. Good night.'

'Good night.'

Mike's mind was in turmoil. He had promised his friends he would be at the party, and he wanted to show that he had recovered from Nkechi's perfidy. He wasn't sure where he stood with Mosun but one thing he knew was that she was a determined lady. There was no way he could get her to attend the party. Then he remembered his friend Ahmed. Ahmed had known her before Mike first met her. Perhaps she won't say no if Ahmed invites her. He phoned Ahmed.

'Good evening Ahmed.'

'Good evening, Mike.'

'I am sorry it's a bit late but I am in desperate need of your help.'

'Okay, what can I do for you?'

'I would like Mosun Martins to attend tomorrow's party in the club house.'

'Mike, just invite her. You are a good friend of hers.'

'It's not that simple.'

'Why not?'

'I have already asked her out?'

'What did she say?'

'She said she couldn't make it because she had a prior engagement. She wants to go to a night vigil service instead.'

'You've got her answer. What else do you want? I am afraid I can't help you.'

'Ahmed, I thought I could count on you.'

'Look Mike, what do you want from this woman?'

'I want to win her love. I believe she is the one.'

'Mike, if you think she is the one, you have to work harder for her love. Obviously, she is very different from Nkechi. She is not crazy about parties. She is a more spiritual person. Is that what you want in your future partner?'

'Ahmed, she is perfect. I want her the way she is. Do you know that when I was on admission in hospital in London, she phoned daily and kept encouraging me. She prayed for me in hospital just before I was transferred from Lagos to London.'

'She did all that?'

'Oh yes, and more. My parents told me she was one of the first persons to suggest that they should transfer me abroad for better treatment when I wasn't making much progress.'

'Mike, you've got the answer to your riddle. Do the right thing.'

'What's the right thing? asked Mike.

'You know the right thing. Forget the party and do the right thing.'

On return from work on Friday, Mike sat in his living room moping. His mum called on him for another matter and immediately sensed that something was amiss. Mike reluctantly shared his thoughts. His mother didn't mince her words.

'Mosun is one hundred times better than Nkechi. If you want this girl, you will attend the night vigil instead of the party. Her faith means a lot to her, so start your relationship by doing something which will impress her.'

The service had just started when Mike walked in Bible in hand and sat in one of the rear pews. After one hour of praise and worship, the presiding reverend asked the members to go round and greet each other. That was when Mosun spotted Mike.

'How long have you been here?'

'I've been here for almost one hour,' replied Mike.

'I hope you are enjoying the service.'

'Oh, yes I am,' replied Mike.

'Come and sit next to me.'

Before long Mike was singing and clapping with the rest of the congregation. The service ended at 4.30 a.m. Mike left for home fully satisfied with himself. He had passed the first test.

CHAPTER 17

Four months went quickly and Mosun resumed at Phoenix Oil as the Director of Operations. Her relationship with Mike had not progressed as rapidly as he would have liked. He had tried every subtle way possible but had not yet succeeded in hitting the sack with her. He quickly discovered that once her mind was made up, she was not for turning. One of the preconditions she gave him was that there would be no mixing of business with pleasure. Consequently, Mike rarely came down to the Phoenix Oil offices. Mosun reported directly to the company's managing director, Mr. Osita, and held monthly strategy and financial review meetings with him and the chairman.

Mike was calculating and pertinacious. He saw his opportunity when his uncle's wife celebrated her 50th birthday in Ibadan. Following their meeting in London, Anita and Mosun had become friends. Anita admired Mosun's sterling qualities and took her under her wings like a younger sister. She hoped her in-law would be sensible and smart enough not to let Mosun slip through his fingers. The birthday celebration was grand and continued late into the night. Mosun was busy all night supervising and directing the catering staff. She did a brilliant job. After the last guests had departed at about midnight, as she flopped on the arm chair exhausted, Mike walked up to her.

'Mosun, it's time to go. I've booked a double executive room for us at The Presidential Hotel.'

Mosun was mute but her mind drifted to what her mother had told her after her last relationship broke up.

Men are like bees looking for nectar to suck. Once they get the nectar they are gone. If you want them to stay, make it difficult for them to get the nectar.

I know what you want but you are not getting it tonight.

'Mosun, it's time to go.'

'I am sorry Mike. You can go on to the hotel. I promised Auntie Anita I was going to help supervise the clean-up. She has offered me her guest room. I'll see you in the morning, good night dear.'

'Good night,' replied Mike, as he trudged along licking his wound.

This woman has outsmarted me again. I'll have to change my strategy.

Mike found it difficult to fall asleep, and when he eventually did, he had a fitful sleep, tossing about in bed. He woke up at dawn, red-eyed. He kept pondering what he was doing wrong. He used to think he was a master tactician but he had now met his match. He got on the phone again to Ahmed.

'Ahmed, how are you and madam? I hope all is well.'

'Mike, to what do I owe this early morning call on a Sunday when you and I should still be in bed.'

'My brother, I am in a fix.'

'What have you done this time?'

'It's not what I have done, but what I haven't done. My woman has outsmarted me again. I came to this party with her and booked a double room for us in the hotel but she conspired with my in-law, Uncle Daniel's wife and slept in her house.'

'How did she do that? What did she say about sleeping in the same room with you?'

'She didn't say anything, but she is now a good friend of my in-law, and was in charge of the entertainment and supervision of house cleaning after the party.'

'You are a lucky man. You've found a good woman.'

'Why is it that I don't feel lucky?'

'Patience man, you have to be patient.'

'Well, she told me that if I really love her, I would wait till she was ready. So, when will she be ready?'

'What do you think?' Ahmed asked.

"She once said she was not interested in fooling around with any man before marriage.'

'So, what are you waiting for?'

'Are you suggesting that I should marry her?'

'That's not for me to say. It's your decision to make. Goodbye and all the best, I am going back to bed'

'Thank you and goodbye,' replied Mike.

Mosun returned to Lagos on Sunday morning, and after a change of clothes drove straight to the office. Her key officers were already waiting for her. They went through all the plans again until they could recite them with their eyes closed. One hour later, Mosun left for the airport in the company of Frank, the travel officer to receive Dr. Franklin King, Vice President of Irish-American Oil Company (Ir-Am Oil) with headquarters in Dallas. Dr. King was one of the resource persons at the Dallas workshop attended by Mosun whilst still at Levron. She had impressed him with her enthusiasm and knowledge during the programme, and they had forged a lasting relationship based on mutual admiration.

When Mosun joined Phoenix Oil, she tapped all her contacts in her quest to take the company to a new prestigious and profitable level. In the search for a technical partner, she sent out feelers to three giant oil companies in North America and the United Kingdom. She finally settled for Ir-Am. She ran her plan past Senator Lawanson and Maxwell Osita and they were bowled over by her presentation. The Irish-American Oil Company had decades of experience in extensive off-shore exploration in North America, and was a technical partner for a Mexican Oil company. It also owned an oil refinery in the Irish Republic. Mosun's plan for Phoenix Oil was in phases. The first phase involved selecting an experienced technical partner to provide technical expertise and bulk of the funding for the exploration of the oil blocks in the Niger Delta. Phoenix Oil's contribution to the partnership would be the ceding of 35 to 40 percent of the ownership of the oil block to the partner. The second phase involved establishing a major foothold in the local petroleum products business with ownership of petrol and gas stations. Finally, as soon as the company strikes oil in the Niger Delta and starts making profit, they would buy substantial shares in an overseas refinery. Once Mosun had the blessing of the Chairman and Managing Director, she went to the United States to seal the deal with the Ir-Am. Phase One was already in operation with heavy machinery and technical experts on the way to their oil blocks. Dr. King was coming to Lagos to formally meet the owners of Phoenix Oil and turn the soil at the foundation laying ceremony of the first Phoenix Petroleum Filling Station.

Dr. King's visit was a massive success, and suddenly Phoenix Oil was a big player in the Oil business. Dr King and Mosun paid courtesy calls on the Governors of the oil producing Delta region and the Federal Minister for Petroleum, Mines and Power. The press gave unprecedented publicity to Phoenix Oil and its Director of Operations, Miss Martins. By the time Dr. King departed after one week in Nigeria, Mosun had become a celebrity. Mosun had worked virtually non-stop for weeks before Dr. King's visit, and the itinerary during his visit was intense. Maxwell and Mosun saw off Dr King at Ikeja Airport on Monday morning, and afterwards she took the day off to rest at home and reflect on the tumultuous events of the past week. She fell asleep as she lay on the sofa listening to a Nat King Cole album.

Mosun was woken up by her phone.

'Hello, who is this? answered Mosun in a sleepy drawl.

'Hello dear, I've missed you. But you were brilliant. Congratulations. I was so proud of you,' replied Mike.

'Thank you. I am sorry I had no time for pleasure last week. I'll make up for it.'

'Let's celebrate your success tonight. I've booked dinner for two at the Atlantic Restaurant. Can I pick you up at 7?'

'Okay, I'll be ready at 7.'

Mike had reserved the executive room for the candle lit dinner with old Motown blues wafting from the surround speakers. The food was sumptuous and they sipped sweet fruity red wine. When they were done eating, Mike asked the waiter to bring a bottle of champagne. As he popped the cork and bubbly spurted out, the music changed to 'What a wonderful world' by Sam Cooke. He poured some of the bubbly and proposed a toast to Mosun. Then went on one knee and produced a diamond ring from his pocket.

'Miss Mosun Martins I love you with all my heart, will you marry me?'

Mosun was flummoxed.

'Please say yes.'

'Yes, yes I will marry you,' she replied, as she pulled him up whilst he gently slipped the ring on her finger. He held her close, their hearts beating as one, as they continued smooching to Sam Cooke's music.

When they finally disentangled, Mosun told Mike her parents were the old fashioned type.

'Mike, we will have to do things the traditional way.'

'That's okay. Just let me know what I have to do,' replied Mike.

'We need to have a proper family introduction and engagement ceremony. Your parents will have to come and meet my parents. Talk to your mum. She will know what to do. Then we will have to see our Reverend for counselling before the Church wedding. Are you happy with that plan?'

'Oh yes, I am,' replied Mike.

They left soon afterwards, both of them truly happy. Mike dropped Mosun at home and hurried back to Ikeja to see his mother. It was already past eleven when he got home and the housekeeper told him that mum had gone to bed more than an hour before. The news will have to wait till the morning. Mike was generally a late riser but by 6.00 a.m. he walked into the kitchen where his mother was giving instructions to the housekeeper.

'Good morning mum.'

'Good morning, Mike. What are you doing up at this time of the day? I hope there is no problem.'

'Mum, can I see you for a minute?' They walked out into the courtyard.

'What is it Mike? I know that something is bothering you.'

'Mum, I've got good news. I've found the girl I am going to marry.'

'Anyone I know? What's her name? The questions came out in a torrent before Mike had a chance to answer the first question.

'Her name is Mo,' replied Mike.

Mo? What sort of name is that? What is wrong with this boy? Couldn't he find someone reliable and compassionate like Mosun.

Then she voiced some of her thoughts.

'Mike, what sort of name is that? Where did you find her?

'Mum, Mo is an abbreviation. That's what I call Mosun.'

'You mean Mosun Martins.'

'Yes mum.'

'Thank you God, thank you.'

'Have you asked her to marry you?'

'Yes, I have.'

'And what did she say?'

'She said yes, but stated that you and dad must come to ask her parents formally. She said they are sticklers for our tradition.'

'Congratulations Mike, she is a good sensible girl, not like that other useless girl.'

'Mum, that's history. Let's forget about that. I know that you and dad like Mosun, so you are getting the daughter you never had.'

'That's true. She is very well brought up. You know she's been calling me mum ever since she met me.'

'So, mum when are you going to meet them?'

'Mike, slow down. We have to agree to a mutually convenient date and of course we can't go empty handed. There are things we have to take along. I'll talk to Mosun in the next few days.'

'Okay mum, but we want to get married soon, definitely before the end of the year. Please give dad the good news. I'm going to get ready for work.'

CHAPTER 18

Senator and Mrs. Lawanson visited Mosun's parents barely two weeks after Mike broke the news to his mother, but this was an informal meeting. A month later, the formal traditional engagement ceremony was held at the Martins family home. Two days later, the cream of the society and top echelons of government thronged the Cathedral Church of Christ on the Marina. The President of the country could not attend but he was represented by the Vice-President. The leader of the House of Representatives and several regional governors were also present. The head of the Senate and his new wife were conspicuously absent. A close friend of Senator Lawanson had sent a message to Senator Osazuwa that the couple would not be welcome at the celebration. The wedding was a grand affair with hundreds of friends and relatives of both families in attendance. The men were clad in three piece flowing robes and the women gaily dressed in traditional *buba* and *iro* with brightly coloured matching head-ties. The Martins family and guests were dressed in royal blue with the Lawanson family and friends opting for maroon attires. Mosun and Mike had quickly established themselves as important players in business circles and the chief executives of several multinational companies and diplomats also attended the wedding.

After the church service, guests were treated to sumptuous dinner at the 5 star Grand Ritz Hotel in Victoria Island. During the reception, the political and business friends of Senator Lawanson seized the opportunity to express their gratitude and loyalty to their benefactor. It was almost as if they were trying to outdo each other with the gifts they showered on the newly married couple. Senator Abisayo stunned the guests when he presented the couple with the keys to a brand new Mercedes Benz ML 350 sport utility vehicle. This must have cost him at least fifty thousand pounds. Then Senator Lawanson topped the lot by giving the couple the keys and title deeds to a newly built detached four bedroom house in Queens Drive, Ikoyi, one of the most expensive and desirable locations in the entire country. He received loud ovation when he announced that he was giving the gift to his two children, because long before the children fell in love, Mosun had treated him and his wife as her parents. The senator recalled Mosun's sterling qualities of reliability and dogged determination, and how she was instrumental in Mike's recovery from the severe injuries sustained in the ghastly motor accident the previous year. After the speeches, gift presentations and toasts, the dancing commenced at about 5pm. Mike and Mosun opened the floor with deft moves, and then beckoned others to join. There was plenty to eat and drink. Shortly after 8 o'clock, Mike and Mosun slipped out of the hall, had a change of clothes in the hotel and were soon on their way to the airport. Senator Lawanson had told them the Grand Phoenix travel officer would be waiting for them at the departure lounge with their passports and flight tickets to Spain for their honeymoon. He had asked them to trust him with the honeymoon arrangements and they did so.

When the couple arrived at Ikeja airport at about 10 p.m., the travel officer was waiting for them. He told them he had completed the checking in of their luggage and would accompany them through immigration. Once through immigration, they were led through an unusual route down a flight of stairs that prompted Mike to ask which airline they were travelling on.

'Lawanson Airlines,' the officer replied, smiling.

'Come off it. Be serious,' replied Mosun.

'Dr. and Mrs. Lawanson, the chairman has a surprise for both of you. All will be revealed in a few minutes.'

As they waited by the door leading to the airfield, a crew car stopped and the doors were opened for the couple to jump in. They sat in the back and the travel officer sat in front. The car sped off to a corner of Murtala Muhammed International Airport where a private plane was being refuelled. The travel officer led the couple up the retractable stairs of the plane. As they entered the plane, two tall handsome men in pilot uniforms stood to greet them. The travel officer spoke first.

'Dr. and Mrs. Lawanson, you are welcome aboard the Grand Phoenix Bombardier executive plane. Please meet the pilot, Captain Joe Jackson from New Jersey, Flight Officer Matthew Mensah from Accra.'

'We are pleased to meet you,' the couple replied in unison. They were still gobsmacked by Senator Lawanson's surprise move.

The pilot took over, and gave a commentary as he showed the couple round the plane.

'This Grand Phoenix plane is a Bombardier Global 5000 executive jet. It is one of the fastest long range jets available today. It can fly 5000 nautical miles non-stop at a cruising speed of 0.85 Mach or 564 miles per hour, at a maximum altitude of 51,000 feet or 16,000 metres. This plane has 18 luxury passenger seats with aft lounge and bedroom. We only took delivery of this plane last week and you are our first official passengers. The chairman has requested that no luxury be spared in making your journey comfortable. We are scheduled to depart just before midnight. The duration of the flight to Malaga is 5 hours. We are going to pop the champagne in a few minutes time to toast your special day. Once we reach a cruising height you can help yourself to a buffet dinner which my colleague will lay out on this table. After dinner, please feel free to retire to the bedroom if you want. If you do so, we'll wake you up half an hour before we land in Malaga, to return to your seats for the descent.'

'Thank you for your hospitality. We've had so much to eat and drink at the reception that we'll give the food a miss, and probably just retire to bed,' replied Mike.

The captain popped the cork off the bottle of champagne and filled the couple's glasses whilst the crew poured themselves orange juice, before he gave a toast to long life and happiness for the newly wedded couple.

The Grand Phoenix travel officer left the plane and the crew shut the door. Fifteen minutes later with everyone strapped in their seats, the plane taxied to the runway. The air traffic was light at this time of the night and there was no delay. The Bombardier hurtled down the runway and was airborne in minutes banking and veering south towards the Atlantic Ocean before turning round and heading North on its way to Spain. Twenty minutes into the flight the pilot switched off the 'fasten seat belt' sign and announced that they had attained their cruising height of 41,000 feet and the forecast was for clement weather all the way to Malaga. From the moment the plane took off, Mike could not keep his hands off his wife. He caressed her body and kissed her repeatedly. Mosun's admonition that he should wait till the seat belt sign was turned off did not dissuade Mike. The moment the captain made the announcement, they unfastened their belts and made for the bedroom eyeing each other and giggling like school children. No sooner were they in the room than they kicked off their shoes and were virtually tearing their clothes off each other. Within a few minutes they were both stark naked. The room was in darkness apart from a small exit door illumination. The dim illumination resulted in silhouettes of their bodies. Mike was seeing Mosun's nakedness for the first time. Her smooth silky black skin glistened in the semi-darkness. Her bosom stood out at right angles to her chest and the curves of her derriere blended smoothly with her back.

'Wow,' exclaimed Mike.

'Do you like what you see?' asked Mosun.

'You are more beautiful than I imagined. You are like a goddess. I am a very lucky man.'

She couldn't reply because Mike promptly enveloped her lips with his, and then lifted her off the ground gently laying her on the bed. By now he was turgid and he gently thrust himself into her. When it was over, he laid his head on her bosom as she gently stroked his face.

'Are you happy?' asked Mosun.

'Happiness? That's putting it mildly. I am ecstatic,' replied Mike.

Mosun smiled as a thought crossed her mind.

The bee finally got its nectar.

They cuddled and fondled each other, and then they were ready again. This time Mike was gentler and took his time. The first encounter could be likened to a volcanic eruption but this was like the gentle flow of a river in mid-stream. Their moaning and utterances were mercifully drowned by the whining of the plane engines and sudden groaning of the engine as the pilot accelerated to clear an area of minor turbulence.

'Thank you Mike.'

'Why are you thanking me?'

'For being considerate and waiting for me, and making this our first sexual encounter a most pleasurable experience.'

'My dear wife, do you know we've just joined a special club.'

'My darling husband, yes I know. We are now in the Mr. and Mrs. club.'

'Not just that. We've just joined the exclusive Mile High Club.'

She smiled but didn't reply. They then fell asleep in each other's arms.

'Dr. and Mrs. Lawanson, this is the Captain speaking. We shall shortly be starting our descent to Malaga International Airport. We expect to be on the ground in thirty minutes. Please return to your seats and fasten the seat belts in five to ten minutes time.'

The couple dragged themselves out of bed and got dressed. They tidied the room as best they could and then returned to their seats, fastening their belts.

As the plane taxied to a stop, the crew emerged from the cockpit and greeted Mike and Mosun warmly. The Captain told them they would be met by a uniformed driver with their name on a placard as they exited the arrival hall. The plane would be back for the couple in a week.

They arrived at dawn before the scheduled holiday flights and therefore had a quick passage through immigration and customs. As they exited the immigration section, they were met by a limousine driver sent by their resort.

'Good morning, Dr. and Mrs. Lawanson.'

'Good morning,' they replied in unison.

'I am Antonio and I'll be taking you to your hotel in Marbella. Would you like me to tell you about the important landmarks as we drive along?'

'Oh yes, that'll be nice,' replied Mosun.

It was almost 7am by the time they left the airport.

'Dr. and Mrs. Lawanson, Malaga International Airport is about 30 miles or 48 kilometres to Marbella. Driving at a steady moderate speed, the journey should take us about 45 minutes.'

About 7 kilometres west of Malaga they drove into a town called Torremolinos.

'This is Torremolinos, the first Costa del Sol resort to be developed back in the sixties. Over the years, the sleepy village has grown into an attractive town with beautiful hotels and shopping centres. There are clean beaches and there is a vibrant night life.

They exited Torremolinos and continued driving on a beautiful seaside road, with the Mediterranean Sea to their left. About 25 kilometres from Malaga, they drove past Fuengirola. The chauffeur resumed his commentary.

'This is Fuengirola, one of the most popular destinations for holiday makers in the Costa del Sol. It was previously a tiny fishing village but has become a vibrant metropolis with many upmarket tapas bars and good restaurants, as well as chic boutiques and fabulous beaches. It looks pretty at night, especially at Christmas when the town is decorated with attractive lights and ornaments.'

They drove past some holiday resorts and were soon on the outskirts of Marbella.

'If you look to your right you'll see that white multi-storey building on the hill. That is the hospital built and donated to the town of Marbella by the late King Fahd of Saudi-Arabia. During his reign, he spent most of his summer months in Marbella. He offered to donate a hospital to the town provided the authorities agreed to reserve the top floor exclusively for the use of the King and his family.'

'Amazing,' replied Mike.

'Oh yes, the Saudi royalty have money and clout,' replied the driver.

Then he continued.

'If you look up the hill on the right, behind all the wooded forest, you will see the minaret of the mosque built by King Fahd, and high above the mosque behind a wall is King Fahd's palace. It's an amazing display of opulence and best of Arabian architecture. It is really a masterpiece. I had the opportunity to view it whilst it was being built, before the King moved into it. Since then, only diplomats or invited guests have been able to gain access to the compound.'

He swung the car round and drove through a big gate.

'Dr. and Mrs. Lawanson, this is Marbella Club Hotel, your

residence for the next one week. This is a golf resort, beauty spa and beach resort all rolled into one. It is an icon of Marbella, established more than half a century ago. This is perhaps the most luxurious hotel in the entire Costa del Sol. This has been a holiday destination for the international jet setters, aristocrats, stars of the entertainment world and business leaders over the years.'

The car came to a stop.

'Thank you, my wife and I thank you very much.'

'You are welcome. If you want to go anywhere, please let the receptionist know. I am available to drive you anywhere you want to go during your stay here.'

Mike and Mosun quickly settled into their suite in the hotel. The receptionist told them that their stay and expenses had been fully covered by Senator Lawanson. For the next twenty four hours they were ensconced in their suite, only opening the door for room service when they were hungry. They ate little, spending most of their time canoodling, and doing what newly married couples do. Mike kept Mosun entertained with his wit; a side of him she did not know existed.

'My dear, if we make a baby on this trip, we won't have any problem with the baby's name.'

'Mike, what do you mean by that?'

'We'll just do what celebrities do.'

'And what is that?'

'They name their children after the place the pregnancy was conceived,' replied Mike.

'No, that is a non-starter. What do you want to call the baby? Bombardier or Marbella?'

'May be Mile High or Sky High,' Mike added, and both of them exploded with fits of laughter.

The couple re-emerged on the second day of their honeymoon and spent most of the day lounging by the swimming pool, occasionally plunging into the pool to cool down. They booked themselves on to the guided tour arranged by the hotel to Tangiers in Morocco. They left by bus early in the morning of day four for Algeciras on the Costa del Sol. The bus trip took one and a half hours. Then the couple with other hotel guests crossed the Mediterranean Sea by high speed ferry. The sea was tranquil and they were able to admire views of the Mediterranean Sea and the Atlantic Ocean across the Strait of Gibraltar. When they arrived in Tangiers, they drove round the town and visited the famous caves of Hercules. They then walked around the medina and bought some souvenirs in Tangier's bazaar. Afterwards, they settled for lunch in a huge traditional tent enjoying Moroccan dishes of fariras soup followed by a main dish of couscous and chicken tagine. As they ate and drank mint tea, they were entertained by traditional snake charmers and live Berber dancing troupes. After several hours in Tangiers, they boarded the ferry to return to Costa del Sol, finally arriving in the hotel late at night. It had been a long hectic day and they slept soundly through the night, waking up late in the morning. The rest of their days in Marbella were spent relaxing in the hotel and treating themselves to the various luxuries on offer, including trying their hands at golf and indulging in beauty treatment at the hotel spa. Soon it was time to return home. They had thoroughly enjoyed themselves and were truly grateful to Mike's dad for his taste and munificence. They had bought special gifts for their parents from their own purse.

Antonio drove them back to Malaga airport. The couple had bought a nice Seiko automatic wristwatch during one of their outings in Marbella, and Mosun gave this to Antonio as they were about to disembark from the limousine at the airport as a mark of their appreciation for his professionalism and for making their stay in Marbella memorable. This was unexpected and he was profoundly moved and appreciative. They whizzed through immigration and were soon on board the Bombardier. This was an afternoon flight and they sat through it watching movies, eating and drinking. When they were in mid-flight, Mosun teased her husband, whispering into his ear.

'Dear, let's rush back to the bedroom to renew our membership.'

'What membership?' Mike asked.

'Membership of the Mile High Club,' replied Mosun.

'You can't be serious.'

'Oh yes, I am,' replied Mosun.

'No, we can't,' Mike replied now getting worried.

'Why not?'

'We've got company. We've got an air steward on this flight.

You don't want anyone gossiping,' Mike implored, now really worried.

Then Mosun erupted with laughter.

'I was only teasing.'

'You are wicked,' replied Mike.

'Do you mean that?' asked Mosun, feigning offence.

'Not really. I mean wicked in a good way. You are killing me softly with your love and wit.'

She smiled and they continued watching the in-flight movies.

When they arrived in Lagos, they were met by the Grand Phoenix Travel Officer who took them to their new home in Queen's drive. They were viewing the house for the first time. The house was tastefully finished but the furnishing was sparse. The living room and one bedroom had been furnished. The kitchen was also fully equipped and furnished. Mike's parents had done this so that the couple could put their own stamp on their home, furnishing it according to their taste. Mosun was quickly on the phone to Mike's parents thanking them profusely for all they did to make the wedding ceremony a success and the excellent honeymoon they arranged. She promised they would visit them the following afternoon, as they were not due to resume work for another three days. Mike reciprocated by phoning his parents in-law thanking them again for consenting to his union with their wonderful daughter and for all they spent during the various ceremonies.

'Mosun, it's a good thing we are still on leave. We'll spend the next week resting and visiting family.'

The following morning the couple had a late lying in, and Mike brought his wife breakfast in bed. They were relaxing in the family living room when they were interrupted by a phone call for Mosun.

'Good morning boss, I am sorry to disturb you on your honeymoon but I've got a special wedding present for you.'

'This had better be good,' replied Mosun.

'Who is that?' Mike asked.

Mosun put the caller on hold.

'It's the Phoenix Oil Operations manager phoning from Port Harcourt.'

'What does he want? Doesn't he know you are on leave?'

'I'll find out in a minute.'

She resumed her phone discussion.

'Mr. Stanley what is the news?'

'Boss, we've struck oil in commercial quantities in block 242.'

'That's brilliant. Excellent news,' replied Mosun.

'Mr. Stanley, we didn't expect to strike oil so soon in that area. We'll have to alter our plans. I'll call you later in the afternoon.'

'Mike, it is extremely good news for the company, not so good for us because I think I have to go to back to work. We've struck a phenomenal amount of oil and I'll have to visit Port Harcourt tomorrow. I'm sorry to interrupt our vacation but I'll make up for it later.'

'I think I'd better return to work as well.'

'That's a good idea Mike, so the company will owe us a week's holiday which we can take later.'

The next day Mosun was on the first flight out of Lagos bound for Port Harcourt. She flew by helicopter to the offshore field.

Meanwhile at the Grand Phoenix headquarters, Mike ran into his father.

'Good morning dad.'

'Good morning Mike. What are you doing here? I thought you were supposed to be on leave.'

Yes dad, we were supposed to be on leave but Mosun flew to Port Harcourt this morning.'

'Why?' asked Senator Lawanson.

'The operations manager called to say Phoenix Oil struck a large amount of oil on a new oil field.'

'That's great news indeed,' replied Senator Lawanson. 'Your wife is a brilliant manager.'

Mosun returned late at night exhausted. The following day she briefed the Chairman and Managing Director of the Phoenix group. They were thrilled to bits. Twenty four hours later she was on the Bombardier executive jet to Dublin. She held high level talks with the management of Irish American Oil Company and agreed on new oil refinery arrangements.

Franchising of the Phoenix petrol filling stations and marketing of petroleum products was the next project in the company business plan. Mosun had decided that the company would have full ownership of the filling stations in Abuja and all the state capitals, but other reputable companies would be granted the franchise to run the filling stations and market the petroleum products in the other cities and towns. About a month earlier, Phoenix Oil ran the franchise adverts in the major newspapers, but the applications had now closed. The country had been divided into three zones - North, West and East for the purpose of the franchising. Two separate companies would be awarded the franchise for each zone, creating an opportunity for six different companies. Senator Lawanson was impressed by Mosun's strategy that no single company would be allowed to have a monopoly of the business.

On return from Dublin, Mosun set up a meeting with the Phoenix Oil marketing manager to review the franchise applications later in the afternoon. Then Mosun's PA came in to her office to deliver a message.

'Ma'am, whilst you were away in Dublin, a certain lady phoned several times. She said she is your good friend.'

'What is her name?'

'Nkechi, she said I should just tell you Nkechi called. She left her phone number and said you should call her.'

'What does she want?'

'I don't know but the telephone operator told me that she had tried to reach Dr. Lawanson but he was out of the office.'

'What? Come again.'

'She had tried to reach your husband but he was out of the office,' repeated the Personal Assistant.

Mosun was furious but did her best to mask her anger. Why on earth was Nkechi trying to get in touch with her husband?

The PA retired to her office and locked the door behind her. Ordinarily, Mosun would not have returned Nkechi's phone call but this was a different situation. She didn't want that woman contacting her husband. She took the phone and dialled the number Nkechi left.

'Hello.'

'Hello, who is that?'

'It's Mosun.'

'Mosun, long time no see. Congratulations on your recent wedding.'

'Thank you. I was told that you've been trying to contact us.'

'Oh yes, I wanted both of you to know that I applied for the

Phoenix franchise, so that you can use your influence to ensure my bid is successful.'

'Well, Mike has no involvement with the oil business. The choice is down to the chairman and me. There is really no need to contact Mike.'

'I am sorry Mosun, but what harm is a phone call among friends.'

'Anyway, Nkechi let's get back to business. What is the name of your company?'

'Queen Holdings. I have ditched journalism for importing and exporting business, but I now want to diversify into petroleum marketing. I am counting on you to give me the franchise for the Eastern zone.'

'Don't worry. I'll talk to my father in-law. You can regard one of the two Eastern zone franchises as yours.'

'Thank you Mosun. Thank you very much.'

The phone conversation ended, and Mosun sank into her chair, ruminating on the events of the past year and the latest telephone conversation.

What does Nkechi take me for? A moron or what? This is a woman you just can't trust, a modern day Jezebel.

Mosun snapped out of her trance and summoned the company telephone operator.

'Mrs. Evans.'

'Yes madam.'

'I understand Mrs. Nkechi Osazuwa was trying to reach me and Dr. Mike Lawanson.'

'Yes, ma'am, but both of you were out of the office.'

'In future all phone calls from anyone calling herself Mrs. Osazuwa or Miss Nkechi Obi, or from any employee of Queen Holdings should be directed to my office. Do you understand this instruction?'

'Yes, Mrs. Lawanson.'

'Good. That will be all.'

The telephone operator returned to her post.

Mosun brought forward her meeting with the marketing manager.

'Good morning, ma'am.'

'Good morning Sam.'

'How many applications did we receive?'

'We received twenty applications, six from the Northern zone, another six from the East and eight from the West.'

'Okay, let's review them quickly,' requested Mosun.

'Let me have that one.'

Mosun picked up the Queen Holdings documents and threw them into her drawer.

'Sam, now we've got only nineteen applications. I want you to go through each application meticulously and score them zone by zone. I also want you to contact the Company House and obtain the names of all the directors of the nineteen companies. We have to be sure that we don't associate with companies with shady characters as chairpersons or directors. When can I have the scores and the list of directors?'

'Tomorrow afternoon.'

'Okay, I'll see you tomorrow afternoon.'

'Yes, madam.'

When Sam left, Mosun retrieved the Queen Holdings application skimmed through and then shredded the document. She had no intention of discussing the matter with either Senator Lawanson or her husband.

One month later, Nkechi had heard nothing from Phoenix Oil and decided to take the bull by the horns. She made a trip to Lagos from Abuja and went straight to the Grand Phoenix headquarters in Victoria Island, arriving around 2 pm. She walked in confidently to the reception desk and asked for Mosun. The receptionist placed a call to Mosun's office. Mosun was furious that Nkechi had turned up unannounced at her office and decided to teach her a lesson. She told the receptionist to ask Nkechi to wait for her in the reception waiting room and she would soon come down to see her. Thirty minutes later Nkechi was still waiting and Mosun had not shown up. Nkechi got up and walked up to the receptionist. She was about to ask the receptionist to try Mosun again when she caught a glimpse of Mosun walking out of the building. She hurried after her, calling out her name. She was less than ten yards behind Mosun who obviously heard her, but carried on walking to her car, got in and asked the chauffeur to drive off. Nkechi was dumbfounded and infuriated. She returned to the receptionist and asked to speak with Mike Lawanson. Mosun had briefed Mike about Nkechi's visit before she left the office.

Mike picked up the phone as soon as the call came through to his office.

'Hello, this is Mike. Who am I speaking with?'

'Hello, this is Nkechi. It is nice to hear your voice again. I am sorry for what happened in the past.'

Mike interrupted her curtly.

'Nkechi, I have put the past behind me. We have both moved on, and that is good. Please do not come to this office again. Do not telephone me or my wife. For your information, Phoenix Oil will not be transacting any business with you or your company. Goodbye.'

With that Mike hung up. Nkechi stood speechless unable to comprehend the events that had just unfolded. She slowly placed the phone down on the receiver and walked sheepishly out of the Grand Phoenix building.

CHAPTER 19

Daniel and Anita Lawanson had played major roles in the wedding ceremony of Mike and Mosun. Anita had been impressed with Mosun's reliability and diligence, and had developed a particularly close relationship with her, even closer than her relationship with Mike who was her husband's nephew. The wedding provided an opportunity for Anita to spend some time with her husband especially because she had missed the last mandatory resident's visit to Saudi Arabia and now had to re-apply for a new visit visa. Daniel was home for only a week. He had to return to Taif two days after the wedding because of an important professional commitment.

The surgeons in various hospitals in Taif met monthly in different hospitals under the aegis of the Taif Surgical Society to discuss interesting and difficult cases, and new developments in surgical practice. These were scientific meetings of the highest quality. Daniel Lawanson was the Chairman of the Taif Surgical Society. The secretary of the society was Mr. Nagendra Ruyat, Consultant in Ear, Nose and Throat Surgery in King Faisal Hospital, Taif. Mr. Ruyat had practised in Taif for five years but was now returning to India to take up the post of Professor of Otorhinolaryngology at the All India Institute of Medical Sciences in New Delhi.

The Surgical Society held a valedictory scientific session in honour of their long serving secretary. Daniel arranged a send-off party in his home for Mr. & Mrs. Ruyat, referred to as Masalama party in expatriate circles. The guests were mainly expatriate doctors and nurses but he had also invited two Saudi clerks who worked closely with him in his hospital. The menu and drinks were varied and rich. Daniel had a lot of support from his surgical colleagues and everyone brought something to eat or drink. Daniel and Nagendra were talking in the kitchen when Mr. Bassey came in with two bottles of *sid*. Daniel raised a big cheer. In abstemious Saudi Arabia the provision of *sid* was celebrated in expatriate parties. It was brewed clandestinely in remote farms and sold surreptitiously through trusted channels. Nobody knew the exact alcohol concentration of *sid* but the strong smell and burning sensation in the throat when ingested undiluted put it at par with the strongest Vodka. Most of the guests spiced up their blackcurrant juice and sodas with a few ounces of *sid* but Khalid and Faisal, Daniel's clerks drank the stuff neat. They were soon intoxicated. They became incoherent but kept drinking. Daniel wrested the alcoholic drinks from them and sat them in a corner, replacing their alcoholic drinks with plain sodas. Shortly afterwards, the inebriated duo fell into slumber.

Daniel and friends half carried them to his guest room to sleep off the alcohol. The party continued uneventful. The revellers started leaving at midnight. By 1.00 a.m. the last of the guests departed. It was only then that Daniel remembered Khalid and Faisal. He went to check up on them in the guest room but found that they had disappeared. He shrugged his shoulders and continued cleaning his house, sanitising was a more appropriate word. In these parts, you didn't leave alcohol lying carelessly around just in case there was an unexpected visitor. In any case the guests had consumed virtually all the *sid* leaving less than a third of a bottle which Daniel intended to quaff next weekend whist watching football on TV. He loaded all the tumblers and plates into the dishwasher and switched it on.

Mr. and Mrs. Ruyat were amongst the last to leave the party. As they drove home, it was Mrs. Ruyat who noticed policemen interviewing someone who looked familiar.

'Dear, that man looks familiar.'

'Which man?' asked Nagendra.

'The man we just drove past, being questioned by the police.'

'Okay, I'll turn round at the next roundabout so that we can have a good look.'

'Priti you are correct. The police are questioning Khalid and Faisal, Daniel's clerks. I think they are testing them for drunkenness.'

As he drove past the police car, he noticed that one of them had been handcuffed and was being shoved into the back of the police car.

'This is serious. They must have been driving dangerously under the influence of alcohol. I must warn Daniel.'

'It's not Daniel's fault,' replied Priti.

'You don't live here. You don't know how the police operate. Once the police start working on the two of them, they'll squeal and Daniel will be picked up. He will be accused of corrupting their boys.'

Nagendra stopped in a safe place and phoned Daniel. He briefed Daniel on what they had just witnessed.

'Thank you. Thank you very much,' replied Daniel.

'So, what are you going to do,' asked Nagendra.

'I don't know but I can't sleep here tonight. I'll have to get rid of the remaining alcohol. Thank you, I've got to go.'

Daniel dropped the phone and rushed to the kitchen and poured the remaining sid down the drain, washing out the bottles with water. He grabbed his wallet and put on an overcoat. He switched off all the lights in the house, slipped out of the back door and scaled the rear wall. No sooner was he on the other side than he heard the police siren approaching the compound's gate. Soon after, he heard loud voices and scrambling feet in his compound. Then he heard the whimpering of someone who sounded like Khalid.

That didn't take long at all. The police didn't take long to break him and get him to lead them to the site of his crime.

Daniel could hear loud rapping on the doors with policemen shouting at the occupant to open the door. Then he saw arcs of flashlights illuminating the sky as the policemen peered through the windows to view the interior of his premises. Daniel's car was not in the driveway because he had parked it round the corner in the driveway of a vacant villa before the party started, to give his friends enough room to park in front of his villa. It sounded plausible to the police when the compound security guards suggested that their target must have driven out with other guests before the police arrived. The police left two officers to guard the house and apprehend Daniel on his return. The police boss could be overheard saying that they would return in the morning with a warrant to search the villa.

Daniel spent the night in a shack on a nearby building site. He slipped away at dawn before the workers arrived, and made his way to the town centre. He picked up a travel bag, a T-shirt and underwear in the souk. He crossed the road to the local bakery where he bought some Afghan bread and kabsa rice. He stuffed all his purchases in the bag, and booked himself into a local hotel, the sort normally occupied by migrant labourers. He would normally not be seen near this hotel but this was an extra-ordinary situation. He phoned the hospital HR department to ask for two days emergency leave. He asked to speak with the hospital director, but he was out of town. The Head of Manpower department, Mr. Gould was also indisposed. He desperately needed to talk to one of them about his predicament. He reclined on the bed ruminating on the events of the past twelve hours. He hadn't slept properly during the night and was so fatigued that in no time at all, he had fallen asleep. He woke up several hours later very hungry. He attacked the kabsa rice, completely devouring it. He washed the food down with bottled water and settled back into another session of introspection. He stayed in his room all day having only bread and water for supper. He dropped off to sleep late at night but woke up two hours later drenched in sweat. He had dreamt he was being chased by policemen in the town centre. He managed to escape his pursuers as he ducked into the souk but his relief was short lived as Napoleon left his usual duty keeping watch over the women and pursued him into the souk, cornering him in a cul de sac and disabling him with a short burst from his sub machine gun. Daniel passed his hands down under the sheet and felt his feet. His feet were still there, intact. This was a horrid nightmare. He had a shower and a change of clothes and then sat out till dawn. As soon as the muezzin called the faithful for the Fajr prayer, he gathered his things and stuffed them in his travel bag and then checked out of the hotel. He had made up his mind to return to work and face the music.

CHAPTER 20

Daniel went straight to the hospital slipping into the surgical department well before other members of staff arrived. He changed into hospital scrubs and went to the ward to see his patients. He then went to the theatre to start operating on his patients. The operations went on most of the day ending just before 5 pm closing time. Daniel dashed down to his office and buried himself in outstanding paperwork. He had forgotten his police trouble. He only checked his wrist watch when the cleaners came in to start their shift.

'Wow, its 6.20 p.m.'

He remembered he didn't come in his car, and only had ten minutes to catch the hospital bus.

He hurriedly tidied his table and dashed to the bus stop. As he was about to board the bus, a man stepped out of the shade and apprehended him.

'Dr Daniel, I am Inspector Saud from the Ministry for the Promotion of Virtue and Prevention of Vice. Please come with me to the police station.'

'Why? What is the problem?' Daniel asked, feigning ignorance.

By now the other members of staff had alighted from the bus and had surrounded the duo. The policeman felt intimidated and spoke into his phone. Within minutes, several police men arrived on the scene. This emboldened the inspector but all the same he was crafty.

'Doctor Daniel is not under arrest. We are only inviting him to the police station to help us with our inquiries.'

Daniel asked one of the hospital workers to inform Mr. Gould and Dr Ali that he had been taken away by the police. He then left with the Inspector.

When they reached the police station Daniel was booked in for interrogation. The police alleged he had organised an illegal mixed sex party and had supplied alcohol to the guests. Daniel refuted the allegations. After one hour of intensive interrogation, the police had gotten nowhere and decided to detain him. There was no police cell in Taif and he was transferred to a prison cell outside the city. The following morning, Daniel was re-interrogated. The police officers pushed a list of party guests across the table. Daniel immediately noticed that only names of the KMC staff and the Ruyats were on the list. He concluded the police must have got the list from Khalid and Faisal. He wasn't going to help them complete the list, so he made up his mind to be reticent with his answers.

'Dr. Daniel, do you recognise the names on that list,' the interrogating officer asked.

'Yes, I do.'

'Were they at the party in your house?'

Daniel realised there was no point lying.

'Oh yes, they were,' answered Daniel.

'Have we left out anyone?'

'No,' replied Daniel.

'Are they all staff of your hospital?'

'Most of them are. In fact all of them work in our hospital, apart from Mr. and Mrs. Ruyat.'

'We will like to speak with Mr. Ruyat. Where can we find him?'

'New Delhi,' replied Daniel.

'This is not a joking matter,' the observing police officer retorted.

'I am not joking,' replied Daniel. 'I believe the Ruyats left the Kingdom yesterday on final exit visas.'

'What a shame. We would have liked to talk to them. O.K. let's go through the list. Who is Maxine Cross?''

She is a theatre nursing sister in my hospital.'

The policeman pointed at another name on the list.

'And who is Claire Peace?'

'She is our hospital matron,' replied Daniel.

'And who is this lady?'

The officer pointed at the name of the last female on the list.

'Dr. Rebecca Cooper is a Consultant Physician at KMC.'

The police officer made some notes. The observing senior officer got up from his chair in the corner and moved with a flounce towards Daniel. He pointed at him and let off a round of expletives in English and Arabic. Then he calmly concluded.

'You are a useless man, a pimp, and you are going to jail for a long time. You cannot pretend you didn't know it is illegal for unmarried or unrelated persons of the opposite sex to gather together in private.'

'Officer, there was no unmarried woman in my house, and all the women came with their husbands.'

'That's a lie,' the interrogator interjected.

'For your information, Dr. Cooper is married to Mr. Bassey, Claire Peace is married to Dr. Rajiv Shah, and Maxine Cross is married to Dr. Richard McKnight.'

'Are you sure?'

'Without a shadow of doubt,' replied Daniel.

The interrogating officer was deflated. That was the first charge thrown out of the window. The superior officer called time out and they exited the room. Daniel stood and stretched his limbs. He knew that he had to be alert. These guys were trying to trip him. The policemen returned half an hour later.

'Dr. Daniel, where did you get the alcohol you gave your guests?'

'Alcohol? Which alcohol? I didn't serve any alcohol.'

'That's a lie and you know it. We arrested two of your guests and they were drunk,' replied the police officer.

'Who?' asked Daniel.

'Khalid and Faisal. We found them drunk after they left your house.'

'They didn't get drunk in my house. All I served were sodas and fruit juice,' insisted Daniel.

Daniel could see that the police were getting frustrated. He knew they hadn't found anything in his house to implicate him, so they desperately wanted his confession. Word had been passed round the expatriate guests they were to insist only sodas and fruit juice had been served at the party, and they had all stuck to this story when they were questioned. The police thought Daniel was lying but couldn't prove it. The police boss was frustrated. He poured invectives on Daniel and his type, and then walked out of the room, ordering his underlings as he left the room to return Daniel to his prison cell.

The KMC driver tried all night to reach Mr. Gould, to no avail. Eventually, he got hold of Dr. Ali but he was away in Riyadh and not due back in Taif for days. He promised to do his best and would contact some friends to intervene. He was soon on the phone to important friends in Taif, calling in favours. By late morning there was so much external pressure by Ali's friends that the police decided to release Daniel. This irked the newly appointed local head of the mutawas, the religious police. He was not going to be thwarted and so before processing of the release papers was completed, he authorised the transfer of Daniel's case to the regional head office in Jeddah. Daniel was immediately transferred under armed escort to the prison in Jeddah, and was promptly charged to court for supply and distribution of illicit alcohol. When Ali returned to Taif, he discovered that his moves had been thwarted and the affair escalated beyond his sphere of influence.

The KMC were informed that Daniel was going to be charged to court in Jeddah for supplying illicit prohibited substance to guests in his house. If Daniel was found guilty, he could be caned and sent to jail for a long time. The hospital found a lawyer to defend him. He was going to plead not guilty. He had no other option. Khalid and Faisal had been released after one week confinement but they did not return to work in KMC. Dr. Ali wanted to know why. He sent out feelers and found out that they had agreed to be prosecution witnesses. This was apparently a precondition for their release from detention. The Taif chief mutawa was bent on using this case to teach expatriates a lesson that they ignore traditional and Sharia laws at their peril.

After Dr. Ali returned to Taif, he placed a call to Anita in Nigeria. He broke the news as gently as possible reassuring her that everything was under control. The hospital had found Daniel a good lawyer, and he was also exploring extra-judicial means of getting him released. No matter what Ali said, it didn't sound good. After all Daniel was in prison custody and she couldn't travel to Saudi Arabia because her exit and return visa had expired. It would take at least another month or two for her to secure another visa, if the process was initiated now. Anita was at work in the Ministry of Education headquarters. She instructed her secretary to cancel her appointments for the day. She closed her office door and sobbed uncontrollably. Her husband was incarcerated but she couldn't see him or speak to him. Ali was going to visit Daniel in Jeddah the following day and would appeal to the prison guards to allow Daniel place a call to Anita but there was no guarantee they would accede to his request. He asked Anita to make herself available the following afternoon in case his plea was successful. Dr. Ali kept his promise. He visited Daniel and was able to obtain permission for Daniel to talk to Anita. They spoke for about five minutes. Daniel sounded confident that he would be cleared and this was reassuring to Anita, and lifted her spirits. She also spoke briefly to Dr Ali, who told her she could keep abreast of developments by phoning him as often as she wanted.

Anita took the rest of the day off and drove down to Lagos to discuss Daniel's situation with her brother in-law, Senator Lawanson and his wife. They all felt Anita should be in Jeddah to co-ordinate the battle for Daniel's release. Her in-laws were dismayed that she was unable to travel to Jeddah even though she had been there several times in the past. Then Senator Lawanson came up with an idea which sounded brilliant. In any case it was the only suggestion on the table.

Ajoke Lawanson was nonplussed.

'Anita, do you mean Daniel was locked up because he entertained guests with alcohol?'

'Yes,' replied Anita. 'That's all he did.'

'Incredible, incredible, just plain incredible' retorted Ajoke repeatedly.

Senator Lawanson ignored his wife's remarks and faced Anita.

'Anita, do you know that Dauda's brother is the Nigerian Deputy Ambassador in Saudi Arabia?'

'Which Dauda?' Anita asked.

'Dauda Adams, your Governor.'

'The Ambassador resides in Riyadh but the Deputy Ambassador is normally resident in Jeddah and runs the Jeddah Consulate. I am sure he has a lot of influence in Jeddah. Appeal to Dauda to ask his brother to use his influence to get Daniel released, even if it means being deported.'

'That's much better than going to jail,' replied Anita. 'I will talk to the Governor tomorrow.'

It was a relieved and more optimistic Anita who set out on the return journey to Ibadan later that night. She would be calling on the Governor in the morning.

Anita arrived promptly at the government secretariat, and made straight for the Governor's office. The Governor had not yet arrived in the office but Anita decided to wait for him. The Governor strode into his office through the waiting room followed by his security men. His eyes skirted round the room quickly but he said nothing and walked straight into his office. Anita was about to remind the Governor's secretary that she had an urgent matter to discuss when the phone buzzed.

'Please send in Mrs. Lawanson.'

'Mrs. Lawanson, the Governor will see you now.'

'Good morning Mrs. Lawanson.'

'Good morning Sir.'

'How are you? How are the education projects?'

'I am well and the projects in the Ministry are on course.'

'How can I help?'

'It's my husband. He's got problems in Saudi Arabia.'

'What sort of problem?'

'He organised a send-off party in his house for a colleague and the police arrested him because they claimed he served alcohol.'

'How did the police get involved?'

'Two of the guests were apprehended by police for reckless driving on the way home, and the police discovered they were drunk. They grassed Daniel and he has been detained for the past week.'

'Arrested for serving alcohol?'

'Oh yes,' replied Anita.

'That is incredible,' replied Dauda, showing considerable dismay.

'I understand your brother is our Deputy Ambassador in Saudi Arabia.' She paused and then continued. 'I would be grateful if you could ask him to intervene in the matter, use his influence to secure my husband's release.'

'That's no problem. I will get in touch with him and let you know what he says. I'll brief you tomorrow night. What's your mobile phone number?'

Anita scribbled on a sheet of paper and handed it over to the Governor.

'Thank you Sir. God bless you.'

Anita heaved a sigh of relief and smiled for the first time during their meeting. Governor Dauda did not miss the beautiful smile and gleaming white teeth. As she got up and walked out of the room, Dauda fixed his gaze on the scintillating motion of her butt.

Wow, this lady is stunning. Just look at her curves, the slim waist and full backside. Daniel is a really lucky man. May be I will get lucky some day. I'll have to work on it. Nothing ventured, nothing gained.

Dauda phoned Anita on Wednesday night as promised.

'Hello, can I speak with Mrs. Lawanson?'

'Hello, this is Anita Lawanson.'

'Mrs. Lawanson, this is Dauda Adams.'

'Thank you Sir for calling as promised.

'I spoke with my brother and he has asked his staff to visit Daniel in prison custody and assist him in any way possible. My brother would like to speak with you so that you can brief him directly and he can discuss the various options with you. What are your plans for the rest of the week?'

'I am travelling to Abuja tomorrow with our Minister of Education to attend the conference of all Education Ministers and their Permanent Secretaries to deliberate on the new secondary school curriculum.'

'Oh yes, I recall that the Minister briefed me about this a few weeks ago. Well, this is an interesting coincidence. My brother plans to be in Abuja for the weekend. He is scheduled to arrive on Friday evening. If you are able to delay your departure from Abuja till Saturday, then I can travel to Abuja on Friday afternoon so that we can meet my brother on Friday night.'

'Of course I'll do that. I'll stay behind when we conclude the conference on Friday morning. I'll extend my Intercontinental Hotel booking by one day.'

'That's fine. Let's have dinner together at the Intercontinental restaurant at 7 p.m. I'll ask my brother to join us at the restaurant at 9 o'clock for drinks. That'll give you the opportunity to update him.'

'Thank you Sir.'

'Goodnight, see you on Friday night.'

Anita was pleased with the developments. She kicked off her shoes and decided to unwind with a Martini. Things were looking up and she was confident her husband would soon be free. She slept soundly for the first time in a week.

All through the deliberations at the education conference, Anita's mind drifted fleetingly to the appointment with the Deputy Ambassador. The first day was hectic but the pace was less frenetic on Friday morning, and the group wrapped up their deliberations and released a communiqué by noon. The participants dispersed and returned to their bases but Anita retired to her hotel to wait for her meeting with Dauda and his brother.

When Anita came down for supper at 7o'clock, Dauda Adams was already sitting at the bar drinking lager beer. He got up as Anita entered and they moved towards a table in the corner of the room. They ordered their food and ate mostly in silence. Dauda tried to make small conversation but Anita had only one thing on her mind, the release of her husband. As they had their dessert, Anita kept checking her watch.

'When are you expecting the Ambassador?' Anita asked.

'It is now 8.00 p.m. and the Jeddah flight should have arrived half an hour ago. He said he would come straight to the hotel from the airport. He should be with us within the hour.'

'That's good,' replied Anita.

'Do you want something to drink while we wait for him?' Dauda asked.

'Apple juice for me,' replied Anita.

'I'll have something stronger. Their service is rather slow. They must be short staffed tonight. I'll get the drinks from the bar.' Dauda stood up and walked towards the bar. Ten minutes later he came back with a glass of apple juice for Anita and a cocktail for himself. Dauda probed her about their deliberations in the education conference. Anita was impressed that the Governor was interested in the development of education. Suddenly Anita yawned and rubbed her eyes.

'I feel sleepy, I am going to my room,' uttered Anita in a drawl.

She got up and took a step but her gait faltered. Dauda quickly got up and slipped his arm round her waist steadying her gait. He picked up her bag and gently led her out of the restaurant towards an obscure hotel elevator. Five minutes later he led her into his room and laid her on his bed. By now Anita was fast asleep. He undressed her completely and then slipped beside her under the sheets. He mounted Anita and satisfied his urge whilst she slept on. Then he fondled her until he was aroused again, and then satisfied his urge once more. At dawn the sun filtered in through slits in the curtain falling on the bed. Anita turned over in bed and stretched her slender arms as she slowly woke up. She was startled by heavy snoring behind her and was aghast as she turned round and saw the almost naked body of Dauda besides her. She looked down and discovered she was completely nude.

Oh my God. What have I done? Did it really happen?

She looked down at her groin and the bed sheet.

Oh no, how did I allow this? I can't remember undressing and leaving my clothes in a mess on the floor. Slowly, she had some recollections but there were gaps. She remembered having dinner but not coming up to Dauda's room. Then it clicked. He had offered to get her a glass of apple juice. Yes, that is it. He must have spiked my drink.

She started crying. At first low level crying but eventually replaced with sobbing and lamentations which woke Dauda.

'What's the matter?' asked Dauda.

'What do you mean by that? How could you? How could you force yourself on me?' lamented Anita.

'I didn't. I thought that is what you wanted. You were a willing partner.'

'Don't give me that. You must have spiked my drink,' replied Anita, raising her voice and now becoming irritated. She poured invectives on him, with little regard for his person or position. He was taken aback by the ferocity of her attack. He apologised profusely and promised redress. She ignored him, dressed hurriedly and stormed out of his room to hers. It was very early in the morning, still not yet six and the corridors were deserted. Anita slipped into her room unnoticed and went straight into the bathroom. She filled the bath with lukewarm water and poured in bath lotion, and then immersed herself in the bubble bath, scrubbing away the filth of the night before. Half an hour later she emerged from the water and got dressed. She hurriedly packed her things and checked out of the hotel. Two hours later she was on a flight to Lagos.

Dauda had breakfast in his room whilst he mulled over the strategy to appease his incandescent Permanent Secretary. He would start by apologising in person and giving a peace offering. When he knocked on her door, there was no response. He went down to the reception desk and asked to be connected to her room but was surprised to learn that she had checked out of the hotel.

Back at work on Monday, Dauda placed a call to the Ministry of Education but was unable to speak to the Permanent Secretary who was said to be off duty due to undisclosed illness.

'Was she truly indisposed or was she still angry'?

This was new territory for him. He had never encountered such indignation and hostility in his previous conquests, and would need to apply all his guile.

CHAPTER 21

On the Tuesday following their return from Abuja, Anita Lawanson accompanied the Minister of Education to the monthly meeting of the Governor with all the Ministers and Permanent Secretaries. This was the forum where major government policies were presented to the heads of the civil service. The meeting went on all morning. Just before the meeting ended, the Governor's private secretary gave a folded piece of paper to Mrs. Lawanson. She flipped open the note and it contained a handwritten message from the Governor. He wanted to see her in his office immediately after the meeting.

Following the meeting, Anita chatted with her colleagues for a little while and then walked down the corridor to the Governor's office. Governor Dauda was waiting for her in his office.

'Good afternoon, Mrs. Lawanson.'

'Good afternoon Sir.'

'Call me Dauda, you can drop the formality when we are alone.'

Then he continued.

'I hope you've forgiven my indiscretion. I respect you a lot. You are intelligent and a consummate professional. I will like to work with you.'

'Thank you for your comments. I try to do my job as well as I can.'

'I've been working on your request. I've already contacted my brother and he has promised to look into your husband's case.'

Then he took his mobile phone and dialled a number.

'Brother, how are you? Mrs. Lawanson is here with me. She wants to know the latest developments about her husband.'

Dauda passed the phone to Anita and they spoke for about five minutes. He reassured her that everything was under control. He had just returned to Jeddah from a briefing with KMC personnel in Taif and would personally visit Daniel in prison and use his influence to secure his release. He said they were all proud of Daniel's professional reputation and the wonderful work he was doing in Taif. He would keep Dauda informed of the progress. Anita thanked him and hung up.

'Thank you for your concern and for keeping your promise.'

'This is only the beginning. I've got more to offer if we can become close,' replied Dauda.

'We are close enough Sir. You know you can always ask me for professional advice,' replied Anita.

'That's not enough. I want us to be closer.'

'That's not going to be possible Sir. I am a married woman and you are also a married man.'

'My wife is unable to give me the intellectual stimulation and advice that you are capable of providing.'

'She is still your wife, and you must honour her,' replied Anita.

'My dear, my wife knows that as a Muslim I am allowed to marry up to four women, so she wouldn't bat an eyelid if I started going out with another woman. Of course I would respect your position and be discreet.'

'It's not a good idea, Sir.'

'I've told you to drop the Sir bit when we are alone. I won't give up because you are so important to me and to this government. I've got a big surprise for you.'

Then her phone alarm went off. She picked up the phone, looked at the message and then silenced the alarm. She had just placed the phone in her handbag when the phone rang. She answered the phone and then turned to the Governor.

'Your Excellency, I've got to go. The Minister and I have an appointment with the Vice Chancellor of the University of Ibadan, and the Minister is about to depart.' This was a good excuse and enabled Anita to escape from what had become an uncomfortable discussion. The meeting with the Vice Chancellor went on till late at night. When Anita returned home, her son was already in bed. It had been a long day and she was exhausted. She went straight to bed without eating or listening to the News at Ten on TV.

The following day Anita got to work bright and early. As she walked in to the Ministry, she wondered why more people than usual jostled to greet her, curtseying as she went along. Then as she walked through her secretary's office, she got up and greeted her warmly.

'Congratulations ma. We rejoice with you. My colleagues have asked me to give you this card.'

Anita was flummoxed.

'Grace, what's this about?'

'Ma'am, haven't you heard?'

'Heard what?'

'It was on the news last night.'

'What was on the news last night?' asked Anita.

'The Head of Service and Secretary to the government had proceeded on leave preparatory to his retirement, and you have been appointed Acting Head of Service and acting Secretary to the Government.'

Anita was speechless.

'Ma'am, you deserve it and we are happy that your qualities have been recognised.'

Then Grace continued.

'Ma'am, I'd like to go with you to the Head of Service office when you take up the substantive post.'

'We'll cross that bridge when we get there. Thank you for the information and your good wishes,' Anita replied, now recovered from the shock. She entered her office and sat down. She saw a big official envelope on her table with the Governor's seal on the flap. She tore it open. Behold, it was the official letter confirming her appointment.

What style of governance is this? What is Dauda up to? I can't reject this elevation. How do I explain it to others when it has already been announced?

Anita's phone did not stop ringing all day. Senator Lawanson was the first to phone from Lagos to congratulate her. Then, Mosun

Lawanson phoned and they chatted on and on. They had grown really close, like sisters. Then her colleagues phoned or dropped in one after the other to congratulate her and pledge their support and loyalty. Her erstwhile colleagues knew it was always a good idea to be in the good books of the new boss. The well-wishers trooped in one after the other all morning. By convention, Anita had to report to the Governor in the afternoon of her first day for inaugural briefing.

Anita walked into the Governor's office promptly at 2 o'clock as requested.

'Mrs. Lawanson, congratulations,' the ebullient Governor shouted across the room as Anita entered his office.

'Thank you Sir,' Anita replied.

'Please close the door behind you, and sit down.'

Anita closed the door and sat across the table from the Governor.

The Governor lifted an internal phone and instructed his personal assistant that he was not to be disturbed until the new Head of Service departed. Anita didn't miss a thing. She noticed that the Governor had not used the term Acting Head of Service. She wondered what he had up his sleeve.

'Congratulations once again Mrs. Lawanson. Can I call you Anita?'

'You are my boss. You can call me Anita if you wish.'

'Good. Anita, didn't I tell you I would surprise you?'

'Yes, you did. I wasn't expecting the elevation.'

'You can rely on me. I always keep my word. The Head of Service retires in three months. The substantive job is yours if you really want it.'

They spent the next hour going through government plans and strategy.

'Anita, that's enough briefing for one day. Let me show you your new office.'

The Governor led the way out of the office through a link corridor to a massive office complex. They walked through a huge waiting room past some offices, and then entered a big office with plush carpets and an ornate mahogany desk in one corner of the room. A luxurious leather three-piece settee was arranged in another corner with a 42 inch plasma TV on the adjacent wall. This looked more like an executive suite in a 5 star hotel than a civil service office. No expense was spared in furnishing the office. It was second only to the Governor's office in opulence.

'This is your new office. Do you like it?'

'Of course, I do.'

'If the furniture is not to your taste, just say so and it will be refurnished to your specification.'

'This is excellent. There is a problem though.'

'What is that?'

'I've got outstanding work in the Ministry of Education which I would like to complete, and I am only Acting Head of Service, so I'd like to keep my office in the Ministry.'

'That's no problem. You can keep both offices for the meantime. Will two days in the Ministry of Education suffice?'

'Yes Sir. Two days will be okay.'

'Good, so you can spend two days in the Ministry office and the remainder of the week here. You'll have to be flexible though, as your new position takes precedence.'

'That's no problem Sir.'

'That's all for now. Let's meet tomorrow afternoon in my office to complete the briefing.'

'Can I have a quiet word Sir?'

They retreated into a corner of the office and Anita spoke in hushed tone.

'Do you have any news about my husband from the Ambassador?'

'I plan to call him again tonight. Don't worry everything is in hand. I trust my brother. He has a lot of clout in Jeddah. Daniel will be home soon.'

'Thank you Sir.'

They parted. The Governor returned to his office whilst Anita held a quick meeting with the administrative staff in the Head of Service complex. She then returned to the Ministry of Education to put finishing touches to a paper she was writing before leaving for home. It was past six o'clock and most of the staff had long gone home before she was ready to leave. She summoned her driver and he drove to the front of the block. Anita waited on the veranda on the lookout for her official Peugeot 504 saloon. Fifteen minutes later, she had still not seen her car. She stormed back to the office and asked her personal assistant to go look for her driver. They were back within five minutes.

'John, didn't you get my message? Where have you been?'

'Ma'am, I was waiting in the car as usual,' replied John.

'What car?' Anita asked.

'Madam, it's your new car.'

'New car?'

'Yes Madam.'

'I was summoned to the transport department to take delivery of your new official car. That brand new Mercedes 280 saloon.' John pointed at a gleaming luxury car which Anita had seen parked a short distance away for the past fifteen minutes but didn't know was meant for her. Anita was speechless.

Surely, Governor Dauda must have had a hand in this.

The car eased away with Anita seated at the back. She sunk into the plush leather seat and kicked off her high heel shoes. She switched on the rear AC control and the cool air hit across her face. She was soon falling asleep.

The following day Anita started juggling the duties of the Ministry of Education Permanent Secretary with that of the Head of Service. At 2 p.m. she returned to the Governor's office to resume her induction and briefing. Before the session started Anita brought up the matter of incarceration of her husband in Saudi Arabia. Governor Dauda again reassured her that the matter was under control.

'I phoned my brother when I got home last night. He had just returned from a visit to the Jeddah Chief of Police.'

Anita shifted in her chair and moved closer to the table.

'What did he say?'

'The Police Chief promised my brother that the case would be withdrawn when the court reconvenes next week. Daniel will be home by the middle of next week.'

'Excellent, that's very good news,' replied Anita.

'I told you that you can rely on me. When I promise something, I always deliver,' the Governor boasted.

The Governor then spent the next two hours completing the briefing of his Head of Service. By the time they finished their meeting both of them were exhausted. Anita got up to leave but the governor beckoned to her to sit down.

'Anita, I hope you haven't forgotten my request.'

'What request Sir?'

'Do you mean you've already forgotten my request for a special relationship?'

'I give you my word that I will work diligently and to the best of my ability. You can count on my loyalty. I will always give you 100 per cent.'

'That I do not doubt. I know you are a consummate professional but we can cement the relationship by taking that extra step.'

'That's going to be difficult Sir,' replied Anita.

'Why?'

'I am a married woman and I love my husband very much. I have never been unfaithful to him.'

'You are an adult with an absent husband and physiological needs. I promise that I will be discreet and respectful, and of course you will be greatly rewarded.'

Anita went silent but her mind was in turmoil.

That's midden. I know what you want but I am not going down that route. You got it once by deceit and guile but I am now wiser.

'Take your time. I don't want to put you under any pressure. Whatever you decide is alright by me.'

Anita was definitely under pressure but was somewhat relieved by this statement.

'Thank you. Thank you very much,' she replied.

Then she was gone.

Anita buried herself in work and this helped to suppress thoughts of Dauda and his lewd proposition. It was difficult to handle because they had to sit down together at least thrice a week. Since the rejection Dauda had become distant and cold. How could they continue to work together in such an atmosphere? Then two weeks after Dauda's request Anita threw a bombshell as they sat down for one of their meetings. They were alone in the Governor's office. Anita had closed the door behind her as she walked into the office.

'Your Excellency, I've got a question for you.'

'Fire on,' replied Dauda.

'Are you still interested in a grown up relationship between us?'

'Oh yes,' replied Dauda. His countenance changed and a smile crossed his face, and he continued.

'That will be a great development, mutually beneficial.'

'Okay, I am ready for the relationship you want, but with conditions,' replied Anita boldly.

'I'll abide by your conditions,' replied Dauda. 'What are the conditions?'

'The first condition is that whatever happens between us, I will not allow my husband to be ridiculed. Therefore, no one else must know about this relationship. The second condition is that we will not have any liaison when my husband is in the country. Thirdly, because we are both so busy, we will only be able to spend time together once a month perhaps a weekend. Finally, I cannot take any chances with the press or the paparazzi and therefore will only spend time with you outside the country. We will have to travel separately.' Anita paused and looked at him.

'So Dauda, what do you say?'

'I agree with your conditions. So, when can we have the first outing?'

'What about London at the end of the month?' replied Anita. 'That'll give us two and a half weeks to plan the trip.'

'That's fine. I was thinking of going for some official business in London.'

'Dauda, I am not mixing business with pleasure. We have to be discreet. One last thing, your aide will have to stay in a separate hotel. They can't know that I am spending time with you.'

'That can easily be arranged,' replied Dauda.

'Very good, I'll confirm the exact date and venue by Friday,' replied Anita.

'Excellent, you've made a wise decision. When we return, you will be greatly rewarded. I think we've had enough deliberations for one day.'

They called it a day and parted.

CHAPTER 22

Governor Dauda left Ibadan for a working trip to Abuja on the last Monday of the month. He held a series of top level meetings with his political godfather the Head of the Senate, some Federal Ministers and even paid a courtesy call on the President. On Wednesday morning, he slipped quietly out of the country flying from Abuja to Accra, and thence to London, arriving at London Heathrow airport late at night. Anita was due to arrive later on Thursday morning by direct flight from Lagos.

Anita had reserved two adjacent executive hotel rooms on the top floor of the Kingdom Hotel on Park Lane. Dauda's reservation was in his name but Anita had reserved her room in her maiden name. Dauda had provided money for the hotel bookings, and payments had been made through secure untraceable accounts. Kingdom Hotel arranged to meet Dauda at Heathrow whisking him off to the hotel in luxury. He was quite impressed with the arrangements, and was bowled over by the splendour and opulence of his hotel room.

I have to admit that Anita has got class. How did she discover this luxurious nest?

Dauda was tired from the tortuous itinerary and soon fell asleep.

He woke up early but lay in bed watching TV. He was startled by the phone ringing. The hotel receptionist spoke to him.

'Mr. Adams, you've got an international call.'

'Put the caller through.'

He reckoned that only Anita knew he was here, so it had to be from her.

'Hello my Governor.'

'Hello my Head of Service. How are you?'

'I am well and looking forward to joining you soon. I've got a problem though.'

'What's that?'

'It's my son. He broke his leg playing football yesterday. I had to be recalled from Lagos and I spent all night with him in hospital. POP was applied and he is now settling down. He has been discharged and is resting at home. I have rescheduled my flight and I am now due to depart on Saturday morning arriving at Heathrow around 5.30 p.m. I should be with you by half past seven.'

'You did the right thing. I'll just have to wait. Family comes first.'

'Thank you for your understanding. I'll see you on Saturday.'

'Bye. See you soon.'

Dauda sat on the edge of the bed despondent. What was he supposed to do in the next two days before Anita's arrival? Watch TV or complete crossword puzzles? This wasn't in the script. He grabbed the TV remote controller and flicked endlessly from station to station. He stomped across the room to the bathroom to freshen up. Half an hour later he returned to the room, got dressed and poured some coffee. He was still moping when there was a knock on the door. He got up and opened the door. It was the chambermaid coming to clean the room. Dauda was blown away by her beauty.

'I've come to clean your room. Are you ready?'

'Oh yes come in and do your work,' replied Dauda.

'Dauda eyed her as she moved round the room dusting the table and emptying the bins. Then she set about tidying the bed. Dauda pretended to be reading a magazine but kept an eye on the chambermaid. She was almost six feet tall, voluptuous with curves to die for, and long sexy legs. He couldn't place her origin. She was either a heavily tanned Caucasian or a mixed race with predominance of the Anglo-Saxon genes. She had impeccable white teeth which dazzled as she spoke. When she bent over to smoothen the bed sheet she was facing Dauda, and he didn't miss her heaving cleavage and boobs as they threatened to escape from the unbuttoned top of her blouse.

Wow! Oh my goodness! This is fantastic.

The chamber maid continued her work unperturbed. If she had noticed Dauda's penetrating eyes, she didn't show it.

I've got to initiate conversation with this lady. You never know, I may hit a jackpot with her. Nothing ventured, nothing gained.

'You've done a really good job in transforming this room within a few minutes. You're just brilliant.'

'Thank you,' replied the chambermaid.

'What's your name?'

'I am Michelle, Michelle Flower.'

I am Dave Adams,' replied Dauda, jazzing up his name so that it sounded more Western.

'Where are you from?'

'London, East London.'

'I mean originally.'

'My father emigrated from Jamaica and my mother is from Belfast.'

'You inherited excellent genes from them.'

Michelle smiled coyly. Then she turned to Dauda. 'What about you? Where are you from, and what do you do?'

'I am from Nigeria.' Then he lied. 'I am a businessman, here on a trip to sign a multi-million pound contract on behalf of my company.'

He steered attention away from himself.

'Can I ask for a favour?'

'It depends,' replied Michelle.

'Can you bring some newspapers up to my room?'

'That's no problem. Which papers do you want?' I can arrange for them to be sent up to your room from the concierge desk.'

'The *Daily Mail* and *Guardian* please, but I would prefer if you brought them up yourself.'

'I'll get the papers when I go for a break in half an hour. I hope that isn't too late.'

'No, not all,' replied Dauda.

Michelle brought the newspapers over an hour later.

'Mr. Adams, the newspapers. Enjoy your reading.'

Dauda brought out a twenty pound note and handed it over to Michelle.

'What is this for?' asked Michelle.

'It's a tip for all your efforts,' replied Dauda.

Michelle was about to say something but Dauda put his finger across her lips to silence her anticipated protest. She muttered her thanks and left.

Dauda sat down to read the newspapers but couldn't concentrate. Michelle's image repeatedly flashed across his face and as he held the newspaper close, he could smell her perfume.

Everything happens for a reason. Anita's delay has turned out to be a blessing. At the last count I must have had a hundred conquests but never a Caucasian. This must be my opportunity to nail one to my bedpost, and I've got to do it before Anita arrives. Tomorrow is the D-day. I have already prepared the ground and I am sure she'll be willing.

Dauda spent most of the day popping in and out of the luxury car showrooms in Park Lane. On a whim he decided he wanted a new luxury car to show off to his family and friends on his return to Nigeria. He went into the Ferrari showroom and was charmed by a 550 Convertible Barchetta in bright tomato red colour. He was suddenly feeling young again. He went for a spin in the Ferrari and was impressed by the power and responsiveness of the sports car. The car would set him back over one hundred thousand pounds but there was a waiting time of three to six months for delivery to Lagos. He didn't want to wait that long. He moved on to the Mercedes-Benz showroom, and was attracted to the Mercedes-Benz S Class 65 Saloon AMG. He had owned other models of Mercedes Benz but none as powerful as this 6 litre executive car. The car was available for immediate shipment. Just before he entered the showroom, he saw the Bentley sign ahead and wanted to have a look before returning to pay a deposit for the Mercedes.

'Good morning Sir.'

'Good morning,' replied Dauda as he walked into the Bentley showroom with a swagger. The salesman could sense the arrogance and confidence that come with being awash with cash.

Dauda looked round and became fixated on a gleaming black coupe in the centre of the hall.

'I want to test drive that car,' said Dauda as he pointed across the hall.

'Tell me about it.'

'This is Bentley Continental GT Coupe. It is a beautiful and powerful luxury car with 6 litres, 12 cylinder engine. It has an automatic transmission, and it has a seven years manufacturer warranty.'

'Good. I want a test drive.'

The showroom manager gently manoeuvred a similar model from the parking lot, and eased the car on to Park lane turned right and drove the car down round Hyde Park on to Knightsbridge. He found a safe place and parked the car, changing seats with Dauda. The car eased away smoothly with flawless acceleration as the gears changed. The manager had to urge him to keep his speed below the speed limit. He pointed the way through Kensington High Street on the approach to the Hammersmith flyover. Just before the flyover he asked Dauda to turn right into a private road. This led to a club with a large parking lot, empty at this time of the day. The manager was a member of this club. Dauda was able to test the power of the engine. As he pressed down hard on the throttle, the 12 cylinder engine responded with a roar and hurtled down the car park like a rocket. After only a few minutes, Dauda switched off the engine and turned to the sales manager.

'Mr. Byrne, let's go back to your office, I'll take the car. How soon can I have one?'

'Next week Sir.'

'That is very good.'

'How much does it cost?'

'Sir, the basic model costs in excess of a hundred grand but this model with full spec, car tax and registration plus free service for two years will add another thirty thousand pounds.'

'I want the top model. I won't be driving it here, so I won't need registration or car tax. I want it shipped to Nigeria.'

'We'll be able to provide one for you at one hundred and forty thousand pounds.'

When they returned to the showroom, the manager asked how Dauda wanted to settle the bill.

'Will you be applying for finance?'

Dauda was visibly angered by this suggestion.

'Mr. Byrne, what's the meaning of that? Do you think I can't afford the car? All right, I've changed my mind. I am going back to buy the Mercedes-Benz I saw earlier.'

Dauda got up and was about to leave the manager's office but the manager dashed round the table and apologised profusely. He even promised to ask his boss to give a special discount. Eventually, Dauda relented.

'So how much discount will you give?' asked Dauda.

Mr. Byrne took his phone and dialled their head office. When he put the phone down, he turned to Dauda.

'Sir, I am happy to inform you that my boss has agreed to give a discount of ten thousand pounds.'

'That's fine. I'll pay a deposit of fifty grand today. Once the car is ready for shipment next week, I'll pay the balance.'

'Is that okay?'

'Yes sir.'

Dauda produced a cheque book and issued a UK bank cheque for fifty thousand pounds.

It was late afternoon by the time Dauda left the showroom feeling accomplished. Mr. Byrne and his staff could only marvel at the source of such wealth. The customer had just put down a deposit equal to the manager's annual salary.

Dauda walked down Park Lane euphoric. He saw a Chinese restaurant and was suddenly hungry. He went in and spent the next one hour going through the various delicacies. It was almost 6 o'clock by the time Dauda returned to the hotel. As soon as he stepped into the hotel and saw a chambermaid, his euphoria vanished. There was the matter of wooing Michelle to contend with. He slept fitfully that night. He was tense, just like a school boy going for his first date.

Dauda got up early on Friday morning, had a shower and got dressed. He needed a caffeine fix and brewed a cup of strong black coffee. He killed the time by watching TV flicking from channel to channel unable to concentrate on any particular programme. He was jolted back to life by a rap on the door just after ten. He opened the door and it was Michelle.

'Are you ready for your room to be cleaned?'

'Yes, I am ready. Please come in.' As Michelle walked into the room, Dauda commented on how beautiful she looked.

'Thank you Mr. Dauda.'

Dauda sat quietly on the sofa pretending to read a book as Michelle went round to make the bed. She bent over in direct view of Dauda and as she tugged at the bed sheet, her bosom heaved almost resulting in wardrobe malfunction. Dauda's pulse raced wildly. He steeled his nerve, got up from the sofa and quietly left the room. It was all a ploy because he returned a few minutes later and craftily locked the door which had been left ajar by Michelle as is the practice with chambermaids. Michelle was backing the door arranging stationery on the table as he returned. Dauda moved swiftly like an Olympic sprinter and he grabbed Michelle from behind, locking her in a vice-like hold across her chest with his powerful right arm, pinning her back against his torso, and simultaneously thrusting his left hand through her cleavage into her bra. Michelle shuddered and panicked.

'Stop it, stop it please,' she begged.

'I like you, I really like you Michelle.'

'No, stop it please,' Michelle pleaded frantically.

'I like you. I want you Michelle. Let's make love.'

'That will cost you a lot,' replied Michelle.

'How much?'

'A thousand pounds,' replied Michelle.

'That's no problem,' replied Mike.

'Okay, let's take it step by step. I want the money upfront.'

Dauda relaxed his grip and turned round to retrieve his wallet from his briefcase. When he turned round to remove the money from his wallet Michelle hit him with full force in his crotch with her knee. He crumpled on the floor with a thud as he let out a frightening piercing cry. Michelle vaulted over his body and flung the door open shouting down the hotel corridor for help. Before she exited the room she had the presence of mind to take a photograph on her mobile phone of the hapless Dauda groaning on the floor struggling to unzip his trousers to let fresh air into his traumatised manhood. She ran down the corridor sobbing as other guests came out of their rooms to find out what was amiss. She pointed at Dauda's room and despite the babble she was able to convey the information that she had been assaulted. The hotel guests poured into Dauda's room as he picked himself up from the floor. He tried to push them out of his room but he was overpowered. The hotel manager soon arrived in the room and escorted Dauda down to his office. He denied sexually assaulting Michelle, and said it was a consensual affair. Michelle insisted she wanted the police notified. One of the first hotel guests to enter Dauda's room gave a statement that the manner in which Michelle ran down the corridor was suggestive of someone who had just undergone a terrifying ordeal. The police were called and they took Dauda away under caution whilst Michelle was taken separately to the station to give her statement. She complained of scratches and soreness on one of her breasts where Dauda had groped her. The police took Michelle to a doctor who examined her and noted there was a scratch across one breast. She noted that this was suggestive of forcible handling of the breast. Scrapings were then taking from Dauda's nails for DNA analysis. The case against Dauda was overwhelming but he continued to deny any guilt. He gave a 'no comment' answer to all the questions he was asked, and demanded his right to a lawyer. The police allowed him to place a call to the Nigerian High Commission in Northumberland Avenue. The High Commissioner and his deputy were at an official function at the Commonwealth office so Dauda's call was diverted to the First Secretary. Dauda gave his version of the events, careful to portray himself as a victim of a set up by a gold digger. The First Secretary got in touch with their legal adviser and both of them were in the police station within two hours of the phone call. The First Secretary tried to get Dauda released by invoking diplomatic immunity. The police rejected the move as it was feared he might interfere with police investigation or abscond.

The interrogation commenced late in the afternoon, with the High Commission lawyer sitting in with Dauda. The police inspector flicked the tape recorder switch, stated the time and date and then listed the names of all those in attendance. He then told Dauda he was now under caution and required to answer all questions truthfully.

'Mr Dauda Adams, please tell us what happened between you and the chambermaid this morning in Room 802 at The Kingdom Hotel.'

'Nothing much, we just had a misunderstanding,' replied Dauda.

'Miss Flower has accused you of trying to rape her.'

'That's a lie. That girl is a big liar. I tried no such thing,' protested Dauda vehemently.

Then he continued.

'Did she tell you she asked for one thousand pounds to be intimate with me?'

'Mr. Adams, I am doing the interrogating and not you. Please tell us exactly what happened from the minute she entered your hotel room till the minute she fled your room crying.'

After one hour, the police had managed to get nothing concrete out of Dauda. Dauda was a politician to the core and was a master of obfuscation. The police inspector switched off the tape recorder and told Dauda that he was not yet ready to tell the truth and was just wasting their time. He and his colleague walked out of the room in a flounce. Dauda's lawyer followed the inspector and the sergeant out of the room. The police inspector slammed his office door behind him and threw his hands up in the air in exasperation. There was a knock on his door.

'Come in.'

'Please sit down Mr. Bullock.'

'Thank you, Inspector.'

'Mr. Bullock, your client does not seem to appreciate the gravity of the charges levelled against him. The complainant has a very strong case with many hotel guests backing her testimony. We are also waiting for DNA results from body fluids on Miss Flower's trousers and scrapings from Dauda's nails.'

'What are our options?'

'The options are clear. If your client comes clean and spares the accuser the torment and anguish of testifying, the prosecutor would be able to consider a plea bargain and try the case in a Magistrate court. As you are aware under Section 3 of the Sexual Offences Act 2003, the sentence for a summary conviction is imprisonment for a term not exceeding six months or a fine not exceeding the statutory maximum or both. But if your client continues with his present attitude, we will commit more police resources to this case and arraign him before the Crown Court for trial by jury. Miss Flower has already said she is ready to testify if necessary. The hotel manager and several hotel guests have already submitted statements and have said they will testify in support of Miss Flower. If your client is found guilty at the crown court, he could be sentenced to ten years in jail.'

Mr. Bullock sighed. After a short pause, he spoke.

'I'll go back and have a serious discussion with my client.'

'Please do.'

Mr. Bullock exited the room and returned to the interrogation room where Dauda was waiting for him.

'Governor Adams, we need to talk.'

They sat down and the lawyer relayed what the police inspector had told him. He was frightened when he heard that he could go to jail for ten years. Surely, nothing would have happened to him if the encounter had occurred in Nigeria. Some of his many conquests had been more blatant.

'What have you decided?' asked Mr. Bullock.

Dauda hesitated. Mr Bullock placed his briefcase on the table, slowly opened it and retrieved a copy of the *The London Evening Echo*, the widely read free London newspaper which he had picked up at the Underground Train Station on his way to the police station. He tossed the paper on Dauda's lap.

'Mr. Adams, I must be honest with you. I'll do my best but you don't have a good case.'

When Dauda held up the newspaper, he saw a photograph of himself being led away by the police at Kingdom Hotel. As he started to read the story of his arrest, he sighed and started sweating profusely.

Dauda Adams started relaying the story from the moment Michelle entered his hotel room, playing down the manner of his aggression and implying that Michelle egged him on. He even believed she was serious when she asked him for a thousand pounds to have intimate relations with him. After he finished, he held the lawyer in both hands. His demeanour had changed. He was clearly frightened.

'Mr. Bullock, I can't go to jail. You have to do whatever you can for me. Money is no object.'

'Okay, I'll tell the police you are ready for a plea bargain.'

'Thank you very much.'

Mr. Bullock exited the room to talk to the police officers.

The police inspector and the sergeant entered the interrogation room at 2 o'clock. The inspector read the rights to Mr. Adams and the questioning commenced. Dauda admitted he had sexually harassed Michelle Flower because he thought she was interested in a relationship with him. He had touched her cleavage but had not indecently assaulted her. He stated that he was ready to plead guilty to these charges in court, and save police time and obviate the need for Michelle to testify in court. The interrogation ended at 2.45 p.m.

The police inspector took leave of Dauda and his lawyer to confer with the crown prosecutor. He returned half an hour later and confirmed that Dauda's plea bargain had been accepted and he would be charged to a magistrate court on the lesser charge of sexual harassment and not the more serious charge of indecent assault.

Dauda Adams was arraigned before the Southwark Magistrate Court for a Summary Trial on Monday. The court was packed full with journalists and other parties well before proceedings commenced. This was the first case of the day and the proceedings commenced promptly at 9 o'clock. Dauda sat grim faced in the dock. The accused was ordered to stand and confirm his identity. The judge read the charges.

'The accused confirmed his identity.'

Then the magistrate continued.

'Mr. Dauda Adams.'

'Yes, your honour.'

'You are hereby charged under Section 3 of the Sexual Offences Act 2003 of sexual harassment by intentionally sexually touching one Miss Flower without her consent and also causing her bodily harm. Are you guilty or not?'

'I am guilty your honour,' Dauda answered quietly, looking sheepish.

The judge beckoned to Dauda to sit down. As he sat, he looked round the crowded court and his eyes rested on a familiar face. He recognised Anita in the court gallery. Their eyes met and she shook her head. He knew what she was thinking and he promptly dropped his head in shame.

Before the judge could make any further pronouncement, Dauda's lawyer stood up to address the court. He made a passionate plea for mitigation, stating that his client was a responsible public servant who had misunderstood the victim and had transgressed due to cultural differences. He had been extremely remorseful and cooperative with the police. He had apologised to the victim and was ready to compensate her financially if necessary. He also appealed to the court to look favourably on the fact that by admitting his guilt he had spared the young lady the torment of testifying in court and having her personal life examined in public.

'The court will reconvene next Friday morning for sentencing. I will consider the submission by counsel to the accused and any character reference that may be submitted to me,' responded the judge.

The deliberations had been swift and the case was adjourned by 11.00 a.m.

Dauda heard rumours that things had gone awry in Ibadan. Some of his colleagues were trying to impeach him. He couldn't do anything from here. He first had to escape going to jail in London and would then deal with the Nigerian problem.

Eventually, Friday came and Dauda was back in the dock. This was again the first case of the day in court number two. The judge entered the court promptly at nine and Dauda and his lawyer stood as the judge announced he was about to deliver his judgement.

'Mr. Dauda Adams, I have considered the submission for mitigation by your lawyer and the statement by the prosecutor that you cooperated fully with the police. I have also noted that you have not wasted the time of this court. I am therefore inclined to temper justice with mercy. I hereby sentence you to pay a fine of five thousand pounds. Your name will also be entered on the sex offenders register. I have spared you custodial sentence because of your remorse and the various submissions on your behalf but if you are ever brought before me for a similar offence in future, I will have no option but to send you to jail without option of a fine.'
Mr Adams jumped up in delight and embraced his lawyer. This was the best outcome possible.

Dauda's joy was however short lived. As he left the court with his lawyer, he was served with a writ for civil suit brought against him by Michelle Flower.

'Mr. Bullock, what is the meaning of this?'

'Mr. Adams, the lady is exercising her right in law to seek redress and compensation for any physical or mental harm suffered by her.'

'What mental harm?' Dauda demanded to know.

'Mr. Adams, this is not the place to address this issue. Let's go to my chambers, and we can look at what options we have.'

They travelled in silence as Mr. Bullock drove them to his law office. One hour after they left the magistrate court, they sat down in Mr. Bullock's office to map out their reaction to the new problem.

'Mr. Bullock, I have to be back in Nigeria as soon as possible. I haven't got the time or stamina for another court case. Please negotiate with the bitch. She is a gold digger.'

'Mr. Adams, mind your language. Be careful what you say in her presence. She can make life very difficult for you.'

Mr. Bullock contacted Michelle's lawyer, Miss Groves. Over the next few days, the two lawyers reached accord. Mr. Bullock agreed that his client would pay £100,000 for physical and mental injury, and £50,000 punitive damages. Mr. Bullock contacted Adams who promptly transferred the sum of one hundred and fifty thousand pounds to Miss Groves company account for the victim, and also settled the two lawyers' bills. As soon as money changed hands, the civil case was withdrawn from the court.

CHAPTER 23

As soon as the deal was sealed, Miss Groves was on the phone to Anita Lawanson who had secretly engaged her to fight Michelle's case and hit Dauda Adams where it would hurt him, in the pocket. After their discussion, she then telephoned Michelle to brief her on the outcome of the compensation negotiations. Miss Groves informed her that she had transferred her share of the compensation money into her account.

'Thank you very much Miss Groves.'

'Thank you Michelle for allowing me to work for you and for being bold and resolute in your pursuit of justice. Take care of yourself and goodbye.'

Michelle left home and went straight to the bank to carry out an important transaction. She then took a bus to Liverpool Street station where she changed on to the underground central line bound for West Ruislip. She disembarked at Greenford station, walked out of the station and turned left into Oldfield Lane South. She checked her London A-Z street map book. She was on time. She walked a short distance down the street and saw the building on the right with a small sign above the door. She pressed the bell and a middle aged woman opened the door.

'Good afternoon Miss.'

'Good afternoon,' replied Michelle.

'I am sorry we have no vacancies, the B & B is full.'

'Oh no, I am not looking for a room. I am here to see one of your guests, Mrs. Lawanson.'

'Is she expecting you?'

'Oh yes she is,' replied Michelle.

The landlady took the phone and spoke to Anita. When she dropped the phone she turned to Michelle.

'When you go up the stairs, hers is the first room on the right. She is expecting you.'

When Michelle entered the room, the two ladies embraced each other. Michelle held Anita tightly and then started to cry.

'Don't cry Michelle. We won, we won.'

'Yes, we won, but why do rich men think they can take advantage of poor girls like me?'

'It is arrogance and the allure of money and power. But we taught this lecherous and mendacious man a lesson he will never forget,' replied Anita.

'Yes we did,' and Michelle relaxed and then started smiling.

'Will you have some tea?' asked Anita.

'Yes please,' replied Michelle. 'Let's celebrate with tea and biscuits.'

As they drank tea and ate biscuits, Anita turned to Michelle.

'Michelle, so what happens next? What are your plans?'

'First of all I want to thank you for everything. Ms Groves has given me my 50 percent share of the compensation and punitive damages. The 75 grand has come in really handy.' She paused and then continued.

'Let me start from the beginning. My parents met in secondary school in London. My father had a black Jamaican Father and a white Welsh mother. My grandparents moved to London from Cardiff after my father was born. My maternal grandparents were both from Ireland and they also moved to East London when my mother was young. My parents lost contact after they left school. My father went to the polytechnic to study civil engineering whilst my mother started working at a departmental store in Oxford Street. Then they ran into each other one day as my father and his class visited Oxford Street for a practical lesson. They rekindled their love immediately they set eyes on each other. Two years later they were married. I was born within a year of the marriage. My childhood was extremely happy. We did what normal families do. My father got a job with a big civil engineering company and my mother continued to work in the departmental store. My parents rented a flat in East London. I went to a Nursery school and then the neighbourhood primary school. I was always well dressed and had plenty of friends from middle class families. My birthdays were marked with expensive parties, and we had regular holiday trips to various parts of the United Kingdom. Three years into the marriage, my parents bought a two bedroom terrace house in East London. We were moving up the status ladder. When I was ten years old everything changed. My father lost his job and he started drinking. Things changed rapidly in our home. My parents started to quarrel. Many nights I pretended to be asleep but I cowered on my bed covering my head with my blanket as my parents quarrelled and swore at each other. It usually started with my father coming home late inebriated. Then one night during a drunken rage my father beat my mother until she collapsed. I can still hear her screams. I was so scared that I jumped from my bed and phoned 999. The ambulance came and took my mother to hospital. The paramedics called the police and my father was locked up. I was taken away to live with my maternal grandparents. When I returned after a few months, he was no longer home. My mother wouldn't talk about what happened but my granny told me he came home another night drunk and abusive. My mother locked him out of the house. Nobody knew where he slept. When my mother finally opened the door in the morning, he was sober and went in quietly into the bedroom, took a travel bag and dumped some of his clothes in it, and walked out. He never returned. Rumour has it that he returned to Kingston Town. I got a birthday card from him when I was eleven, but I have not heard from him since. '

'I am sorry to hear your story,' Anita stated.

Before Anita could continue, Michelle raised her hand to stop her, and then continued her story.

'After my father left, money became tight. My mother struggled to make the mortgage payments and put food on the table, so she took a second job which she did whenever she was off duty in her main job or on leave. The holidays stopped. We just couldn't afford them. My mother was determined that whatever happened she would not compromise on two important issues, she would not lose the house and I would get a good education. She has never remarried and has worked two jobs ever since. I learnt that my father was very brilliant. I must have inherited his brainy genes because I have always done well in my examinations despite the hard times. I had eight A scores at GCSE and three As at GCE advanced level. I always wanted to be a lawyer, and applied to study law at the University of London. I was offered a place last June. I am not sure if I can afford to go. I'll probably ask for deferment for a year whilst I save more money at work. That decision is for another day. Right now I am elated. When I got the cheque for 75 grand, I asked my mum what the mortgage balance was. We phoned the building society and I cleared the balance. So my mum now owns the house, and I've told her to give notice to her second employer. She no longer needs to work two jobs.'

'What was the mortgage balance?' Anita asked.

'Sixty nine thousand five hundred pounds,' replied Michelle. 'The payment is gone but it is money well spent because when my mum dies the house will pass to me.'

'That's a good decision,' stated Anita.

'Oh yes, and I've got an even bigger surprise for my mother. She has not had a holiday in over ten years, so I am going to book a two weeks holiday for both of us when she is on leave. I have paid a deposit on a Mediterranean Cruise. That will set me back two thousand pounds, so I'll still have three thousand pounds balance in my account.'

'That's brilliant and very thoughtful of you. What's next?'

'I'll rest for a week and then go back to work,' replied Michelle.

'Do you mean the Escort Agency where I came to recruit you for the sting operation?'

'Oh yes. It's not the safest job but it pays well. I can take care of myself. Growing up on the tough streets of East London, I had to learn to protect myself from bullies and perverts. After my dad left, my uncle took me to a martial arts school and I got a black belt in judo. I still practise the art.'

'Michelle, I admire you and your determination. I really want you to leave that job and start your law studies this year.'

'I can't. I can't afford it. Maybe next year but not this year,' replied Michelle.

'I'll pay your fees.'

'You'll do what?' Michelle asked, not sure she heard her well.

'I'll pay your fees and give you reasonable allowance for the duration of your course as long as you pass the exams.'

Michelle embraced Anita again, and showered her with praise.

'Thank you. Thank you and God bless you.'

'How much will the course cost?'

'It's a three year full-time course. Tuition fee is 3,000 pounds per annum, and I reckon another three thousand pounds will be sufficient for books, transport and other expenses. I intend to live at home so I don't have to pay for an expensive student flat in central London.'

'That makes six thousand pounds per annum,' stated Anita.

'Yes,' replied Michelle.

'Okay, let's make it eight thousand. I'll pay 3 grand to the university and 5 grand into your account every year for three years. I'll set up the special account today. Better still, let's go to the bank now to set up the standing order because I am off to Saudi Arabia tomorrow.'

'Mrs. Lawanson, that's a total of twenty four thousand pounds.'

'Yes it is,' replied Anita.

'Why are you doing this? Twenty four grand is a lot of money.'

'You deserve this and more. You helped me to teach that brute a lesson and all the travels and hotel bills cost me less than half of the seventy five grand that came to me. I really didn't want to profit financially from the situation, so I feel you need the money more than I do. There are only two preconditions.'

Michelle's heart sank and she sat up straight.

'What are these preconditions?'

'The first is that you quit that escort job immediately.'

'That's no problem. I'll quit. What is the second?'

'You give an undertaking that you'll take the studies seriously. Be the best that you can.'

'I will. I promise.'

'Okay, let's go to the bank. Have you got the university admission details?'

'I've got all the details on the request for admission deferment I was about to post to the university,' replied Michelle.

'Can I have the letter?'

'You don't need that anymore.'

Anita collected the letter and they left for the bank. Anita set up the standing order and they parted ways. Anita promised to keep in touch with her. Anita returned to the B&B. The following day she left on a Saudi Arabian Airlines flight to Jeddah.

CHAPTER 24

The Saudi Arabian Boeing 747 landed at King Abdul Aziz International Airport in Jeddah early on Sunday morning. Anita slipped on her black abaya during the flight and covered her hair with a black scarf. It was a low travel season and she went through immigration processing fairly rapidly. She was so thrilled to see her husband that she flung herself into his arms as she exited the arrival hall, momentarily forgetting where she was. There were disapproving glances from bystanders and she quickly controlled herself.

'My darling I have missed you so much.'

'Me too,' replied Daniel.

'Wait till we get home, I've got a special treat for you.'

'I wasn't expecting any less,' replied Daniel.

'I've taken the day off work.'

He hauled her suitcase into the boot of his car and gently eased the car out of the car park. Soon they were on the Makkah road leading from Jeddah to Taif. As Daniel drove, he cast furtive glances at his wife. He had come to appreciate her more during his incarceration. He had learnt from Dr Ali and the Nigerian Deputy High Commissioner of all the moves she made to get him released. They drove in silence as Anita drifted in and out of slumber. She was too tense and had not slept properly on the flight despite travelling in the first class cabin. As Daniel started driving up the hill towards Al-Hada, Anita woke up. The one hour sleep since they left Jeddah had refreshed her.

'Darling, there are rumours that your boss has been convicted of sex offences in London.'

'Bad news travels fast. How did you hear that?'

'It was from one of the High Commission staff who came for treatment in my clinic yesterday.'

'It is true. He was convicted at the magistrate court for sexual harassment and causing bodily harm. His name has also been placed on the sex offenders register. Can you imagine the disgrace? He was fortunate that the High Commission got him a good lawyer otherwise he would have gone to jail.'

'How do you know that?' enquired Daniel.

'I attended one of the court sessions and I spoke to the girl he assaulted. He actually tried to rape the girl, a hotel chambermaid, but came a cropper. He is a lecherous old man and does not deserve to be our Governor.'

'Do you really detest him so much?' Daniel asked.

'He tried it on with me but I dealt with him severely,' replied Anita.

'What did you do to him?'

'I'll spare you the details but suffice it to say I taught him a lesson he will never forget. You know I don't take nonsense from anyone. He will never again make a pass at any other man's wife.'

Anita decided that there was no point in spelling out the details of Dauda's misdemeanour in the Abuja hotel. She wasn't complicit and there was no point in souring their time together. In any case it was true that she had taught him a bitter and costly lesson. Anita decided to steer the discussion away from that angle.

'Do you know what really shocked me about the man?'

'What?' Daniel asked.

'He is a liar, what our people call bold faced liar. His mendacity knows no bounds.'

'Why do you say so?'

'Your brother advised me to solicit his help in contacting the Deputy High Commissioner in Jeddah to use his influence in effecting your release. I did so and he promised to contact his brother. He didn't contact him promptly, and did not follow up the matter even though he lied that he did.'

'How are you sure?'

'I wanted to know how truthful our Governor was but he failed woefully. Immediately you were released, before it became public knowledge, I went to him to urge his brother not to forget his promise. He said he would phone him again that day. Do you know that he came back the following day to tell me that his brother had sent his top official to see you in detention after our discussion, and also that his brother had gone to see the Chief of Police in Jeddah who promised you would be released the following week?'

'Anita, that is incredible.'

'The man is a prolific liar. He just cannot be trusted. And your brother trusted him implicitly and invited him to join his team as his running mate.'

'Politicians are very smart. You never fully know their true nature until they get into power. Power and money is a potent combination – it can be a force for good or evil, depending on the individual,' Daniel replied philosophically.

'My dear, let's forget about politics and politicians. How did you come to be released so miraculously?'

'That's the right word. It was actually a miracle. It's a long story and I'll tell you all about it when we get home, after we've rested and you've given me what you brought.'

She giggled.

Daniel eased his foot on the throttle and slowed the car as they entered Taif. Twenty minutes later he drove into the KMC staff quarters. The old faces were on duty at the security gate. Daniel slowed down to be recognised. As the guard lifted the barrier, he greeted Anita warmly. She responded with a smile and a wave. When they entered their villa, they just dumped Anita's things on the floor and hugged each other. Anita became very emotional and was in a flood of tears.

'I never thought I would ever step into this house again,' blurted Anita in between her sobbing.

'All is well,' replied Daniel.

'I don't want to leave you alone again. When are you returning home finally?'

'We'll deal with that later. Right now we have a more important matter to deal with. There is the issue of the package you promised.'

The couple canoodled as they stumbled their way up the stairs into the bedroom.

It wasn't until well after noon that they finally came down for lunch.

After lunch Anita revisited the detention saga.

'So how did the release come about?'

'This is what happened. You will recall that last year I successfully treated the mother-in-law of Prince Rasheed and he was so impressed that he gave us that fantastic holiday in London. She came back for a follow up clinic the week I was arrested, with some minor complaints. She was seen by one of the general surgeons who examined her and placed her on some drugs. She did not respond to the treatment and told her daughter she had not received proper treatment. Her daughter phoned Prince Rasheed that her mother was still ill and needed to see a proper doctor. She pleaded with her husband to arrange an appointment with me. He contacted my department but was told I was incarcerated in Jeddah on some trumped up charge. Prince Rasheed then got in touch with Dr Ali who confirmed the story.

Prince Rasheed summoned the Jeddah Chief of Police to Riyadh. The case against me was thrown out and I was released the same day and driven by the police to Taif. The following day I returned to work and Princess Aisha brought her mother to see me. I diagnosed urinary tract infection and dehydration. I placed her on appropriate antibiotics with instruction that she must drink fluids liberally. I urged her to stay in their palace in Taif so that she could return to see me after four days. By the time she returned to the clinic she was symptom free. They were still in the clinic when Princess Aisha phoned Prince Rasheed to tell him that I had cured her mother of her ailment. She asked him to thank me himself. I demurred and stated that I was only doing my job but she insisted and we had no choice. Prince Rasheed thanked me profusely and again apologised for the indiscretion of the religious police. So that is how the masalama party fallout was resolved.'

'That's amazing. Really amazing,' commented Anita.

Meanwhile back in Nigeria the fallout from Dauda's UK conviction was playing itself out. From the moment he was arrested, it was front page news. Photographs of Dauda being led away by police from Kingdom Hotel was splashed across the front page of several newspapers the day after his arrest. A gossip magazine published by a political opponent even managed to get hold of the mobile phone photograph of the Governor crouching in the corner of the hotel room holding his crotch after Michelle had kneed him in the groin before she escaped.

An emergency meeting of the House of Assembly was convened. The opposition legislators moved a motion that the Governor should be suspended from office because he had brought the honourable position of Governor into disrepute. His supporters argued that these were merely rumours peddled by his enemies and detractors. In any case, even if it was true that he was arrested, he was innocent until proven guilty. The opposing groups argued their cases with fervour. It was a stalemate until the Monday he pleaded guilty. Dauda's supporters tried all tricks to stymie the opponents but in the end his adversaries prevailed, and Dauda was suspended from office of Governor. The goal of the opposition was removal from office through impeachment for dishonourable and disreputable behaviour. They set the process in motion. Some were hoping that the British authorities would solve their problem by giving him a custodial sentence. If he was jailed, return to office would be impossible and a new Governor would have to be chosen.

The High Commission officials and Mr. Bullock shielded Dauda from developments in Nigeria whilst the court case was on. Immediately the case was determined Dauda realised something was amiss when he tried unsuccessfully to contact the Governor's office in Ibadan. He took a taxi to the High Commission in Northumberland to thank the High Commissioner and his staff for all their help, and to find out what was happening back home. As he sat waiting to see the High Commissioner, his eyes drifted to a pile of Nigerian newspapers on the table. His heart sank when he picked up the first one. His photograph was on the first page. As he read through he became despondent. He looked through the pile and most of the dailies had something uncomplimentary to say about him. He got up and made some excuse to the secretary. He left a note thanking the High Commissioner but stated that he had to leave because an emergency had arisen. In reality, he was confused and ashamed. He wandered aimlessly around central London. He saw a pub and went in to drown his sorrow. He downed pint after pint of John

Smith's bitter. By the time he left the pub two hours later, he had consumed five pints of bitter. When he got outside and the breeze hit his face, he suddenly felt light headed and needed a snooze. He took a taxi to his new hotel. During the trial Mr. Bullock had been informed that he had been barred from Kingdom Hotel, and his belongings had been handed over to the lawyer. He was now staying in a small nondescript hotel near Victoria Train Station. He woke up a few hours later with a splitting headache. He popped two Paracetamol tablets and washed them down with a glass of water. He had made up his mind to call in favours owed him. Dauda had made up his mind to fight his adversaries with everything he had. As for the rats in his party, he would deal ruthlessly with them when he returned to power. He had campaigned vigorously for Senator Osazuwa in the past and had also carried out some dirty tricks on his behalf. The Senate leader owed him.

It was early evening when Dauda got through to the Senate leader. Senator Osazuwa confirmed Dauda's suspension as Governor. What was more worrying was the motion for his removal as Governor. This motion was moved earlier in the day by one of the opposition legislators. Undoubtedly, the opposition National Congress Party would vote solidly in support of the motion, but they didn't have the numbers for two-thirds majority required for impeachment. Unfortunately several members of the ruling party had openly castigated the Governor and were likely to vote along with the opposition. The Senate leader promised to send his boys to Ibadan to work on the party members, but he advised Dauda to return home as soon as possible. Dauda reassured him he would be on the next available flight to Abuja or Lagos. Dauda felt much better after the phone call. Dauda had seen a travel agency near the Victoria Station. He slipped on his jacket and walked down to the agency. He got there just before the agency closed for the day.

'Good evening Sir. How can we help?' the travel agent asked.

'Good evening. I want to buy a flight ticket to Nigeria.'

The agent tapped on his keyboard and smiled.

'Oh yes, we've got a seat on the British Airways flight to Abuja leaving Heathrow at 11o'clock tomorrow morning.'

'I'll take it,' replied Dauda.

'It'll cost you four hundred and seventy nine pounds.'

'You don't mean it. What class is that?' Dauda asked.

'It's an economy seat.'

'No way. I can't travel economy class. It's got to be first class travel.'

'Okay sir. There is no empty first class seat on any direct flight for the next three days, but we can get you a seat on Emirates with stopover in Dubai. The flight leaves tomorrow night at ten. There is a five hour stopover in Dubai before the flight departs for Abuja.'

'I'll take it.'

'How are you paying Sir?'

'I'll pay by bank debit card.'

Dauda returned to the hotel and found a letter redirected from The Kingdom Hotel to his attorney, who had sent it on to his new hotel through a courier. When he opened it, he found a demand notice for payment of the balance on his Bentley luxury car. The car had been delivered to the showroom in accordance with Dauda's instructions before the debacle in the hotel. He didn't finish reading the letter. He ripped the letter in two before tossing it into the bin. Acquiring a luxury car was the last thing on his mind at the moment. He had just received a phone call from a loyalist updating him of the ruckus in the House of Assembly between the dwindling number of his supporters and those bent on impeaching him.

Meanwhile, the PPN whips and enforcers descended on Ibadan. They used a combination of blackmail and sweeteners on the aggrieved party legislators. They reminded the legislators that they were due for re-election the following year, and nomination to stand again was not automatic. The leadership would look favourably on supporters of Governor Adams.

CHAPTER 25

'**H**ello, good morning, is that Grand Phoenix?'

'Good morning. This is Grand Phoenix. How can I help?' replied the receptionist.

'This is Tan Azeez, Minister of Finance, Western State. I would like to speak with Senator Lawanson.'

'I'm afraid he is not in the office. Can I take a message Sir?'

'No thanks, but can I talk to Dr. Lawanson.'

'Hold on Sir.'

'Good morning Sir, this is Dr. Mike Lawanson.'

'Good morning, this is Tan Azeez. I need to see the Senator urgently.'

'Dad is attending a meeting in the city and then travels abroad tonight. Can I book an appointment for you to see him when he returns next week?'

'No, this is an emergency. I must see him today. I am leaving Ibadan right now. Where can I meet him?'

Before Mike could answer, he continued.

'I've got vital new information on David's murder which I want to share with your father. Next week is too late. He needs to take action now.'

'Okay, let's meet at my father's house at 4 o'clock. I'll make sure dad is at home. Do you know how to get there?'

'Of course, I have been there several times in the past.'

Mike reached his father and conveyed the message to him.

Mike and his father were back in the Ikeja family house by 3 o'clock. Mr. Tan Azeez drove into the compound at 3.30 p.m.

It was apparent that this was not a social call. It was serious business, and Senator Lawanson usually held such in his private library where he would not be disturbed. Tan was led into the library by the housekeeper. As he walked in, the Senator and Mike stood up to greet him but Tan fell flat on his face, prostrating fully in front of Senator Lawanson, a traditional sign of complete submission and respect.

'Please get up Tan,' remarked the Senator.

Tan remained prostrate and begged for forgiveness.

'Sir, I wish to ask for your forgiveness. As you listen to my story, I don't want you to think that I am unworthy of your past support and endorsement. Please be patient with me and hear me out. It will become apparent why I took the decision that I made.'

'Okay, please get up. Let's hear what you've got to say,' remarked the Senator.

Mr. Azeez sat down, cleared his throat and started telling his story.

'Dauda Adams and I have known each other for over twenty five years. We first met at the Polytechnic where we were classmates. We were nonconformist and joined a fraternity where we swore oath of allegiance to each other and rather brazen in our attitude and activities. Dauda left the college after the Ordinary Diploma and joined the civil service, but I stayed for another two years to obtain the Higher Diploma in Finance. I worked in the private sector after my graduation and slowly rose through the ranks to become an Accountant in a multinational drug company. Dauda and I kept in touch with each other. About seven years ago he decided to go into politics and it wasn't long before I followed him into local government politics. We became councillors on the platform of the PPN. When we went into politics, Dauda took me to a shrine where we renewed our oath of allegiance. We swore to look out for each other and our families. We virtually became blood brothers. When the campaign for the last governorship elections started and Dauda indicated his interest, I became his campaign manager. The understanding was that I could choose whatever portfolio I wanted. We didn't have the funds to run a successful campaign so we sourced funds from some rich businessmen and religious leaders, many of them from the North with business interests in the West. We gave the commitment that their business interests in the West would be protected.

'Three and a half years ago we all gathered in Jos for the National convention of our party. You are aware of how the party nomination panned out. David won the nomination and Dauda became his running mate. It looked like an excellent team. Perhaps you do not know, but David and Dauda were classmates in primary school. We were celebrating when Dauda called me aside. He had a stern look. I asked him what was wrong. He said some kaffirs had defiled the Holy Koran and our financiers were very upset. They had decided that the offenders had to be taught a lesson. Our sponsors had discovered where the offenders would meet that night and we were charged with recruiting the band of faithful followers to discipline them. Dauda secretly recruited scores of thugs and local miscreants. A stash of money had been shared by the gang with the promise of more after the event. At about 10 p.m., we congregated on the outskirt of the village where David and his friends were holding their night vigil service. Dauda and I wore masks so that we couldn't be identified by any of the boys. Not that any of them seemed to care. They all appeared to be intoxicated. I suspect that their recruiter had given them an intoxicant to drink or smoke. The church service was going on behind closed doors when Dauda gave the sign for the boys to attack the worshippers. First they disabled and set their vehicles on fire. The ruckus continued for about half an hour in the car park in front of the small gospel church. Suddenly it dawned on us that they had stopped singing and had gone quiet. Then Dauda led the charge into the church. When Dauda shouted, God is great in Arabic, death to the infidels, the mob surged forward with their machetes and axes and started hacking at the door. Within minutes the door splintered and they gained access to the church. I was surprised that they went in with such force. This was not what Dauda had promised me. About twenty minutes later they exited the church and retreated after setting the church on fire. I could only guess at what transpired in the church. Dauda was not forthcoming, and he just told me we had to leave before the cops arrived. The miscreants vamoosed on foot and just melted into the surroundings, and we disappeared in the hired car we had concealed on the other side of the village.

'The following day I was shocked when the press reported that David and the Sexton had been murdered in a religious sectarian attack the previous night. I confronted Dauda immediately and accused him of perfidy. He swore that it was a terrible mistake. He insisted that David wasn't supposed to be in the church service. He wasn't the target but once they broke into the church and they discovered that the main target had escaped through the rear window into the bush, he could not restrain the boys. He said he tried to protect David but the boys would have none of it, and hacked him to death. The old man was pushed and must have died of shock.'

'Oh my God,' shouted Senator Lawanson, interrupting Tan.

'David must have suffered terribly. What a gruesome way to die.'

Tears welled in the Senator's eyes and he dabbed his eyes with a handkerchief. Mike was also struggling to control his emotions.

'Tan, this is very difficult for me. Why didn't you say anything when the case was being investigated by the police?'

'Sir, I wasn't convinced that Dauda was innocent but because he swore repeatedly that it was a terrible mistake, and then invoked the oath of silence. I had no choice but to keep quiet.'

'So why are you speaking up now?' asked Mike.

'Yes, I will also like to know. What happened to the oath of allegiance?' Senator Lawanson demanded to know.

'Dauda broke the oath. He betrayed my trust in the most despicable manner possible.'

'What happened?' Senator Lawanson demanded to know a second time.

'I'll come to that later Sir. We need to deal with the matter at hand first.'

'And what is that?' asked Mike.

'Dauda must be removed from power. He is a criminal. He is a convicted felon. Right now he is rallying the forces. His mentor, the Senate Leader has sent his men to Ibadan and they are using a combination of money and blackmail to castrate the House of Assembly. The PPN is in disarray in Ibadan. The opposition is standing firm but they don't have the numbers to impeach him. Dauda's supporters have falsified the London judgement. They are now saying that because he was not jailed, he was acquitted. If they are not countered, I am afraid Dauda may regain the Governorship.'

'What do you want me to do about it?'

'Sir, you are the only person who can stop the disarray and miscarriage of justice in the house. All you have to do is instruct your supporters and Dauda is toast. Once he is out of power, he can be arrested and tried for David's murder. From what he did to me and my family, I am convinced that nobody defiled the Koran. It was all contrived, an excuse by Dauda to eliminate David.'

'You are one of his aides, one of his most senior ministers. Why didn't you quit his government if he was so despicable?' asked the senator.

'It was difficult but after my daughter died I knew that I had to be wise, to be calm and pretend to be dumb, choosing the time and place of my revenge. The time has now come. I am willing to testify against him in court but I need you to ensure he does not escape justice.'

'Mike, what do you think?'

'Dad, Mr. Azeez has made a good point. If he returns to power we won't be able to arrest him. He will have immunity from prosecution, and once he gets wind of the case he'll destroy whatever evidence may remain and eliminate real and perceived enemies. We must make sure the House proceeds with his impeachment.'

That was it. Senator Lawanson picked up the phone and gave instructions to his lieutenants. They swung into immediate action and started working on party members in the House.

'Thank you Sir,' remarked Tan after the Senator dropped the phone.

'Now that we have taken care of that matter, I would like to know why you hate him so much.'

'I want him to feel the pain he inflicts on others. He needs to pay for what he did to my family, and what he has done to other families. Dogo for one has suffered irreparably.'

'Who is Dogo?' asked the senator.

'Dogo is the man who was convicted for the murder of David.'

'What happened to him? Where is he now?'

'He is languishing on death row in Jos prison.'

'Are you saying he was not guilty?'

'I don't know. What I know is that Dauda recruited him to lead the thugs and miscreants. He corrupted the poor man by flashing obscene amount of money in his face. On the day of the attack, both of them went into the Church armed and when they exited two men lay dead. Only two men, Dauda and Dogo know who actually killed David. During the trial Dogo denied killing David, insisting that a masked man hacked him to death. Of course when he said that, he was ridiculed by the prosecution. Dauda and I wore masks so that none of the miscreants could identify us. I believe Dogo was fingered by Dauda, and he was made a scapegoat. Dauda has no scruples. He will use anyone and anything to get what he wants, and if you stand in his path, he'll drive right through you like a juggernaut.'

'Mike, I am famished. Tell your mum to get us something to eat.'

'Nothing for me please,' replied Tan.

'We've been talking for the past two hours, and we need a break,' the Senator reiterated.

'You still have to tell us what Dauda did to you.'

'Okay Sir, I'll have a glass of soda or tonic water and some snacks.'

Mike disappeared and came back minutes later with refreshments for the three of them. They tucked into fried fish and barbecued chicken wings washed down with soft drinks.

CHAPTER 26

'This is a very personal story. The only thing I've got left are the memories, so I make sure I guard the memories jealously. I need to protect the name and memory of my daughter, so I want your commitment and Mike's that what I am about to tell you will stay within these four walls.'

'I promise,' replied the Senator.

'What about you Mike?'

'I promise to keep whatever you tell us about your family secret' replied Mike.

'Okay, this is it. After my secondary school education, I enrolled in the State Polytechnic at Apata to study Finance and Business Management. I met Dauda Adams who wanted to become an engineer. That was about thirty years ago. We became friends and as I told you earlier we joined one of the college fraternities. We led a chequered lifestyle holding parties and wooing the female students. Dauda had worked in the Police Force before enrolling, and had money to burn. He also had a Volkswagen Beetle car which was a rarity in those days, and led to many of the girls drooling and falling over each other to go out with us. After two years, Dauda passed his Ordinary Diploma and left the school. I stayed back for the Higher National Diploma.

'After Dauda left the Polytechnic, I mellowed somewhat. My outlook became more mature and less obscene. First I didn't have money to throw around like the Dauda days, but more important was the arrival of a petite beauty on the campus. The day I set my eyes on her, I wanted to befriend her. I didn't waste any time and approached her at the earliest opportunity. She was polite and well spoken. She said her name was Funmi Williams. Her father was a Professor of English at the University. She was quickly warned off any relationship by older students who knew my track record. The more she resisted, the more determined I was to win her heart. After almost a year, my persistence paid off. She agreed to attend the college end of year party with me. I was at my best, polished and respectful. My friends could not believe the transition from a lout to a gentleman. I had passed the first test but the ultimate test was winning over her father. She had told me that as an only child, her father meant everything to her. She would never disobey her father. During the Xmas holidays, Funmi invited me to the birthday party of an aunt. Professor Williams, vigilant and perspicacious correctly assessed the situation and called Funmi aside to find out who her guest was. Funmi said we were just friends from school, so her father asked me to join his table. I could not extricate myself and he engaged me in discussion, cleverly finding out things about me. He was a staunch Christian and he asked me which Church I attended. I told him I was a Muslim, though not a practising one. I thought that would assuage him but I was wrong. That was the end of the discussion. He excused himself and called Funmi to one side. When Funmi returned I sensed a change in her countenance. She was colder, not her usual bubbly self. She made excuses for no longer paying attention to me. I became uneasy and shortly afterwards I left the party.'

'I met up with Funmi on campus the following week after days of avoiding me. I tried to find out what I had done wrong but she was not forthcoming. I didn't give up and eventually one of her close friends and roommate told me her father had forbidden her from seeing me because it was taboo for the daughter of a Church choirmaster to start a relationship with a Muslim. He would never give his blessing should we decide to get married. Funmi's father had quoted a traditional proverb, "you don't sniff at what you are not going to eat." The friend begged me to leave Funmi alone. I was downcast and went into a period of introspection.'

'I have always been a fighter. It may take some time for me to make up my mind but once I do, I don't give up. I did my research and the following Sunday morning I pitched up in her Church and worshipped with the congregation. Unfortunately, Funmi did not attend the service. I learnt later that she had gone home for the weekend. The following Sunday, I attended the Church service again. This time Funmi was there but she barely acknowledged my greeting as we left the service. I persevered and continued attending the Church service. One Sunday two months after I started attending the Church, Funmi smiled and stopped to talk to me as we walked out of the Church.'

Mike interrupted Tan.

'Do you mean you attended the service weekly for two months despite being ignored?'

'Oh yes I did. If you want something so badly, you fight for it. If you don't give up eventually you will succeed.'

'So, what happened next,' Mike asked.'

'Tajudeen, what are you looking for in Church?' Funmi asked.

'I came here to worship along with you,' I replied.

'Tajudeen was my birth name, but I dropped it soon after I met Funmi and became known as Tan, short for my middle name Tanimola afi Oluwa, literarily meaning no one knows tomorrow except God.'

'Let me get back to the story. Funmi told me I was wasting my time because I couldn't worship God in Church on Sunday and then Allah in the mosque on Friday. She told me that I needed to know who I worshipped and why. She gave me a Bible and invited me to Bible Study during the week. I started attending the weekly Bible fellowship in addition to the Sunday service. Soon after that I became baptised and took the name Timothy. Funmi was a very smart girl. She invited her father to worship with us on the day I was billed to read the Bible to the congregation during the service. He was gobsmacked when I walked to the lectern and started reading the Bible. I greeted Funmi's father as I departed the service and he smiled in return. I had a spring in my step as I walked to the bus station. I knew the battle to win Funmi's heart was half won. The following year, just after I obtained my Higher National Diploma and Funmi passed the Ordinary Diploma, Professor Williams walked his daughter down the aisle and gave her away in marriage to me. We were overjoyed. We were soul mates and did everything together. I forgot to tell you that Dauda Adams was there at the beginning. He attended the wedding service and the reception. He was happy for us although he asked me before the wedding why I ditched the religion of my forefathers.'

'Our marriage was blissful. I joined the Accounts department of a multinational company as a trainee Accountant, whilst my wife went back to college for a degree in education. The day she acquired her bachelor's degree was one of the happiest days of my life. The happiest was the day I married my wife. We were particularly happy for my parents-in-law. They were proud that their daughter had achieved her life's ambition of getting a university degree. My wife started teaching in the government secondary school in the town. Our joy knew no bounds when six months later she became pregnant. The first trimester was uneventful. As the pregnancy progressed she started putting on weight, and then her feet started to swell and she became unwell. Her blood pressure became elevated and she had to be admitted into the Teaching Hospital. The doctors made a diagnosis of toxaemia of pregnancy and gestational diabetes. That was a frightening combination of complications of pregnancy. She was confined in hospital for most of the third trimester, yet the symptoms and signs did not abate. The doctors had a top level meeting with me and I agreed that although I wanted a live baby, my wife's life and health was more important. So they operated, a caesarean section was performed even though she was only thirty three weeks pregnant. The baby was premature and underweight and was managed in the neonatal intensive care unit for several weeks. The moment the baby was delivered, Funmi's blood pressure slowly returned to normal. Unfortunately the diabetes did not disappear, and she would have to receive treatment for diabetes mellitus for the rest of her life. We named the baby Ope Oluwa meaning thanks be to God. My wife and I had a meeting with the doctors and we learnt that there was a good chance the pre-eclampsia would return in subsequent pregnancies and the high blood pressure may be uncontrollable. There was a risk of intracranial bleeding or stroke from sustained uncontrolled high blood pressure. I was not willing to take any chance with my wife's health and wellbeing, so we agreed we would not have any more children. Ope was enough for us. She gained weight rapidly, becoming a strong infant, ahead of her peers in achieving various growth milestones. She was extremely beautiful. She had her mother's face and complexion. Her grandparents doted on her. My father died when I was a child, so I came to regard my father in-law as my dad, and called him dad. Dad died tragically in a road traffic accident two years after Ope was born. It was hard for Funmi to accept the loss. She had been so close to him and he seemed to have a solution to all problems. We never imagined that the end would come so soon. We stayed strong for my mother-in-law's sake, and for several months we brought her to live with us. Eventually, she wanted her independence and returned to her home, but we were never far from her.'

'After dad died I went back to my Accountancy job and Funmi resumed her teaching career. Ope continued to thrive. We saw Dauda from time to time. He was now a fledgling local politician. I went with him to one of the local PPN meetings and joined the political party but continued my full time job. Shortly afterwards Dauda won his first election and became a councillor in Ibadan. Dauda suddenly became affluent and more influential in the city. The more I went to these meetings, the more I got attracted to politics. Eventually I resigned from the company and became a full time politician, Most of Dauda's mentors were rich and powerful Muslim leaders, and Dauda often went for Jumat prayers with them on Fridays. One day Dauda mischievously called me Tajudeen in the presence of his mentors. They were surprised and said they thought I was a Christian. Before I could answer Dauda told them I was a Muslim but I only accompanied my wife to Church now and then. I was confused and didn't know what to say. That Friday afternoon, I went with them to the mosque. That is how I started living a double life, the mosque on Fridays and Church on Sundays. After a few weeks, I couldn't do it anymore. I confessed to my wife and begged her to allow me to return to the religion of my father. I promised not to interfere with her Christian worship. She was upset and agonised over the situation for several days. She sought her mother's advice and in the end Funmi gave me her blessing. I would never have tried that if dad was still alive.'

'My political fortunes improved and I also became a councillor. I continued as a Muslim but I fully kept my word and allowed my wife and daughter to go to Church. My mother-in-law passed away when Ope was twelve years old. A few months after her burial my wife suddenly informed me that she wanted to convert to Islam. I suspect the wives of some of my friends had been preaching to her and had given her a copy of the Koran, because she was knowledgeable about Islam when I quizzed her. She said she wanted us to do things together as we used to do when we first got married. So, both of us became practising Muslims. Ope followed her mother into Islam. Ope excelled in her studies and was acclaimed as a sensible level headed girl. She was head prefect in her secondary school in her final year. When I became Minister of Finance in Dauda's government, Ope gained admission into the university to study law at the age of eighteen.'

'During Ope's first summer vacation, Her mother and I decided to go for the Umra, the lesser Hajj in Mecca. We didn't want to leave an eighteen year old girl alone at home for a whole week. Dauda had a daughter who was only a few years older than Ope, and Dauda's wife was my wife's good friend. When my wife asked if Ope could stay with them, she gladly agreed. Ope stayed with the Adams for the week. She said it was a bit lonely when Dauda's daughter travelled to London on holidays two days after Ope arrived to stay with the family. Still we were grateful that our daughter had a safe place to stay.'

'The rest of the summer vacation was uneventful. Ope got a vacation job in the Governor's office and we got on with our lives. Soon the holidays ended and Ope returned to the university. One night, someone from the university health centre phoned our home to explain that Ope had taken ill suddenly and had been transferred to the teaching hospital. Funmi was away in Abuja for a teachers' conference, so I went alone to see her. I was shocked when I saw my normally bubbly daughter looking gaunt and pale. She could hardly speak and was burning with fever. I was also perplexed that she was on the gynaecological ward because the nurse who spoke to me on the phone gave me the impression that she had typhoid fever. I sat by her side for hours without any obvious improvement despite the intravenous fluids and antibiotics they were pumping into her veins. The nurses were not very forthcoming. They kept reassuring me that she would get better and that I should go home to get some rest and return the following morning to see the Consultant. I didn't believe them and at 11.00 p.m. I suddenly remembered that when the medical director came to my office to solicit government assistance for new equipment the hospital wanted to buy, I had promised we would give the hospital some funding so I reckoned he owed me. I retrieved his card from my wallet and phoned him. He was about to go to bed but he said he would be there within an hour. He was on the ward within thirty minutes. All the nurses who had been reticent suddenly became more forthcoming. The medical director asked me to sit in whilst the ward sister briefed him in the sister's office.'

'The ward sister started briefing the medical director.'

"Sir, Ope must have undergone a termination of pregnancy in some rundown clinic or by a quack."

'She turned to me and said': "This is what is known in common parlance as criminal or illicit abortion. She now presents with clinical signs and symptoms of septicaemia, blood poisoning in layman's term. The Gynaecology registrar reviewed her earlier tonight and said if she does not improve by the morning, she will undergo a laparatomy. A CT scan has already been booked for 8.00 a.m. tomorrow morning."

"Can I ask a big favour?"

"Go on Sir," replied the medical director.

"My wife is not in town. When she returns tomorrow I intend to tell her my daughter has got typhoid fever. That is the provisional diagnosis from the health centre. She will be devastated if anyone mentions criminal abortion."

"We will respect your wishes Sir," the nursing sister replied.

'I thanked both of them, and I then phoned my wife. I told her our daughter was in hospital with typhoid fever and she should try and catch the first flight out of Abuja. The driver would be waiting for her at Lagos airport. I reassured her that there was no reason to panic because Ope's condition was improving. I then returned to keep vigil by her bedside. When Ope opened her eyes, all she said was that she was sorry, very sorry for letting us down. When I asked who impregnated her and where she attempted the termination, she wouldn't answer. She was quiet for about an hour and appeared to be sleeping. When she opened her eyes it was about 5.00 a.m., she was very weak but I could read from her eyes that she wanted to say something. I moved near and placed my ears near her mouth. She summoned all her strength and uttered the shocking words.'

"Governor Adams, Mr. Dauda Adams made me pregnant and gave me money for the abortion. It started last summer when I stayed in his house."

'Oh my goodness, we caused this. If only we hadn't asked her to stay in Dauda's house. I bet that is why he sent his daughter to London, so he could have easy access to Ope. The man is the devil's incarnate.'

'As I was lost in my thoughts, her condition suddenly deteriorated, she became extremely pyrexial and breathless. I pressed the emergency alarm bell, and the night nurses rushed in and started working on her. I was asked to step outside and within thirty minutes she was on the way to the operating theatre. There was no time to wait for a CT scan any longer. The operation was prolonged and they were still in the theatre when my wife arrived in the hospital just after 9.00 a.m. Shortly after Funmi arrived, the medical director came round and took us to an empty waiting room. I could sense that the news was bad but Funmi wasn't expecting it. The medical director broke the news gently and expertly. The surgeons had tried their best but the infection and blood poisoning was too far gone as the bowel had perforated spewing its contents into the abdominal cavity. Ope was too weak and had not survived the complications of her condition.'

'Funmi let out a yowl, and then collapsed on the floor sobbing. I tried to be brave but tears still streamed down my face. I picked her up and we held each other and sobbed convulsively. The medical director was good. He stayed with us and expressed soothing words. My wife wiped her face and then asked when we could see our daughter. My wife hadn't yet accepted that Ope was dead. It was easier for me to accept because I saw the condition she was in before surgery. The medical director asked us to give him some minutes to ensure the body was made decent for us to view. Ope's corpse was laid in the recovery room with a single white sheet covering her body up to her lower neck. Her hair had been oiled and combed. She looked angelic. It looked like she was sleeping. We kissed her face, prayed and then left for home. The burial was arranged by our friends and relations.'

'Nine months after Ope died, my wife collapsed at work and was rushed to the teaching hospital. She was unconscious by the time she reached the hospital. She was admitted to the Intensive Care Unit but she did not recover. The doctors said she died of diabetic keto-acidosis but I know that she died of a broken heart. When our daughter died, my wife stopped caring about herself.

She stopped taking pride in her appearance, but worse still she stopped complying with doctors' instructions. I tried to get her to see a psychologist but she refused. I even got a psychiatrist to come and see her at home but she refused to see him. When she stopped taking her drugs or checking her blood sugar I knew that it was only a matter of time before she died. Unfortunately, when she passed on my life also ended. The only thing keeping me going was the desire to ensure that the guilty do not go unpunished. I was biding my time, and the time to strike has come.'

'Wow, you are great man. I admire you for your patience and wisdom. I agree that if you had tried to expose him at the time, nobody would have prosecuted him because of the immunity clause for governors. He would then have moved to eliminate or discredit you. He is a very evil man and I will do all in my power to ensure he does not return to office so that he can be tried for my brother's murder. I know he can't be nailed for what he did to your daughter, but we will nail him for David's murder.'

CHAPTER 27

Senator Abisayo had rallied the troops in the West and all the wavering legislators were now standing firm. The House of Assembly would meet the following day to deliberate on the motion for impeachment and vote on the motion if there was enough time, otherwise the voting would be fixed for another day. Nothing was being left to chance. A group which called itself 'Committee for Good Governance in Nigeria' had taken two full page adverts in the centre spread of the most widely read daily newspaper. The first page featured the photograph of Dauda Adams being led away by the Metropolitan Police after his arrest in Kingdom Hotel, and the photograph taken by Michelle of the half clothed Dauda holding his crotch on the hotel floor. The full judgement was reproduced on the second page of the advert. If any legislator was thinking of speaking in support of Dauda, they quickly changed their minds after the publicity onslaught. Legislator after legislator condemned Dauda for bringing the esteemed office of Governor into disrepute. Before they broke for lunch, the voting took place. Only two-thirds majority was needed to remove the Governor but ninety percent of the legislators voted for his impeachment.

Dauda Adams was waiting for news of the deliberations at the party regional headquarters in Ibadan. As soon as news of his removal from office was confirmed, special branch officers from Abuja descended on the PPN headquarters.

'We are looking for Mr. Dauda Adams,' a plain clothed officer asked the receptionist.

'Who are you?' the receptionist demanded to know.

He flashed his ID badge, and the receptionist waved him on.

'He is on the third floor, the party secretary's office.'

Some of the special branch officers ran up the stairs while one stayed with the receptionist so that Dauda could not be warned by phone.

'Mr. Dauda Adams, I am arresting you for the murder of Mr. David Lawanson. You have the right to remain silent. You have the right to a lawyer. You do not have to say anything but anything you say may be used in evidence against you in the court of law.'

The police then led Dauda down the stairs and he was driven straight to Lagos airport from where he was put on the plane to Abuja. When news of the arrest reached Mrs. Adams, she immediately got in touch with Senator Osazuwa on the phone, and then set out for Lagos. She had been told that Dauda was arrested by Special Branch officers from Lagos, so she drove straight to Force CID headquarters in the Ikoyi area of Lagos. If she thought she would receive any favours she was in for a shock. Her husband had fallen from grace and bad news spreads fast. When she arrived at the Force CID gate she was kept waiting for an hour before receiving clearance to enter the premises. After another hour at the reception desk, she was none the wiser about her husband's whereabouts. It appeared she would have to seek legal assistance before the police produced her husband. She left Force CID dejected. On the way home she placed another call to the Senate Leader. She didn't get through but left a message she had been unable to see Dauda in Lagos. Early the following morning, the Senate Leader returned the call. He told her that he was being detained in the police headquarters in Abuja and he had arranged for a Senior Advocate of Nigeria to represent Dauda. She was extremely grateful and relieved and said that she would soon be in Abuja.

The police interrogated Dauda in the presence of his lawyer. He was reticent and denied all the allegations. Despite the opprobrium poured on him by the press following his conviction in London and removal from office in Ibadan, Dauda still thought he would be exonerated. He did not know the strength of the case against him.

His lawyer, Chief Samson Morgan was one of the best advocates in the country and had helped many high profile accused go scot free in the past. Dauda displayed unusual arrogance and confidence all through the questioning. He clearly irritated the interrogating police officers. The police terminated the questioning after two frustrating hours. Chief Morgan tried to arrange bail but this was refused. The police were determined to exercise their right to hold the accused for 48 hours. The Divisional Police Officer (DPO) was furious after he was briefed about Dauda's arrogance. He would teach him a lesson he would not forget. He asked his men to put Dauda in a room in the 'M republic.' Dauda was detained in a decrepit cell on the outskirt of the compound next to a stagnant pond and a refuse dump. The room had a small open window with steel bars at the top of the wall. Dauda was tired from the day's ordeal and lay on the hard plank bed. As he tried to sleep, a mosquito flew past his ear and landed on his cheek. He dealt himself a heavy slap crushing the insect as it bit him. As he inspected the blood smear on his palm, another mosquito bit him on his neck, and another zoomed past his ear. Then scores of mosquitoes descended on the room like red arrow pilots during an air show. There was no mosquito net and he spent all night swatting and battling the insects. Apparently M republic stood for Mosquito republic, and the cell was reserved for difficult and uncooperative customers. The mosquitoes did not retreat until it was daylight. Dauda had been unable to get any sleep and by morning his eyes were blood-shot and he had a splitting headache.

When he returned to the interrogation room later that morning he could hardly keep his eyes open. Although he did not provide any useful information, he was now polite and respectful. It seemed that he had now realised that the fear of the mosquito cell was the beginning of all wisdom. He was rewarded that night by being moved to a normal cell where he was able to sleep without the menace of mosquitoes.

48 hours after Dauda was arrested, he was charged to court. He was brought before Justice John Paul and two other judges at the Abuja High Court. His supporters had been hoping that the case would be allocated to one of the more amiable judges. Justice John Paul, a doctor of law from Harvard was widely known as a stickler

for protocol and discipline. His greatest attribute was his eidetic memory. He could recall events and testimonies of witnesses accurately weeks and months after the events. His summing up was always meticulous and incomparable. Attorneys had to be at their very best when appearing before him otherwise they would be ridiculed. This was the man who would decide Dauda's fate. Right from the outset, the judge informed the court that he had cleared his diary, and therefore expected the lawyers and the prosecution would work towards speedy resolution of the case. Frivolous calls for adjournment would not be tolerated. The first appearance was brief. The accused stood to confirm his name. The Director of Public Prosecution (DPP) read the charges and explained that the State would provide evidence that Dauda Adams conspired with others at large to murder Dr. David Lawanson and the Church Sexton, Papa Abraham, and also to commit arson. Chief Samson Morgan stood up to announce he was representing the accused. The judge adjourned the case till Thursday morning. The prosecution and defence team had two days to finalise their strategies. The prosecution had submitted the names of their prosecution witnesses. Tan Azeez and Dogo Kontagora were the chief prosecution witnesses. The defence team had the right to know and was given the list of the witnesses.

Senator Lawanson was in court for the preliminary hearing. After the case was adjourned, he went in to discuss the next line of action with the DPP. It was then that he learnt that the defence had received a list of their witnesses. He almost wet his pants. He was surprised that the DPP did not fully understand what Dauda and his group were capable of. He tried not to panic but he quickly took his leave and rushed home. He had to find a safe home for Tan, but he was in Abuja whilst Tan was in Ibadan. He phoned Tan and briefed him on the need to stay vigilant and alert. Tan agreed that he had to be careful till the case was over. The Senator told him he would send the Secretary to the government to see him later in the day.

Anita put on tight jean trousers and jeans jacket, wig and sunglasses. Unless you were a close friend or relation, you wouldn't have recognised her. As Secretary to the Government she had a licensed firearm. She hardly ever carried it but this was one occasion when it might come in handy. She tucked the Smith & Wesson double action .45 semiautomatic compact pistol into the inner pocket of her jacket. She jumped into an unmarked government SUV and headed for the College Road residence of Tan. She arrived at the gated entrance just after 6 p.m. Tan had briefed his security man he was expecting an important female visitor. She honked once and the gate swung open. She paused to talk to the security man asking him to contact her if ever there was any problem with her brother in-law, his boss. She left her card and asked him to keep it securely and then gave him a hefty tip. The briefing was over in less than five minutes, and she then drove onwards to the side of the house backing her car into the garage as the garage door was open. She opened the rear door of the SUV and hauled the travelling bag containing the gifts she had brought for him. Tan came out and helped to carry the bag into the house through the inner garage door. Tan called the security man on the intercom and told him he didn't want to receive any more visitors once his guest had departed. He was tired and would be retiring to bed for the evening. Thirty minutes after she arrived, Anita drove out again. The security man again thanked her profusely. He looked across the driveway to the main house and noticed that the lights were switched on in the downstairs living room. The boss was probably having his supper or listening to the news on TV. One hour later the living room lights went off, and the lights came on in the bedroom upstairs. Oga must be tired. He is already in his bedroom.

The security man looked at his watch and it was only 8 o'clock. One hour later, the bedroom lights were switched off. The security man sat down in his gate house and started munching his meal of beans and gari with cow hide. He took his time, savouring every mouthful and ate slowly. When he was done, he stretched his limbs and yawned loudly. He walked round the compound to keep himself awake. It was now almost 11 o'clock and it was getting a bit windy and chilly. Perhaps it was going to rain tonight. He hurried to his gate house, and thrust his hand behind his bags packed in one corner and retrieved a bottle of his favourite drink, known as *ogogoro* in local parlance. It was a local brew, stronger than vodka and guaranteed to drive away the cold. He pulled opened the cover, and took a swig of the hot stuff. It warmed him up and he felt good.

'*I dey kampe,* I feel good,' exclaimed the security man.

He sat on the doorstep of his security house, struggling to stay awake. Suddenly, he could hear a commotion outside the gate and looked through a peep hole in his gate house. He saw a gang of fierce looking men wielding guns. This didn't look good. He wasn't going to wait to find out who they were or what they wanted. He slipped behind the gate house and crawled into a hole which led to a culvert beneath the road. He was already outside the compound half immersed in effluent from the houses in the neighbourhood. The men were walking on the road just above him and were now banging on the gate. One of them was particularly irked that the gate had not been opened promptly.

'Where is this stupid gateman?'

'I saw him opening the gate for a guest earlier this evening, and he hasn't gone out. When we get in I'll shoot him in both feet to teach him not to be so disrespectful in future.'

'Tiger, we don't want to make too much noise so as not to wake the target. Just climb over the gate and open it for us.'

The security man shuddered and shivered when he heard this. These were assassins looking for his boss. Fear gripped him and he spontaneously wet his pants. Not that it mattered too much as he was already immersed in dirty water. Few minutes later the men entered the compound and their voices receded as they approached the main house. He thought he heard one of them rifling through his things and thought. That must be the one looking for me, to teach me a lesson.

The gang came with their own locksmith and the steel external doors only delayed their entry. Fortune had smiled on the gang. There was power failure in the neighbourhood and the standby electricity generators were providing electricity to several houses in the area with the noise from the generators masking their break in.

The men knew where Tan's bedroom was located. They had been properly briefed. Two of them were in the bedroom within minutes whilst the remaining two stood guard by the front and rear doors just in case their target managed to escape from his bedroom and wanted to make a dash for dear life. The fifth intruder stood guard by the main gate whilst the designated driver sat at the wheel. Tan was fast asleep when they tiptoed into his bedroom. He was sleeping with his back to the door, almost completely covered by a blanket. The first man pumped six bullets into the chest of the victim. The other assassin did not believe in wasting his bullets. He fired only a single shot into the back of Tan's head. The victim must have died instantly because he did not stir or utter a single sound. The bed sheet was soaked in blood.

'Gringo, let's go. The man is dead.'

'Okay, let's grab a few things here and ransack the sitting room so the police will think it's a robbery gone wrong.'

Gringo grabbed a Rolex wrist watch from the table and they both made their way to the sitting room, where they turned over the chairs and removed valuable electronic gadgets.

'Boys, let's go. The idiot is dead.'

One hour after they arrived at the house they were gone. The security man waited another half hour before he crawled out of his hiding place. He ran to the house and was shocked when he saw the state of the house. He ran up the stairs and peeped into Tan's room. He almost collapsed when he saw the bullet riddled body on the bed. He exited quickly and changed into dry clothes. He waited for the first sign of dawn, retrieved the card Anita gave him, locked the gate and made his way to her house. He arrived at Anita's residence just before 6.00 a.m. The police guards kept the dishevelled man at the gate for several minutes. Then he remembered the card and when he produced it and said she was expecting him. They phoned the main house and he was allowed in. He relayed the traumatic ordeal as best he could. Anita asked if he had told anyone else and he said no. She asked him to keep quiet about the whole thing as it was now a police matter, and she didn't want him to be wrongly implicated. He was not to return to the building until further notice. Anita organised a private ambulance and by 9.00 a.m. she arrived at the house with her police guards and ambulance staff. The corpse was removed in a body bag to the morgue, and the house was sealed off by the police as it was now a crime scene. Anita briefed Senator Lawanson.

The Director of Public Prosecution was in Jos to interview Dogo Kotangora at the prison on Wednesday morning prior to being transferred to Abuja later in the day. The Senator's men had earlier visited Dogo and he had given an undertaking to testify and avenge the perfidy of the man in the mask. As the prisoners went for morning exercise, there was ruckus at the bottleneck hallway. No one knew what started it but when it was all over and the warder's regained control, Dogo lay dead in a pool of his blood. Someone had slashed his neck and severed his carotid artery. He must have died within minutes.

The country was still digesting the news of the murder of Tan Azeez by armed robbers when the rumour mill became rife with the story of the death of Dogo, the second major prosecution witness in the trial of Dauda Adams.

'We failed. We failed miserably,' lamented Senator Lawanson when he heard the news. The DPP was dejected when he reached the prison and learnt that Dogo had been killed that morning. He remembered the Senator's warnings that Dauda was a formidable and dangerous foe. He placed a call to Senator Lawanson. The Senator implored him not to be despondent, and requested that they meet in Lagos later in the day to reassess the situation and plan the way forward. They fixed an appointment for 2 o'clock at a secret meeting house.

CHAPTER 28

Abuja High Court One was packed full with journalists, politicians and members of the public well ahead of 8.00 a.m. when the proceedings were due to commence. Hundreds of stragglers were kept outside a safe cordon created by the police. Dauda was brought in by two armed policemen at 7.45 a.m. His handcuffs were removed as soon as he sat down in the dock. He stood up and looked towards the public gallery with a smirk on his face. He waved to his supporters and they responded with loud cheers. He had heard the news of the demise of his adversaries and felt confident that the tide had turned in his favour. Senator Lawanson and his family were seated barely two rows behind him on the prosecution side. He looked at them with disdain and then gave arrogant thumbs up.

At exactly 8 o'clock, Justice John Paul entered the court followed by two other judges. With the court declared open, the DPP proceeded to address the court.

'My Lords, the State is ready to open the case against Mr. Dauda Adams. The State will prove beyond reasonable doubt that three years ago Mr. Dauda Adams and others at large unlawfully killed one David Lawanson and Papa Abraham in the village of Tomas near Jos. The State hereby calls on the first prosecution witness, Mr. Tan Azeez.'

The old man sitting next to Senator Lawanson stood up and walked briskly to the witness stand. Dauda and the defence team looked on with disbelief. Dauda was wondering what the jokers were playing at.

The whole country had been told that Tan was dead and lay in a morgue. So who was this impostor?

When the witness reached the witness stand, he tore off his facial mask meticulously made by a theatre arts specialist and then removed his wig. The spectators and the defence team were aghast. There were murmurings of disbelief. Then there was a massive noise in the front of the court as Dauda collapsed and landed awkwardly on the floor. The policemen and the defence team rushed to his aid. His political aide vaulted the barrier and joined the first aiders. Dauda was cold and clammy. Ambulance men arrived at the scene pretty quickly and resumed the resuscitation. Justice John Paul announced that the court would go on a one hour recess. Ten minutes into the resuscitation, Dauda Adams came round fully. As he was brought up into his chair, he sighted Mr. Lucky Johnson, his political assistant amongst the first aiders. He lunged at him with the agility of a tiger in full pursuit of a prey and dealt him a heavy slap which sent the hapless man tumbling. Then Dauda went into a tirade.

'You are an incompetent fool. I thought you said you had taken care of the matter.'

'We did,' Lucky answered meekly, partially recovered from the bashing.

'You did? Then what is that rat doing here?'

'Mr. Adams, please keep quiet. You are complicating our case,' Chief Morgan admonished. Unfortunately, Dauda wasn't done.

'Don't mind the idiot. This is what happens when you send a boy to carry out a man's job.'

Dauda's wife shouted at him to keep quiet and follow his lawyer's directive. This worked and he sat mute in his chair. Lucky made his way to his seat. The court settled down and the case resumed after the recess.

Mr. Azeez took the oath and the DPP was about to begin the cross examination when Chief Morgan stood up and asked to approach the bench. The lead judge was irritated because he had warned all counsels that he would not tolerate any obfuscation. All the same, he allowed the defence counsel to approach, and the DPP followed. Chief Morgan told the judge that there had been a breach of trust between him and his client and he wanted to withdraw from the case. The judge refused the application and asked the lawyer to mend the breach between him and his client.

The DPP commenced the questioning.

'Please can you tell us your name and job description?'

'I am Tanimola Azeez, known by most people as Tan Azeez. I am the Minister for Finance in the Western State.'

'Do you know the accused and how long have you known him?'

'I have known Mr. Dauda Adams for about thirty years. We were classmates in the Polytechnic, and have kept in touch with each other over the years. When he became the Governor of the West three years ago, he appointed me his Minister for Finance.'

As Tan relayed his past relationship with Dauda, the accused sank in his chair. His head dropped. He looked like a defeated man.

'Mr. Azeez, please tell the court what happened in Jos during the convention of the People's Party of Nigeria, and in the village of Tomas on the night Mr. David Lawanson was selected as the People's Party of Nigeria's candidate for the governorship election.'

'My Lords, Mr. Adams and I travelled together with the late David Lawanson and Chief Olu Thomas to Jos for the PPN convention. Chief Thomas had been chosen at our local meeting in Ibadan to run as David's deputy. We got to Jos some days ahead of the convention to do our ground work and cement relationships. We quickly realised that the executive committee of the party was going to favour Christian-Muslim tickets in regions where there was a mix of religions like ours. David and Olu were both Christians, but our opponents had a Muslim-Christian team vying for nomination.'

Chief Morgan rose and interrupted the evidence.

'Objection, my Lords.'

Justice John Paul turned to him.

'On what basis are you objecting?'

'My Lord, the evidence by the witness is irrelevant.'

The DPP intervened before Chief Morgan could continue.

'My Lords, the witness is trying to build a foundation of the close relationship between him and the accused.'

'Objection overruled, witness can continue,' the judge ruled.

'My Lords, as I was saying when we realised the other team was likely to be favoured by the executive despite all the hard work we had put in, we sat down to serious deliberations. We had only one option. Chief Thomas was magnanimous and stepped down but asked for one dispensation. He wanted to be allowed to choose his replacement from the party. There were five of us in the inner caucus and we all thought that was reasonable. Mr. Dauda Adams was a campaign operative and not a member of the inner caucus. Chief Thomas nominated his half-brother Alhaji Lookman Thomas who was the majority leader in the House of Assembly. He was a distinguished and respected party member. Three of us in the group supported Chief Thomas but David Lawanson made no comment. When we pressed him for his opinion, he rambled on and on about his respect for Alhaji Lookman Thomas but was of the view that he would prefer Mr. Dauda Adams as his running mate. We were very surprised because Dauda was junior to Lookman in the party, but David said he was comfortable with Dauda as they had been classmates in primary school even though they had lost touch with each other in the intervening years. In the end we reached a compromise, Chief Thomas would be rewarded with a shot at membership of the Federal House of Representatives and David was allowed to pick Dauda as his running mate. We campaigned together and were successful. David would stand for Governor and Dauda would be his deputy. It was agreed that if we won the election, I would become the Minister of Finance.'

'Mr. Azeez, please tell the court what happened after the election,' the DPP asked.

'As soon as the party nomination results were announced in the morning, Dauda came to me with the report that some non-believers had defiled the Holy Koran and our financiers wanted us to give them a good hiding, teach them a lesson they would never forget. He would recruit the mob to carry out the assaults but we would go with them to ensure they carried out the operation appropriately. I was aghast but he told me I had nothing to fear, as we would not be identified; we would wear masks. That night we made a rendezvous with the gang of thugs and miscreants on the outskirts of Tomas village. One of the thugs was clearly their leader, a burly six footer who I later came to know as Dogo Kotangora. We were led by the masked Dauda Adams and descended stealthily on the worshippers in the gospel church. The vehicles parked in front of the church were damaged and set ablaze. I stood behind with a small boy who I restrained from joining the ruckus because I reckoned he was too young to partake in such mayhem. From the distance, the church entrance was illuminated by the burning cars, as we watched two men gain entrance into the church. One of them was the masked Dauda. The little boy, Sule, told me the other man was his older brother Dogo. So, only Dogo and Dauda went into the church.

Dauda and Dogo exited the church and we disappeared. Dauda was quiet as we went back to our hotel rooms. I was shocked when the newspapers reported the following day that David Lawanson and Papa Abraham, the church Sexton had died in a religious uprising the previous night. I rushed to Dauda's room and challenged him. He broke down in tears and admitted that although unplanned, Dogo had accidentally killed the two men. I didn't know what to believe but subsequent events which I have here on tape prove conclusively that Dauda planned and executed the murder of his old classmate and friend.'

Tan held a cassette tape aloft and waved it in the air.

There was loud murmuring in the court when Tan made this pronouncement.

The DPP stood up and addressed the court.

'No further questions for the witness but I would like the court to listen to the tape presented by the witness and then to accept it as exhibit one.'

'Objection my Lords, this is not admissible in law. We cannot vouch for the authenticity of this tape,' Chief Morgan protested.

'My Lords, I plead that the court be allowed to listen to the tape before deciding whether it is authentic or not.'

Justice John Paul gave his ruling.

'Okay, I will allow it but if the content is irrelevant, I will not hesitate to order that the cassette player be stopped.'

The DPP produced a cassette player and inserted the tape. He depressed the play button and Tan's voice came on. He could be heard questioning Dauda as to why he shopped Dogo to the police. Dauda replied that Dogo's family had been well taken care of financially. He said that in life there were losers and winners, and Dogo was a loser and so was David Lawanson. Tan was never to bring up the matter of David's demise again. After all he had kept his promise by making Tan Minister of Finance. Tan verified the date of this conversation by asking them to get ready for an important State event that evening. The DPP switched off the cassette player and then removed the cassette.

'My Lords, experts have verified the voices on the tape as those of the witness and the accused. I wish to submit this tape as exhibit one.'

The judges accepted the exhibit.

'Any questions for the witness from the defence counsel?' the lead judge asked.

'Oh yes my Lord.'

Chief Samson Morgan proceeded to question Tan. Tan was intrepid and perspicuous. The more the counsel probed, the deeper the hole he dug for the accused. After only ten minutes, the attorney gave up.

'No further questions, my Lord.'

'The witness may step down,' declared the lead judge.

The DPP stepped forward.

'The State calls the second witness, Sule Kotangora.'

Sule corroborated Tan's testimony regarding the night of the murder. Then he stated that his brother had confided in him that when he and the masked man entered the church, the masked man rushed forward and hacked the younger man, who his late brother later discovered was David Lawanson, to death with his machete. Nobody touched the old man. When he saw his colleague being butchered, he held his chest, screamed and keeled over. When he moved near to check on the old man's condition, he was dead.

Chief Morgan tried to discredit Sule but he stood his ground.

'My brother would not lie to me. He swore that the masked man killed the younger man.'

Chief Morgan had been weighed down by the evidence against his client and the demeanour of the accused. By the time the proceedings ended that day, Dauda's goose was cooked. At 5 p.m. the judge adjourned the case till the following morning.

Dauda was returned to prison custody. As the people trooped out of the courtroom, a police officer walked to Dauda's aide and read him his rights.

'Mr. Lucky Johnson, I am arresting you for the attempted murder of Mr. Tan Azeez and for attempting to pervert the course of justice. You have the right to remain silent, but anything you say may be used in evidence against you in the court of law. You have the right to a lawyer during interrogation.'

This was a direct result of the outburst by Dauda Adams in court during the recess. Lucky Johnson was taken away in handcuffs.

When they reached the police headquarters, the interrogating police inspector set the scene in the presence of Lucky's lawyer.

'Mr. Lucky Johnson, I am afraid that Mr. Dauda Adams has helped us to complete the jig saw puzzle of the attempt on Mr. Tan Azeez's life and the murder of Dogo Kotangora. All you have to do is reconfirm your role in the whole saga and we will look favourably on your cooperation and perhaps this could be reflected in sentencing.'

'No comments,' replied Lucky.

'Mr. Johnson, it may interest you to know that we have already arrested two of the hired assassins. During the operation, they helped themselves to Mr. Azeez's music system and other valuables. The police caught them as they were trying to sell these items. The men are squealing. They know that the penalty for murder is death by hanging.'

'But they didn't kill anyone,' replied Lucky.

'Don't forget that Dogo died.'

'I had no hand in that operation,' replied Lucky.

'What did you have a hand in? If you don't tell us the truth, you'll go down with the hit men for murder and attempted murder. It may take a long time but eventually we'll find you and the hit men guilty and you'll die by hanging. The best result is life imprisonment. You will spend the rest of your life doing hard labour in a prison on the verge of the Sahara desert in very inclement weather. It is baking hot in those towns with temperatures soaring to 50 degrees centigrade in the hot season, and blinding sandstorms in the harmattan season.'

Lucky was terrified. He looked at his lawyer who intervened.

'Can we have a ten minute break whilst I speak privately with my client?'

The police officers obliged and left the interrogating room. When they returned, the lawyer addressed the policemen.

'My client wants a plea bargain. Before he says anything that may incriminate him he wants assurance he will be tried on a lesser charge for his cooperation.'

'We don't make the decision, but if you say everything that you know and agree to testify against Dauda Adams for authorising the whole operation we'll appeal to the DPP to drop the attempted murder charge and replace it with a minor charge of attempting to pervert the course of justice.'

'Will I know the DPP's decision before I testify?' asked Lucky.

'Of course, you will.'

'Okay, that's good enough for me. After the preliminary hearing when it became known that Mr. Azeez and Dogo would testify against Mr. Adams, he managed to slip a note to me with instructions that Mr. Tan Azeez had to be eliminated that night or by morning at the latest. As a political organiser, I know some of these boys. They have their uses when we need some muscle or unorthodox control or discipline of our adversaries. We knew they had firepower but we had never used them to eliminate anyone. This time when I contacted their boss, he was only too willing to carry out the assignment. They were supposed to eliminate Azeez. Apparently, they failed, but we didn't know until Tan appeared in court.'

'How did you pay the men?'

'We paid them from a special security account set up by Governor Adams, sorry ex-Governor Adams.'

'Do you know who could have arranged Dogo's death?'

'I have no idea. Perhaps it was a coincidence, or perhaps someone else was given that project.'

'So, are you willing to testify in court that Dauda Adams authorised the murder of Tan Azeez?'

'I will, providing the DPP meets his side of the bargain.'

'Okay, you will hear from the DPP tomorrow morning and you may be required to testify for the prosecution in the afternoon.'

Both parties were satisfied and the interrogation concluded.

CHAPTER 29

The court reconvened on Friday morning. The court was packed as usual. Before the proceedings commenced, the DPP approached the bench and spoke in a hushed tone to the judges. The judges summoned the lead defence counsel. No one else heard what they were saying but it was apparent that whatever it was, they reached accord, as the DPP and Chief Morgan soon returned to their desks.

The DPP called the next witness and continued to build up the case against Dauda Adams. The defence by normally ebullient Chief Morgan was puny and perfunctory. Just before the court went on lunch recess, the DPP stood up and made an announcement which startled and dismayed almost everybody in the court room.

'The State calls Mr. Lucky Johnson to the witness box.'

As Lucky walked to the box, Dauda could not contain his fury. He jumped up and vented his spleen at his aide.

'Aargh!, Lucky, you have joined my detractors. God will punish you.'

The lead judge was irritated and warned the accused.

'Defence Counsel, please control your client. If there is any further outburst, I will charge the accused for contempt of court.'

Dauda sat down slowly, murmuring to himself as he did that a man's enemies are those of his household.

The DPP ignored Dauda and pressed on with his questioning as soon as Lucky took the oath to tell the truth and nothing but the truth.

'Please tell the court your name and official position.'

'I am Lucky Johnson, Political Assistant and Special Adviser to the former Governor of the Western State, Mr. Dauda Adams.'

'How long have you worked for Mr. Adams, and what is the nature of your work?

'I have worked for Mr. Adams for the past four years, from the time of the gubernatorial election, and continued to do so until his removal from office. My remit is mainly to ensure the safety and security of my boss.'

'Is it true to say that in general you would carry out his instructions without questioning?'

'That is correct,' replied Lucky.

'What instructions did he give you with regards to Mr. Tan Azeez at the commencement of this trial?'

'When it became apparent that Mr. Tan Azeez was going to testify against Mr. Adams, he gave me instructions through a coded written message that Mr. Tan Azeez was to be eliminated as soon as possible.'

There was loud murmuring in court. The court was called to order and the questioning resumed.

'Do you still have the instruction?'

'No Sir, I tore the sheet of paper and flushed it down the toilet. Our operational rule is never to keep anything which may incriminate us.'

'Is there any proof that Mr. Dauda Adams gave any such instruction?'

'Last Tuesday as Mr. Tan Azeez stood to testify, Mr. Adams collapsed and a recess was called. When he came round in court and saw me, he poured invectives on me and slapped me before he was restrained. Many people, including your good self and Chief Morgan were witnesses to Mr. Adams accusing me of incompetence for failing to arrange the murder of Mr. Azeez as instructed by him.'

'No further questions for this witness.'

'The defence counsel may proceed to question the witness,' declared Justice John Paul.

'My Lord, the defence has no question for this witness.'

Lucky Johnson stepped down and the court went on a one hour recess for lunch.

After lunch, the defence counsel declined to call the accused to the witness box. The DPP proceeded to summarise the case against the accused. He then stated that Dauda Adams had always been a mendacious and manipulative fiend. It was the height of perfidy that he planned and personally executed a friend who plucked him out of obscurity and gifted him with the exalted position of deputy Governor. He then manoeuvred himself into the position of chief investigator, manipulating the courts to convict a hapless small fry. My Lords, Mr. Dauda Adams is a devious and evil man and the State has proved conclusively that he killed Dr. David Lawanson, and that he also attempted to eliminate Mr. Tan Azeez. The State asks the court to pass the maximum sentence of death by hanging on the accused.

Chief Samson Morgan then began his summing-up. His submission was more like a plea for mitigation rather than defence. This was a bad case and he knew it. Mr. Dauda Adams had not helped his cause by losing control in court and blurting out incriminating statements. The lead judge then adjourned the case for one week to allow them consider all the evidence and write their judgement.

The week passed quickly. When they arrived in court the following Friday, the court was guarded by heavily armed policemen. There was the expectation that a momentous event was about to unfold. Justice John Paul announced that the verdict was unanimous. He spent thirty minutes delivering the judgement. It was a harsh critique of the life style of Dauda Adams. The judge told Dauda that he was dishonest and dangerous. There was no evidence that anyone had defiled the Holy Koran. He had lied and exploited religion to achieve his political ambitions. He had committed a heinous crime, eliminating someone who extended the hand of friendship to him. By his actions he did not qualify to be called a normal human being and therefore should be put away for the rest of his life, where he could no longer wreak havoc on innocent people. He then sentenced him to life in prison without parole.

As the sentence was pronounced, Dauda turned round and saw his wife and daughter sobbing in the public gallery but there were loud cheers and jubilation amongst the Lawanson supporters. He was cuffed and led down to the holding cell on his way to start a new life in Abuja prison.

The first night of the rest of his life was momentous. He could not sleep in his solitary cell, and stayed awake all night mulling over his life. In a few weeks he had fallen from the lofty position of His Excellency the Governor to a resident of the commander in-chief's prison. He agreed with the judge that he had been a victim of his inordinate ambition. Morning came and he had a splitting headache. After breakfast he reported to the Health Centre and was given two Paracetamol tablets for his headache. He was then given the opportunity to phone his family. He had a few minutes to talk to his wife. He desperately needed some money and she also wanted to see him because they had not been able to have a proper discussion since he returned from his ill-fated London trip. Visiting time was the following Saturday afternoon and she would be there.

Nike Adams was at the prison gate well ahead of the visiting time of 4 o'clock. She was first in the queue of visitors. She looked a bit apprehensive, not sure exactly what to expect but she had the premonition that the visit would not end well. The huge metal gate swung open at 4.00 p.m. and the visitors were led through to the identification and examination room. Nike was frisked by a female prison officer and then led through to a chair in a vast meeting hall. She sat and waited whilst the warder peered through the door to another room and called her husband.

'Dauda Adams.'

'Sir,' replied Dauda.

'Your visitor is here.'

'Thank you Sir,' he replied.

Nike marvelled at the vicissitudes of life. Two months ago, Dauda was a Governor with all the trappings of power and affluence but he was now a common prisoner, the lowest of the low. Dauda had adapted quickly, and learnt to give the warders the utmost respect. She was still lost in thought when Dauda pulled a chair and sat in front of her.

'Good afternoon dear, thank you for coming.'

'Good afternoon dear,' replied Nike.

'What is life like inside? How is the food? Are you able to sleep soundly at night?' Nike rattled off the questions without waiting for him to answer.

'Not too bad, the first night was bad but I have now readjusted and I sleep fairly well. I exercise a lot and get myself so tired that I drop off to sleep almost as soon as I hit our wooden bed. Did you bring the money?'

'Oh yes I did. This is it.'

She bent over and passed a bundle of one hundred Naira notes carefully packed and concealed in a copy of the Holy Koran to him, whispering in his ear as she handed over the package.

'Twenty thousand Naira in hundred Naira notes.'

'Thank you, thank you very much,' replied Dauda.

The couple were quiet for the next five minutes. They were startled by the announcement over the tannoy that the visitors had thirty minutes to go.

'Dauda, I need to know the truth. Did you kill David as alleged during the trial?'

'No, I didn't,' replied Dauda.'

'Then, how did he die?'

'It was an accident,' replied Dauda.

'What sort of accident?' Nike demanded to know.

'Nike, trust me it was an accident. Dogo was the one involved, not me.'

'Okay, let's assume it was an accident. Why did you guys go there to attack them in the first place?'

Dauda was mute. When he didn't offer any answer, his wife pressed on.

'What was that accusation about trying to eliminate Tan Azeez?'

Dauda did not offer any response

'And Dogo is dead too. Did you have a hand in that too?'

'No, I had no hand in that,' replied Dauda.

'Why don't I believe you? I don't think I know you anymore. Perhaps I never knew you. I must have been living with a stranger all these years.'

'Don't be like that. We need to stand together, and look to the future,' stated Dauda.

'What future? There is no future for us. You don't seem to

realise you were sentenced to life imprisonment. You've destroyed our future by your greed and criminality.'

'I am sorry I've put you in this predicament. Please give my love to our daughter. I will be expecting you on the next visiting day in a fortnight.'

Nike did not reply. She just shrugged her shoulders. Shortly afterwards the horn blared and visiting time was over. Dauda hugged Nike and she departed.

'Goodbye my dear,' shouted Dauda, waving as Nike walked briskly out of the room. She did not reply or look back.

Over the next week, the Prison Governor received many applications for special visits from political heavyweights in Abuja. He managed to fend off most of them but a few still managed to see Dauda bringing gifts and money. The Governor was peeved but couldn't do much about it. Then the police detectives from Jos came to question Dauda about the murder of Dogo in prison. This presented an opportunity for the prison Governor to be rid of this problem. He contacted the Comptroller of Prisons and argued that it would be easier for the police to investigate Dogo's murder if Dauda was transferred to Jos Prison. The prison boss agreed, and the Governor was directed to arrange the transfer within a week. The visiting time had just expired and Dauda was still moping at the failure of his wife to visit as expected when a burly warder came into his cell and gave him the news that he was to be transferred to Jos the following afternoon. He was immediately overcome with fear and he swooned feeling faint and only managing to steady himself by holding on to the cell door. The warder exited the cell and locked the door behind him. Dauda sat in the corner and held his head in his hands. His mind went straight to Dogo. He was being thrown into the lion's den. How would he cope in Dogo's backyard? His anonymity had been compromised by the trial. He was sure some of the inmates would be Dogo's friends. There was the other matter of the assassins his boys paid. They would still be in prison, and may want to silence him so that they are never exposed. He didn't know them but they knew him. He was now very afraid and was sweating profusely.

That night, Dauda was granted the opportunity to phone his family before his transfer but instead he placed a call to the residence of the Senate leader.

'Hello, good evening?

'Good evening,' replied the voice from the other end.

'Mrs. Osazuwa.'

'Yes, who is speaking?'

'Nkechi, it is me, Dauda Adams.'

'How are you?' Nkechi asked, not sure what else to say.

'I am not so good and that is why I want to speak to the leader.'

'I am afraid he is not in, he's gone for a meeting,' Nkechi lied. The Senate leader was sitting by her listening to the nine o'clock news on TV.

'Please tell him that I need him to intervene on my behalf to stop my transfer to Jos. I have just been informed that I am being transferred to Jos prison tomorrow afternoon. He can stop it by calling the Comptroller of Prisons. I can't go to Jos, I am afraid I won't survive it.'

'Okay, I will relay your concerns. Good night.'

She dropped the phone before he could reply. Nkechi turned to her husband.

'Dear, did you get a gist of that phone call from Dauda Adams?'

'Not exactly, what does he want?'

'He is being transferred to Jos prison tomorrow but he doesn't want to go. He wants you to intervene on his behalf.'

'And how will I do that?'

'He wants you to call the Comptroller of Prisons to cancel the transfer.'

'The man is an idiot, a moron. He complicated his case by his lack of control and stupid outburst in court during a recess.'

'Are you going to call your friend, the Comptroller?'

'I am not going to waste my breath on him. If he phones again, tell him I have travelled out of town.'

Dauda didn't phone again. Even if he wanted to, the prison authorities didn't give him an opportunity. He was woken up early in the morning before the daily prison roll call and put on the 'Black Maria,' the police van for moving convicts. By noon Dauda Adams was in Jos prison. His processing took some time and he was finally locked up in his cell around 1 p.m. News travelled quickly in the prison. Suspicion was raised by the amount of buzz around the new prisoner, and his solitary confinement. Dauda was tired and aching all over from being bounced up and down on the hard seat during the long trip from Abuja to Jos on the pot hole riddled road. He fell asleep in his cell as soon as he was locked in and did not appear for lunch. He woke up in time for supper and one of the warders led him to the dining area. He ate quietly, but he got the sense that other inmates were watching him intently. As he retired, a fierce looking inmate walked across his path, looked him over and Dauda thought he saw him draw a finger across his throat mimicking the act of slashing a throat with a knife. Dauda hurried to his cell and sat on his wooden bed rubbing his neck as if to assure himself that it was still intact.

Dauda lay awake for most of the night ruminating on his life, his various antics and misdemeanours, which had led to this point and him being trapped like a wild animal. He could sense imminent retribution from Dogo's friends. He looked around furtively at breakfast.

Look at that group in the corner with one of them pointing towards me. They must be talking about me. One of them is the man who wanted to slash my throat, he thought.

He gobbled down his food and returned to his cell. He felt he had now confirmed his suspicion.

Dauda didn't leave his cell for lunch. He missed supper as well. The following day he bluntly refused to leave his cell despite all attempts by the prison warders to get him to go for his meals or the one hour open air exercise. On Wednesday, the situation was reported to the prison Governor who summoned the Prison Doctor. Dauda was taken to the prison clinic.

'Good morning Mr. Dauda Adams, I am Doctor Fred Jonathan. How are you?'

'I am not feeling too well. I can't sleep well.'

'Why can't you sleep well?'

'I keep thinking of the inmates who want to kill me.'

'Who are these people?'

'They are my enemies. I see them every time I go for meals.

They stand in groups talking about me. One of them pointed at me the other day, and another threatened to slash my throat.'

'Mr. Adams, these are paranoid delusions. They are not real. You have nothing to fear. I will prescribe something for you to take tonight to calm you down and ensure you sleep soundly tonight, and I will be back to see you tomorrow morning.'

Dauda was admitted overnight in the prison sick bay and kept on suicide watch on instruction of the Doctor. Dauda slept soundly and had a hearty breakfast. He was looking much better when the Doctor arrived to review his case. Dauda was discharged from the sick bay, but the watch and his nocturnal medication continued for the next week. After the week, he was discharged fully fit and expected to return to normal prison life.

As Dauda went out for one of his rare open air exercise sessions, someone tapped him on the shoulder. He turned round and it was a fellow inmate.

'The boss wants to see you.'

'Who is the boss? The Prison Governor? Dauda asked.

'What's your name again?' the inmate asked.

'Dauda Adams.'

'Mr. Adams let me advise you, and you will do well never to forget what I am about to tell you.'

'Go ahead,' replied Dauda.

'The Prison Governor is responsible for keeping you locked up, but the real boss who determines whether your life inside is bearable or miserable is General B. Don't mess with him. Don't argue with him. Just do whatever he says. Even the warders don't mess with him. The few inmates who tried to mess with him in the past are now six feet under.'

'What does B stand for?'

'I don't know, and I have never been bold enough to ask. I just call him General. When he arrived in the prison three years ago, I overheard two warders talking about him. He was a bouncer in a top class night club in Jos. One night, two revellers were slightly intoxicated and started harassing other guests. General B was called in to eject them. He was polite but firm with the offenders. They were recalcitrant and one of them slapped General B. General B grabbed the offender and snapped his wrist. Those nearby heard the crackling sound as the carpal bones were hyper-extended and forced to touch the dorsum of the forearm. He collapsed in agony in a corner. His colleague was infuriated and squared up to General B. As he landed a blow, the general grabbed the man's throat in both hands and held it in a vice-like grip. He lifted him off the floor as the hapless man's feet kicked and dangled in the air. Witnesses pleaded in vain with the bouncer. When he finally let go, he had snuffed the life out of his victim. The court cleared him on the count of causing grievous bodily harm to the first victim on the basis of self-defence but gave him a life sentence for culpable homicide of the second victim. So you see why I said he is not a man to be trifled with. That's him seated on the bench in the corner of the field with his body guards standing behind him. Another thing, don't sit down unless he asks you to. Okay, don't keep him waiting, go and see him.'

Dauda hurried on to see General B.

'Good morning Sir,' Dauda greeted General B as he approached the bench.

'Good morning,' replied General B. Then he beckoned to Dauda to sit down.'

Dauda sat gingerly. He was in awe of the man mountain in front of him. He reckoned that General B must be around 6 feet 6 inches tall, with bulging muscles glistening in the morning sun. His biceps were bigger than the thighs of most adult men. He looked like a hybrid between a super heavyweight boxing and wrestling champion. He had the confident and relaxed look of a powerful and untouchable person. He signalled to his bodyguards and they disappeared.

'Mr Adams, how are you?'

'I am fine General B. Well, not exactly, but I am trying to adjust.'

'I understand you were admitted to the sick bay.'

'How did you know that?'

'This is my territory. I have ears and eyes everywhere.'

'I think some inmates are stalking me and this has worn me down. I haven't been able to sleep, I am not eating properly, and I rarely leave my cell.'

'Why do you think this is happening?'

Dauda was reticent.

'Is it to do with Dogo's death?' asked General B.

Dauda was shocked.

'You look surprised. I told you I know everything happening in my territory.'

'Yes. I don't know who these people are but I suspect they may be Dogo's friends. I think I am being blamed for his death.'

'Are you responsible?'

'What?' asked Dauda.

'Are you responsible for Dogo's murder?'

'Not directly. I was in a fix and I asked my minders to take care of the situation. I left the details to their discretion. I swear I didn't tell them to kill him.'

'So, you think someone is out to get you.'

'I think so. I really think so and my instincts are usually right,' replied Dauda.

'I can guarantee your safety.'

'Can you?' asked Dauda.

'Of course I can. I am not called General B for nothing.'

'Can I ask you about something intriguing?'

'Go ahead.'

'What does B stand for? How did you get the name?'

'You are a brave man. No other inmate has ever asked me that question. I like your courage and I'll tell you the story.'

'Many years ago in my late teens, I was a tearaway living in Lagos doing odd jobs at the Apapa quayside. One day I got into an argument with a fellow dock hand. This guy was a known rough hand, a local bully. I apologised and tried to walk away from the altercation. As I did so, he followed me and gave me a thunderous slap which sent me reeling. I was smaller than him but I have never been a coward. I turned round and faced him. He swung a blow at me but I have always been nimble. I dodged and he lurched forward. I connected with an uppercut. The victim's neck was hyper-extended by the blow. There was a crunching noise as his mandible slammed against his upper jaw, and as he collapsed on the ground he spat out some blood and a tooth. He didn't get up and had to be carried to the port medical centre for treatment. When the police arrived to investigate the altercation, one of the spectators reported that the victim was the aggressor but I had defended myself with a single "bazooka" blow. From that day on, my mates started calling me Bazooka. That's the origin of the B name. The name stuck when I moved up North to Kaduna.'

'Dauda, let's get back to your problem. Do you want me to protect you?'

'Yes, General'

'It will cost you but that should be no problem. You are a rich man and can easily afford my charges.'

'One of my bodyguards will escort you from your room at every meal time and when inmates have shared programmes like the open air exercise. You will also have the honour of sitting at my table during meals. All these benefits will cost you only 2,000 Naira a week. What do you say?'

'I agree,' replied Dauda.

'Adams, one last point.'

Dauda looked on intently.

'This does not make us friends. We are not mates and you must never forget who the boss is. This is a straightforward business contract. You pay and I provide security. As long as you are in credit, nothing will happen to you.'

'That is clear, General. How do I pay?'

General B beckoned to one of his bodyguards, who then approached the bench.

'This is "Bulldog" and you can hand over the money to him tonight in the dining room. Wrap it in this napkin and place it on your tray. He'll sit next to you and swap the trays. Don't start eating the food when you sit down as this may irritate him. Wait for him to swap the trays before you eat.'

As Dauda got up and retired to his cell, Bulldog walked just one step behind him. This was a very public statement that Dauda was now under the protection of the General.

Bulldog showed up in front of Dauda's cell at supper time and they walked together to the dining hall. They switched trays and the bodyguard picked up the wrapped napkin, pocketed it and continued with his meal. Dauda was now accompanied wherever he went by his minder. Dauda was more relaxed and slept well. The arrangement continued for several months. Each time Dauda had the opportunity to use the prison phone, he asked for replenishment of his funds from his friends and erstwhile political mates. His wife and daughter had never visited him in Jos. He initially persisted in phoning them but gave up after it became apparent that they didn't want to talk to him and had changed their telephone numbers. With time his friends became fewer, and those who were willing to visit him in Jos even fewer. Nine months into his sentence, the visits dried up completely and with this the replenishment of his funds. By the tenth month, Dauda began to fall into arrears with his payments to General B. He had only managed to come up with 1,000 Naira. General B summoned Dauda to a meeting and warned him that he had defaulted on his side of the contract. He would continue to protect him on credit till the next visiting day in two weeks-time because of their longstanding business relationship, but Dauda would need to catch up with his payments after the next visiting day. Dauda promised to deliver. Unfortunately, no one visited Dauda and he therefore could not meet his contractual obligation. The General quietly but promptly withdrew personal protection from Dauda. It soon became clear to other inmates that Dauda was no longer under the protection of the General. Yet, the aura and fear of the General was such that no one dared to harass Dauda for the next one month. He walked freely without hindrance, and he became relaxed and settled down to life in the prison.

One morning, approximately eleven months after Dauda was transferred to Jos prison, there was ruckus in the shower room. The General and his bodyguards were conspicuously absent, relaxing in their cells. By the time the prison warders rushed to the shower rooms, Dauda Adams lay on the floor making a gurgling sound and bleeding profusely from a cut to the neck. The warders tried to stem the bleeding but were unsuccessful. The attacker had slashed his jugular vein and common carotid artery. Dauda died on the bathroom floor within minutes. There was a bloody mess all over the shower room floor. When the matter was reported to the Prison Governor, he checked his diary and noted that it was exactly a year to the day that Dogo Kontagora was killed in a similar way. Undoubtedly, this was retribution. Dogo's friends must have had a hand in this. All inmates were locked in their cells and police detectives called to investigate. They didn't make any headway. No inmate was willing to talk. They all claimed they had seen nothing suspicious. The corpse was removed to the morgue and a post mortem examination carried out. The prison authorities contacted his family in Ibadan but Dauda's wife was not interested in collecting the corpse.

When the trial ended, Mrs. Adams became a recluse hardly venturing out of the house. Two months later, the daughter of her best friend, one of the very few people she still trusted was getting married and she had to attend the traditional wedding ceremony. Tan Azeez also attended because the groom's father was his bosom friend. Mrs. Adams refused to acknowledge the presence of Tan at the ceremony. She refused to shake Tan's hand during the official introduction of family members and special guests. As they left the event, Tan overheard Mrs. Adams explain to her friend that she could not greet a traitor. No matter what her husband did, a childhood friend should not have grassed him. Tan had no option but to use an intermediary to set up a meeting with Mrs. Adams. By the time Tan finished relaying the story of her husband's escapades with his daughter and showing her the love notes and other incriminating evidence that he found in his late daughter's belongings, she was cursing Dauda and apologising profusely to Tan for the hurt her husband caused the Azeez family. When their daughter was critical and uncompromising in her view that they had to visit Dauda in Jos prison, Mrs. Adams had no option but to spill the beans. She was shocked and disgusted with her father's moral bankruptcy and depravity, and quickly ditched the idea of visiting him.

This was why neither of them was interested in collecting his corpse after the Jos prison authorities contacted them. A week after he died, his body still lay in the morgue and the prison authorities collected the corpse and buried it in an unmarked grave in Jos cemetery. The news of his death was reported as a footnote in some newspapers. Very few people were sorry for him. Most people thought this was retributive justice.

CHAPTER 30

After Dauda Adams was led away from the court to begin his sentence, there were mixed feelings amongst the Lawanson family. They could not celebrate because surpressed feelings and hurt had been unearthed during the course of the trial but they were pleased that justice had been served. David's widow broke down in tears after the sentence was pronounced. This was payback for a man she had always regarded as a family friend but who had robbed her of life with her soul mate. Anita had sat next to her all through the trial. As Justice John Paul read the sentence the tension was palpable, David's widow held Anita's hand and squeezed tight until Anita's fingers almost went numb. Thereafter Anita hugged her and held her tightly as both of them cried uncontrollably, with tears streaming down their faces. The Senator came round to commiserate with his sister-in-law, and invited the whole family to lunch in his expansive villa in Abuja. David's widow excused herself. She said she had been away from her twin children for far too long and had to return home immediately to be with them. Mike Lawanson drove her to the hotel to pick up her travelling bag and then took her to the airport to catch her flight to Lagos. Mike waited for the flight to depart and then joined the rest of the clan in Senator Lawanson's mansion.

The family chatted in small groups laughing and drinking. The moment Mike returned from the airport, Senator Lawanson called the family to order. There was a minute silence to honour the memory of their departed member. Then the buffet luncheon was declared open. Mike's mother and wife were in charge of the food whilst Mike manned the bar. Eating and drinking went on for hours. After they had their fill Senator Lawanson called the men and they retired to the library, whilst the women chatted in the living room.

'Daniel, when are you going back to Saudi Arabia?'

'Brother, I am leaving Lagos next week Thursday so that I can be back in Taif at the beginning of the week.'

'Why not leave on Saturday or Sunday?'

'That's too late. Our weekend is Thursday and Friday and the week starts on Saturday.'

'Really?'

'Oh yes,' replied Daniel.

'Daniel, we need you back here.'

'Brother, to do what?'

'The family needs you and our great country needs you too.'

'Okay, I'll come home more regularly to see the family but the country doesn't need me. I am a surgeon, and there are hundreds, maybe thousands of surgeons in Nigeria.'

'You don't understand,' replied Senator Lawanson. 'We need you in government.'

'Me? That is impossible. I am a doctor not a politician.'

'That's where you are wrong. The country needs good people in politics, people with integrity and vision, not idiots and criminals like Dauda. If the likes of Dauda Adams can be governor, what stops you from aspiring to be a governor or even the president?'

'Brother, I have told you I am not a politician. I wouldn't even know where to start.'

At this juncture, Mike butted in.

'Uncle Daniel, that is no problem, I will assist you. I will put my political machinery at your disposal. My old campaign team will gladly work for you, and don't forget that dad has a formidable political machine.'

'What about funding the campaign? I am comfortable and have some savings but not enough to fund a long campaign.'

'Daniel, that's no problem, I will fund your campaign.'

'Brother, you seem to have an answer for every question.'

'That's because it's a very good idea and I have thought long and hard about it.'

'Perhaps my wife won't like the idea.'

'Why don't we ask her,' replied Senator Lawanson.

'Okay, let's join them in the living room.'

The men moved into the living room interrupting the women who were having a sing along to the latest release by the country's highlife music maestro. The women stopped singing. They knew their patriarch had something important on his mind. He was the first to speak.

'Anita, please come and sit next to me.'

She did.

'Daniel and Mike, please sit down anywhere you like.'

Then the Senator spoke. It was more like a legal submission than mere discussion.

'Anita, we've been talking to your husband. We tried to get him to call it a day in Saudi Arabia and return home very soon. We gave him three good reasons why he should return home soon. First one is that you and Ade need him. It is not ideal for a young family to be away from each other for too long. I bet you miss him terribly when he is away.'

He paused, and watched Anita. She nodded her head in agreement. Then he continued.

'This family needs him. There are times when the family needs his presence but he is away in Saudi. I recall how confused we were when Mike had his accident. We desperately needed his professional advice. We missed his presence. Finally, this country needs him. Mike and I think he should stand for a senatorial seat in next year's election. Daniel claims he is a doctor not a politician. We told him we'll support him and help to organise his campaign. Daniel wants to know your opinion. So, what do you think?'

'Daniel, I know that you'll be a brilliant senator. I'll support you fully if you want to stand.'

'You should know me better than others. I am a surgeon and not a politician. Furthermore, what do I tell Prince Rasheed?'

'Who is Prince Rasheed?' asked Senator Lawanson.

Anita replied.

'Prince Rasheed is the Saudi Minister of Works and Planning. He is a very influential member of the Saudi Royal family. He is

Daniel's friend and has stated on several occasions that Daniel is the best doctor in Saudi Arabia. Daniel treats his family and they come all the way from Riyadh to Taif to see him. Sometimes they send a royal plane to Taif to bring Daniel to Riyadh to see senior royals.'

'That's wonderful. Congratulations brother. You'll have to find a diplomatic way to tell your royal friend that your country also needs you.'

'This is arm twisting. And even my wife is involved in the conspiracy. I have built an excellent surgical team in Taif.'

'My brother, don't think too much about your employer. If they find an equally good doctor ready to accept less pay, they wouldn't hesitate to ditch you. Come and use your skills in your own country.'

'Mike, get me the champagne. Let's give a toast to the future Senator Daniel Lawanson.'

The revelry continued till late when they retired to bed. The following day some members of the clan returned to Lagos in the Grand Phoenix Bombardier business jet. Mike and Mosun returned by commercial flight. Senator Lawanson had an unwritten rule. His nuclear family never travelled together in the same aeroplane. Senator Lawanson moved quickly to set the wheels in motion. He took Daniel to the state headquarters of their party where he joined the party officially. The party rules state that members cannot stand for elections unless they have been members for at least one year. The nucleus of Senator Lawanson's committee of friends had been invited and Daniel met all of them. By the time they left the party headquarters, Daniel realised that there was no going back. When they returned to the Senator's residence, Mike and Mosun were still there.

'It's late. I thought you guys would have departed,' Daniel addressed Mike.

'You are leaving for Ibadan tomorrow morning and then you are off to Saudi soon. I want you to meet my friend before you leave.'

'Who is he?'

'He is my old classmate, now an honourable member of the Federal House of Representatives.'

'Okay, where is he?' asked Daniel.

'He is talking to mum in the family living room.'

He led Daniel to the living room and introduced him to Ahmed.

'Mummy, I'll come back to see you another day. I'd like to talk to Brother Daniel before I go home.'

'Okay, goodnight Ahmed.'

'Goodnight ma.'

'Brother, Mike has briefed me about your intention. Have no fear, Sir. My local office and staff will be at your disposal. Your nomination and election in this area is a foregone conclusion. Daddy is not known as 'The Kingmaker' for nothing. Here is my business card. Please phone me if you want anything to be done here whilst you are away in Saudi Arabia. I am thinking of going for umra soon. If my plans materialise before you leave Taif, I'll phone you when I get to Mecca. I understand Mecca is less than an hour by road to Taif.'

'That's okay. I'll be pleased to see you. I am not allowed to step on Mecca's soil though, but you can take a taxi from Mecca to Taif KMC and you can spend a few days with me in Taif. I'll then drive you back to Jeddah through the ring road which bypasses Mecca.'

Daniel scribbled his Taif address and phone number on a sheet of paper and handed it over to Ahmed.

Ahmed bade him farewell and then left for home.

As Anita and Daniel retired to the guest room, Daniel was unusually quiet. Anita nudged him.

'What's the matter dear?'

'I am scared. What have I let myself into?'

'There is no need to worry. You have a good support team. Your brother is a formidable tactician and many of the top politicians owe him. You'll be all right.'

'If you say so,' replied Daniel.

'Daniel, you have to start believing in yourself. In my position, I have met most of the opposition. They are no match for you.'

'Okay, I believe,' replied Daniel.

'Daniel, that's enough politics for one day. Come here let's go to bed.'

They canoodled and then fell asleep in each other's arms.

They returned to Ibadan on Sunday. Daniel spent the days before his departure rekindling old relationships and acquaintances.

Daniel returned to Lagos on Thursday morning and called on his brother to bid him farewell before travelling to Saudi Arabia.

'Brother, I am intrigued by something that happened during the trial.'

'What is that Daniel?'

'How did you know that Dauda would try to eliminate Tan?'

'You can call it sixth sense but that type of intuition comes from several years experience as a political gladiator. In politics as in war, it is dangerous to underestimate your adversary. If Dauda could kill a childhood friend for power, it would be foolish not to expect him to try something desperate to save his skin. I knew that Tan was the chief prosecution witness. Without Tan's evidence, Dauda would walk free. So I decided from the start that Tan had to be protected at all cost.'

'Why didn't you rely on police protection?'

'I had no doubt that the police would do their best but their best was not likely to be adequate. For one, they wouldn't be able to deploy the resources that we put in. Secondly, Dauda used to be a policeman and there might be friends or rogue agents sympathetic to his plight in the police force.'

'That's true,' replied Daniel.

'So how did you get him out of his house without the private security guard and neighbours knowing about it?'

'Credit for that goes to your wife. She is a brilliant and courageous woman.'

'What role did Anita play?'

'We suspected that goons might have been sent to stake out Tan's residence prior to an attempt on his life once his name was mentioned in court as a prosecution witness. Your wife volunteered to smuggle him out of his house. She visited him in his house in Ibadan the same evening, backing her SUV into the open garage. Tan and Anita dressed the mannequin she brought in Tan's clothes and carefully laid it in a sleeping position on the bed, and then planted fake liquid blood in plastic bags next to the torso. They then covered the body up to the neck with a bed sheet so that only the wig was visible. They were careful to ensure that the body backed the door. Apparently when the assassins blasted the torso with bullets, they ruptured the plastic bags and the bed sheet was soaked in the fake blood. They departed thinking they had killed Tan.'

'Wow! That's amazing,' exclaimed Daniel.

Then he continued.

'Where did you get the mannequin and the fake blood?'

'Anita got the stuff from her theatre arts group.'

Daniel marvelled at his wife's ingenuity.

'So, how did Tan get out of the house?'

'What do you think?' asked Femi Lawanson.

'Anita?' asked Daniel.

'Of course,' replied Femi.

'Your wife hid him in the boot of her car and drove him all the way to a safe house we had arranged. He was driven to Lagos in disguise the same night. The following morning he was flown secretly to Abuja in the company plane. The police never knew where he was, and the first time he was seen in public after the abortive attempt on his life was when he appeared in court.'

'Brother, this sounds like a secret service operation.'

'We had no choice. Dauda had shown that he was evil and had a great reach and so we had to be smarter than him. Without your wife we could not have succeeded. You are a very lucky man. With such a woman by your side, you are destined for great things in politics.'

Daniel had been talking to his brother for over an hour whilst Anita chatted with Femi's wife. She looked at her wristwatch and remembered that Daniel's flight was due to depart in three hours. She took her leave and interrupted the men in the library.

'Daniel, it's time to go if you don't want to miss your flight.'

They bade the senior Lawansons good bye and then left for the airport.

Daniel was back at the clinic on Saturday morning. He booked an appointment to see the Medical Director during his lunch break. His clinic had been overbooked as usual and it overran. By the time he finished his consultation, lunch was over and the Medical Director had gone home. He would see him later. Daniel finally managed to see Dr. Ali after his post-surgical ward round on Wednesday.

'Welcome back Dr. Daniel.'

'Thank you, Dr. Ali.'

'I understand you've been trying to see me.'

'Oh yes, I have an important matter to discuss with you.'

'What is the matter?'

'Dr. Ali, I have enjoyed my time in Taif tremendously. Even when I had the encounter with the religious police, you and the staff were amazing and I will always be grateful.'

Dr. Ali shifted in his chair. He seemed to know what was coming but it still hit him like a hurricane when Daniel told him he wanted to leave KMC.

'Dr. Daniel, we've got a hospital to run and patients to treat. We can't let you go just like that.'

What you didn't say is that you've got money to make. Your profit is more important than my freedom. I'll have to be calm and smart, Daniel thought.

'Dr. Ali, I didn't say I want to leave immediately. I'll give the required three months notice in accordance with my contract.'

'Daniel, what is your current monthly salary?'

'Fifty thousand Riyals,' replied Daniel.

'That is over nine thousand pounds tax free, plus a full month salary at the end of the year as your bonus.'

Daniel nodded to indicate he agreed with the statement.

'We'll increase your salary by fifty per cent. That is seventy five thousand riyals monthly.'

'Thank you, but it's not about money,' replied Daniel.

Dr. Ali's countenance changed.

'I think the Head of Manpower should be here.'

He picked up the phone and punched some buttons.

Mr. Gould came on the line. Dr. Ali told him they had a crisis and he had to come to his office immediately. Mr. Gould arrived within minutes.

'Dr. Daniel, please tell Mr. Gould what you have just told me.'

'Mr. Gould, you and Dr. Ali have been so kind to me. I wish I didn't have to make this request but every good thing must come to an end one day. My wife and child need me back at home, and I have decided to return to Nigeria. I wanted to speak with you as friends before submitting my letter of resignation. I intend to give three months notice as required by my contract.'

'Doctor, that will be difficult,' replied Mr. Gould.

'No, Mr. Gould, it is impossible. We cannot allow Dr. Daniel to leave without suitable replacement.'

Mr. Gould turned to Daniel.

'Our urology service is a key part of our practice. We have clients from all over the country, some of them very important personalities as you know, and it will be negligent of us not to ensure that we have a good Consultant Urologist in service.'

'But my contract states that all I have to do is work three months notice once I resign in writing,' replied Daniel.

'If you read the appendix of the same contract, you will see a clause where it is stated that if a replacement is not found within the three months notice period, the employer reserves the right to ask the employee to work for a further three months.'

Daniel opened his mouth to protest but no sound came out. He was surprised and alarmed.

This reaction did not go unnoticed, and Mr. Gould responded.

'Dr. Daniel, it takes at least three months to advertise such senior positions and conduct an interview. If we find a suitable candidate, it is usually at least three months before the successful candidate can take up the job. If we don't get a suitable candidate, it is back to the drawing board, and another three to six months delay.'

'Thank you,' was all Daniel could say. He got up and left the office without uttering another word. He trudged along despondent. Hussein saw him on the corridor and greeted him but Daniel only grunted in reply. That was unlike Daniel and Hussein knew something was seriously wrong. It wasn't long before he discovered what was amiss. Daniel came to the Manpower Department and submitted his letter of resignation, giving the statutory three months notice. He left the office without saying much.

Daniel sat quietly in his villa pondering on events of the day when someone knocked on his front door. He looked through the peep hole and saw Hussein. He opened the door and invited him in.

'Mr. Hussein, I am sorry I was not very communicative earlier today. That was not very polite.'

'I understand your situation.'

'Can I offer you a drink?' Daniel asked.

'I'll have some cold water.'

Daniel served him some ice cold water and opened a can of cola for himself.

They sat down watching TV. Suddenly, Hussein turned to him.

'Dr. Daniel, please be careful. What I am going to tell you is strictly confidential and must not be repeated outside these walls. These guys are good when you are on their side but they can be vicious if you cross them. They are dangerous enemies to make. Do not forget that first and foremost, they are businessmen. I can tell you that since you joined KMC two years ago, the profit from the department of surgery has doubled.'

'So what should I do? My family needs me and I want to return home.'

'Your best bet is to find a suitable replacement.'

'What? I am not a head hunter.'

'You heard me well. The easiest way for you to depart in three to six months is to recruit a good urologist, preferably from Europe or the United States, otherwise you could still be here in a year. Don't forget that your passport is held in our Travel department, and when you are leaving finally the hospital will have to obtain a Final Exit Visa for you from the Ministry of Interior.

Let me tell you a true story. Before I came to Taif, I worked in Qassim province in the North. We had a brilliant British Asian surgeon who wanted to return to England after five years of service. He gave his notice but the hospital authorities begged him to stay. He was a brilliant surgeon and there was no ready replacement for him. They offered him more money but he rejected the offer. He continued to work his notice. Two weeks to the end of his notice, the relations of a young woman he had operated upon three years before complained about her treatment and demanded financial compensation. The woman had come in with severe lower abdominal pain which our surgeon correctly diagnosed as Appendicitis. He booked her for laparascopic appendix removal. Reports had it that the inflamed appendix was stuck to other tissues and key hole surgery was impossible. He converted to open laparatomy and successfully removed the appendix. She had a fairly stormy immediate post-operative period but was discharged home well in ten days. It was agreed by all those present in the theatre that the surgeon had done a brilliant job.'

'So, what did the relations complain about?' Daniel asked.

'The girl's father claimed that he consented only to pin hole surgery, but the surgeon had left long mutilating scars on her lower abdomen which would hinder her chances of getting a husband. The doctor contested this assertion vehemently. He claimed he had written down clearly on the consent form that he would try to do laparascopic surgery but if this failed he would convert to open surgery.'

'All they needed to do was look up the consent form in the patient's case note,' stated Daniel.

'They did but there was no consent form in the case note. It was rumoured that someone had removed the consent form.'

'Oh my goodness,' shouted Daniel.

'Not only that Dr. Daniel. We found out later that someone in the hospital had instigated the complaint.'

'So, what happened,' asked Daniel, now thoroughly terrified.

'The surgeon's employment and pay ended when his three months notice elapsed, but the trial by a panel including Ministry of Health representatives and Sharia judges lasted six months. He was not working and he could not leave the country. In the end he was found guilty and asked to pay thirty thousand Riyals compensation to the patient. Some colleagues contributed money and he repatriated the balance from the UK. He was only allowed to leave the country after he paid the fine.'

'Thank you. Thank you very much. I now know what to do.'

Hussein had been a great help. Daniel felt much better and he set to work right away. Riyadh time is three hours ahead of London, and although it was well after closing time in Taif, people were still at work in the UK. Daniel placed phone calls to his colleagues in London and Cardiff, trying to find a Consultant Urologist interested in relocating to Taif. His friends would ask around and contact him if anything positive came up. Then he phoned the membership secretary of the Royal College of Surgeons who advised him to contact the immediate past President, Professor Huw Davies in Cardiff. Why hadn't he thought of this? Professor Davies had been one of his teachers during his post-fellowship urology training at The University Hospital of Wales in Heath Park. The professor had just gone for a meeting so Daniel left a message, he would call again the following day just after lunch. Thursday was only a half-day and Daniel was back home by noon. At exactly 3 p.m. he phoned Professor Davies. He was in and his secretary connected them.

'Good afternoon Sir. This is Mr. Daniel Lawanson, one of your old students.'

'I remember you. How are you? What have you been up to?'

'I have been working in Saudi Arabia but I am now planning to return to Nigeria. That is why I have called to enlist your help.'

'How can I help?'

'I am seeking your help to find a Consultant Urologist to take over my job in Taif.'

'I'll ask around. What is the pay like?'

'I am on fifty thousand Riyals tax free every month.'

'What is that in Sterling?'

'That is just over nine thousand pounds, plus free fully furnished three bedroom villa, one first class ticket for my wife, child and I from Saudi Arabia to point of hire every year. After each completed year, I get a month's salary as bonus.'

'Okay. I'll ask around. We are in the process of appointing my replacement as I retire towards the end of the year. My wife and I want to go sailing and scuba diving.'

'Sir, then this is the place for you. You can take up this job, earn good money and join the expatriate sailing and diving club in Jeddah. I learnt that the Red Sea is one of the best diving sites in the world. They say the red vegetation and organisms in the Red sea constitute one of the wonders of the world.'

'I've heard about the beauty of the Red Sea,' stated Professor Davies.

Daniel drove home the advantage.

'There is another popular diving site in Yanbu on the western coast.'

'Can you send me the hospital and job details by post so that I can discuss the pros and cons with my wife?'

'I'll do better than that. I'll take your fax number and fax the hospital brochure and relevant details to you within the next half hour. Can I give you a hint?'

'Yes, go on,' replied Professor Davies.

'When I gave notice of my resignation they offered to increase my salary, so if you decide to take on this job ask for 75 thousand Riyals monthly. They'll reject it and tell you they can only pay 50 or

55 grand. Stand firm. They'll contact me and I'll negotiate on your behalf and tell them you were my Professor. We should be able to settle for somewhere between 65 and 70 grand.'

'65 grand sounds extremely attractive. I'll talk to my wife. Send the fax and call me again tomorrow at the same time.'

'Goodbye Professor.'

'Goodbye Daniel.'

When the phone rang on Friday at noon, Prof. Davies was waiting. He grabbed the phone immediately it rang. He had convinced his wife it was time to move to warmer climes and enjoy their hobbies on regular basis. He could retire a few months ahead of time and be in Taif in four months if the pay was right. Daniel agreed he would stay behind and work alongside the professor for a few weeks after his start date.

It was a different Daniel who walked into the Manpower Department on Saturday morning. He smiled and winked at Hussein as he walked in to see Mr. Gould. He gave Mr. Gould the Professor's secure phone number. Mr. Gould phoned the number immediately. Professor Davies came on the line. Within minutes of the conversation, Mr. Gould was smiling. Then came the issue of remuneration and Mr. Gould frowned.

'Professor Davies, I'll get back to you in an hour or two. I need to discuss this matter with the hospital board.'

Mr. Gould dropped the phone and turned to Daniel.

'Mr. Lawanson, he seems a suitable candidate but he is asking for too much money.'

'How much?' Daniel asked.

'Seventy five thousand Riyals monthly. We can't afford that.'

'He was my teacher. He is better than me, and should consequently be paid more than I am paid to reflect his experience and expertise.'

'Okay, we can pay him a little more than you earn but not seventy five thousand.'

'What is your best offer?' Daniel asked.

'Let me talk to Dr. Ali. Can you come back in an hour?'

'*Mafi mushkila,*' replied Daniel.

Daniel returned in an hour. Dr. Ali was in Mr. Gould's office. Mr. Gould spoke as Dr. Ali nodded to show his approval.

'Mr. Lawanson, we've considered the situation and the best offer is sixty grand.'

'I don't think he'll accept sixty grand, make it seventy grand and I'll convince him to accept.'

Dr. Ali intervened before Mr. Gould could speak.

'We'll meet him half way. Sixty five thousand Riyals monthly is our final offer.'

'I'll call him later and implore him to accept sixty five grand.'

'So, when is he ready to start?' asked Dr. Ali.

'He said if his terms are met he can start in four months. He wants me to stay back for two weeks after he arrives so that I can hand over properly to him.'

'Will you do that?' asked Dr. Ali.

'I will,' replied Daniel.

'*Mumtaz*. That is excellent,' replied Dr. Ali.

The three men stood up and shook hands. Mr. Gould escorted the two men out of the office, with the three of them smiling. Hussein was happy. He knew that their differences had been resolved.

Four months later, Professor Huw Davies resumed in KMC as the new Consultant Urologist. One of the things he did was to schedule an appointment for Princess Aisha's mother. They attended the appointment and Daniel formally handed over her care to Professor Davies. Princess Aisha gave Daniel a gold plated Mont Blanc pen and a 21 carat white gold necklace, set with sapphires for Anita.

Daniel returned to Lagos barely five months after he gave a commitment to leave Saudi Arabia. He kept himself busy by volunteering three days a week at the Catholic Hospital in Ibadan. He ran clinics and operation sessions. The rest of the working week was spent in his political office. Daniel won the PPN nomination for the senatorial election. Ahmed and the Lawanson political machinery swung behind him. His medical missionary work did not go unnoticed. He won the election in a landslide. His NCP opponent lost his deposit.

They celebrated with a party hosted by Senator Femi Lawanson at his Lagos home. As the festivities continued in the compound,

Senator Femi Lawanson, his family and close friends retreated briefly to the main living room.

'Ladies and gentlemen, thank you for honouring our invitation.'

He stood beside his brother and held up his arm.

'I present to you Senator Daniel Lawanson.'

Then he turned to his brother.

'Brother, congratulations. I know that you will serve your constituents well and never forget where you have come from.'

He beckoned to his brother to sit down, and then turned round to address the gathering.

'Ladies and gentlemen, the political dynasty is in good hands. When the time comes for me to join my ancestors, and the mantle falls on my brother, I can go in the knowledge that the future is in safe hands.'

The Kingmaker sat down beaming with smiles. He had manipulated events like a chess grand master and had fulfilled his ambition of ensuring that the Lawanson family remain a force to reckon with in the political life of the country.

ACKNOWLEDGEMENTS

When *The Kingmaker* was published in 2009, several readers claimed that a sequel was necessary. *Behind the Mask* is a fulfilment of that dream.

I am grateful to my wife, Iyabode, for her support and patience during all the time I have spent writing this story despite my heavy commitments with my medical practice. I thank all my children, my siblings, their spouses, some of my colleagues at work, my friends in Government College Ibadan Old Boys Association Europe Chapter and others who encouraged me to keep writing. I want to single out my twin daughters for special thanks, Funlola for painstakingly undertaking the initial editing of the manuscript, and clarifying the legal system in England, and Funlayo for invaluable advice and suggestions.

I thank my lawyer friends Messrs Dupe Fadina and Seun Oloke-Ogun for explaining the difference between the criminal code in use in Southern Nigeria and the penal code in operation in Northern Nigeria.

Finally, I am extremely grateful to my publisher Mr. Damola Ifaturoti and staff of the AMV Publishing Services for excellent professional advice and support without which this work of fiction could not have been so brilliantly finished and published.

Other Novels by the Author

The Kingmaker

The Long Road to Damascus

For more information, visit: www.daredemuren.com

9 780989 491716